D1115217

CORRALLED

NEW YORK TIMES BESTSELLING AUTHOR

B.J. DANIELS

Recycling programs
for this product may
not exist in your area.

ISBN-13: 978-1-335-40657-6

Corralled
First published in 2012. This edition published in 2022.
Copyright © 2012 by Barbara Heinlein

Stockyard Snatching
First published in 2016. This edition published in 2022.
Copyright © 2016 by Barb Han

Harlequin Enterprises ULC
22 Adelaide St. West, 41st Floor
Toronto, Ontario M5H 4E3, Canada
www.Harlequin.com

Printed in U.S.A.

CONTENTS

CORRALLED   7
B.J. Daniels

STOCKYARD SNATCHING   215
Barb Han

B.J. Daniels is a *New York Times* and *USA TODAY* bestselling author. She wrote her first book after a career as an award-winning newspaper journalist and author of thirty-seven published short stories. She lives in Montana with her husband, Parker, and three springer spaniels. When not writing, she quilts, boats and plays tennis. Contact her at bjdaniels.com, on Facebook or on Twitter, @bjdanielsauthor.

Books by B.J. Daniels

Harlequin Intrigue

Whitehorse, Montana: The Clementine Sisters

Hard Rustler
Rogue Gunslinger
Rugged Defender

The Montana Cahills

Cowboy's Redemption

HQN

Sterling's Montana

Stroke of Luck
Luck of the Draw

The Montana Cahills

Renegade's Pride
Outlaw's Honor
Hero's Return
Rancher's Dream

Visit the Author Profile page at Harlequin.com for more titles.

CORRALLED

B.J. Daniels

This is for my little brother, Charles Allen Johnson, who, like the rest of the Johnson family, has always given me something to write about.

Chapter 1

As he heard the music, he slowed his Harley, the throb of the engine catching the beat coming from the out-of-the-way country-western bar.

His kind of place.

He had been headed back to his hotel before that. But drawn to the music, he parked his motorcycle out front and pushed through the door into the dimly lit room. A clamor of glass and conversation competed with the band onstage.

Like him, most everyone inside was dressed in jeans and boots. The dance floor was packed, the air scented with beer and perfume as he stepped up to the bar and ordered a cold one.

Later he would recall sensing her presence even before he turned, a draft beer in hand, and first laid eyes on her.

He shoved back his Stetson, leaning against the bar, as she made her way through the crowd on the dance floor as if heading for the door. Her tight jeans hugged her hips as they swayed to the music, her full breasts pressing into the fabric of her Western shirt.

His gaze went to her boots, a pair of fancy Tony Lama's so fresh out of the box that he could almost smell the new leather. That alone would have made him steer clear. Then he saw her face. It wasn't classically beautiful or even unusual enough to hold most men's attention.

No, but her expression of total bliss caught him like a well-thrown lasso. She stopped him in his tracks as he watched her. She was clearly lost in the music and he couldn't take his eyes off her.

When she finally looked up, her gaze locked with his. Her eyes were the color of worn jeans, her lashes dark and thick like her hair cascading from beneath her straw cowboy hat. She'd tied her hair back with a red ribbon, but loose tendrils had escaped and now framed her face.

As she started past him, impulsively he stepped in front of her. "I think you owe me a dance."

Her lips turned up in an amused smile. "Is that right?"

He nodded and, leaving his leather jacket on the bar stool, took her hand. She didn't put up a fight as he led her out onto the dance floor as one song ended. If anything, she seemed curious.

"You sure you can keep up with me?" she said challengingly as a fast song began.

He grinned, thinking the woman had no idea who she was dealing with. He was Montana born, raised on country music and cowboy jitterbug. But to his surprise, she had no trouble staying with him, giving back everything she got. He loved the way she moved with the music, all grace and sexy swing.

Everything about her surprised and thrilled him, especially the way they moved together. It was as if they were one of those older couples he'd seen in Montana bars who had danced together for years.

When the song ended and a slow dance began, she started to draw away, but he dragged her back and into his arms. She looked at him, that challenge still lighting those washed-out blue eyes of hers.

"What makes you think I don't have friends I need to get back to?" she asked as he pulled her closer, the two moving as one to the sweet sounds coming off the guitar player's strings.

"Why would you want to go back to them—if there really are people waiting for you—when you can dance with me?"

She laughed. It had a musical quality that pulled at him just as he'd been drawn to the bar band earlier.

"You are quite full of yourself," she said as if not minding it all that much.

He shook his head. "I just know there is nothing I want to do tonight but dance with you," he said honestly.

She grew serious as the song ended and another boot-stomping tune began. Her gaze locked with his as he let go of her.

"Up to you," he said quietly. Her answering smile was all invitation.

He took her hand and whirled her across the middle of the dance floor as the music throbbed, the beat matching that of his heart as he lost himself in the warm spring night, the music and this woman.

He made only one mistake as the band took a break not long before closing. He offered to buy her a drink, and when he turned back, she was gone.

As he stepped to the front door of the saloon, he was in time to see her pull away in an expensive silver convertible sports car, the top down. She glanced over at him as she left and he saw something in her expression that made him mentally kick himself for not getting her number. Or at least her name.

As she sped off, he walked back to the bar to finish his drink. He told himself that even if he had gotten her number or her name, he was only in Bigfork until tomorrow. He had to get back home to the ranch and work. But damned if he wouldn't have liked to have seen her again.

When he pulled on his leather jacket, he felt something in the pocket that hadn't been there earlier. Reaching his hand in, he pulled out a key. It wasn't like any he'd ever seen before. It was large and faux gold and had some kind of emblem on it. He couldn't make it out in the dim light of the bar, but he had a pretty good idea who'd put it in his jacket.

Finishing his beer, he pocketed the key again and left. As he climbed onto his bike, all he could think about was the woman. He couldn't remember a night when he'd had more fun or been more intrigued. Did she expect him to know what the key went to or how to find her? She expected a lot from this country boy, he thought with a smile.

He was still smiling as he cruised back to his hotel. The key was a challenge, and Logan Chisholm liked nothing better than a challenge. But if she was waiting for him tonight, she'd have a long wait.

The next morning Logan woke to see the key lying on the nightstand next to his bed. He'd tossed it there last night after taking a good look at it. He'd had no more idea what it went to than he had at the bar.

Now, though, he picked it up and ran his fingers over the raised emblem as he thought about the woman from the bar. He needed to get back to Whitehorse, back to work on his family's ranch, Chisholm Cattle Company. The last thing he needed was to go chasing after a woman he'd met on a country-western bar's dance floor miles from home.

But damned if he could leave the Flathead without finding her.

"Have you ever seen one of these?" Logan asked the hotel clerk downstairs.

"I'm sorry, Mr. Chisholm, I—"

"Isn't that a key to the Grizzly Club?" asked another clerk who'd been standing nearby. "Sorry to interrupt," he said. "But I have a friend who stayed out there once."

"The Grizzly Club?" Logan asked.

"It's an exclusive gated community south of here," the clerk said. "Very elite. You have to have five million dollars to even apply for a home site inside the development. A lot of famous people prefer that kind of privacy. There are only a few of these gated communities in Montana."

Logan knew about the one down by Big Sky. He thought about the woman at the bar last night. He couldn't see her living there, but he supposed it was possible she'd hooked up with some rich dude who'd invented computer chips or made a bundle as a famous news broadcaster. Or hell, maybe she invented the chip.

It wasn't like he really knew her after only a few dances on a spring Friday night at a country-western bar, was it?

He thought it more likely that she was a guest at the club. At least he liked that better than the other possibilities. "So you're saying this key will get me into the place?"

The clerk shook his head. "That key is to the amenities once you get inside. You don't need a key to get in the gate. There is a guard at the front gate. If someone lost their key, the guard might be able to tell you who it belongs to. I noticed it did have a number on it."

Logan didn't like the sound of a guard, but what did he have to lose? "How do I get there?"

Outside, he swung onto his bike and headed down Highway 35 south along the east side of Flathead Lake. The road was narrow, one side bordering the lake, the other rising steeply into the Mission Mountain Range. Flathead was the largest freshwater lake in the western United States, just slightly larger than Lake Tahoe. This morning it was a beautiful turquoise blue. Around the lake were hundreds of orchards making this part of Montana famous for its Flathead cherries.

The Grizzly Club sign was so small and tasteful that he almost missed the turn. The freshly paved road curled up into the mountains through dense, tall, dark pines. Logan always felt closed in by country like this because it was so different from where he lived. The Chisholm Cattle Company ranch sat in the middle of rolling Montana prairie where a man could see forever.

At home, the closest mountains were the Little Rockies, and those only a purple outline in the distance. Trees, other than cottonwoods along the Milk River and creeks, were few and far between. He loved the wide-open spaces, liked being able to see to the horizon, so he was glad when the trees finally opened up a little.

He slowed as he came to a manned gate. Beyond it, he could make out a couple of mansions set back in the trees. Was it possible one of them was owned by the woman he'd met last night? That could explain the new boots, since few people in this kind of neighborhood were from here—let alone lived here year-around.

He tried to imagine her living behind these gates even for a few weeks out of the year and decided she had to be visiting someone. A woman like that couldn't stand being locked up for long, he told himself.

The guard was on the phone and motioned for him to wait. Logan stared through the ornate iron gate and realized that the woman he was looking for could work here. And that expensive sports car convertible she was driving? She could have borrowed her boss's car last night.

He smiled. And like Cinderella, she'd had to get the car back before morning or suffer the consequences. Now that seemed more like the woman he'd met last night, he thought with a chuckle.

The guard finished his conversation and turning, perused Logan's leathers and the Harley motorcycle. He instantly looked wary. Logan realized this had been a mistake. No way was this man going to let him in or give him the name of the woman connected to the key. More than likely, the guard would call security. The best he could see coming out of this was being turned away—but only after he'd made a fool of himself.

Fortunately, he didn't get the chance. From the other side of the gate, he saw the flash of a small silver sports car convertible coming through the trees. The top was still down. He caught a glimpse of the driver.

She'd done away with her cowboy attire, including the hat. Her hair blew free, forming a wave like a raven's wing behind her as she sped toward the gate. She wore large sunglasses that hid most of her face, but there was no denying it was the woman from the bar.

"Never mind," Logan said to the guard and swung his bike around as the gate automatically opened on the other side of the guardhouse and the sports car roared out.

Logan went after her.

He couldn't believe how fast she was driving, taking the curves with abandon. He saw her glance in her rearview mirror and speed up. Logan did the same, the two of them racing down out of the mountains and onto the narrow road along the lake.

This woman is crazy, Logan thought when she hit the narrow two-lane highway and didn't slow down. She wanted to race? Then they would race.

He stayed right with her, roaring up beside her when there was no traffic. She would glance at him, then gun it, forcing him to fall behind her when an oncoming car appeared.

They were almost to the town of Bigfork when she suddenly hit the brakes and whipped off the road onto a wide spot overlooking the lake. She'd barely gotten the car stopped at the edge of the rocky cliff, the water lapping at the shore twenty feet below.

Logan skidded to a stop next to her car as she jumped out and, without a word, climbed onto the back of his bike. Wrapping her arms around his waist, she leaned into him and whispered, "Get me out of here."

After that exhilarating race, she didn't need to ask twice. He was all the more intrigued by this woman. He roared back onto the highway headed north toward Glacier National Park. As she pressed her body against his, he heard her let out a sigh, and wondered where they were headed both literally and figuratively.

Caught up in the moment, he breathed in the cool mountain air. It smelled of spring and new beginnings. He loved this time of year. Just as he loved the feel of the woman on the bike behind him.

The sun was warm as it scaled the back of the Mission Mountains and splashed down over Flathead Lake. At the north end of the lake, Logan pulled into a small out-of-the-way café that he knew catered to fishermen. "Hungry?"

She hesitated only a moment, then nodded, smiling, as she followed him into the café. He ordered them both the breakfast special, trout, hash browns, eggs and toast with coffee and watched her doctor her coffee with both sugar and cream.

"Are you at least going to tell me your name?" he asked as they waited for their order.

She studied him. "That depends. Do you live around here?"

He shook his head. "East of here, outside of a town called Whitehorse." He could tell she'd never heard of it. "It's in the middle of nowhere, a part of Montana most tourists never see."

"You think I'm a tourist?" She smiled at that.

"Aren't you?" He still couldn't decide if she was visiting the Grizzly Club or lived there with her rich husband. But given the way she'd left that expensive sports car beside the lake, he thought his present-day Cinderella theory might not be that far off base.

Maybe he just didn't want to believe it, but he was convinced she wasn't married to some tycoon. She hadn't been wearing a wedding ring last night or today. Not only that, she didn't act married—or in a committed relationship. Not that he hadn't been wrong about that before.

"Don't you think you should at least tell me your name?" he asked.

She looked around the café for a moment as if considering telling him her name. When those pale blue eyes came back to him, she said, "Blythe. That's my name."

"Nice to meet you, Blythe." He reached across the table extending his hand. "Logan. You have a last name?"

Her hand felt small and warm in his. She didn't clean houses at the Grizzly Club, that was definite, he thought, as he felt her silky-smooth palm. Several silver bracelets jingled lightly on her slim tanned wrist. But she could still be a car thief.

"Blythe is good enough for now, don't you think?"

"I guess it depends on what happens next."

She grinned. "What would you like to happen next?"

"I'm afraid I have to head back home today, otherwise I might have had numerous suggestions."

"Back to Whitehorse," she said studying him. "Someone waiting for you back there?"

"Nope." He could have told her about his five brothers and his father and stepmother back at the ranch, but he knew that wasn't what she'd meant. He'd also learned the hard way not to mention Chisholm Cattle Company. He'd seen too many dollar signs appear in some women's eyes. There was a price to be paid when you were the son of one of the largest ranch owners in the state.

"Someone waiting for *you* back at the Grizzly Club?" he asked.

"Nope."

Their food arrived then and she dived into hers as if she hadn't eaten in a week. She might not have, he realized. He had no idea who this woman was or what was going to happen next, but he didn't care. He liked her, liked watching her eat. She did it with the same kind of passion and abandon she'd shown dancing and driving.

"I've never seen that part of Montana," she said as they were finishing. She wiped her expressive mouth and tossed down her napkin. "Show me."

He raised a brow. "It's a five-hour drive from here." When she didn't respond, he asked, "What about your car?"

"It's a rental. I'll call and have the agency collect it."

He considered her for a moment. "You don't want to pick up anything from your house?"

"It's not my house, and I like to travel light."

Logan still wasn't sure she was serious about going with him, but serious or not, he was willing to take her up on whatever she was offering. He liked that he had no idea who she was, what she wanted or what she would do next. It had been too long since a woman had captivated him to the point that he was willing to throw caution to the wind.

"Let's ride then." As they left the café, he couldn't help but notice the way she looked around as if afraid of who might be waiting for her outside. He was reminded of how she'd come flying out of the Grizzly Club. Maybe she really had stolen that car she'd been driving and now he was harboring a criminal.

He laughed to himself. He was considered the rebel Chisholm brother. The one who'd always been up for any adventure, whether it was on horseback or a Harley. But as they walked to his motorcycle, he had a bad feeling that he might be getting into more than even he could handle.

Chapter 2

Sheriff Buford Olson hitched up his pants over his expanding belly, reached back into his patrol car for his Stetson and, closing the door, tilted his head back to look up at the hotel-size building called the Main Lodge.

Buford hated getting calls to come out to the Grizzly Club. It wasn't that he disliked the rich, although he did find them demanding and damned irritating.

It was their private security force, a bunch of punk kids, who made his teeth ache. Buford considered anyone under thirty-five to be a kid. The "club" had given these kids a uniform and a gun and turned them into smart-ass, dangerous punks who knew diddly-squat about law enforcement.

Buford always wondered why the club had to call him in if their security force was so capable. It was no secret that the club liked to handle its own problems. The people who owned homes inside the gates didn't want anyone outside them knowing their business. So the whole idea was to sweep whatever trouble the club had under one of their expensive Persian rugs.

Worse, the folks who owned the club didn't want to upset the residents—or jeopardize new clientele—so they wanted everyone to believe that once they were behind these gates they were safe and nothing bad could happen.

Buford snorted at the thought, recalling how the general manager had asked him to park in the back of the main lodge so he wouldn't upset anyone. The guard at the gate had said, "Sheriff Buford, right? I heard you were here for a complimentary visit."

A complimentary visit. That had made him contrary enough that he'd parked right out front of "the Main Lodge." Now, though, as he started up the wide flagstone steps, he wished he hadn't been so obstinate. He felt his arthritis bothering him and, worse, his stomach roiling against the breakfast his wife had cooked him.

Clara had read in one of her magazines that if you ate a lot of hot peppers it would make you lose weight. She'd been putting hot chile peppers in everything they ate—and playing hell with his stomach.

The general manager he'd spoken to earlier spotted him and came rushing toward him. The diminutive man, whose name Buford couldn't recall at first, was painfully thin with skin that hadn't seen sunlight and piercing blue eyes that never settled more than a second.

"I thought I told you to park in the back."

Buford shrugged. "So what's the problem?" he asked

as he looked around the huge reception area. All the leather, antler lamps and chandeliers, thick rugs and gleaming wood floors reminded him of Clara's designer magazines.

Montana style, they called it. The Lodge Look. Buford was old enough to remember when a lot of places looked like this, only they'd been the real McCoy—not this forced Montana style.

"In here," the general manager ordered, drawing him into a small, claustrophobic office with only one window that looked out on the dense forest. The name on the desk read Kevin Andrews, General Manager.

Kevin closed the door and for the first time, Buford noticed how nervous the man appeared. The last time Buford had been called here was for a robbery inside the gates. That time he'd thought Kevin was going to have a heart attack, he'd been so upset. But once the missing jewelry, which turned out only to have been misplaced, was found, all was well and quickly forgotten.

Buford guessed though that it had taken ten years off Kevin's life from the looks of him. "So what's up? More missing jewelry?"

"This is a very delicate matter. I need you to handle it with the utmost care. Do I have your word?"

Buford felt his stomach roil again. He was in no mood for this. "Just tell me what's happened."

The general manager rose from his chair with a brisk "come with me."

Buford followed him out to a golf cart. Resigned that he had no choice but to ride along, he climbed on. Kevin drove them through the ritzy residence via the narrow paved roads that had been hacked out of the pines.

The hotel-size houses were all set back from the road, each occupying at least ten acres from Buford's estimation since the buildings had to take up three of those acres with guest houses of another half acre. Each log, stone and glass structure was surrounded by pine trees so he only caught glimpses of the exclusive houses as Kevin whipped along the main road.

Finally he pulled down one of the long driveways, coming to a stop in front of a stone monstrosity with two wide wooden doors. Like the others, the house was all rock and logs with massive windows that looked out over the pines on the mountainside and Flathead Lake far below.

Buford saw with a curse that two of the security force's golf carts were parked out front. One of the garage doors was open. A big, black SUV hunkered in one of the three stalls. The others were empty.

Getting off the golf cart, he let Kevin lead him up to the front door. Bears had been carved into the huge wooden doors, and not by some roadside chainsaw artist. Without knocking, Kevin opened the door and Buford followed him inside.

He was hit at once with a familiar smell and felt his stomach clutch. This was no missing jewelry case.

With dread, he moved across the marble floor to where the walls opened into a football field–size living room with much the same furnishings as the club's main lodge. The two security guards were standing at the edge of the room. They had been visiting, but when they saw Kevin, they tried to act professional.

Buford looked past them to the dead man sprawled

beside the hearth of the towering rock fireplace. The deceased was wearing a white, blood-soaked velour robe and a pair of leather slippers on his feet. Apparently nothing else.

"Get them out of here," Buford ordered, pointing at the two security guards. He could only guess at how many people had already tromped through here contaminating the scene. "Stay back and make sure no one else comes traipsing through here."

He swore under his breath as he worked his way across the room to the fireplace and the dead man. The victim looked to be in his late fifties, but could have been older because, from the tightness of his facial skin, he'd had some work done. His hair was dark with distinguishing gray at the temples, a handsome man even in death.

It appeared he'd been shot in the heart at point-blank range. An expensive handgun lay on the floor next to the body in a pool of drying blood. Clearly the man had been dead for hours. Buford swore again. He'd bet that Kevin had contacted the Grizzly Club board before he'd called the sheriff's department.

Around the dead man were two different distinct prints left in his blood. One was a man-size dress shoe sole. The other a cowboy boot—small enough that Buford would guess it was a woman's. It was her prints that held his attention. The woman hadn't walked away—she'd run—straight for the front door.

At the motorcycle, Blythe tied up her hair and climbed on behind the cowboy. She didn't think about what she was doing as she wrapped her arms around him. All she knew was that she had to escape, and wherever Logan was headed was fine with her. Even better, this Whitehorse place sounded like the end of the earth. With luck, no one would find her there.

She reminded herself that she'd thought this part of Montana would be far from the life she wanted so desperately to leave behind. But she'd been wrong.

Running didn't come easy to her. She'd always been a fighter. But not today. Today she only wanted to forget everything, hang on to this good-looking cowboy on the back of his motorcycle, feel the wind in her face and put her old life as far behind her as possible.

An image flashed in her mind, making her shudder, and she glanced down at her cowboy boots. She quickly wiped away a streak of dark red along the sole as Logan turned the key and brought the Harley to life.

She felt the throb of the engine and closed her eyes and her mind the way she used to tune out her mother when she was a girl. Back then it was to close out the sound of her mother and her latest boyfriend arguing in the adjacent room of the small, old trailer house. She had learned to go somewhere else, be *someone* else, always dreaming of a fantasy life far away.

With a smile, she remembered that one of her daydreams had been to run away with a cowboy. The thought made her hold on to Logan tighter as he shifted and tore out of the café parking lot in a shower of gravel.

Last night dancing with Logan she'd thought she was finally free. It was the best she'd felt in years. Now she pressed her cheek into the soft warmth of his leather jacket, lulled by the pulse of the motorcycle, the feel of the wind in her hair. She couldn't believe that he'd found her.

What had she been thinking giving him that damned key? She'd taken a terrible risk, but then she'd never dreamed he would come looking for her. What if he had gotten into the Grizzly Club this morning before she'd gotten out of there?

She shook off the thought and watched the countryside blur past, first forest-covered mountains, then wide-open spaces as they raced along the two-lane highway that cut east across the state.

She'd gotten away. No one knew where she was. But still she had to look back. The past had been chasing her for so long, she didn't kid herself that it wasn't close behind.

There were no cars close behind them, but that didn't mean that they wouldn't be looking for her.

For a moment, she considered what she'd done. She didn't know this cowboy, didn't know where he was taking her or what would happen when they got there.

This is so like you. Leaping before you look. Not thinking about the consequences of your actions. As if you weren't in enough trouble already.

Her mother's words rang in her ears. The only difference this time was that she wasn't that fourteen-year-old girl with eleven dollars in the pocket of her worn jean jacket and her only possession a beat-up guitar one of her mother's boyfriend's had left behind.

She'd escaped both times. That time from one of her mother's amorous boyfriends and with her virginity. This time with her life. At least so far.

That reckless spirit is going to get you into trouble one day. You mark my words, girl.

Wouldn't her mama love to hear that she'd been right. But mama was long dead and Jennifer Blythe

James was still alive. If anything, that girl and the woman she'd become was a survivor. She'd gotten out of that dirty desert trailer park where she'd started life. She would get out of this.

"Who's the victim?" Sheriff Buford Olson asked, sensing the Grizzly Club general manager hovering somewhere at a discreet distance behind him.

"Martin Sanderson," Kevin said. "It's his house."

Buford studied the larger bloody footprint next to the body. At a glance, he could see that it didn't match the soles of the two security guards or the general manager's, and unlike the other smaller print, this one headed not for the door, but in the opposite direction.

As he let his gaze follow the path the bloody prints had taken, Buford noted that the man had tried to wipe his shoe clean of the blood on an expensive-looking rug between the deceased and the bar where he was now lounging.

Buford was startled to see the man making himself at home at the bar with a drink in his hand. How many people had those dumb security guards let in?

"What the hell?" the sheriff demanded as he pushed himself up from where he'd been squatting beside the body. The "club" gave him a royal pain. He moved toward the bar, being careful not to step on the bloody footprints the man had left behind.

Buford didn't need to ask the man's name. He recognized Jett Akins only because his fourteen-year-old granddaughter Amy had a poster of the man on her bedroom wall. On the poster, Jett had been wearing all black—just as he was this morning—and clutching a fancy electric guitar. Now he clutched a tumbler, the dark contents only half full.

The one time his granddaughter had played a Jett Atkin's song for him, Buford had done his best not to show his true feelings. The so-called song had made him dearly miss the 1960s. Seemed to him there hadn't been any good music since then, other than country-western, of course.

"Mr. Atkins found the body," Kevin said from the entryway.

Jett Atkins looked pale and shaken. He downed the rest of his drink as the sheriff came toward him. Buford would guess it wasn't his first.

"You found the body?" he asked Jett, who looked older than he had on his poster. He had dark hair and eyes and a large spider tattoo on his neck and more tattoos on the back of his hands—all that was showing since the black shirt he wore was long-sleeved.

"I flew in this morning and took a taxi here. When I saw Martin, I called the club's emergency number." His voice died off as he looked again at the dead man by the fireplace and poured himself another drink.

Buford wanted to ask why the hell he hadn't called 911 instead of calling the club's emergency number. Isn't that what a normal person would do when he found a dead body?

He turned to Kevin again. "How many people were in this house?"

"Mr. Sanderson had left the names of six approved guests at the gate with the guard, along with special keys for admittance to all the amenities on the grounds," Kevin said in his annoyingly official tone. "All of those keys have been picked up."

"*Six* people? So where are they?" the sheriff demanded. "And I am going to need a list of their names." Before he could finish, Kevin withdrew a folded sheet of paper from his pocket and stepped around the sunken living room to hand it to him.

"These are the names of the guests Mr. Sanderson approved."

Buford read off the names. "JJ, Caro, Luca, Bets, T-Top and Jett. Those aren't *names*." He had almost forgotten about Jett until he spoke.

"They're stage names," he said. "Caro, Luca, T-Top and Bets. It's from when they were in a band together."

Stage names? "Are they actors?" Buford asked, thinking things couldn't get any worse.

"Musicians," Jett said.

He was wrong about things not getting worse. He couldn't tell the difference between women's or men's names and said as much.

"They were an all-girl band back in the nineties called Tough as Nails," Jett said, making it sound as if the nineties were the Stone Age.

"You don't know their *real* names?" Buford asked.

"They are the only names required for our guards to admit them," Kevin said. "Here at the Grizzly Club we respect the privacy of our residents."

Swearing, Buford wrote down: Caro, Luca, T-Top and Bets in his notebook.

"What about this JJ?" he asked. "You said he picked up his key yesterday?"

"*She.*"

Buford turned to look at Jett. "She?" he asked thinking one of these women account for the woman's cowboy-boot print in the dead man's blood.

"JJ. She was also in the band, the lead singer," Jett said.

The sheriff turned to the club manager again. "I need full legal names for these guests and I need to know where they are."

"Only Mr. Sanderson would have that information and he... All I can tell you is that the five approved guests picked up their amenities keys yesterday. This gentleman picked his up at the gate today at 1:16 p.m.," he said, indicating Jett.

"Which means the others are all here inside the gates?" Buford asked.

Kevin checked the second sheet of paper he'd taken from a separate pocket. "All except JJ. She left this morning at 10:16 a.m."

Buford glanced over at the body. 10:16 a.m. That had to be close to the time of the murder, since the dead man's blood was still wet when a woman wearing cowboy boots appeared to have knelt by the body, then sprinted for the front door.

Blythe pressed her cheek against Logan's broad back and breathed in the rich scents on the cool spring air. The highway rolled past in a blur, the hours slipping by until they were cruising along the Rocky Mountain front, the high mountain peaks snow-capped and beautiful.

The farther Blythe and Logan traveled, the fewer vehicles they saw. When they stopped at a café in the small Western town of Cut Bank along what Logan said was called the Hi-Line, she was ravenous again.

"Not many people live up here, huh," she said as she climbed off the bike. A fan pumped the smell of grease out the side of the café. She smiled to herself as she realized how much she'd missed fried food. All those years of dieting seemed such a waste right now.

"You think *this* is isolated?" Logan said with a chuckle. "Wait until you see where we're headed. They say there are only .03 people per square mile. I suspect it's less."

She smiled, shaking her head as she tried to imagine such wide-open spaces. Even when she'd lived in the desert there had been a large town closeby. Since then she'd lived in congested cities. The thought of so few people seemed like heaven.

Blythe could tell Logan wanted to ask where she was from, but she didn't give him a chance as she turned and headed for the café door. She'd seen a few pickups parked out front, but when she pushed open the door, she was surprised to find the café packed.

One of the waitresses spotted her, started to come over, then did a double take. She burst into a smile. "I know you. You're—"

"Mistaken," Blythe said, cutting the girl off, sensing Logan right behind her.

The girl looked confused and embarrassed. "I don't have a table ready. But you look so much like—"

Blythe hated being rude, but she turned around and took Logan's arm. "I'm too hungry to wait," she said as she pulled him back through the door outside again.

"Did you know that waitress?" Logan asked, clearly taken aback by the way she'd handled it. "She seemed to know you."

She shook her head. "I must have one of those faces or that waitress has been on her feet too long. I didn't mean to be abrupt with her. I get cranky when I'm hungry. Can we go back to that barbecue place we passed?" She turned and headed for the bike before he could press the subject.

"You sure you've never been to this town before?" he asked as he swung onto the bike.

"Positive," she said as she climbed on behind him. It wasn't until he started the bike that she let herself glance toward the front windows of the café. The young waitress was standing on the other side of the glass.

Blythe looked away, promising herself that she would make it up to her one day. *If she was still alive.*

She shoved that thought away, realizing she should have known someone would recognize her even though she looked different now. It was the eyes, she thought, and closed them as Logan drove back to the barbecue joint.

It wasn't until later, after they'd settled into a booth and ordered, that she tried to smooth things over with Logan. She could tell he was even more curious about her. And suspicious, as well.

"When I was a little girl I used to watch old Westerns on television," she said, hoping to lighten both of their moods. "I always wanted to run away with a cowboy."

"So you're a romantic."

She laughed softly as she looked across the table at him. There were worry lines between the brows of his handsome face.

"Or was it the running away part that appealed to you?" he asked.

"That could definitely be part of it. Haven't you ever wanted to run away?"

"Sure." His Montana blue-sky eyes bore into her.

"Most people don't have the luxury of actually doing it though."

"Good thing we aren't most people," she said, giving him a flirtatious smile.

"Oh? You think we're that much alike? So tell me what *you're* like and I'll tell you whether or not you're right about me."

"No big mystery. I like to dance, drive fast, have a good time and I'm always up for an adventure. How else could I have ended up living that little-girl fantasy of running away with a cowboy?"

"How else indeed," Logan said, but he was smiling.

"Has anyone looked in this house for the four approved guests who are unaccounted for?" the sheriff demanded.

Kevin was reaching for his phone to check with his security personnel when Buford caught a glint out of the corner of his eye. Turning toward Sanderson's body, he saw something glittering on the lapel of the dead man's robe that he hadn't noticed before.

Stepping over to the body again, he crouched down next to Sanderson and inspected the lapel. Someone had attached a safety pin to the left-hand lapel of the dead man's robe. As Buford looked closer, he found a tiny piece of yellow paper still attached to it.

The killer had left a note? Or was it possible that Sanderson had left a suicide note?

The thought took him by surprise. He'd been treating this like a homicide. But what if it had been a suicide, complete with note?

If so, then why would anyone take it? To protect

Sanderson? To purposely make it appear to be a homicide?

A history buff, Buford thought of a famous death that perplexed historians still. Captain Meriwether Lewis of the famed Lewis and Clark Expedition through Montana had suffered from depression that was thought to be the cause of his apparent suicide. But there were still those who believed he'd been murdered.

Very perplexing, Buford thought as he moved to a small desk in the kitchen. On it was a yellow sticky note pad. The top sheet had been torn in half horizontally, leaving the glued piece and a ragged edge. The paper was the same color as the tiny scrap still caught on the safety pin.

A blue pen lay beside the pad. Unfortunately there was no slight indentation on the pad. Whoever had written the note had ripped the scrap of paper off first before writing the note.

"Did anyone remove something that had been pinned to the deceased's robe?" he asked. Both Kevin, the two guards and Jett swore they hadn't. From their surprise at the question, Buford suspected they were telling the truth.

But *someone* had taken the note.

Chapter 3

"So tell me about your life in this isolated place where you live," Blythe said, steering the conversation away from her as they waited for their barbecue sandwiches.

Clearly Logan was itching to know who he'd let climb onto the back of his bike. Not that she could blame him. But she wasn't ready to tell him—if she ever did. Better to split before that.

"Not much to tell," he said, as if being as evasive as she was. "I spend most days with cows. Seems I'm either chasing them, feeding them, branding them, birthing them, inoculating them or mending the fence to keep them in."

"Sounds wonderful."

He laughed. "You obviously haven't worked on a ranch."

The waitress brought their orders and Blythe dived into hers. As she stole a look across the table at him, she thought about how he'd come looking for her at the Grizzly Club, how he hadn't batted an eyelash when she'd suggested going with him, how he hadn't really asked anything of her—not even what the devil she was doing taking off across Montana with a stranger. He probably thought she did this kind of thing all the time.

A thought chilled her to her bones. What if it was no coincidence that he'd come into her life last night?

No, she thought as she studied him. The cowboy had no idea who she was or what he was getting himself into.

She jumped as her cell phone blurted out a song she'd come to hate. Worse, she hadn't even realized she still had the phone in her jacket pocket. She'd thought she'd left it along with her purse and the keys in the car.

Logan was looking at her expectantly. "Aren't you going to take that?"

She had no choice. She reached into her pocket. As she pulled out the phone, the scrap of wadded up yellow note paper fell out. It tumbled under the booth.

The first few refrains of the song began again. She hurriedly turned the phone off without even bothering to check who was calling. She had a pretty good idea, not that it mattered.

The song died off, the silence in the café almost painful, but she saw a girl at the counter looking at her frowning slightly as if trying to either place the song—or her. The girl, Blythe had noticed earlier, had been visiting with the cook.

"What if that was important?" Logan asked.

"It wasn't."

She picked up her fork and began eating again, even though she'd lost her appetite. She could feel his gaze on her. She thought about the scrap of notepaper she'd dropped and what had been written on it. She had shoved it into her pocket earlier and forgotten about it.

"Won't someone miss you?"

"I really doubt it." She moved her food around her plate, pretending to still be interested in eating, and fortunately he let the subject drop. As soon as she could, she excused herself to go to the bathroom. When she returned, Logan was up at the counter paying for their meal.

The girl at the counter was staring at her again as if it wouldn't take much to place where she knew her from. She had to get that stupid song off her phone.

Blythe glanced toward the booth. She couldn't see the scrap of notepaper. Nor could she get down on her hands and knees to look for it without raising all kinds of questions.

Not to worry, she assured herself. The note would get swept out with the garbage tonight. What had she been thinking hanging on to it anyway?

That was just it. She hadn't been thinking. She'd just been running for her life.

Buford caught Jett making a call on his cell. "Hey, I don't know who you're trying to call, but don't. You'll get a chance to call your lawyer, if I decide to arrest you."

"Arrest me?" Jett said pocketing his phone. "*I* didn't kill him."

Buford heard a noise from down a long hallway toward the back of the house. He turned to see three women headed toward the sunken living room—and the murder scene.

He moved quickly to cut them off as the tall blonde in front glanced at his uniform and asked, "What's going on?"

"I'm Sheriff Buford Olson," he said introducing himself and shielding the woman from Martin Sanderson's body. "Where did the three of you come from?"

"The guesthouse out back," the blonde said frowning. "Where's Martin?"

"I need to speak to each of you." Buford turned to the club's general manager, amazed Kevin and his security force hadn't thought to search the house, let alone the guesthouse out back. "Kevin, can you suggest a place I can speak with these women?"

"Mr. Sanderson's library. Or perhaps his office?"

The sheriff motioned for Kevin to lead the way. They backtracked down the hallway toward the back of the huge house, the same way the women had come. Buford left the general manager in the plush library with instructions to say nothing to the other two women, while he took the blonde across the hall to Sanderson's office.

"What is this about?" she wanted to know.

"If you would have a seat," he said. "I need to ask you a few questions, beginning with your name."

She sat down reluctantly and looked around as if searching for something. At his puzzled frown, she said, "I was hoping there would be an ashtray in here." She pulled out a pack of cigarettes, seemed to think better of it and put them back into her jacket pocket.

Buford studied her as she did so. She said her name was Loretta Danvers, aka T-Top because of a hairdo she'd had ten years ago when she played in the band Tough as Nails. She was thirty-something, tall, thin and bleached blond. In her face was etched the story of a hard life.

"So what's this about?" she asked again.

"Martin Sanderson is dead," he said and watched her reaction.

She laughed. "Isn't that the way my luck goes? So the reunion tour is off? Or was it ever really on?"

"The reunion tour?"

"He was putting our old band together for a reunion tour. At least that's what he said." She pulled out her cigarettes, shook one out and lit it with a cheap lighter. "Guess he won't care if I smoke then, will he." She took a drag, held it in her lungs for a long moment and then released a cloud of smoke out of the corner of her mouth away from him. "With JJ onboard, we could have finally made some money. I knew it was too good to be true. So who killed him?"

"Do you know someone who wanted him dead?"

She laughed again. "Who *didn't* want him dead?"

You, apparently, Buford thought, since with Sanderson gone, so apparently was any chance of a reunion tour.

Logan didn't start having real misgivings until after Blythe's phone call. He hadn't even realized that she'd brought her cell phone until it had gone off. It wasn't until then that he'd recalled that she'd said she would have someone pick up the car she'd left beside Flathead Lake, but he hadn't seen her call anyone. In fact, he'd gotten the impression when the phone began to play that song that she hadn't even remembered that she had the phone with her.

Who had been calling? Someone she hadn't been interested in talking to. Even the ring tone with that pop-rock-sounding song didn't seem like her. Was it even her phone?

He'd realized then too that Blythe hadn't only left an expensive sports car convertible behind. She'd apparently left her purse, as well. What woman left behind her purse in a convertible beside the road? Or had she left it at the Grizzly Club?

After recalling the way she'd come flying out of club, he couldn't shake the feeling that maybe she wasn't as freewheeling as he'd originally thought— and instead was running from something serious. What did he really know about this woman he was taking back to Whitehorse with him?

Every time he'd started to ask her anything personal, she'd avoided answering one way or another. When he'd seen her reach for her cell phone, he'd noticed that she'd dropped something under the booth. He saw her look for it, then, as if changing her mind, go to the restroom. He had waited until the door closed behind her before he'd retrieved what she'd dropped.

It was nothing more than a crumpled scrap of paper from a yellow sticky notepad. He felt foolish for picking it up from under the booth and, as the waitress came by to clear the table, he'd hastily pocketed it without even looking to see if anything was written on it.

He'd been at the counter paying for the meal when Blythe had come out of the restroom. He saw her glance toward the booth. No, glance down as if looking under the booth to see what she'd dropped? Or hoping to retrieve it?

The woman intrigued him. Not a bad thing, he told himself as they left the café and climbed back on his motorcycle. He'd take her to Whitehorse and, if he had to, he'd buy her a bus ticket to wherever she needed to go. All his instincts told him that she needed to get away from something and he was happy to oblige. Chisholm men were suckers for women in trouble.

As she wrapped her arms around him and leaned into his back, he started the motor and took off. He tried to relax as the country opened. He felt as if he could breathe again. Whatever was up with this woman, he would deal with it when the time came.

A few hours later when he crossed into Whitehorse County, he'd forgotten about the scrap of paper in his pocket. He was too busy breathing a sigh of relief. He liked leaving, but there was nothing like coming home.

He breezed into the small Western town, thinking it would be a mistake to take her out to the house until they'd talked. At the very least, shouldn't he know her last name? He had always preferred not to take a woman to his house. Actually, he'd never met one he liked well enough to take home.

It didn't take but a few minutes to cruise down the main drag of Whitehorse. The town had been built up along the railroad line more than a hundred years ago. He waved at a few people he knew, the late afternoon sun throwing dark shadows across the buildings. He pulled into a space in front of the Whitehorse Bar and cut the engine.

"Could we just go to your house?" she asked without getting off the bike.

He looked at her over his shoulder. She had the palest blue eyes he'd ever seen. There was something vast about them. But it was the pain he saw just below the cool blue surface that took hold of him and wouldn't let go.

"You sure about this?" he asked.

She held his gaze and nodded. "Haven't you ever just needed to step out of your life for a while and take a chance?"

He smiled at that. Born a cowboy, riding a horse before he could walk, and now astride a Harley with a woman he probably shouldn't have been with. "Yeah, I get that."

She smiled back. "I had a feeling you might."

All his plans to get the truth out of her evaporated like a warm summer rain on hot pavement. He started the bike, flipped a U-turn in the middle of the street and headed out of town, hoping he wasn't making his worst mistake yet.

Buford asked former drummer Loretta Danvers to return to the guesthouse for the time being until he could talk to the others. Then he called in the next woman.

"Which one are you?" he asked the plump redhead.

Bets turned out to be Betsy Harper. He quickly found out that she'd played the keyboard in the former all-girl band and hadn't been that sorry when the band broke up. Now, the married mother of three said she played the organ at church and kept busy with her sons' many activities.

She looked relieved more than surprised when he told her that Martin Sanderson was dead.

"Then there isn't going to be a reunion tour," she said nodding. "I can't say I'm sorry about that. I was dreading being away from my family."

Both women had mentioned the tour. "You don't seem upset by Mr. Sanderson's death," Buford said, surprised since of the three, Betsy Harper had a more caring look about her.

"I feel terrible about that," she said. "But Martin wasn't a nice man."

She didn't ask how he'd died, nor did she offer any suggestions on who would want him dead. Her only question was when she would be able to return to her husband and kids.

Buford sent her back to the guesthouse and brought in Karen "Caro" Chandler, former guitarist and singer.

She was a slim brunette with large soft brown eyes. She was the only one who looked upset when he told her that Martin Sanderson was dead.

"How did he die?" she asked, sounding worried.

"He was shot."

She shuddered. "Do you know who…?"

"Not yet. It's possible he killed himself."

She looked so relieved he questioned her about it. "I was just worried that JJ might have…done something to him."

The elusive JJ. "Why would you say that?" he asked.

"Everyone in the business knew she was trying to get out of her contract."

The business being the music business, he guessed.

"Then there were those accidents onstage during her most recent road tour," Karen said. "Martin made it all sound like it was a publicity stunt, but I saw JJ interviewed on television. She looked genuinely scared. I was worried about her."

"You kept in touch with her over the ten years since the band broke up?"

"No," she said quickly with a shake of her head. "I'm sure the others told you that we didn't part on the best of terms. The band broke up shortly after JJ left. She was obviously the talent behind it."

Both Loretta and Betsy had made it clear they hadn't been in contact with JJ since the breakup, either.

"Not that I blamed JJ," she said quickly. "Who wouldn't have jumped at an opportunity like that if Martin Sanderson had offered it to them?"

Buford sent Karen to the guesthouse after the interview. All three had claimed the same thing. They'd all arrived by taxi together and had been together the entire time—except for when they'd gone into separate rooms in the guesthouse to sleep.

They said Martin had told them to relax and take advantage of the club's facilities. He would meet with them the next afternoon at two. He had said he had other business to take care of this morning and didn't wish to be disturbed.

All said they had come to Montana because Martin Sanderson was paying their expenses and promising them a reunion tour of their former band.

"What about this morning?" the sheriff had asked each of them. They had gone to bed early, had breakfast in the guest quarters and hadn't heard a sound coming from the main house.

The blonde, Loretta, said she'd been the first one down to breakfast but that she'd heard the showers running in both rooms as she'd passed. The other two, Betsy and Karen, had come down shortly thereafter.

The three hadn't been apart except to go to the bathroom since then.

Buford figured any one of them could have sneaked out to go to the main house and wasn't ruling any of them out if Martin Sanderson's death was found to be a homicide.

"Where is the other member of your former band?" Buford asked and checked his list. "Luca."

"Dead," the blonde said. "Talk about bad luck. Stepped out in front of a bus."

"How does Jett fit in?" he'd asked Betsy.

"Didn't he tell you? He used to hang around the band, flirting with all of us, but in the end, he left with JJ when she left the band. As far as I know, they're still together. At least according to the tabloids I see at the grocery checkout. I don't read them, mind you."

All of them swore they hadn't seen JJ and claimed they weren't even aware that she had arrived yet. When he'd checked the other rooms of the house, he found a guest room at the far end of the house where someone had obviously spent the night. The room was far enough away from the living room that Buford suspected a gunshot couldn't be heard.

He waited until the coroner and crime scene techs took over before he interviewed Jett Atkins. By then, Jett had had enough to drink that he was feeling no pain.

"So did one of them confess?" he asked with a laugh. "I didn't think so. They know who killed Martin. JJ."

"Why do you say that?"

Jett looked shocked. "It's been in all the trades for

months. JJ wanted out of her contract. Martin refused. We all knew it was coming to a head. Why else would he threaten to put her old band back together?"

"*Threaten?* I thought he flew everyone up here to make arrangements for the tour," the sheriff said.

Jett howled with laughter. "There is no way JJ would ever have agreed to that. No, he was just trying to bring her back in line. Those women hate JJ. She not only broke up the band, she also became successful. I would imagine JJ went ballistic when Martin told her that either she played ball or he would force her into doing a reunion tour with women who would have stabbed her in the back just as quickly as looked at her."

"Martin Sanderson could make her do that?"

"He *owned* her. He could do anything he wanted. The only way she could get out of that contract was to die. Or," Jett added with a grin, "kill Martin."

"Do you think this JJ knew that Martin had already flown the band members to Montana?" Buford asked. All except Luca, whoever she had been.

"Doubt it, since apparently he had them staying in a separate guest house," Jett said. "I can't say I blame JJ for killing him. He really was a bastard."

"What about you?" Buford asked.

"What about me?"

"What are you doing here?"

"Martin invited me." He grinned. "More leverage. I'm sure he planned to leak it to the press. He wanted it to look like JJ and I were back together."

"You weren't?"

He shook his head. "It was just a publicity stunt. Martin loved doing them. But JJ and I would have had to go along with it, since he held our contracts."

"So you were signed with him, as well. How does his death affect that?"

Jett smiled widely. "Freedom. With Martin dead, JJ and I are both free. Well, at least I am. I owe her a great debt of gratitude."

When Buford was finished interviewing all of them, he asked them not to leave town. Betsy called for a taxi and the four of them left together, but the sheriff could feel the tension between them.

As he watched them leave, he wondered where the missing JJ was and why they all seemed to think she had killed Martin Sanderson.

Blythe knew she was taking a chance going home with this cowboy. But that's how she'd always lived her life. She was convinced that if she hadn't, she'd still be living in her mother's trailer in the middle of the desert with some abusive drunk like her mother had.

She had learned to take care of herself. She'd had to even before she'd left home at fourteen. There'd been too many nights when her mother would pass out and Blythe would hear the heavy footsteps of whatever boyfriend her mother had brought home from the bar coming down the hallway toward her room.

She'd been eleven when she started keeping a butcher knife under her pillow. She'd only had to use it once.

Blythe shoved that memory away as she watched the small Western town disappear behind them. The air was cooler now as Logan sped along the blacktop of a two-lane. The houses, she noted, were few and far between, and the farther they went, the less she saw of anything but open country.

The land ran green in rolling hills broken only occasionally by a tree or a rocky point. In one such tree, a bald eagle watched them pass. Several antelope stood silhouetted against a lush hillside. Further down, a handful of deer grazed on the new green grass. One lifted his head at the sound of the motorcycle. His ears were huge, reminding her of Mickey Mouse ears at Disney World.

Blythe stared at all the wild things they passed, having never seen them before except in magazines or on television.

As Logan turned onto a gravel road, slowing down a little, she saw cattle in the distance, dark against the horizon. Closer, a couple of horses loped along in the breeze.

When she looked up the road, she saw where the road ended. She really was out in the middle of nowhere. Alone with a man she'd didn't know. For all she knew, he could be more dangerous than what she'd left behind.

She could hear her mother's slurred words, the words she'd grown up with all those years ago.

"You think you're better than me?" The harsh cigarettes-and-booze laugh. "I can see your future, little girl. No matter how you try to fight it, you're headed for a bad end."

She *had* tried to fight it, and at one point, she'd actually thought she'd beaten her mother's prediction. But by then her mother was long dead and buried and there was no one there to hear her say, "See Mama, you were wrong. Look at your little girl now."

Blythe laughed softly. Wouldn't her mother love to be here now to see that all her predictions had come true. She would have been the first to tell her daughter that if you flew too high, too fast, you were headed for a fall.

Clearly, she'd proven that she had too much of her mother's blood in her. She'd flown high all right, but ultimately, it had caught up with her. She was now in free fall. And the worst part was, she knew she deserved it.

As Logan turned down an even smaller road, she stared at the stark landscape and wondered what she'd gotten herself into this time. Logan, she thought, must be thinking the same thing.

Maybe they were more alike than he thought.

The last of the day's sun had slipped below the horizon but not before painting the spring green rolling hills with gold. The sky, larger than any she'd ever seen, had turned to cobalt blue. Not even a cloud hung on the horizon.

At the end of the road, she caught a glimpse of an old farmhouse. Past it were an older barn and some horses in a pasture.

The house, she saw as they drew closer, had seen better days but she could tell it had recently been given a fresh coat of white paint. There was a porch with a couple of wooden chairs and curtains at the windows.

"It's not much," Logan said as he parked the motorcycle out front and they climbed off.

"It's great," she said meaning it. She couldn't see another house within miles. She'd never been in such an isolated place. Here she could pretend that she'd escaped her old life. At least for a little while.

As he opened the door, she noticed that he hadn't bothered to lock the house when he'd left. Trusting soul. She smiled at the thought. The kind of man who brought home a perfect stranger. Well, not perfect, far from it. But still a stranger.

Buford was glad to have turned the case over to the state crime techs. This would be a high-profile case and while he would still be involved, it was no longer solely on his shoulders.

It would be getting dark soon and he was anxious to get home for supper. He just hoped Clara would lay off the hot peppers. The woman was killing him.

Unfortunately, he couldn't quit thinking about the case, especially what might have been pinned to the man's robe. Too bad someone had taken the note.

He told himself the crime techs would be especially thorough on this one, since clearly Martin Sanderson was somebody. Not only did he own a place in the Grizzly Club, he was apparently some hotshot music producer from Los Angeles.

The club liked to play down the identities of their owners, how much money they had and how they made it. No need to announce it anyway, since the residents probably all knew much more about each other than any of the staff or people outside the club ever could. After all, if they had the dough to buy a place behind the gate, then they were instantly part of the club, weren't they? Clearly Kevin was merely staff.

Buford stopped at the guardhouse to ask about the woman visitor who'd at least said she was JJ when she'd picked up her key. He found it irritating that the residents who left the names of their guests didn't even want the guards to know exactly who was coming for a visit.

"These are people who have to be very careful,"

Kevin had said when Buford had questioned why they needed so much secrecy. "They worry that they could be kidnapped or their children kidnapped. They aren't like you and me."

"They die when they're shot in the heart just like you and me," Buford pointed out and warranted himself a scowl from Kevin.

At the gate, the guard was more than glad to talk to the local sheriff about the guest allegedly known as JJ. He described a dark-haired good-looking woman. "She left in a hurry, I can tell you that. She barely waited for the gate to open."

"What was she driving?"

The guard described a silver sports car convertible. "I can give you her license plate number. We take those down on anyone coming or going."

Buford thanked him as he glanced at the plate number the guard gave him. It began with a 7, which meant a local Montana Lake County plate, probably a rental. "How did the woman seem to you when she left?"

"I didn't speak to her, barely got a glimpse of her."

"She was going *that* fast?" he asked in surprise since there were speed bumps near the gate.

"Well, she was moving at a good clip, but I was also about to check the guy on the motorcycle who was coming in just then."

"A club resident?"

He shook his head. "Not one I'd ever seen. But I didn't get a chance to talk to him. As I started toward him, he swung around and took off after the woman in the sports car."

"He *followed* her?"

The guard hesitated. "I saw him look at her as she left and then he seemed to go after her."

"He *knew* her?" Buford asked.

"I got the feeling he did."

"You didn't happen to get the plate on the motorcycle, did you?"

"No, but I'm sure our cameras caught it."

Buford waited. It didn't take long before the guard produced the bike plate number. He pocketed both, anxious to run them. But as he left the guard station his radio went off, alerting him of an accident on the road back to town.

A car had left the highway and crashed in the rocks at the edge of the lake. Firefighters and emergency medical services were on their way to the scene.

Buford turned on his flashing lights and siren. It was going to be a long night the way things were going.

As Blythe stepped into Logan's farmhouse, she wasn't sure what she would find. She half expected a woman's touch. She'd taken him for being about her own age, early thirties, which meant he could have been married at least once or at least lived with someone. But she was pleased to see that there was no sign that a woman had ever lived here.

"Like I said, basic," he noted almost apologetically.

"I like it. Simple is good." He had no idea how she'd been living.

She walked around, taking it in. The place was furnished with apparently the only thought to being practical and comfortable. There was an old leather couch in front of a small brick fireplace, an even older recliner next to it and a rug in front of the couch on the worn wooden floor. The kitchen had a 1950s metal and Formica top table and four chairs. Through a door she spotted a bathroom and stairs that led up to the second floor, where she figured there would be bedrooms.

"Why don't I show you up to your room in case you want to freshen up," Logan said, shrugging out of his leather jacket.

She couldn't help noticing his broad shoulders, the well-formed chest, the slim hips, the incredibly long legs. It brought back the memory of being in his arms on the dance floor and sent a frisson of desire through her.

Logan headed up the stairs and she followed. Just as she'd figured, there were two bedrooms, one with a double bed, one with no furniture at all, and another bathroom, this one with a huge clawfoot tub.

One bed. She realized she hadn't thought out this part of her great escape. That was so like her. Not that the idea of sharing his bed hadn't crossed her mind. After all, she was the one who'd wanted to run away with him. What did she expect was going to happen?

He must have seen her expression. "You can have this room," he said motioning to the bed. "I'll take the couch."

"I don't want to take your bed."

He didn't give her a chance to argue the point. "I'll see what's in the fridge. Are you hungry? You didn't eat much at the last place we stopped. I could fry up some elk steaks."

She smiled, giving herself away. She couldn't explain this ravenous hunger she had except that maybe she was just tired of going to bed hungry and for all the wrong reasons.

"You've never had elk, right?"

"How did you know?" she said with a laugh.

"You're going to love it."

"I thought you raised *beef*," she said.

"I try to kill an elk every year or so. A little variety, you know?"

She thought she did know.

"There are towels in the cabinet in the bathroom. I just put clean sheets on the bed before I left. Holler if there is anything else you need," he said, and tromped back down the stairs, leaving her standing in his bedroom.

She glanced at the bed, tempted to lie down for a while. The ride here had taken five hours, which wasn't bad, but she hadn't slept well last night and for some time now she'd been running on fear-induced adrenaline.

The memory of what she had to fear sent a shaft of ice up her spine. She shivered even in the warm bedroom. The weight of her life choices pressed down on her chest and she had to struggle to breathe. Did she really think that she could escape the past—even in this remote part of Montana, even with this trusting cowboy?

"There's a price that comes with the life you've lived." Not her mother's voice this time. Martin Sanderson's. "And sweetheart, your bill has come due."

Chapter 4

The ambulance was there by the time Sheriff Buford Olson reached the accident scene. He parked along the edge of the narrow road where a highway patrolman was directing traffic. A wrecker was in the process of pulling the blackened car up from the rocky shore where it had landed, but he could still smell smoke.

As Buford walked to the edge of the road, he could see where the car had gone off, dropped over the steep edge of the road to tumble down the rocks before coming to a stop at the edge of the lake.

He noticed no skid marks on the pavement or in the dirt at the shoulder of the road. The driver hadn't even tried to brake before going off the road and over the rocky precipice?

"The passengers?" he asked as he spotted one of the ambulance drivers.

"Just one." The man shook his head.

Buford walked over to one of the highway patrolmen at the scene and asked if there was anything he could do to help.

"Pretty well have it covered," the officer said. "Looks like the driver was traveling at a high rate of speed when she missed the curve, plummeting over the edge of the road and rolling several times on the rocks before the car exploded."

Buford turned to watch the wrecker pull the car up from the edge of the lake, then asked to see the patrolman's report. He did a double take when he saw the license plate number the highway patrolman had put down.

He hurriedly pulled the slip of paper the security guard at the Grizzly Club had given him. It matched the sports car the woman guest had been driving earlier that morning.

"You get an ID when you ran the plate?" he asked the patrolman.

"The car was a rental. Rented under the name of Jennifer James yesterday."

JJ? Had to be, since the license plate was the same one the guard had given him.

As Buford left the scene, he couldn't help thinking how coincidental it was that one of Martin Sanderson's guests was now also dead. Of course, it could be that the woman had been killed because she was driving too fast away from the murder scene. That would have made a great theory if it hadn't been hours since she'd left the Grizzly Club driving too fast then too—before she'd apparently gone off the road and died at the edge of the lake.

So where had she been during those missing hours?
The crash had occurred only miles from the Grizzly
Club turnoff. And why hadn't she tried to brake?

Martin Sanderson had approved six guests. Jett Atkins was accounted for and possibly JJ, along with
three members of the all-girl band. Luca was apparently dead.

But it was the elusive JJ who captured his thoughts.
That and the safety pin and missing note on Sanderson's robe.

Unfortunately, the woman who'd been driving this
car was now on her way to the morgue and she might
have been the only other person in the world who knew
what that note said and why Martin Sanderson was
dead.

Logan went downstairs and dug some steaks out
of the freezer. He had no idea what Blythe was doing
here or what she was thinking. Or what she might be
running from, but she was sure as the devil running
from something.

He told himself it didn't matter, although he feared
he could be wrong about that. Apparently the woman
wanted a break from whatever life she'd been living.
He didn't even know what that life had been or if he
should be worried about it. But she triggered a powerful protective instinct in him that had made him throw
caution to the wind.

Too bad she didn't trust him enough to tell him
what was going on, he thought, then remembered the
scrap of yellow paper he'd retrieved from under the
booth table back at the café. He quickly reached into
his pocket.

"Logan?"

He started at the sound of her voice directly behind him. It was the first time she'd said his name. It was like music off her tongue. His hand froze in his pocket as he turned.

"Would you mind if I took a bath?"

He withdrew his hand from his pocket sans the note and smiled. He'd seen the gleam in her eye when she'd spotted his big clawfoot tub. "You're in luck. There's even some bubble bath up there. A joke housewarming gift from my brothers."

"You have brothers?"

"Five."

She raised a brow. "Wow. Sisters?"

He shook his head. "Take as long as you want. I have steaks thawing for steak sandwiches later."

"Thanks." She started to turn away. "And thanks for bringing me here." With that she ran upstairs. A moment later he heard the water come on in the bathroom.

Thinking of her, he told himself there was something strong and carefree about this woman he'd brought home and, at the same time, vulnerable and almost fragile. Whatever she wanted or needed from him, he'd do his damnedest to give to her. Right now, though, it was just the use of his tub, he thought smiling, and tried not to imagine Blythe with her slim yet lush body up to her neck in bubbles.

He waited to make sure she didn't come back down before he withdrew the scrap of paper and pressed it open to see what was on it.

Logan wasn't sure what he'd expected to find on the piece of notepaper—if anything. He'd hoped it would be a clue to this woman.

He was disappointed.

There were only two words on the yellow note paper, both written in blue pen. *You're Next.*

He stared at them for a moment. Next for what? He had no idea. The words didn't offer any clue to Blythe, that was for sure. He wadded up the scrap of paper and tossed it into the garbage, pushing it down where it couldn't be seen. He felt foolish for retrieving it, worse for thinking it might be important.

Charlie Baker let out a string of profanity when he saw all the flashing lights on the highway ahead. Cops. The stupid woman had gotten pulled over for speeding.

He swore again as his line of traffic came to a dead stop and he saw a highway patrolman walking down the line of cars toward him. Realizing regrettably that he had no way of getting out of the traffic, he quickly checked himself in his rearview mirror.

Charlie and his girlfriend had been on the road from Arizona for four days. He knew he looked rough. Hopefully not so rough that the officer would run the plates on this stolen pickup, especially with a warrant already out on him.

As the cop neared, Charlie put his window down, wishing he hadn't listened to Susie. Earlier he'd stopped to take a leak beside the road. It had been her idea to take that sports car after she'd found the keys on the floorboard—and the purse lying on the passenger seat.

He had looked around, pretty sure that whoever it belonged to had walked down to the lake and would be coming back any minute. They'd argued about taking the car, but Susie said the owner deserved to have it stolen—hell, was *asking* to have it stolen.

Once she opened the glove box and realized it was a rental, there had been no more argument. "I'm taking it. It might be my only chance to drive a car like this and it sure as hell beats that old pickup you *borrowed*."

She'd been bitching about the vehicle he'd stolen since they left Arizona and he'd been getting real tired of it.

"We can dump the pickup," she'd said. "It's probably going to break down soon anyway."

"We'll talk about it away from here," he'd said. There was something about this that made him uneasy. Who just left such an expensive car beside the road with the keys and a purse in it?

But there was no arguing with Susie. She got in the car and started it up, revving the engine too loud.

Charlie hadn't wanted to be around when whoever had rented the car came racing up and found Susie behind the wheel. He'd taken off in the pickup, yelling at her that he'd meet her down the road at the campground where they'd spent last night.

Only she hadn't shown. Back at the camp, he'd fallen asleep and lost track of time. Susie should have shown hours ago. He figured she'd probably taken off in that convertible and left him high and dry. But he'd decided he'd better go look for her, since if she was in trouble, he knew she'd rat him out in a heartbeat, and now here he was with a cop heading for him.

The officer stepped to his window. "There's been an accident. It could be a little bit before we get the road cleared."

That damned Susie had gone on a joyride and left him. Or, he realized, she could be caught in the traffic on the other side of the wreck just like he was. "What kind of accident, officer?"

"A car went off the road." He was already walking away.

Charlie watched him head down the highway to tell the other drivers of cars piling up behind him. Or, he thought, Susie might have wrecked that convertible. With a curse, he waited a minute before he got out of the pickup and worked his way along the edge of the trees to where a few people had gathered on the side of the road.

It was almost too dark to see what was going on, but as he drew closer, he smelled smoke. Joining the others gawking at the scene, he saw what was left of the pretty silver sports car convertible that Susie just had to drive being lifted up onto the back of a wrecker's flatbed.

"Did the driver get out?" he asked the man standing next to him.

"Trapped in the car. I heard the EMT say she was burned beyond recognition."

As Charlie turned to walk back to his pickup, he took an inventory of his emotions, surprised how little he felt other than anger. He should have known Susie wouldn't know how to drive a car like that. *He* should have driven it. Served her right.

But he knew if he had taken the car, he wouldn't have met Susie at the campground. He would have just kept going, leaving her and the stolen pickup behind. Susie probably knew that, he thought as he climbed into the truck and waited for the highway to clear so he could get the hell out of this state.

He had been getting real tired of Susie anyway. Fortunately, he'd insisted on taking everything from the purse she'd found in that expensive convertible. The cash and credit cards were going to come in handy.

Charlie smiled to himself. He'd never had good luck, but sometimes things had a way of working out for the best, didn't they.

Buford had to stop by his office on the way home and was shocked that he had a half-dozen calls from reporters. As tight-lipped as the Grizzly Club was, he couldn't believe word had gotten out this quickly. But people liked to talk—especially when it was something juicy like the death of a wealthy man from the Grizzly Club. And he'd already caught Jett on his phone.

He decided to see how bad it was. He picked up one of the messages and dialed the number.

"Is it true that JJ was killed tonight on the road just outside of Big Fork?" the reporter asked.

Not about Martin Sanderson? "I'm sorry but I can't…" He realized she'd called the victim JJ. "The accident is under investigation." He hung up frowning.

Who would have given a reporter that information? No one at the scene, even if they'd overheard that the car had been rented to a Jennifer James. Who knew that Jennifer James was known as JJ?

Jett, he'd bet on it. Buford had insisted on the cell phone numbers of Jett and the three members of the former band in case he needed to ask them any more questions. He'd warned all of them not to leave town until the investigation was complete.

None of them had been happy about the prospect of staying around, since they couldn't stay at the Grizzly

Club and had been forced to take a cheap motel instead. Betsy had called him to tell him where they were staying, as per his request.

As he grabbed his phone to call, Buford felt his stomach rumble. He was starved. He'd picked up a couple of cheeseburgers at a fast-food restaurant on his way back to his office. Clara would kill him. He was supposed to be on a diet. But she was killing him anyway with those darned chili peppers. He'd prefer to drop dead after eating a cheeseburger any day than keep living with his belly on fire.

He dialed the cell phone number Jett had given him. Jett answered on the third ring and didn't sound all that happy about hearing from him so soon.

"I just had a reporter call me," Buford said. "You didn't happen to—"

"I haven't talked to anyone."

Maybe. Maybe not. From what he'd seen of his granddaughter's rock 'n' roll idol, Jett liked publicity and he didn't seem to care if it was good or bad. He'd talk to anyone, even the tabloids, and he'd admitted that he let Martin use him and JJ for publicity stunts.

"What about the others?"

"Nope," Jett said after getting confirmation from the three women. Buford could hear the background noises. Apparently they were all in a restaurant together.

"Not even about the accident?" Buford said.

"*Accident?* Is that what you're calling it?" Jett snapped. "I should have known JJ would get away with this. She's always gotten away with whatever she did. Have you found her? Is that what she claims? That she *accidentally* killed Martin?"

So he didn't know about the car wreck. Which meant neither did the others, and they couldn't have called the press. But they were certainly quick to blame JJ for murder even before all the facts were in.

Buford decided to let Jett and the women read about the wreck in the morning papers. "I'll let you finish your supper then. Wait, one more question. Why did JJ want out of her contract?"

Jett sighed. "You really don't know much about the music business, do you? Martin discovered JJ, took over her career, made her a star. She wanted more control over her career and her life, but she was making him a ton of money. He would never have let her go though. She knew that."

"Does she also go by the name of Jennifer James?" He asked the real question he had wanted to ask, hoping to confirm what he *did* know.

"Yes," Jett said impatiently, as if everyone knew that. "Is that all?"

"For now," he said and hung up.

He started to call it a night. But then he remembered the man on the motorcycle that the guard thought had chased after the infamous JJ.

When he ran the number, Buford got a surprise.

Logan had the steaks cooked and everything ready for a late supper when Blythe came down wearing his robe and smelling of lilac bubble bath. Her wet, long, dark hair was pulled up on top of her head and he was struck by how beautiful she looked. Everything about her took his breath away. As little as he knew about her, he felt they were kindred souls somehow.

"Tell me about this part of Montana," she said as they ate. It was dark outside, the sky filled with millions of sparkling stars and a sliver of silver moon. A breeze stirred the curtains at the kitchen window. The house felt almost cozy.

He told her about the outlaw era that brought such infamous luminaries as Kid Curry, Butch Cassidy and the Sundance Kid to the area. "It was the last lawless place in Montana."

He told her how the railroad had come through and brought settlers who were given land and a time limit on improving the acres if they wanted to keep it.

"It was a hard place to survive. Not many of them made it. You had to be hardy."

"Like your family?" she asked.

He smiled at that. "Chisholm roots run deep, that's for sure." He didn't tell her how his ancestors had brought up a herd of cattle from Texas and each generation had helped build up Chisholm Cattle Company to what it was today.

Longhorns hadn't done well because of the tough winters. Once they'd changed to Black Angus cattle, the ranch had thrived.

"I saw the horses out in the pasture," she said. "Are they yours?"

"Do you ride?"

She laughed and shook her head. "But I've always wanted to."

"Tomorrow I'll teach you," he said on impulse.

"Really?" She looked excited about the prospect. There was a peacefulness to her that he hadn't seen since they were on the dance floor last night.

"I think you'll like it, and when you're ready, I'll show you more of my part of Montana by horseback."

"I'd love that," she said and finished her sandwich.

"You liked the elk?" he asked amused at the way she ate. He had joked that she acted as if she wasn't sure where her next meal might be coming from, but now wondered if that wasn't the case. She'd said that the sports car she'd been driving didn't belong to her. For all he knew, she might not have anything more than the clothes on her back.

Maybe she *had* been a guest at the Grizzly Club, but he had a bad feeling he'd been right and she'd borrowed a car she shouldn't have.

He shook his head at the thought that he might be harboring a criminal. And such a beautiful, engaging one at that.

As they finished the elk steaks, Logan looked across the table at his guest and saw how exhausted she was. He felt a strange contentment being here with her like this. It surprised him. He never brought any of his dates back to his house. But then this woman wasn't exactly a date, was she?

"There's a quilt up on the bed that my great grandmother made," he said. "You look like you're ready to crawl under it."

She smiled, appearing almost as content as he felt.

He got up and cleared the dishes, putting them in the sink, then he went to the closet and pulled down the extra blankets he kept there. Winters in this old farmhouse were downright cold, and there were many nights when he'd fallen asleep in front of the fire—the only really warm place in the house.

Dropping them on the couch, he turned to find her

standing in the kitchen doorway. "Don't you want me to help you with the dishes?" She looked cute wearing his robe. He watched her pull it around her, hugging herself as if even the spring night felt cold to her. It slid over her curves in a way that made him realize he would never look at that robe the same way again.

"The dishes can wait. Why don't you get some sleep? I'll saddle up the horses in the morning and we'll get you ridin'."

She seemed to hesitate for a moment, then smiled gratefully. "Thank you. For everything."

He nodded. "It's nice to have you here." It was true, but still he hadn't meant to say it, let alone admit it. He'd never been without female company if he'd wanted it. But he often found women confusing. He preferred his horse.

Not this woman though.

Even after she went upstairs, he could smell lilac and felt a stirring in him at the mere thought of her. He'd felt drawn to her from that moment he'd seen her expression on the dance floor. He recalled the way she had moved to the music.

As he heard her close his bedroom door, he groaned to himself. He must be losing his grip. His brothers would think him a damned fool. Not just for bringing a woman he knew nothing about back to his house, but for letting such a beautiful woman go to bed alone—and in his bed.

Whatever her reason for being here, it wasn't because she couldn't resist him, he thought with a laugh. Logan Chisholm wasn't used to that, either.

As he lay down on the couch and pulled a blanket over him, he told himself she would be gone in the morning—and probably with his pickup and any cash she could find.

But as he heard her moving around upstairs, he found himself smiling. He could always get another truck.

Chapter 5

The motorcycle that the guard at the Grizzly Club said had gone after the woman in the silver sports car was registered to Logan Chisholm, the address Chisholm Cattle Company, Whitehorse, Montana.

Sheriff Buford Olson let out a low whistle. Hoyt Chisholm was one of the wealthiest ranchers in the state, so it was no surprise his son might be visiting the Grizzly Club. Or even that he might know the woman who'd been visiting Martin Sanderson, as the guard had suggested.

So what had he been doing on this side of the Rockies? Visiting his friend JJ? Did that mean that Logan Chisholm also knew Martin Sanderson?

Buford picked up the phone. His stomach growled again and he noticed how late it was. He'd call him tomorrow. Probably a waste of time anyway, since Logan Chisholm hadn't actually gone into the Grizzly Club.

But Chisholm had seen Jennifer James leaving and possibly followed her. He might know where she'd gone between the time she was seen leaving the club and going out in a blaze that evening beside Flathead Lake.

Sighing, Buford put the phone back. He was starved and it was late. Also, he didn't relish telling Logan Chisholm about the dead woman—that was if Logan even knew this JJ. Chisholm was probably still in the Bigfork area, which meant he would read about it in the papers.

There was always the chance that if Chisholm knew something about either death, he would come forward with any information he had. Buford had never heard much about Hoyt Chisholm's sons except that they were adopted and there were a bunch of them. Which meant they hadn't been in too much trouble. With a father as well known as Hoyt Chisholm, it would be hard to stay out of the headlines if the sons had run-ins with the law. Even Chisholm's money could only do so much when it came to the press.

It certainly hadn't been able to keep Hoyt's name out of the headlines when he'd lost first one wife, then another. The first wife had drowned, the second had been killed in a horseback riding accident, the third had disappeared, recently turning up dead, murdered.

Buford had followed the case with interest. Hoyt had been arrested, but later cleared. An insurance investigator by the name of Agatha Wells had been arrested for the third wife's murder. Last Buford had heard, Agatha Wells had been sent to the state mental hospital for evaluation and had escaped.

It had been nasty business, since Hoyt Chisholm had recently taken a fourth wife, Emma. The insurance investigator had come after her as well, abducting her at one point. Later Agatha Wells was believed to have drowned in the Milk River after being shot by a sheriff's deputy on the Chisholm ranch. Her body, though, had never been found.

He hoped Logan Chisholm didn't have any connection to Martin Sanderson's death. The Chisholm family had been through enough.

Picking up his hat, Buford pushed himself up out of his chair. He'd spent too much time on his feet today and he ached all over. As he turned out his office light, all he could think about was his big leather recliner waiting for him in front of the television. He had a lot on his mind. And he couldn't quit thinking about that note that had been pinned to Martin Sanderson's body. He'd give anything to know what it said. He had a feeling it would solve this case.

So much about the case nagged at him. Why had Martin Sanderson invited all of the members of the former Tough as Nails band to Montana and left keys for them when he had to know that the one called Luca was dead?

And what, if anything, did this Jennifer James, JJ, have to do with it?

It wasn't until he got home to discover his granddaughter visiting that he found out just who JJ had been.

Betsy Harper glanced around the table in the motel restaurant dining room, marveling at how little they had all changed. Loretta was still brassy, loud and demanding. Karen had always been quiet, never letting anyone know what she was thinking.

And Jett was Jett, she thought with no small amount of bitterness. He had barely acknowledged her, but what did she expect? He'd dumped her for JJ ten years ago and done her a favor in retrospect.

He would have made a lousy husband, an even worse father. Still, he'd been her first, and she somehow thought that might have made a difference to him. Apparently, it didn't.

"So what do you think of this whole mess?" Jett asked after he'd joined them in the motel restaurant dining room.

They'd decided to all stay at the same motel. Jett had joked about keeping enemies close. Betsy supposed that was how he felt. Just like JJ, he'd definitely betrayed them all, some of them more than others.

Conversation had been stilted. Loretta had gone on for a while complaining about how bad her life was. As if they couldn't just look at her and see that she was hard up for money. Loretta blamed Martin and was convinced Tough as Nails could have been great if he hadn't broken up the band.

"I'm not sorry Martin's dead," Loretta said now. "I just wish I'd shot him."

"Who says you didn't?" Jett said. "We all think it was JJ, but maybe she didn't do it."

"I think she did it," Betsy said. "Why else would she take off the way she did?" Jett had told them that JJ had been staying in a wing of the main house and that he'd seen her prints in Martin's blood—and so had the sheriff.

"Maybe she ran to avoid *us*," Karen said without

looking up from her meal. "If like you said Martin was threatening her with this reunion tour… She was probably afraid that we all hated her."

Jett laughed. "Like you don't. I would have loved to have seen her face when she found out what Martin was up to. I'm surprised she didn't kill him with her bare hands."

"I can't believe she agreed to a reunion tour," Betsy said.

Karen gave her a you-can't-be-that-naïve look. None of them knew just how naïve she'd always been about a lot of things.

"Jett just said JJ knew nothing about it," Karen said impatiently to her. "There was never going to be a tour. It was just Martin messing with us again."

"Well, he's dead now." Jett waved the waiter over. "Anyone else want to drink to that? I'm in the mood to celebrate. Champagne," he told the waiter.

"You're the only one who thinks this is a celebration," Karen said. "A man has been murdered and you're all ready to string JJ up for it."

"Well, if one of *us* didn't kill him, then who else was there?" Jett said. "We're the only ones who had motive, opportunity and means, since there was a handgun on the floor beside him. I heard the sheriff check. It belonged to Martin."

"But JJ is the only one missing, isn't she?" Loretta pointed out.

The waiter brought the champagne and glasses. Jett poured himself a glass and lifted it for a toast. "Here's to JJ, wherever she might be. If she was here I would thank her."

No one else reached for a glass, but that didn't keep Jett from emptying his.

As he set his down, his gaze settled on Betsy. She felt the heat of his look as he asked, "What do you girls have planned to amuse yourselves until we can get out of this godforsaken place?"

Karen felt disgusted being around Jett again. She hated that they were all acting as if nothing had happened ten years ago.

Betsy was the worst. Jett had broken her heart. Karen remembered how despondent she'd been. She'd had to hold Betsy's hand through that horrible time while keeping her own pain and anger to herself.

Now as she watched Jett turning his charm on Betsy, she wanted to throw something at him. Throw something at Betsy, too. Hadn't the woman learned what a no-count Jett was? He used people, then discarded them. One look at Jett and Betsy should have known the man hadn't changed.

"I, for one, am going to turn in early," Karen said tossing down her napkin and rising. "I regret ever coming here."

"You came because you felt like you owed us," Loretta said snidely.

Karen turned on her. "It wasn't your guilt trip that made me change my mind and come after you pleaded with me," she snapped. "I did it because I got tired of listening to you whine."

"Now, ladies," Jett said.

"There are no ladies here," Loretta said with a laugh. "I think I *will* have a drink, Jett. That is, if you're buying." She picked up one of the champagne glasses and held it out. He happily filled it.

"I didn't want to come, either," Betsy said. "But I also didn't want to be the one band member who ruined it for the others."

"How could we have had a reunion tour without Luca anyway?" Karen said.

"Bands do tours all the time without the original members," Jett said.

"There wasn't going to be a reunion tour," Karen snapped as she started to step away from the table.

"Then why get us here?" Betsy said, sounding surprised and disheartened.

Karen was tired of Betsy's apparent naïveté. No one could be that sweet and innocent, she thought as she walked away.

Behind her, she heard Jett say, "I think he was hoping one of you would kill JJ."

Loretta's laugh and words followed Karen out of the room. "What makes you think we didn't?"

Emma Chisholm stood at the window looking out at the rolling prairie. Chisholm land as far as the eye could see. She'd fallen in love with this place, the same way she had with Hoyt Chisholm, only months ago.

Of course, she hadn't had any idea what was in store for her when she'd agreed down in Denver to run off with him to Vegas for a quickie marriage. They hadn't known each other. They hadn't cared. Love does that to you. He'd told her the ranch was large and isolated.

"Sounds wonderful," she'd said, and he'd laughed. "Some women can't take that kind of emptiness."

"I'm not some women." But she'd heard the pain

in his voice and known there had been others before her who he'd taken back to the ranch. All she'd known then was that they hadn't lasted. A man in his late fifties would have had at least a wife or maybe even two, she'd thought then.

It wasn't until she'd come to Whitehorse, Montana, and met Aggie Wells that she'd found out she'd underestimated Hoyt's history with wives—and pain. He'd been married three other times, all three ending tragically, as it turned out.

Former insurance investigator Aggie Wells had brought the news along with a warning that Emma was next. "He killed his other wives. I can't prove it," Aggie had said, "but I keep trying. Watch yourself."

Emma hadn't believed it. She knew Hoyt soul deep, as they say. He wasn't a killer. She'd just assumed like everyone else that Aggie was either obsessed with her husband—or just plain crazy.

That was months ago, she thought now as she looked out across the land and realized she'd been living with ghosts—the ghosts of her husband's exes and now Aggie's ghost.

So why did she still expect to see one of them coming across the prairie with only one goal in mind, killing her, the fourth and no doubt final wife of Hoyt Chisholm?

No one knew about the ghosts she'd been living with. As much as she and her husband shared, she couldn't share these thoughts with Hoyt.

"Aggie Wells is dead," Hoyt had said. "She was shot. You saw her fall into the river. She didn't come up."

But when the sheriff had dragged the river, they hadn't found her body.

"She got hung up on something, a root, a limb, an old barbed-wire fence downriver," Hoyt said. "When the river goes down this summer, we'll find her body. But until then, she's gone, okay?"

But it hadn't been okay, because Emma had come to know Aggie, had actually liked her, maybe worse had believed in her heart that the woman might not be crazy. Nor dead. If anyone could survive being shot and even drowned, it would be Aggie.

The insurance investigator wasn't the only ghost Emma now lived with though. Hoyt's first wife, Laura Chisholm, was the ghost that caused her sleepless night. Aggie had come to believe Laura hadn't drowned that day on Fort Peck Reservoir but was still alive and vengefully killing Hoyt's wives.

Aggie had even provided photographs of a woman who looked so much like what Laura Chisholm would look like now after all these years that it had made Hoyt pale. Seeing the effect the photographs had had on her husband had made a believer out of Emma. And if you believed Laura Chisholm was alive, then you also had to believe that she had murdered not one but possibly all of Hoyt's other wives—and would eventually come for Emma herself, like the living ghost she was.

Hoyt didn't believe it. At least that's what he said. But if that were true, then why would he continue to insist on someone hanging around near the ranch house so Emma was never left alone?

She laughed softly at a thought. Didn't Hoyt realize that she was never really alone? Either Aggie's ghost or Laura's was always with her—at least in her thoughts. She was merely waiting for one of the ghosts to appear. Either Aggie trying to save her again or Laura determined to kill her.

"What are you baking?" Hoyt asked as he came into the kitchen and pulled her from her thoughts.

"Gingersnaps," she said, stepping away from the window and back to her baking. Baking was the one thing that took her mind off the waiting. She was always baking or cooking or cleaning. Hiring help had proved to be difficult after all the trouble here on the ranch. Suspicion hung over the place like thick smoke.

"I hate seeing you work so much," Hoyt said now. "I've called an agency in Billings. We have that guest-room at the far wing. What would you think about live-in help? No one wants to drive all the way out here from Whitehorse. I think this will work better."

She didn't correct him. It wasn't the drive and he knew it. Maybe people in Billings didn't know about the Chisholm Curse, as it was called.

"I don't need any help. You know I like to keep busy," Emma said, but she could tell he was determined to hire someone. Normally she would have put up a fight, but the truth was, having someone living in the house and helping sounded like a blessing. That way Hoyt and his sons could go back to running this ranch instead of babysitting her.

Hoyt came up behind her, put his arms around her and pulled her close. She closed her eyes and leaned back into him. Never had she felt such love.

"Dawson just left for home," her husband said, nuzzling her neck. Her stepson Dawson had been assigned to Emma duty that day, which meant he'd spent the day pretending he had things to do around the ranch's main house and yard. Did any of them really believe they were fooling her?

Certainly not Hoyt, she thought as she turned off the mixer and let him lead her upstairs to their bedroom. The cookies could wait. Being in her husband's strong arms could not.

She knew as he closed the bedroom door that he believed their love was like a shield that would protect them. She prayed he was right, but alive or dead, his first wife and Aggie Wells were anything but gone for good.

Former insurance investigator Aggie Wells had come close to dying. She still wasn't her old self. For months, she'd felt her strength seep out of her and now wondered if she would ever be the same again.

She told herself she was lucky to be alive. If the bullet had been a quarter of an inch one way or the other it would have nicked a vital organ and she would have drowned in that creek.

It surprised her that she'd survived against all odds. How easy it would have been to give in to death. She still had nightmares remembering how long she'd had to stay underwater to avoid the sheriff's deputies catching her.

That memory always came with the bitter bite of betrayal. She'd trusted Emma Chisholm. That stupid, stupid woman. Aggie had been trying to save her life and what did she get for it? Shot and almost drowned.

In her more charitable moments, she reminded herself that she *had* abducted Emma just months before that day on the river. Still, she'd risked capture to bring Emma important information about Laura Chisholm.

Also, Emma had seemed as surprised as Aggie had that day when they'd heard the sheriff and her deputies coming through the trees. Maybe Emma hadn't informed them about the meeting by the river. At least that's what Aggie liked to believe. She liked Emma and now there was nothing she could do to save her. *The die is cast,* she thought. After surviving the cold water and the bullet wound, Aggie had gotten pneumonia and barely survived.

Her weight had dropped drastically and she didn't seem to have any strength to fight it. She told herself she was bouncing back, but a part of her knew it wasn't true. Worse, she feared she would never see this case through.

A small, bitter laugh escaped her lips. It wasn't her case, hadn't been for years. The insurance company she'd worked for had fired her because she hadn't been able to let the Chisholm case go.

She couldn't really blame them. She'd gotten it all wrong anyway. When Hoyt Chisholm's first wife, Laura, had allegedly drowned in Fort Peck Reservoir, Aggie had been convinced Hoyt had killed her.

He'd remarried not long after. He had adopted six sons who needed homes, and if any man was desperate for a wife, it would have been him. Tasha Chisholm had been killed in a horseback-riding accident.

Aggie couldn't believe he'd kill another one. And then along came Krystal. Did he really think he could get away with a third murder?

Krystal Chisholm had disappeared not long into the marriage. By then Aggie had been pulled off the case, but that hadn't stopped her. She couldn't let him get away with killing another wife.

The first two deaths appeared to be accidents—at least to the unsuspecting. The third wife's disappearance could never be proved to be anything more than that.

"But I knew better," Aggie said to herself. Her faint voice echoed in the small room of what had once been a motel and was now a cheap studio apartment where she'd been hiding on the south side of Billings.

She'd hit a brick wall in her covert investigation back then. The insurance company had warned her off the case. But eventually they found out and fired her.

Fortunately, she'd saved every dime she'd ever made, so money wasn't a problem. She'd taken on private investigations when she felt like it. She was good at what she did, putting herself in someone else's shoes until she knew them inside and out.

Thankfully, she'd helped people who, when called on, couldn't say no to helping her. Like the surgeon she'd had to call after she was shot.

She might have given up the Chisholm cases—if Hoyt Chisholm hadn't married a fourth time all these years later. Aggie had no choice but to warn Emma Chisholm. The woman was blind in love.

"Just as you had no choice but to abduct her once you figured out who the murderer really was," Aggie said to the empty room, then pulled herself up some in the threadbare recliner where she sat.

Only a little sun spilled in through the dirty window between the two frayed and faded curtains. The light bothered her now. Her illness had seemed to affect her eyes. She drew her attention away from the crack in the curtains, feeling too weak to get up and close them tighter.

But no one believed her. Instead, law enforcement was convinced that Aggie herself had killed Hoyt's second and third wives in an attempt to frame him for murder.

She scoffed at that. This was about obsession. Not Aggie's with this case, but Laura's with Hoyt. Aggie understood obsession, she knew how it could take over your life.

If only the sheriff had listened to her. Instead, she'd been arrested and sent to the state mental hospital for evaluation. They thought *she* was crazy?

Aggie smiled to herself as she remembered how she'd slipped through the cracks, sending another woman to the state mental hospital who actually needed the help.

Her smile faded quickly though as she reminded herself that she had failed. That day beside the river she had brought Emma the proof that Laura Chisholm was alive and living just hours away in Billings as a woman named Sharon Jones.

But when she'd come out of her fever, surfacing again at death's door, she'd asked the doctor if a woman named Sharon Jones had been arrested.

"I had hoped and yet I knew better," she said to herself. Laura was like a warm breeze in summer, drifting in and out unnoticed. She had to be to stay hidden all these years, appearing only to kill and then disappear again.

The doctor had given her the bad news. Sharon Jones hadn't been arrested and now she'd disappeared again. "I went by the house you asked me to check," the doctor told her. "It was empty. No sign of anyone."

Laura Chisholm was still on the loose. She would

take another identity and when the time was right, she would strike again. Emma Chisholm was going to die and there wasn't anything Aggie could do about it.

Chapter 6

It was late by the time Logan headed for the barn to saddle his horse the next day. He must have been more tired than he'd thought. He couldn't remember sleeping this late in the day since college.

Once saddled, he rode down the half-mile lane to pick up his mail from the box on the county road. As much as he loved being on the back of his motorcycle, he loved being on the back of a horse just as much.

It was a beautiful Montana spring day, the sky a brilliant blue, no clouds on the horizon and the sun spreading warmth over the vibrant green land. He loved this time of year, loved the smells, the feel of new beginnings.

He wondered if that was what his houseguest was looking for. She'd apparently bailed—at least for a while—on her old life, whatever that was. He hadn't slept all that well last night knowing she was upstairs. And this morning he had no more idea what she was all about than he'd had when he'd met her the other night at the bar. He hadn't heard a sound out of her by the time he'd left. For all he knew she'd sneaked out last night and was long gone.

At least she hadn't taken his pickup.

He'd already decided to take a few days off work and, if she hadn't bailed on him as well, show her his part of Montana if she was still up for it. But then what, he wondered? Eventually, he had to get back to work. His father and brothers would be wondering what was going on. The last thing he needed was for one of them to show up at the house, he thought as he reached the county road.

Logan realized Blythe didn't really know who he was, either. He felt almost guilty about that—even though she had been anything but forthcoming about herself. He wanted her to like him for himself and not for his family money. Of course, it could be that she already knew who he was—knew that night at the bar when he'd asked her to dance. His family had certainly been in the news enough with that mess about Aggie Wells.

He pushed away the memory, just glad that it was over. With Aggie Wells dead, that should be the end of speculation about his father's other wives' deaths.

Logan thought instead of Blythe and his reservations about her. He recalled her new cowboy boots. She wouldn't be the first woman who'd come to Montana to meet herself a cowboy. Even better a rich one.

But with a self-deprecating grin, he reminded himself that she hadn't even made a play for him. Maybe that was the plan, since it seemed to be working. He couldn't get her off his mind.

Swinging down from the horse, he collected his mail and the newspapers that had stacked up since he'd been gone. He glanced at today's *Great Falls Tribune,* scanning the headlines before stuffing everything into one of his saddlebags, climbing back into the saddle and heading home.

As he rode up to the house, he saw her come out onto the porch.

"Good morning," he called to her as he dismounted, relieved she hadn't taken off. Even without his pickup.

"Out for a morning ride?"

"Just went down to get the mail and my newspapers," he said as he dug them out of the saddlebag. "You up for a ride?"

She eyed the horse for a moment. "Do you have a shorter horse?"

He chuckled as he turned toward her. "I have a nice gentle one just for you." He noticed that she was wearing one of his shirts. It looked darned good on her. "Want to ride or have something to eat first?"

"Ride."

Logan knew he would have granted her anything she wanted at that moment. She was beautiful in an understated way that he found completely alluring. Her face, free of makeup, shone. There was a freshness about her that reminded him of the spring morning. She seemed relaxed and happy, her good mood contagious.

"Let's get you saddled up, then," he said, and led her out to the barn.

"This isn't going to be like a rodeo, is it?"

He laughed. "No bucking broncos, I promise. Don't worry, you're in good hands."

He showed her how to saddle her horse, then led it outside and helped her climb on.

"I like the view from up here," Blythe said, smiling down from the saddle. "So what do I do now?"

He gave her some of the basics, then climbed on his own horse. At first he just rode her around the pasture, but she was such a natural, he decided to show her a little piece of the ranch.

"This is what you do every day?" she asked, sounding awed.

He laughed. "It's a little more than a ride around the yard."

"You said you chase cows." She glanced around. "So where are these cows?"

"They're still in winter pasture. We'll be taking them up into the mountains pretty soon."

"You and your brothers. You ranch together?"

Her horse began to trot back toward the barn, saving him from answering. He rode alongside her, giving her pointers. She had great balance. It surprised him how quickly she'd caught on, and he wondered if she really had never ridden before.

"You're a natural," he said when they reached the house. It was late afternoon. They'd ridden farther than he'd originally planned, but it had been so enjoyable he hadn't wanted to return to the house.

"I had so much fun," she said as she swung down out of the saddle. "I wish we could do it again tomorrow." She groaned, though, and he could tell she was feeling the long ride.

"We can do it again tomorrow, if you're up to it," he said, liking the idea of another day with her.

"You probably need to start chasing cows again and I should be taking off, though, huh?" She looked away when she said it.

He really needed to get back to work, but he said, "I can take a few days off." As she helped him unsaddle the horses and put the tack away, he wondered again how long she planned to stay and where, if anywhere, the two of them were headed.

He knew he wouldn't be able to keep his family from Blythe long. Since his father, Hoyt, had remarried after years of raising his six sons alone, all six sons were expected to be at supper each evening. His stepmother, Emma, wanted them to spend time together as a family, and she was a great cook. It was just a matter of time before the family heard he was back and started wondering why he hadn't been around.

Loretta was waiting for the others late the next morning down in the coffee shop. She'd already had a cup of coffee, which had only managed to make her more jittery. How long was the sheriff going to keep them here? She was broke and wondering how she was going to pay her motel bill, let alone eat.

Not to mention the latest news she'd just heard before coming down to the coffee shop. JJ had been killed yesterday in a car accident.

As Betsy and Karen joined her, she said, "You heard?"

"It's on all the news stations," Karen said.

"You and JJ had been closer than the rest of us," Loretta said, noticing that Karen had been crying.

"They were best friends when they were kids, huh," Betsy said.

That was news to Loretta.

"We grew up next door to each other," Karen said. "People thought we were sisters." She smiled at the memory, her eyes filling with tears.

"Must have been hard when she left the band," Loretta said. "So did she keep in touch with you?"

"No." Karen looked away.

"I thought it was just us," Betsy said. "But then none of us kept in touch either after that first year. Not surprising, I guess."

"Yeah, after everything that happened," Loretta agreed. She'd called Betsy a couple of times but felt like she'd gotten the cold shoulder. Karen, who she thought always acted as if she thought she was better than everyone, she hadn't even bothered to call.

"So we know what Betsy's been doing the last ten years, cranking out kids," Loretta said. "What about you, Karen?"

"I work in New York as a magazine editor."

Beat the hell out of Loretta's bartending job and part-time drumming gigs.

"So you never married?" Betsy asked.

"Three times. None of them stuck," Loretta said. "What about you, Karen?"

Karen shook her head.

"You got married quick enough after the band split," Loretta said to Betsy. "But I get the feeling you're still carrying a torch for Jett." Loretta couldn't help herself, even though Karen shot her a warning look.

"Jett made the rounds among us," Karen said pointedly, "but I don't think any of us were ever serious about him."

"Is that right?" Jett said shoving Karen over as he joined them in the booth.

Loretta didn't miss the look Jett and Betsy exchanged. He was up to his old tricks, she thought, and wondered what Betsy's husband would have to say about it. That was, if anyone bothered to tell him.

She discarded the idea. What did she care? She hadn't come here to bond with her former band members. She'd come for the money and now there wasn't any.

"You all heard about JJ?" Jett said, glancing around the table. He looked solemn for a moment before he asked with a grin, "So which one of you killed her?"

"Why would any of us want to kill JJ?" Karen asked with obvious annoyance.

Jett shrugged. "Jealousy. I've already told the sheriff to check the brakes on her rental car."

"Jealous? Not over you," Loretta said.

"Maybe," he said still grinning. "But I definitely felt some professional jealousy. JJ became a star while the rest of you—"

"Did just fine," Karen said. "Let's not forget that JJ, according to the tabloids, had been trying to get out of her contract. I don't think her life was a bed of roses."

"So we're all supposed to feel sorry for her?" Loretta asked. "Excuse me, but she dumped us. Sold us right down the river. I, for one, haven't forgotten or forgiven." When she saw the way everyone was staring at her, she added, "But I had nothing to do with her driving her car off a cliff."

"I'm sure it was just an accident," Betsy said.

"Sure," Jett replied with a chuckle. "Just like Martin getting shot through the heart."

Buford's phone had been ringing off the hook all day. As hard as Kevin had tried to keep the news of Martin Sanderson's death from the media, he'd failed.

"Mr. Sanderson's death is under investigation," the sheriff said. "That's all I can tell you at this time."

When his phone rang yet again, he'd snatched it up, expecting it would be another reporter.

"You knew about JJ's accident last night," Jett Atkins said the moment Buford picked up.

He recognized his voice but said, "I'm sorry, who is this?"

"Jett Atkins. You knew JJ was dead when you called me last night."

"The accident was under investigation."

"It's splashed all over the papers, television and internet. You could have told me last night. Instead I have to see it on TV."

"Well, you know now." Buford didn't have the time for the rock star's tantrum.

"They killed her. JJ was too good a driver. You'd better check the brakes on that car. I already warned them that I was going to tell you."

Buford loved nothing better than being told what he needed to do. But he was reminded of the lack of skid marks on the highway. It had appeared that the driver of the car hadn't braked.

"Who are *they?*" he asked, even though he suspected he knew.

"Her former band members. The more I've thought

of it, the more I think one of them killed Martin and then sabotaged JJ's car and killed her, as well."

"I thought you were convinced JJ killed Martin," he reminded him.

"Well, she could have after what he did to her. But if anyone is murderous, it's the members of her former band. They hated her enough as it was. Once they found out that JJ wasn't doing any reunion tour—"

"They knew that for sure?"

"I don't know. But if Martin told them and they figured out that he'd used them—"

"Mr. Atkins—"

"Check the brakes on her car. I'm telling you one of them or all three of them killed her. You should have seen their faces this morning at breakfast when I asked them which one of them did JJ in."

Buford groaned. "Please let me do the investigating."

"Let me know what you find out about the brake line."

"You must be starved," Logan said after he and Blythe returned from their horseback ride. They'd eaten elk steak sandwiches late the night before, but that had been hours ago now. "I'll make us something to eat."

"Can I help?" She had picked up the newspapers he'd brought home earlier.

"No, you've had a strenuous enough day. Anyway, it's a one-man kitchen. I'm thinking bacon, scrambled eggs and toast." He liked breakfast any time of the day, especially at night.

"Yum." She sounded distracted.

He left her sorting through the newspapers on the couch and went into the kitchen. The sun had long set, the prairie silver in the twilight. Blythe must be exhausted. He hadn't meant to take her on such a long ride. But she'd been a trooper, really seeming to enjoy being on horseback.

It wasn't until the meal was almost ready that he realized he hadn't heard a peep out of her. She must have fallen asleep on the couch.

He put everything into the oven to keep it warm and was about to go check on her when he smelled smoke. Hurriedly, he stuck his head into the living room to find her feeding the fire she'd started in the fireplace.

"I hope you don't mind," she said quickly, no doubt seeing his surprise. "I felt a little cool."

"Sure," he said, but noticed she'd used one of the recent newspapers he hadn't had a chance to read instead of the old ones stacked up next to the kindling box by the fireplace. Also she'd made a pitiful fire. "Here, let me help you."

She'd wadded up the front pages of the most recent *Great Falls Tribune* and set the paper on fire, then thrown a large log on top. The paper was burning so quickly there was no way it would ignite the log.

He pulled the log off. The newspaper had burned to black ash.

"Oh, I'm sorry. You probably wanted to read that," she said behind him.

"Probably wasn't any good news anyway," he said not wanting to make her feel bad.

"Don't bother to make a fire," she said. "I'm fine now. What is that wonderful smell coming from the kitchen?"

He studied her a moment. "You're sure?"

She nodded.

He told himself it was his imagination that she looked pale. Earlier she'd gotten some sun from their long ride and her cheeks had been pink. Now all the color seemed to have been bleached out of her. She seemed upset.

"Maybe I'll teach you how to build a fire while you're here, too."

Her smile wasn't her usual one. "That's probably a good idea."

As they went into the kitchen, he couldn't shake the feeling that her purpose in burning the newspaper had nothing to do with a chill. It seemed more likely that it had been something she'd read in the paper.

Logan tried to remember the headlines he'd scanned before riding back to the house. Scientists were predicting a possible drought after low snowfall levels. A late-season avalanche had killed a snowmobiler up by Cooke City. Some singer named JJ had been killed in a car wreck in the Flathead Valley.

He couldn't imagine why any of those stories might have upset her and told himself he was just imagining things. Who got upset about an article and burned the newspaper?

"Are you sure I can't help?"

He started at the sound of her voice directly behind him and checked his suspicious expression before he turned. "Nope, everything is ready." When he studied her face, he was relieved that her color had come back. She looked more like that laid-back, adventurous woman who'd climbed onto his motorcycle yesterday.

"I hope you're hungry," he said as he handed her a plateful of food.

But something had definitely ruined her appetite.

"Blythe," Logan said after they'd eaten and gotten up to put their dishes in the sink. He touched her arm, turning her to face him. She was inches from him. She met his gaze and held it. "Tell me what's going on with you." He saw her consider it.

But then her expression changed and even before she closed the distance between them, he knew what she was up to. Her lips brushed over his cheek, the look in her eyes challenging. She put her palm flat against his chest as she leaned in again, lips parted and started to kiss him on the mouth.

He grasped her shoulders and held her away from him. "What was *that?*" he demanded.

"I just thought…"

"If you don't want to tell me what's really going on with you, fine. If you want to make love with me, I'm all for it. But let's be clear. When you come to my bed, I want it to be because you want me. No other reason."

Disbelief flickered across her expression. He knew he was a damned fool not to take what she was offering—no matter her reasons. The woman was beautiful and just the thought of taking her to bed made his blood run hotter than a wildfire through his veins.

He wanted her. What man wouldn't? But he wouldn't let her use sex to keep him at a distance. Even as he thought it, he couldn't believe it himself. Why did he have to feel this way about this woman?

Her eyes burned with tears. "I appreciate everything you—"

"Don't," he said. "I'm glad you're here. Let's leave it at that. I'm going to check the horses."

Blythe couldn't escape upstairs fast enough. Just his touch set something off in her, while the kindness in his eyes made her want to confess everything. She had wanted to bare her soul to him.

Instead, she'd fallen back on what she'd always done when anyone got too close. She had tried to use the same weapon her mother had: sex. To her shock and surprise, Logan wasn't having any of it. He'd shoved her away and what she'd seen in his gaze was anything but desire. Anger burned in all that blue. Anger and disappointment. The disappointment was like an arrow through her heart.

He'd gone out to check the horses and she'd hurried upstairs to run a bath before she did something crazy like confess all. How would he feel about having a murderess under his roof? Worse, a coward? She'd gotten at least one person killed, maybe two, if she counted Martin.

Even the hot lilac-scented water of the clawfoot tub couldn't calm her. She was still shaken and upset about the almost kiss. Logan had seen right through her. Another man, she thought, would have taken what she was offering and not cared what was going on with her. But not Logan.

He saw through her. No doubt he'd also figured out why she'd burned the newspaper. She couldn't believe what she'd read in the paper. A young woman had apparently stolen her rental car, lost control and crashed, the poor woman, and now everyone thought it had been her and that she was dead?

Not her. *JJ.* The fantasy performer that Martin Sanderson had created. Now they were both dead.

She'd seen the way Logan had looked at her when she'd attempted to destroy the news articles in the fireplace. But she couldn't let him see either story—not the one about JJ's sports car convertible ending up down a rocky embankment, catching fire and killing its driver or about Martin Sanderson's murder.

When the bath water cooled to the point where she was shivering, she got out and, wearing Logan's robe, went to his bedroom. On the way, she listened for any sound of him on the couch below. Nothing. Maybe he was still out with the horses.

Still embarrassed, she was glad she didn't have to face him again tonight. Once in his bedroom, she moved to the window of the two-story farmhouse and looked out at the night. She still felt numb. What had she thought would happen when she left everything in the car beside the lake?

Nothing. She hadn't thought. If she had, she would have realized that someone could have come along, found the car, the keys, her purse and thought she'd killed herself in the lake. Instead, someone had taken the car and died in it.

How could she have ever suspected something like that was going to happen? Still she felt to blame. Someone else was dead because of her.

She remembered what it had said in the article. The police had speculated that the woman had been driving too fast and had missed the curve. Officers were investigating whether drugs and alcohol might have been involved.

Not her fault.

She sighed, close to tears, knowing better. Just like Martin Sanderson being dead wasn't her fault. Now she wished she'd been able to keep the newspaper article, to read it again more closely, but she'd panicked. If Logan saw it he might connect the car she'd been driving with this woman's death—and her. She wasn't ready to tell him everything. If she ever was.

Maybe the best thing she could do was clear out. He didn't need her problems, and eventually those problems were going to find her here. She didn't kid herself. All burning the articles had done was buy her a little time. Logan was too smart. He was going to figure it out. Eventually the police would figure it out, as well.

Isn't it possible Fate is giving you a second chance? JJ was dead and she was alive.

She had wanted out of her life and she'd been given a chance to start over. A clean slate. With everyone thinking she was dead, she could start life fresh. Did it matter that she didn't deserve it?

As she turned away from the bedroom window, she recalled her conversation with Martin. "I would give anything to do it differently."

He'd laughed. "You're what? Barely thirty and you're talking as if your life is over? Save the drama for when you get paid for it. I'm not letting you out of your contract. Period. If you keep fighting me, I'll make you do a reunion tour with your former Tough as Nails band."

She'd been shocked he would even threaten such a thing. "You wouldn't do that."

"Wouldn't I?"

"You can't make me," she'd said, knowing that Martin Sanderson could destroy her and he knew it.

"I'll sue you, and take every penny I made for you."

"Take it. I'm done," she'd said and meant it.

He'd studied her for a moment. "Okay, you're not happy. I get it. So let's do this. Take some time tonight to unwind. Go into town. Have some fun. Then sleep on it. If you feel the same way in the morning, then... well, we'll work something out that we can both live with."

She remembered her relief. She'd actually thought things might be all right after all. Isn't that why she'd gone to that country-western bar that night? And luck had been with her. She'd met Logan Chisholm.

But by the next morning everything had changed. Martin was dead and she'd realized that she had worse problems than getting out of her contract and a tour with her former band members.

She didn't know what she would have done if Logan hadn't shown up when he did at the Grizzly Club. It had been desperation and something just as strong— survival—that had made her abandon her car and get on the back of his motorcycle. She had wanted to run away with him. Just ride off into the sunset with the cowboy from her girlhood dreams.

Now another swift change of luck. Everyone thought JJ was dead.

Especially her former band members.

Even if they suspected she was still alive, they wouldn't think to look for her in this remote part of Montana.

A bubble of laughter rose in her chest as hot tears burned her eyes. She was too exhausted to even think, let alone decide what to do tonight. She would decide what to do tomorrow. She moved to the bed. She was a survivor. Somehow she would survive this, as well. Or die trying.

As she climbed between the sheets, she didn't fight the exhaustion that pulled her under. The last thing she wanted to think about was what a mess she'd made of that old life. Or the look on Logan's face when she'd tried to kiss him.

Sheriff Buford Olson was in his office when he got the call from the coroner's office.

"I've just spoken with the state crime investigators. Martin Sanderson's death has been ruled a suicide," the coroner said without preamble. "He was dying. Cancer. His personal physician confirmed my findings. He'd known he had only a few weeks to live."

Buford ran a hand over his thinning hair. All the evidence had been there indicating a suicide—except for the note. Because someone had taken it.

The moment he'd seen the safety pin with the tiny piece of yellow sticky note stuck to it, he'd thought suicide. But again, without the note...

Martin Sanderson had been shot in the heart—and not through the robe. For some unknown reason suicide victims rarely shot themselves through clothing.

The gun found at the scene was registered to Sanderson. Its close proximity to the body, the lack of evidence of a struggle, the powder burns around the wound, the gun powder residue on the victim's hands and the sleeves of his robe all pointed toward suicide.

Even the angle of the shot appeared to be slightly upward, like most suicides. Another sign of a possible suicide was the single shot to the heart. All the scene had needed was a reason for the suicide, and now the coroner had provided it. Sanderson was dying. If only they had that damned note, this case could have been tied up a lot sooner.

"Good work," the mayor said when Buford gave him the news. "Case closed. I'll alert the media."

Closed as far as the mayor was concerned, Buford thought after he hung up. But there was that missing note and the mystery of who—and why—the person had taken it. If it had been Sanderson's guest Jennifer "JJ" James, then they would never know what the note said.

Buford told himself it didn't matter. Martin Sanderson's death had been ruled a suicide. The infamous JJ had died in a car wreck. All the loose ends had been neatly tied up. What more did he want?

With a curse, he called the garage where Jennifer James's car had been taken and asked the head mechanic to check to see if someone might have tampered with the brake line.

Chapter 7

The next day Logan was still angry with himself and Blythe. Why wouldn't she let him help her? Stubborn pride? He, of all people, understood that.

What bothered him was that the night he'd danced with her, he'd seen a strength in her that had drawn him. Now though she seemed scared. What had happened between their last dance and now? Something, and whatever it was had her on the run and hiding out here with him.

He couldn't help but feel protective of her. Whatever she needed, he would do his best to give it to her if she would just let him. He was worried about her. But he told himself the woman he'd danced with was too strong and determined to let whatever had happened beat her. Maybe she just needed time.

As for what had happened last night... He'd wanted

to kiss her, wanted her in his arms, in his bed. He was still mentally kicking himself for pushing her away. He could imagine what his brothers would have said if they'd heard that he turned down a beautiful, desirable woman.

But Blythe wasn't just any woman.

And he'd meant what he'd said last night. He wanted more than just sex with her. Logan chuckled, thinking again about what his brothers would say to that.

Speaking of his brothers, he thought with a curse. One of the Chisholm Cattle Company pickups was coming down the lane in a cloud of dust. As the truck drew closer, he recognized his brother Zane behind the wheel.

He glanced toward the stairs. Blythe hadn't come down yet this morning. He'd hated the way he'd left things last night. But by the time he'd come in after mentally kicking himself all over the ranch yard, her door upstairs had been closed, the light off.

Late last night, unable to sleep, he'd decided that whatever Blythe was running from had something to do with an article in yesterday's newspaper. He'd ridden down this morning, but today's paper hadn't come yet. Maybe the best thing to do was go into town to the library so he could go through a few days' papers on the internet. He couldn't imagine what she was hiding, just that she was here hiding because of it.

Now, though, he had a bigger problem, he thought as he stepped out onto the porch and walked down the steps to cut his brother off at the pass.

"Hey, what's going on?" Zane asked as he climbed out of the pickup. "Dad said you called and needed a few more days off."

"Is there a problem?"

"We're shorthanded, that's the problem," his brother said as he glanced toward the house. "Dad wants one of us staying around the main house to keep an eye on Emma until some agency in Billings can find someone to come up here and live in the guest wing."

"He's still worried about Emma?" Their lives had been turned upside down the past six months, but should have calmed down after Aggie Wells had drowned in the creek. Once winter runoff was over, they'd find her remains and then that would be the end of it.

Logan knew his stepmother had been put through hell and all because of his father's past. But then again, she should have asked a few more questions before she'd run off with him for a quickie marriage in Vegas.

He thought about Blythe and realized he'd put himself in the same position Emma had. What did he know about the woman now sleeping in his bed? And had he let that stop him?

"You know Dad," Zane said.

"Can't today. Sorry."

"Oh?" His brother looked past him. "Emma was worried you were sick. She wanted to send some chicken soup along with me. I got out of there before she baked you a cake, too."

"I'm fine."

Zane looked at him suspiciously. "How was the Flathead?"

"Pretty this time of year."

His brother laughed. "I see you bought yourself some new clothes."

Logan looked to where Zane was pointing and swore

under his breath. Blythe had left her jean jacket with the embroidered flowers on it lying over the porch railing.

His brother was grinning from ear to ear. "I knew you wanting time off had something to do with a woman."

Just then, as luck would have it, Blythe came out the front door onto the porch.

Zane let out a low whistle. "It's all becoming clear now," he said under his breath. "Aren't you going to introduce me?" When Logan said nothing, his brother stepped around him and called up to the porch, "Hello. I'm Logan's brother Zane, but I'm sure he's told you all about me."

Blythe smiled. "As a matter of fact, I think he said you were his favorite."

Zane laughed. "I like her," he said to Logan. "Why don't you bring her to supper tonight. I'll tell Emma to set another plate."

Logan could have throttled him. Zane knew damned well that if he'd been ready to tell her about the family, he would have already brought her by the house.

"Oh, and I'll cover for you today, but I'll expect you back to work tomorrow. You get babysitting duty." With that Zane climbed into his pickup, waved at Blythe and drove away.

Sheriff Buford Olson was about to leave his office for the day when he got another call from the coroner's office. What now, he thought as he picked up.

"The woman's body found in that car accident wasn't Jennifer James," the coroner said in his usual all-business tone. "This woman was in her early twenties. The crime lab took DNA from a hairbrush Jennifer James left at the Grizzly Club. This Jane Doe is definitely not the woman the media calls JJ."

"We have no idea who she is?"

"She was wearing a silver bracelet with the name Susie on it. I would suggest sending her DNA to NDIS to see if they have a match. That's the best I can do." The National DNA Index System processed DNA records of persons convicted of crimes, analyzed samples recovered from crime scenes as well as from unidentified human remains and analyzed samples for missing person cases.

"Thanks," Buford said, still processing this turn of events. If JJ hadn't died in her rental car, then where was she? She'd have to be on the moon not to hear about the accident that had allegedly claimed her life at the edge of Flathead Lake. So why hadn't she come forward?

He'd barely hung up when he got a call from a gas station attendant in Moses Lake, Washington.

"Is this the sheriff in that town where JJ was killed?" a young female voice asked.

"Yes?" he said, curious since the dispatcher had motioned to him that he might actually *want* to take this call.

"Well, I wasn't sure if I should call or not, but I just had this guy in an old pickup buy gas? The thing is, he used one of JJ's credit cards. It has her on the front, you know one of those photos of her with her guitar, the kind you can get on certain credit cards? I have all her CDs, so I recognized her right off. The man tried to use the card at the pump but it didn't work so he brought it in and when it was denied again, he just took off."

Buford felt his heart racing, but he kept his voice calm. "Did you happen to get the plate number on the pickup?"

"Yeah. He didn't look like the kind of guy JJ would have dated, you know?"

"Yeah." He wrote down the license plate number she gave him and thanked her for being an upstanding citizen. She gave him a detailed description of the pickup driver. He told her to hold on to the credit card and that he'd have someone collect it from her shortly.

Even before he ran the plates on the pickup, he suspected it would be stolen—just like the credit card. It was.

Buford put an all points bulletin out on the pickup and driver, then sat back in his chair and scratched his head. JJ wasn't dead. At least her body hadn't been found, and right now Logan Chisholm might be the only person who could tell him where she went that day after leaving the Grizzly Club.

When he called directory assistance and no listing was found, he put in a call to the Chisholm Cattle Company.

Logan didn't want her meeting his family, Blythe thought with no small amount of surprise. She'd been so busy hiding her former life and who she'd been from him, she'd never considered that he might be hiding her from his family and friends.

"You can get out of it," she said as Zane drove away.

"Out of what?" Logan asked, clearly playing dumb.

She smiled. "Out of taking me to supper with your family."

"It isn't what you think." He dragged his hat off and

raked his fingers through his thick blond hair. He wore his hair longer than most cowboys, she thought, but then again she didn't know many cowboys, did she? His eyes were the same blue as the sky. She'd met her share of handsome men, but none as appealing as this one.

"You don't have to explain. We just met. We don't even know each other. There is no reason I should meet your folks." Even as she said it, she was curious about his family. Curious about Logan. She felt as if she'd only skimmed the surface, but she liked him and wouldn't have minded getting to know him better—if things were different.

The thought surprised her. She hadn't had roots since she left home at fourteen and thought she didn't want or need them. But being here with Logan had spurred something in her she hadn't known was there.

"Is there any coffee?" she asked as she turned back toward the house.

"Blythe, it isn't that I don't want you to meet them."

In the kitchen, she opened a cupboard and took down a cup. She wasn't kidding about needing some coffee. She felt off balance, all her emotions out of kilter. She could feel him behind her, close.

She turned to him. "Look, you don't really know me. Or I you. I don't even know what I'm doing staying here. I should go." She started to step past him, but he closed his hand over her arm and pulled her close.

His alluring male scent filled her, making her ache with a need to touch him and be touched. She turned to find him inches from her. He took the coffee cup from her hand and set it on the counter. Then he pulled her to him.

He felt warm, his shirt scented with sunshine and

horse leather. His hands were strong as they cupped her waist and drew her close. As his mouth dropped to hers, she caught her breath. She'd known, somewhere deep inside her, that when he kissed her it would be like rockets going off. She hadn't been wrong.

Logan deepened the kiss, his arms coming around her. He stole her breath, made her heart drum in her chest, sending shivers of desire ricocheting through her. She melted into his arms. He felt so solid she didn't want him to let her go.

As the kiss ended, he pulled back to look into her eyes. "I've wanted to do that since the first time I saw you."

Her pulse was still thundering just under her skin. She wanted him and she knew it wouldn't take much for him to swing her up into his arms and carry her upstairs to that double bed of his. Just the truth.

She took a step back, letting her arms slip from around his neck. She almost didn't trust what she might say. "I'm sorry about last night."

He shook his head. "I just want us to be clear. I want you. I have from the moment I laid eyes on you at the country-western bar."

"I want you, too. And I want to tell you everything. I just need some time to sort things out for myself."

He grinned and shoved back his Stetson. "And I want to take you home to meet my family, but I need to warn you about them."

"No, don't spoil it. Let me be surprised," she joked.

"I called my stepmother. We're on for tonight. But you might change your mind about everything once you meet them all."

She knew it was crazy, but she was relieved he

wanted her to meet his family. It was dangerous. What if one of them recognized her? Blythe knew she had worse worries than that.

And yet, right now, all she wanted to think about was meeting Logan's family. "I need to go into town and get myself something to wear." She hadn't been this excited about a date in a long time.

Logan seemed to hesitate, as if he was thinking about kissing her again. Desire shone in his eyes. Her own heart was still hammering from the kiss. She *did* want him. More than he could know. But he wanted more from her than a roll in the hay. When was the last time she'd met a man like that?

"I better go start the truck," he said.

She was glad now that she'd stuffed a few hundred dollar bills into the pocket of her jeans before she'd left Martin Sanderson's house that awful morning. It seemed like weeks ago instead of days.

Blythe took a sip of the coffee, needing the caffeine to steady her after the kiss. She hadn't slept well last night, and the sound of the vehicle coming down the road this morning had made her heart race until she reminded herself that not a soul in the world knew she was here—other than Logan.

Now his brother Zane knew, and soon so would his family. But they knew her as Blythe. She heard the pickup door slam, the engine turning over, and downed the rest of the coffee. She felt nervous about meeting Logan's family and unconsciously touched a finger to her lips.

She couldn't help smiling as she thought of his kiss. *You're falling for this cowboy.*

No, she told herself, as messed up as her life was,

she couldn't let that happen. Once he knew the truth
about her, that would be the end of it. Maybe she should
go to the door and call him back in and tell him everything. Nip this in the bud before it went any further and
they both got hurt. Tell him before she met his family.

Logan would be hurt enough once he knew everything. How long did she really think she could keep
that old life a secret anyway? What if someone in town
recognized her?

Blythe put down her cup and pushed out through the
screen door to the porch to pick up her jean jacket from
where she'd left it. As she did, she looked out at this
wide-open land. It was like her life now. Wide open.
Now that she had this new life—at least for a while—
she was surprised by what she wanted to do with it.

She had put away most of the money she'd made
in an account where she could get to it. She could do
anything she pleased, go anywhere in the world. To
her surprise, though, she realized she didn't want to
leave here, didn't want to leave Logan. She wanted to
meet his family.

Couldn't she just enjoy this life for a little while?

As she headed out to the pickup, she saw him sitting behind the wheel. He smiled at her and her heart
took off in a gallop as she climbed into the cab next to
him. She knew this couldn't last, but was it so wrong
for just another day?

Logan had some time to kill while he waited for
Blythe to shop for clothes. He'd offered to buy her anything she needed, but she'd told him she had money.

"Nothing fancy," he'd warned her. "You're in the
real Montana now."

After he'd left her, he'd headed to the library. He felt a little guilty, but he had to know what had been in the newspaper Blythe had burned. She was in trouble. He felt it at heart level. The only way he could help her was to know what had her running scared. Something in that newspaper had upset her. He was sure of it.

It didn't take him long at the library to find the section of the paper Blythe had burned. He scanned the articles. One caught his eye—the one about the woman who'd been killed in a car wreck at the edge of Flathead Lake. Was it possible Blythe had known the woman? He read the name. Jennifer James. Apparently she was best known as JJ, a rock star who shot to meteoric fame.

According to the story, she'd missed a curve and crashed down a rocky embankment, rolling multiple times before the car burst into flames and finally came to rest at the edge of the lake. The infamous JJ was believed to have been driving at a high rate of speed. It was not determined yet if she was under the influence of drugs or alcohol.

All it said about this JJ person was that she had led a glittering life in the glare of the media after her sky-rocketing career. She had died at the age of thirty.

It wasn't until he focused on the sports car convertible that he knew he'd been right about something in the newspaper upsetting her.

The sight of the car stopped him cold. That and a sentence in the cutline under the photograph. JJ had been discovered by legendary music producer Martin Sanderson. Sanderson was a resident of the Grizzly Club, an exclusive conclave south of Bigfork.

That's when Logan saw the second headline: Famous Music Producer Found Dead.

He quickly scanned the story until he found what he was looking for. Martin Sanderson had been found dead in his home Saturday.

Saturday? The day Logan had gone to the club looking for the mysterious woman from the bar. The day Blythe had come tearing out of the gate to race down the highway like a crazy woman, then climb on the back of his motorcycle and ask him to take her away with him.

He hurriedly read the article. Investigators from the Missoula Crime Lab had been called in on the case. They thought it was a homicide? He checked to see the estimated time of death. Saturday morning.

Logan groaned. No wonder she'd wanted to get as far away from the Flathead as possible. She'd known the sheriff would be looking for her.

The article mentioned that Sanderson had discovered the recently deceased JJ who, according to sources, had been visiting Sanderson at the Grizzly Club.

His heart began to pound as he reread the first newspaper article. Who had died in the car? Someone named Jennifer James better known as JJ, according to the story. He double-checked the car photo. It was the same make and color as the one Blythe had left beside the highway two days ago. No way was that a coincidence. Add to that the connection to the Grizzly Club...

Logan shook his head. Blythe had to have known this woman. But then why not say something? Because she felt guilty for leaving the car for her friend? They both must have been staying at the Grizzly Club with Sanderson.

So who was this JJ? From the grainy black-and-white photo accompanying the short article, it was impossible to tell much about her, since she was duded out in heavy, wild makeup and holding a garish electric guitar.

Logan glanced at his watch. He'd told Blythe he would pick her up back on the main drag after running a few errands of his own. He still had thirty minutes, enough time to see what else he could learn about the woman who had been killed.

He typed in Pop Singer JJ. Pages of items began to come up on the computer screen. He clicked on one and a color photograph appeared.

His breath rushed out of him as he stared at the photograph in shock. Blythe. No wonder he hadn't recognized her. He wouldn't have ever connected the woman who'd climbed on the back of his motorcycle with this one even without the wild makeup and masks she wore when she performed.

He thought about her that first night at the Western bar in her new cowboy boots. There had been a look of contentment on her face as she'd danced to the music. No, she'd looked nothing like this woman in the publicity photo.

It didn't help that he wasn't into her kind of music. He'd never heard of JJ or a lot of other singers and bands she'd performed with, since he was a country-western man himself.

But who was this woman staying with him really? The infamous JJ? Or the woman he'd come to know as Blythe? He had a feeling that whoever she was, she was still wearing a mask.

At least now he knew why she'd run. It had to have something to do with music producer Martin Sanderson's death. Had she killed him?

He didn't want to believe he'd been harboring a murderer. But with a curse, he reminded himself that everyone thought she was dead and she had let them. She'd seen the article. She knew someone else had died in her car. If she was innocent, then why hadn't she said something? Why hadn't she come forward and told the world she was still alive?

Aggie Wells woke coughing. Sun slanted in the crack between the curtains. She'd fallen asleep in her chair again and lost another day. But what had brought her out of her deathlike sleep was that same horrible nightmare she'd been having for weeks now.

She sat up, fighting to catch her breath.

The doctor had said that the pneumonia had weakened her lungs. The gunshot wound had weakened her body. Add to that failure and she felt like an old woman, one foot in the grave.

"You have to call Emma," she said when she finally caught her breath.

Call and tell her what? That you had a horrible dream—most of it unintelligible, but that you've seen how it all ends?

Aggie realized how crazy that sounded. She had nothing new to tell Emma or the sheriff. No one believed that Laura Chisholm was alive, let alone what she was capable of doing.

The nightmare seemed to lurk in the dark shadows

of the room. Aggie pulled her blanket around her, but couldn't shake the chill the dream had left in her bones.

She remembered glimpses of the nightmare, something moving soundlessly in a dark room, the glint of a knife. Aggie shuddered. She hadn't seen Laura in the shadows, but she'd sensed something almost inhuman.

Aggie reached for the phone, but stopped herself. She was sure the sheriff would be tracing any calls coming into the ranch. Hoyt might answer. She might not even get a chance to talk to Emma at all.

And what would be the point? She didn't know where Laura Chisholm had gone or who she had become. She just knew the killer was headed for Chisholm ranch soon and Emma would never see her coming.

All calling would accomplish was to give the sheriff Aggie's own location. She couldn't bear the thought of spending what was left of her life in the state mental hospital or behind bars in prison.

In her weakened state, she didn't have the energy to escape again. Nor could she go out and find Laura Chisholm again for them. Just the thought of Laura Chisholm made the hair stand up on the back of her neck. She shifted in her chair. She realized sitting there that somehow she'd gone from being the hunter to the hunted.

It wasn't what Laura was capable of that terrified her. It was that the woman could somehow be invisible—until it was too late for her prey. It took a special talent to go unnoticed. To seem so safe that she didn't even stir the air, didn't appear to take up space, didn't seem to exist in any form other than a ghost.

Maybe the worst part was that Aggie *knew* Laura.

She'd become Laura when she'd believed Hoyt Chisholm had killed his first wife. Aggie had worn the woman's same brand of perfume and clothing, had her hair cut in the same style, had learned everything she could about Laura. She'd tried on the woman's skin.

She *knew* Laura and, she thought with a shudder, Laura knew *her*.

A lot of people thought Aggie Wells was dead.

Laura Chisholm wasn't one of them.

In Aggie's nightmare, Laura found her.

Chapter 8

Logan's cell phone rang, echoing through the small, quiet library. He quickly dug it out, saw that it was his stepmother calling and hurried outside to take it. "Hello."

"Where are you?" Emma said sounding excited about having company tonight.

"In town. Blythe—" She might be the pop rocker JJ, but he thought of her as Blythe and knew he always would. "Had to get something to wear for tonight."

"You didn't tell her she had to dress up, did you?" Emma scolded.

"Just the opposite. But she's a woman. You know how they are."

His stepmother laughed. "We're looking forward to meeting her."

Logan wanted to warn Emma not to get too attached

to her—just as he'd been warning himself since she'd climbed on his motorcycle. Since finding out who she really was, he was even more aware that she would be leaving soon, possibly prison. If innocent, back to her old life. No woman gave up that life to stay in his old farmhouse—no matter what she said.

"So you're still in town," Emma said.

"I have to pick up Blythe at the clothing store in about fifteen minutes and then we were headed back to my place."

"Don't do that. Come on over to the main house so we can visit before supper," she said. "Anything you want to tell me about this woman before you get here?"

He chuckled. "Nothing that comes to mind."

"Oh, you," Emma said. "Zane says she's lovely."

"She is that." And mysterious and complex and let's not forget a star—and quite possibly a murderer. Right now a star who is being immortalized because she died so young.

"Is this serious? Your brother seems to think—"

"Zane really should stop thinking," he snapped, realizing that Blythe wouldn't just be lying to him tonight at supper at the main ranch. She would be lying to his family. Involving them in this mess.

"I didn't mean to pry," Emma said, sounding a little hurt.

"You did, but that's what I love about you," he said softening his words. Emma was the best thing that had happened to their family. She only wanted good things for all of them.

"I just remembered an errand I have to run," Logan said, and got off the phone.

He checked his watch and then hurried back in the

library. He wanted to check today's paper and see if there was anything more about Martin Sanderson's and JJ's deaths.

Logan found the most recent edition of the *Great Falls Tribune.* Both JJ and Martin Sanderson had made the front page.

Mayor Confirms Music Producer's Death a Suicide

A tidal wave of relief washed over him as he quickly read the short update. Blythe might be JJ, but at least JJ wasn't a murderer. He knew that should make him happier than it did. There was a long article about JJ, about her humble beginnings, her rise to stardom, her latest attempts to get out of her contract and how she had died too young.

Her fans had been gathering across the country, making memorials for her. Logan remembered the waitress at the Cut Bank café and swore. The woman had recognized her. That's why Blythe had made them hightail it out of there.

But if she hadn't killed Martin Sanderson, then what was she running from? Was her life that bad that she'd rather let even her fans believe she was dead rather than come forward? Better to let them think she had died in a fiery car crash?

He realized that the whole world believed that the infamous JJ was dead. Everyone but him, Logan thought with a groan.

The only thing to do was call the sheriff over in the Flathead and let him know that JJ was alive. He started to reach for his cell phone and stopped himself. He couldn't do anything until he confronted her.

As he left the library, he recalled what she'd said to him when they'd reached Whitehorse that first night.

"Have you ever just needed to step out of your life for a while and take a chance?"

Is that what she was doing? Just taking a break from that life? Good thing he hadn't gotten serious about her, he told himself as he drove down the main drag and saw her waiting for him on the sidewalk ahead.

As he pulled in, she turned in a circle so he could see her new clothes. She was wearing a new pair of jeans, a Western blouse and a huge smile.

It was easy to see why he would never have recognized her even if he had followed pop rock. She looked nothing like the JJ of music stardom. Her dark hair was pulled back in a ponytail, her face, free of makeup, slightly flushed, her faded-denim blue eyes sparkling with excitement.

He felt a heartstring give way at just the sight of her.

"What do you think?" she asked as she slid into the cab next to him. "I don't want to embarrass you at supper. Is it too much?"

"You look beautiful."

She beamed as if that was the first time anyone had ever told her that.

"Emma called." Logan was going to tell her that supper was canceled but she instantly looked so disappointed, he couldn't do it. He had let her pretend to be someone she wasn't this long, what were a few more hours? "She wants us to come on by."

"If it's okay with you, sure," she said brightening. "Can you believe it? I'm nervous about meeting your family."

She wasn't the only one who was apprehensive, Logan thought as he drove out of town. At least he wasn't taking an alleged murderer to meet his family.

But he didn't have the faintest idea who this woman really was or what she was doing in Whitehorse. Once supper was over and they were back at the house—

"I have great news," she announced as he started the motor. "I have a job. I saw a Help Wanted sign in the window just down the street, I walked in and I got the job."

He stared at her. The sign down the street was in the window of a local café. "You took a *waitress* job?" He'd expected that she would tire of being the dead star soon enough and come out of hiding. He'd never expected this.

"I've slung hash before," she said sounding defensive. "It's been a while, but I suspect it's a little like riding a bike."

He didn't know what to say. Did she really hate her old life that much? Or was she still hiding for another reason?

"Tomorrow, if you'll give me a ride to town, I'll find myself an apartment so I can walk to work. As much as I've loved staying with you…"

Logan had driven out of Whitehorse, the pickup now rolling along through open prairie and sunshine. He hit the brakes and pulled down a small dirt road that ended at the Milk River. Tall cottonwoods loomed over them, the sunlight fingering its way through the still bare branches.

As he brought the truck to a dust-boiling stop, he said, "You can drop the front. I know who you are, JJ. So what the hell is really going on?"

Sheriff Buford Olson couldn't believe he was still sitting in his office waiting for phone calls. His stomach grumbled. He'd missed lunch and he didn't dare go down the hall to the vending machine for fear of missing one of those calls he'd been waiting for.

When his phone finally rang, he was hoping it would be Logan Chisholm. It wasn't.

"We picked up Charlie Baker," the arresting officer told him. The man who'd tried to use JJ's credit card at the gas station in Moses Lake, Washington. "He has several warrants out on him from Arizona and he's driving a stolen pickup."

"I just need to know where he got the credit card he tried to use for gas in Moses Lake," Buford said.

"He says his girlfriend took it from a purse she found in a convertible parked next to Flathead Lake. He swears the car keys were on the floorboard and that his girlfriend took the car, wrecked it and died."

"Did he say what his girlfriend's name was?"

"Susie Adams."

Now at least Buford knew who was lying in the morgue. What he didn't know was where JJ was, why she left her car beside the lake or why she hadn't turned up yet.

He thought about what Jett had said about checking the brake line on her rental car. Jett thinking that someone had tampered with the car bothered him.

First Jett was so sure JJ had killed Martin. Now he was sure that JJ had been murdered. The man just kept changing his tune. Why was that?

After Buford hung up from talking to the officer who'd picked up Charlie Baker, he called the garage and asked for the head mechanic.

"Tom, anything on that convertible yet?"

"You had it pegged," the mechanic said. "Someone tampered with the brakes."

That explained why the woman driving the car hadn't appeared to brake.

As he hung up, Buford wondered how it was that Jett had suspected foul play. Was he also right that one of JJ's former band members was behind this? Apparently they all had it in for JJ, including Jett.

The big question now was: where was JJ? And how long before whoever tried to kill her tried again?

Blythe turned to him, those blue eyes wide with surprise, then regret.

"We both know your name isn't Blythe."

Her chin came up. "It's Jennifer *Blythe* James."

The afternoon sun shone into the truck cab, illuminating her beautiful face. "Why didn't you just tell me you were this JJ?" he said with a curse.

Her smile was sad. "I'm sorry I kept it from you."

"Why did you?"

She shook her head. "It's such a long story."

He shut off the engine. "I have nothing but time."

Looking away, she said, "You wouldn't believe me if I told you."

"Try me."

With a sigh, she turned to face him again. "I saw a chance to put that life behind me—for even a little while. I took it."

"Who was Martin Sanderson to you?"

"He was my music producer. Basically he owned me and my music," she said with no small amount of bitterness.

"You knew he was dead before you got on the back of my bike, didn't you?"

She nodded. "I didn't kill him, if that's what you're thinking."

"That was exactly what I thought, but his death has been ruled a suicide."

The news took her by surprise. "*Suicide?* No, that can't be right. Martin wouldn't—"

"Apparently he had cancer and only weeks to live."

She shook her head, letting it all sink in, then she smiled. "The bastard. That explains a lot. He insisted I come to Montana so we could talk about him letting me out of my contract. He was threatening to destroy my career—such as it was—and take everything I've made. I didn't care. I just wanted him to let me go."

"Did he?"

"Just before I met you that night at the bar," she said with a nod. "He told me to go have some fun and that if I didn't change my mind, then he would try to work something out with me in the morning." She let out a humorless laugh. "He knew he wouldn't be around by then."

"So you don't know how he left it."

She shook her head. "It doesn't matter. I'm done. If he sold my contract to someone else, let them take me to court. If they want, they can take every penny I made. I don't care." She smiled. "I have a job as of today. I don't need more than that."

Logan liked her attitude. He just wasn't sure he believed she could go from being rich and famous to being poor and unknown.

"Anyway, it probably doesn't matter," she added with a shake of her head.

"What do you mean, it probably doesn't matter?"

Again she looked away. He reached over to turn her to face him again. "What aren't you telling me? What was the real reason you ran away with me?"

"I told you. It was my girlhood fantasy to run away with a cowboy," she said.

He shook his head. "The truth, Blythe."

She swallowed, her throat working for a moment, then she sat up a little straighter as if steeling herself. "Someone has been trying to kill me."

Buford felt his belly rumble again with hunger. Clara was still putting hot chile peppers in everything, but he was building up a tolerance apparently. He couldn't wait to get home for supper, but he didn't want to leave until he heard back from Logan Chisholm.

When his phone rang, he thought for sure it would be Chisholm calling him back. He'd left a message at the ranch and been assured by Emma Chisholm that she would have her stepson call as soon as she saw him.

Instead the call was from a waitress from a café in Cut Bank, Montana.

"I saw in the newspaper that JJ was dead?"

"Yes?" Apparently she hadn't seen the latest edition.

"Well, that's weird because I saw her that day, you know, the day it said she died?"

Buford thought of the missing hours between when she'd left her car beside the lake and when she'd left Martin Sanderson's house.

"What time was that?"

"It was late afternoon."

Cut Bank was hours from Flathead Lake. "Where was this that you saw her?"

"Here in Cut Bank at the café where I work. I recognized her right off, even though she pretended it wasn't her. I guess I scared her away. I should have been cooler."

"Scared her away? You saw her leave?"

"Yeah, I watched her and her boyfriend leave on his motorcycle."

Bull's-eye, Buford said under his breath. "What did the boyfriend look like?" He listened as she described a blond cowboy on a Harley, the same description the guard at the Grizzly Club had given him. Logan Chisholm.

"Did you see what direction they were headed?" he asked.

"East."

East, toward Whitehorse, Montana. East, toward the Chisholm Cattle Company ranch.

Buford thanked her for calling. The moment he hung up, he called Sheriff McCall Crawford in Whitehorse.

Blythe had feared how Logan would take the news. She had to admit he'd taken it better than she'd suspected. He was angry with her, but it was the disappointment in his expression that hurt the most.

"Someone is trying to kill you?" He sounded skeptical. She couldn't blame him. She didn't want to get into this with him, but she could see he wasn't going to take no for an answer.

"I started getting death threats a few months ago. I didn't think too much about it. People in the glare of the media often get letters from crazies." She shrugged, and she could see that he was trying to imagine the life she'd been living.

"Something happened to convince you otherwise," he said.

"There were a series of accidents on the road tour. The last time I was almost killed when some lights fell. You have to understand. I had wanted to quit for months. I guess that was just the last straw."

"You went to the police, of course."

"I did, but then Martin leaked the story to the media and it turned out looking like a publicity stunt. For a while, I thought it was. I thought Martin had hired someone to scare me back in line."

"Martin Sanderson really would have done something like that?" Logan asked, clearly unable to comprehend it.

She let out a humorless laugh. "Martin was capable of anything, trust me."

Logan took off his Stetson and raked a hand through his hair. "The note you dropped at the café in Cut Bank, is that part of this?"

She couldn't help her surprise.

"Yeah, I picked it up. It didn't seem important until now. *You're next?*"

"It was pinned to Martin's robe the morning I found him lying dead next to the fireplace. I thought whoever had killed him—"

"Was coming after you next." Logan nodded. "That explains the way you came flying out of the club and why you climbed on the back of my motorcycle."

"Not entirely. When I saw you... I wanted to run away with you and would have even if none of this had happened." She could tell he wanted to believe that, but was having a hard time.

"You thought whoever killed him left the note for you."

She nodded.

"Why do I get the feeling that you know who's after you?"

She looked into his handsome face. It had been so long since she'd opened up to anyone. When had she become so mistrustful? She'd told herself it was the dog-eat-dog music business that had turned her this way. It was hard to know who your friends were, since it felt as if everyone wanted a piece of you.

But she trusted Logan. He hadn't asked anything of her. Still wasn't.

"I made a lot of mistakes in my life, especially when I signed with Martin Sanderson. Ten years ago, I was in a small all-girl band called Tough as Nails with some friends. Then Martin 'discovered' me." She couldn't keep the regret from her voice. "I wanted to get away from my life so bad then that I signed on the dotted line without thinking, let alone reading the contract. I dumped the band and my friends, latched onto that brass ring and didn't look back."

He frowned. "So you think this is about your former band members? Why now? Why wait ten years? Unless something changed recently."

She loved how quickly he caught on. "Martin was waiting up for me the night after I met you at the bar. He had some news, he said. He was planning to get Tough as Nails back together for a reunion tour and he'd invited them to Montana to knock out the details. He said after that, then he would let me out of my contract."

"You refused."

"I didn't trust him, let alone believe him. I'd lost track of the other members of the old band. As far as I knew, they'd all moved on, and since I hadn't heard anything about them, I'd just assumed they weren't involved in the music industry anymore." She looked out the side window for a minute. "Also we hadn't parted on the best of terms. They felt like I deserted them. I did."

"Still that doesn't seem like enough to want you dead."

She laughed. "You really don't know the music business." She quickly sobered. "But you're right. There *was* more. There was this young musician who was part of a band that we used to open for. His name was Ray Barnes. He'd been dating my best friend in the band and the others, as well. When I left, he left, too. With me. Today he's best known as Jett Atkins."

Jett Atkins. Logan remembered seeing JJ with Jett in one of the photographs he'd uncovered on the library internet. "So you and Jett are—"

"History. A long time ago. But another one of my regrets."

"Who was the girl he was dating?"

"Karen Chandler, or Caro as we called her. But I think he might have been seeing the others at the same time. He was like that." Logan heard her remorse, saw the pain. He could understand why she had wanted to start her life over. "I don't want to believe it is Karen, but I hurt her badly. She and I grew up together. I should have fought harder for the band. After I left, it fell apart. Any one of them probably wants me dead."

Logan shook his head. "Isn't it possible the band would have fallen apart even if you'd stayed?"

"We'll never know, will we? But if Martin was telling the truth, then he got their hopes up. He was threatening to tell them I refused to be part of the band anymore, that I was too good for them. It wasn't true, none of it. He admitted he had never planned a reunion tour of Tough as Nails. He was just using them to get back at me."

Martin Sanderson really had been a bastard. He played with people's lives with no regard for them. Logan could understand why Blythe had wanted out, why she had felt desperate. Especially after Martin had apparently killed himself. Had he tried to make it look as if she had murdered him? Then why the note, he asked, voicing his thoughts.

"When I found Martin dead and saw the note pinned to his body…" She shuddered. "I couldn't be sure his killer wasn't still in the house and that I *was* next."

"So you think he wrote the note? Or someone else?"

She shrugged. "Maybe it was his final hateful act."

"I'm glad I was there when you needed me, but you can't keep running from this, Blythe. You have to find out who's after you—if they still are—and put an end to it. The Flathead County sheriff is going to figure out that you weren't in that car, if he hasn't already."

She nodded. "I would have told you the truth, but I wanted you to like the girl who always wanted to ride off into the sunset with a cowboy."

"I *do* like her," he said as he reached across the seat for her. "I like her a lot." He cupped her cheek, his thumb stroking across her lips.

She leaned into the warmth of his large callused

hand and closed her eyes. Desire thrummed through her veins.

"Blythe?" His voice was low. The sound of it quickened her pulse.

She opened her eyes. Heat. She felt the burn of his gaze, of his touch.

He dragged her to him and dropped his mouth to hers. She came to him, pressing against him with a soft moan. Her arms wrapped around his neck as he deepened the kiss and her blood turned molten.

"I want you," she whispered when he drew back. "Here. *Now.*"

Chapter 9

"Come on," Logan said as he opened the pickup door and pulled Blythe out behind him. Warm sunlight filtered through the new leaves of the cottonwoods. A warm spring breeze whispered softly in the branches as he led her along the riverbank.

At a small grassy spot, he turned and drew her close. His face was lit by sunlight. She looked into Logan's handsome face and felt her pulse quicken.

She'd wanted this from that first night they'd danced together at the country-western bar. There was something about this man. Being in his strong arms, she'd never felt safer—and yet there was a dangerous side to him. This man could steal her heart and there was nothing she could do about it.

As he pulled her closer, she swore she could feel the beat of his heart beneath his Western shirt. Her nipples ached for his touch as they pressed against the lace of her bra. His kiss, at first tender, turned punishing as the fever rose in both of them.

She grabbed the front of his shirt and tore it open, the snaps giving way under her assault. She pressed her palms to his warm, hard chest, breathing in the very male scent of him along with the rich primal scents of the riverbottom.

Logan pulled back, his gaze locking with hers, as he tantalizingly released each of the snaps on her Western shirt. She felt her blood run hot as his gaze dropped to her breasts. He freed one breast from the bra, his mouth dropping to the aching nipple. She arched against him, moaning softly like the trees in the spring breeze.

As he slid her shirt off her shoulders, he unhooked her bra freeing her breasts, and pulled her against him. Blythe reveled in the heat, flesh against flesh, as they stripped off the rest of their clothing, then dropped down in the sweet, warm grass.

Later she would remember the wonderful scents, the soft sounds, the feel of the Montana spring afternoon on her bare skin. But those sensations had been lost for a while in the fury of their lovemaking. It was Logan's scent, his touch, his sounds that were branded in her mind forever.

Logan let out a curse as he checked the time. They had been snuggled on the cool grass as the sun disappeared behind the Bear Paw Mountains in the distance.

They got up, brushing off their clothes and getting dressed by the edge of the river.

"This might have been a better idea after the family

supper," Logan said, but he was grinning. He picked a leaf out of her hair, laughed and then leaned in to kiss her softly on the mouth.

"Keep that up and we won't make supper at all," she said, teasing. She would have been happy to stay here by the river forever.

Once in the pickup, she snuggled against him again as he drove toward the family ranch. Logan seemed less nervous about taking her home to meet his family. That was until they turned and passed under the large Chisholm Cattle Company sign and started up the road to the house.

She felt him tense and realized that she hadn't been paying any attention as to where they were going. Looking up now, she saw a huge house come into view. She tried to hide her surprise. She couldn't help but glance over at Logan.

"Nice place," she said playing down the obvious grandeur. Was this why he didn't want her to meet the family? He didn't want her to know that they were obviously well off? The irony didn't escape her.

As the front door of the house opened, a short, plump redhead in her fifties stepped out onto the porch.

"My stepmother, Emma," Logan said as he parked and cut the engine. Opening his door, he reached for Blythe's hand and she slid out after him. He squeezed her hand as they walked toward the house as if he was nervous again. She squeezed back, hoping there wasn't any reason to be.

"This must be Blythe," Emma said, pulling her into a warm hug. "Welcome to our home."

She felt herself swept inside the warm, comfortable living room where she was introduced first to

Logan's father, Hoyt. He was just as she'd pictured the rancher, a large man with blond hair that was turning gray at the temples, a sun-weathered face and a strong handshake.

The brothers came as a surprise. Blond and blue-eyed, Colton resembled Logan and Zane and their father, but the other three had dark hair and eyes and appeared to have some Native American ancestry.

"You really do have five brothers," she whispered to Logan as they were being lead into the dining room.

"We're all adopted," Logan said.

That came as a surprise too, and she realized how little they knew about each other. It was the way she'd wanted it, actually had needed it. But that was before. Now she found herself even more curious about him and his family.

With the fiancées of the brothers Tanner, Colton, Marshall and Dawson, the dining room was almost filled. She was thinking how they would have to get a larger table if this family kept growing and at the same time, she couldn't help thinking of her own family table—TV trays in front of the sagging couch.

What was it like growing up with such a large family? She felt envious of Logan and wondered if he knew how lucky he was. A thought struck her. How could he ever understand her and the life she'd led? He'd always had all this.

Dinner was a boisterous affair with lots of laughter and stories. She couldn't remember a more enjoyable evening and told Emma as much.

"I'm new to the family myself," Emma confided. "Hoyt and I were married a year ago May."

Blythe could see that the two were head-over-heels

in love with each other. On top of that, it was clear that everyone at the table adored Emma, and who wouldn't?

"This meal is amazing," Blythe said. "Thank you so much for inviting me."

Logan had been quiet during supper. She wondered if he was always that way or if he felt uncomfortable under the circumstances. He wouldn't want to lie to his family, so keeping her secret must be weighing on him.

But when their gazes met, she saw the spark she'd seen earlier by the river and felt her face heat with the memory of their lovemaking.

"So I understand that Logan has taught you to ride," Hoyt said drawing her attention.

"She was a natural," Logan said sounding proud.

"I had a wonderful instructor and I loved it," she gushed. "I love the freedom. All this wide-open country, it's exciting to see it from the back of a horse."

"Where are you from that you don't have wide-open country like this?" Emma asked.

Blythe had known someone was bound to ask where she was from. "Oh, we had wide-open country in southern California. Desert. It's not the same as rolling hills covered with tall green grass and huge cottonwoods and mountains in the distance dark with pine trees."

"What do you do for a living?" Hoyt asked. Emma shot him a look. "I don't mean to be rude," he added.

"I'll get dessert," Emma said, rising from her chair.

Blythe smiled and said, "I don't mind. I've done a lot of different things, but today I got a job in town at the Whitehorse Café. I'll be waitressing."

"Waitressing's a good profession," Emma said, and shot her husband a warning look.

Blythe excused herself and went into the kitchen to help Emma get the dessert. The rest of the meal passed quickly and quite pleasantly.

It wasn't long until she was saying how nice it was to meet everyone, how wonderful the meal was and promising to come back.

"Oh, Logan, it slipped my mind earlier," Emma said as she pressed a bag full of leftovers and some freshly baked gingersnaps into his arms as they were leaving. "You had a call earlier from a Sheriff Buford Olson from Flathead County. He needs you to call him. I put the number on a slip of paper in the bag with the food. He said it was important."

Logan had seen Blythe's panicked expression when Emma mentioned the call from the sheriff in Flathead County. He drove out of the ranch and turned onto the county road wondering why the sheriff was calling him, and realized the guard at the Grizzly Club had probably taken down the plate number on his motorcycle.

He glanced over at her, saw she was looking out at the night and chewing at her lower lip. "The sheriff knows. Or at least suspects I know where you are."

Blythe nodded. "I'll call him."

What if she was right and someone really was trying to kill her? She was safe here.

"It's too late now. Let's call him in the morning," he said.

They made love again the moment they reached the

house, both of them racing up the stairs to fall into his double bed.

Lying staring up at the cracked ceiling, Logan smiled to himself. His body was damp with sweat and still tingling from her touch.

Blythe was lying beside him. She sighed, then let out a chuckle.

Logan glanced over at her and grinned. "What's so funny?"

"Us," she said. "We both lied about who we are. You were afraid I was after your money. I was afraid you would only be interested in JJ."

"Pretty funny, huh," he said.

She nodded.

He studied her for a moment, then pulled her over to spoon against her backside. His breath tickled her ear, but she giggled, then snuggled closer.

"I love the feel of you. I can't remember a time I've felt happier."

Logan felt the same way. He breathed in her warm scent, languishing in her warmth and the feel of her flesh against his, and tried not to worry.

But if she was right and someone wanted her dead, then as soon as everyone knew she was alive, Blythe wouldn't be safe. He couldn't bear the thought of any harm coming to her.

She would be safe here with him.

That was if she didn't go back to her old life.

The thought was like an arrow through his heart.

Of course she would go back.

He felt his heart break. He'd fallen for this woman from the moment he'd seen her on that dance floor only days ago.

* * *

"We can't keep living like this," Emma Chisholm said after everyone had left. She'd said this before, but this time she saw that Hoyt knew she meant it.

"The house is armed to the teeth with weapons," she continued. "You never leave my side or have one or two of my stepsons here watching me."

She wasn't telling him anything he didn't already know, but she couldn't seem to stop. "You have done everything but build a dungeon and lock me in it. I can't leave here without an armed guard. You're killing me, Hoyt, and worse, I see what it is doing to you."

He nodded as if he knew she not only meant it, but that he could see the strain this had put on their family.

"I know you're sick to death of me hanging around," he said.

"It's not you. It's knowing that you should be working this ranch and not babysitting me. Your sons are going crazy, as well. They need to be on the back of a horse in wild country, not cooped up here in this kitchen. And I need to do something besides bake!"

He smiled then as if he'd noticed the extra weight she was carrying. "I like your curves."

"Hoyt—"

"I have some news," he said quickly. "I was going to tell you tonight. I found a woman through that service in Great Falls. She sounds perfect, older, with experience cooking for a large family. The service explained how isolated we are out here and that it would be a live-in position and she was fine with that."

Emma didn't necessarily like the idea of someone living in the house with them. But the house was large. The woman would have her own wing and entrance and they would all have plenty of privacy. Anyway, what choice did Emma have?

She knew Hoyt flat out refused to leave her alone. It was nonnegotiable, as he'd said many times. If this was the only way she could have some freedom, she would take it. It was at least a step in the right direction.

"Wonderful. I could use the help," she said agreeably.

Hoyt eyed her suspiciously. "She comes highly recommended. She will be doing the housework and helping with the cooking, if you let her. She'll accompany you wherever you need to go."

Emma mugged a face, but was smart enough not to argue.

He smiled and moved to embrace her. "I'm so sorry about all of this."

"Stop that. None of this is your fault."

His expression said he would never believe that. "If Laura is alive, if she's what Aggie believed she was, then it has to be my fault. I failed her. Failed all of us, especially you."

Emma was surprised to hear him even entertain the idea that his first wife might be alive. He'd sworn he didn't believe it. Apparently she wasn't the only one living with ghosts.

She shook her head and took her husband's face in her hands. "Listen to me. We can't know what's in another person's heart let alone their mind, even those closest to us. You said yourself that Laura was like a bottomless well when it came to her need. No human can fill that kind of hole in another person."

He leaned down to kiss her.

"So when do I meet my new guard?" she asked.

"She's coming at the end of the week."

Emma hated the idea, but at least Hoyt and his sons could get back to running the ranch. She would deal with the housekeeper and find a way to get some time away from the ranch—alone.

She couldn't live her life being afraid, thinking every person she met wanted to kill her. Emma had lost some of her old self and she intended to get it back.

Not that she was going to take the gun out of her purse that was always within reach. She was no fool.

Aggie Wells had been dozing in her chair. She jumped now at the sudden tap on her door. Holding her breath, she waited. Another light tap.

Aggie realized it was probably her doctor friend coming back to check on her. He'd wanted to put her in the hospital but she'd refused, knowing that would alert the authorities and be the end of her freedom.

With effort, she pushed herself up out of the chair and moved to the window. Parting the curtain, she peered out, surprised that it was dark outside.

Even in the dim light, she could see that it wasn't the doctor. It was the elderly woman who lived in the unit at the end of the building. The old woman was horribly stooped, could barely get around even with the gnarled cane she used. She wore a shawl around her shoulders, a faded scarf covering most of her gray hair.

Aggie had seen her hobbling by, headed for the small store a few blocks away. She'd thought about helping the woman but everyone who lived in the old motel units kept to themselves, which was fine with her.

The old woman tapped again, so bent with age and

arthritis that she probably saw more of her shoes than she did where she was going. For a moment she leaned into the door as if barely able to stand, then tapped again, swaying a little on her cane, and Aggie realized she must need help or she wouldn't be out there.

Aggie quickly opened the door. "Is something wrong?" she inquired, reaching for the elderly woman's arm, afraid the woman was about to drop onto the concrete step.

But the moment she grabbed the arm she realized it wasn't frail and thin but wiry and strong.

Aggie had always been a stickler for details. Too late she noticed that while everything else was like the old woman's who lived a few doors down, the shoes were all wrong.

Chapter 10

The woman Aggie Wells had opened the door to brought the cane up, caught her in the stomach and drove her back into the room. She quickly followed her in, closing and locking the door behind them.

As the formerly stooped woman rose to her full height, she shrugged off the shawl and faded scarf. Aggie saw why she'd been fooled. The shawl and faded scarf were *exactly* like the old woman's who lived in the last unit.

She let out a cry of regret, knowing that the old woman wouldn't be in need of either again.

Aggie had stumbled when she'd been pushed and fallen, landing on the edge of the recliner. Weak and gasping for breath, she now let herself slide into the seat while she stared at the old woman's transformation into a woman nearer her own age. It was a marvel the way Laura Chisholm shed the old woman's character.

"We finally meet," she said to Laura, realizing the woman must have known where she was for some time. Laura had been watching and waiting for just such an opportunity.

Only the shoes would have given her away, had Aggie noticed them before she opened the door. Laura Chisholm's feet were too large for the old woman's shoes. When she'd disposed of the poor old woman, taken the shawl and scarf and cane, she'd had to use her own shoes.

There was a time when Aggie wouldn't have been fooled. She would have noticed the small differences and would never have opened the door. But that time had passed, and a part of her was thankful that she had finally gotten to meet a woman she'd unknowingly been chasing for years.

"Aggie Wells," Laura said, as if just as delighted to meet her.

How strange this feeling of mutual respect, two professionals admiring the other's work.

"Just tell me this," Aggie said, not kidding herself how this would end. "Why?"

"Why?" Laura cocked her head almost in amusement. There was intelligence in her blue eyes but also a brightness that burned too hot.

"Do you hate Hoyt that much?"

Laura looked surprised. "I *love* Hoyt. I will *always* love him. Haven't you ever loved someone too much and realized they could never love you as much?"

Aggie hadn't. Other than her job. "Let me guess, everything was fine until he adopted the boys."

Laura's face darkened. "I wasn't enough. First it was just three boys, then three more. He said he had enough love for all of us." She scoffed at that.

"You could have just divorced him and made a life for yourself."

Laura smiled. "Who says I haven't?"

"But you couldn't let go. You've been killing his wives." There was no accusation in her voice. She was just stating what they both knew.

Laura looked down at the thick gnarled wood cane in her hand, then up at Aggie. "If I couldn't have him, no one else could, either."

"Why didn't you just kill him?"

The woman looked shocked at the idea. "I *loved* him. I couldn't do that to him."

But killing his wives was another matter apparently. "I'm curious. How did you get away that day at the lake?"

Laura frowned and waved a hand through the air as if the question was beneath Aggie. "I told Hoyt I was afraid of water, that I couldn't swim. He believed anything I told him. I grew up in California on the beach and learned to scuba dive in college. I set everything up beforehand, the scuba gear, the vehicle on a road a few miles from the spot where I would go overboard. I simply started an argument with Hoyt and let the rest play out. When he realized that I'd filed for divorce, it made him look guilty. I thought he would never remarry. I was wrong."

She shrugged, and Aggie realized what Laura had been able to do since then was much more impressive. Laura had dedicated her life to making sure Hoyt found no happiness with another woman.

Just as Aggie had dedicated hers to chasing the truth. Other people had balance in their lives, they had their job, their family, their friends, but not her and Laura. They'd both sacrificed their lives for something intangible: a cockeyed sense of being the only ones who could get justice.

Was this woman's quest any crazier than her own? Aggie had lost the job she loved because she couldn't let go of that thin thread of suspicion that something wasn't quite right about Laura Chisholm's death.

Had she been able to let go, where would she be now? Certainly she wouldn't be wanted for murder, nearly committed to a state mental hospital and about to die at the hands of the real killer.

And Laura? Had she felt loved, wouldn't she still be with Hoyt, raising six sons, getting old with him in that huge house on the ranch?

"We don't choose this, it chooses us," Aggie said seeing the truth of it.

Laura nodded as if she had been thinking the same thing.

Then again Laura might simply be crazy.

The difference now was that Laura would win.

"Has it been worth it?" That was the real question Aggie had wanted to ask. She watched Laura lift the thick wooden cane and step toward her.

"Worth it?" Laura asked as she closed the distance between them. A smile curled her lips, her eyes now bright as neon. "What do you think?"

Aggie's last thought was Emma. She said a quick prayer for her. The fourth wife of Hoyt Chisholm didn't stand a chance against a woman this obsessed.

* * *

Logan woke to find his bed empty. For just an instant, he thought he'd dreamed last night. But Blythe's side of the bed was still warm, her scent still on his sheets. He heard the soft lap of water in the tub of the adjacent bathroom, then the sound of the water draining, and relaxed.

A few moments later Blythe came out, her wonderful body wrapped in one of his towels. He grinned at her and pulled back the covers to pat the bed beside him.

"Sorry, but I have to call the Flathead sheriff, then get to work, and so do you," she said, reaching for her clothes. "Zane said you have Emma duty today."

He couldn't believe she was really going to go to that waitress job, but he was smart enough not to say so. With a groan, he recalled that she was right. He had Emma duty today. He much preferred working on the ranch than hanging out at the house. Today, though, he much preferred staying in bed with Blythe. He reached for her, thinking they had time for a quickie.

She giggled, pretending to put up a fight.

At the sound of a vehicle coming up the road, they both froze. "Are you expecting anyone this morning?" she whispered.

He shook his head and reluctantly rose from the warm bed to pull on his jeans. Going to the window, he looked out and felt a start. It was a sheriff's department patrol SUV coming up the road. He watched it grow closer until he could see the sheriff behind the wheel. She had someone with her.

He swore under his breath as he hurriedly finished dressing.

"Who is it?" Blythe asked sounding worried.

"The sheriff. She has someone with her. I'll go see what they want."

"You know what they want."

He gave her a smile he hoped was reassuring, kissed her quickly and went downstairs. He'd wanted to call the sheriff before anyone found out that JJ was staying with him. He figured it would look better for Blythe.

As the patrol car came to a stop in front of his house, he stepped out onto the porch. "Sheriff," he said as McCall Crawford climbed out. He felt as if he'd seen too much of her during the mess with his father's former wives.

"Logan."

His gaze went to the big older man working his way out of the passenger seat. He was big-bellied, pushing sixty, his face weathered from years in Montana's sun.

The man merely glanced in Logan's direction before reaching back into the patrol car for his Stetson. As he settled it on his thinning gray head, he slammed the patrol car door and stepped toward the house.

"This is Sheriff Buford Olson from the Flathead County," McCall said. "We're here about Jennifer James. JJ?"

Logan nodded as the door opened behind him and Blythe stepped out.

Jett Atkins groaned at the sound of someone knocking on his motel room door. It was that damned sheriff, he thought as he went to the door. Sheriff Buford Olson acted as if he wasn't all that sharp. But Jett wasn't fooled.

He hurriedly hid the suitcase he'd had by the door.

The sheriff hadn't told him he could leave town yet—even after Martin Sanderson's death had been ruled a suicide. It was that damned JJ. The sheriff had said he was waiting for the coroner's report.

All Jett knew was that he'd had enough of this motel room, this town, this state. He wanted to put as much distance as he could from whatever Martin had been up to with JJ's former band members.

But when he opened the door, it wasn't the sheriff. Loretta stood in the doorway.

"What are you—"

She didn't give him a chance to finish as she pushed past him. He closed the door and turned to find her glaring at him. It reminded him of all those years ago when the two of them had dated. Well, he wouldn't really call it dating. More like what people now called hooking up.

"Where's JJ?" she demanded.

"What are you talking about? She's dead."

"You haven't seen the news today?"

He hadn't. He was sick of sitting in this room with nothing to do but watch television. Last night he'd packed, determined to leave town no matter what. Then he'd finished off a half quart of Scotch and awakened with a hangover this morning. He hadn't even turned on the TV.

"No, why?" he asked now. Loretta said she sang in a bar and nightclubs. He knew she was just getting by. He'd shuddered at the thought, since it was his greatest fear. At least she hadn't been famous and had the rug pulled out from under her. Most people hadn't even heard of her or Tough As Nails.

"That body that was found in JJ's rental car turned

out to belong to some woman from Arizona. The cops think the woman stole JJ's car and crashed it. I heard just now that they are investigating the crash as a homicide."

He had to sit down. He lowered himself to the edge of the bed. "You're saying someone tried to kill JJ but killed some other woman instead? Then where is JJ?"

"That's what I just asked you."

"I haven't seen her. She was gone by the time I reached Martin and found him dead…" He stared at Loretta. "I wasn't joking about one of you wanting her dead."

Loretta rolled her eyes. "If I wanted to kill her, it would be more personal than a car wreck. I'd want to be the last person she saw before she died."

He shuddered. "Maybe you were."

She scoffed at that. "I vote for Betsy. That sweet act of hers? I've never bought it. It's women like that who kill, you know."

He didn't know. He figured any of the three were capable of it. Especially if they acted together.

"Or Karen," Loretta said, as if she'd been giving it some thought. "After all, JJ was her best friend—or so she thought. Also, I heard that Martin went to Karen first." She nodded at his surprise. "Karen had the talent. But I heard she turned him down flat, saying she could never desert JJ."

Jett let out a low whistle. "Then JJ deserted her without a thought."

Loretta shrugged. "There is another possibility," she said eyeing him intently. "You."

He laughed. "Why would I want to kill JJ?"

"According to the tabloids, she dumped you."

"Do you really believe *anything* you read in them?" he challenged. "Anyway, that was just the spin Martin put on it after *I* dumped JJ." He could see Loretta was skeptical. "You have no idea what it's like to date someone with her kind of star power. It was exhausting."

"She did outshine you, didn't she?" Loretta said with no small amount of satisfaction.

"Well, whoever tried to kill JJ…apparently they failed," Jett said. "And now she's disappeared."

"So it would appear," Loretta said mysteriously.

"If you know where she is, then why were you asking me?" he demanded.

She smiled. "I just wanted to see if you knew where she was. You don't. She'll turn up. She owes me for this mess and I intend to get my money out of her, one way or another." With that she left, slamming the door behind her.

"We were going to call you this morning," Logan said as Sheriff Buford Olson's gaze went to Blythe.

"Is that right?" he said, not sounding as if he believed it for an instant. "I think we'd better sit down and talk about this."

"Do you mind if we come in?" McCall asked.

Logan shook his head. "Come on in. I'll get some coffee going."

"So why don't we start with you telling me who you are," Buford said after they'd all taken chairs and cups of coffee at the kitchen table.

Blythe braced herself as she looked into the sheriff's keen eyes. "My name is Jennifer Blythe James, but I think you already know that."

"JJ," he said. "Okay, now tell me what you're doing here."

"Getting on with my life," she said.

"You do realize that you left the scene of a death without calling anyone, then left the scene of an accident that resulted in another death, not to mention let everyone believe you were dead."

"At first I panicked," she admitted. She had felt no need to clear her name. Not her name, JJ's. How strange. JJ had become a separate persona over the past ten years. Blythe had lost herself and only found that girl she'd been the other night at a country-western bar dancing with Logan Chisholm.

But she doubted the Flathead sheriff would understand that.

"I'd been getting death threats and having some close calls on my music tour," she continued. "I was convinced someone was trying to kill me. Martin had made it appear that the incidents were nothing more than a publicity stunt. I left the tour and came to Montana to try to talk him into letting me out of my contract. I'd had enough."

Sheriff McCall Crawford sipped her coffee and didn't say a word. Clearly, she'd just come to bring the Flathead sheriff.

"Did you talk him out of it?" Buford asked.

Blythe shook her head. "I thought I had. But that night when I returned to the house, he told me he had contacted the members of my former band and was going to make me do a reunion tour with them if I didn't go back on my music tour. I told him to stuff it and left the room."

"Did you hear the shot that killed him?"

"No, that house is too large, I didn't hear a thing. I didn't know he was dead until I came back down to the living room the next morning and saw him."

"Saw him and the note pinned to him," Buford said. "What did the note say?"

She had to quell a shudder at the memory. *"You're next."*

The sheriff studied her. "Why did you take the note?"

"I don't know. I grabbed it before I thought about what I was doing, wadded it up and stuck it in my pocket. I guess it made everything a little less real. Then I realized that whoever had killed him could still be in the house. So I ran. I thought if I could get far enough away from there, go some place that no one knew about…"

"That was pretty shortsighted," Buford said.

She nodded and glanced at Logan. "I just wanted to escape my life for a while. By the way, Logan didn't know anything about what I was running from or even who I was."

"Did you recognize the handwriting on the note?" Buford asked.

A chill snaked up her spine. Hadn't she known how vindictive Martin was? How deceitful? The man had made his fortune using other people and their talents.

"No," she said. "I just assumed the person who'd killed him was the same one who'd been threatening me. Now I think he might have written the note himself."

"Why would he do that?" Buford asked.

"He wanted me to fear for my life. I think he killed himself hoping I would be under suspicion for his death." If it hadn't been for fate and a car thief, she might have been arrested.

"You're that sure he wrote the note," the sheriff said. "What about his other guests?"

"Other guests?" she echoed.

"You weren't aware your former band members were staying in the guesthouse just out back?"

She could feel the color drain from her face. Reaching for her coffee, she took a drink, burning her tongue.

"So you didn't know that Karen, Loretta and Betsy had already arrived?" he said.

She shook her head.

"Is it possible one of them found the body and wrote the note?" he asked.

Blythe couldn't speak. She looked from her coffee cup to him and knew he saw the answer in her eyes.

"You said there had been death threats before this? Do you have copies of those?" he asked.

"No, I threw them away. They didn't seem…serious at the time."

"A death threat that didn't seem serious?" Buford asked.

"I've had them before and nothing happened. Other musicians I've known have gotten them. They aren't like, 'I'm going to kill you.' They're more vague, like, 'You have no idea what you're doing to the kids listening to your horrible music. Someone should shut you up for good.' That sort of thing."

"I have a granddaughter who listens to your music," Buford said. "She listens to Jett Atkins, as well. I think whoever wrote that note might have a point."

"That's another reason I wanted out of my contract," she said. "Martin had total control of my career as well as the music. I hated what I was singing. I signed the contract with him when I was very young and stupid."

"Your former band members aren't the only ones in Montana. Your boyfriend, Jett, is here, as well," Buford said.

"He's not my boyfriend."

The sheriff nodded. "No love lost there either, huh?"

"If you're asking if I have enemies—"

"I know you do," Buford said, cutting her off. "The brakes on your rental car had been tampered with. The death of the woman driving it has been ruled a homicide."

Blythe felt all the air rush out of her. She shot to her feet and stumbled out of the room.

"If you know someone is trying to kill her," she heard Logan say as she pushed open the screen door and stepped out onto the porch. Blythe didn't catch the rest. Logan couldn't blame the sheriff. She was the one who'd run. If she'd called the sheriff the moment she'd found Martin's body—

She heard the screen door open behind her. The next moment, Logan's arms came around her.

"Don't worry," he said as he drew her close. "I'm not going to let anyone hurt you."

"You can't arrest her given the circumstances," Logan said when he and Blythe returned to the kitchen and the two sheriffs sitting there.

Buford studied him for a moment, then turned his attention to Blythe. "You should know that at least one member of your old band is dead. Lisa Thomas."

"Luca?" Blythe said.

"Apparently she died recently," Buford said. "In a hit-and-run accident."

Logan saw Blythe's expression. She had to be thinking the same thing he was. It had been no accident.

"I'm going to talk to the former members of your band again," Buford was saying, "but in the meantime…"

Blythe glanced at her watch. "In the meantime, I have a job in town I need to get to."

The sheriff raised two bushy eyebrows, but it was McCall who spoke before Logan could.

"Are you sure that's a good idea?" the Whitehorse sheriff asked. "You seem to have a target on your back."

"It's a terrible idea," Logan interrupted, but he saw the stubborn set of Blythe's jaw.

"What am I supposed to do, sit around and wait for someone to come after me again?" she demanded.

Buford chuckled as he rose slowly from the kitchen chair. "What kind of job did you say this was?"

"Waitressing." She raised her chin defiantly.

"Making it easy for whoever wants you dead to find you, huh?" He nodded smiling.

Logan stared at her. "You're using yourself as *bait?* Have you lost your mind?"

"Could I speak with you outside?" she asked.

"You betcha," he said taking her arm and leading her back out to the porch. "What the hell, Blythe?"

"I don't expect you to understand this," she said. "But ten years ago I signed away all control of my life when I took Martin Sanderson's offer to make me a star. I have that control back and it feels really good."

"You're right, I don't understand. There is someone out there who wants you *dead*."

She nodded. "And I might have kept running like I did when I left my car beside the lake and climbed on the back of your motorcycle. But you changed that. I don't want to run anymore."

"You don't have to run. You can stay here. I will—"

Blythe leaned into him and brushed a kiss across his lips silencing him. "I need a ride to town. I hate being late my first day of work. Is that offer to lend me a pickup still open?"

He didn't know what to say. It was clear that she'd made up her mind and there was no changing it. He swallowed the lump in his throat, trying to fight back his fear as the two sheriffs came out onto the porch. All he could do was reach into the pocket of his jeans and hand her his truck key.

"I'll get one of my brothers to come pick me up," he said his voice tight.

"You sort it out?" Buford asked as Blythe headed for his pickup.

"Find out who is after her," Logan said between gritted teeth. "Find them before they find her." Meanwhile he was going to do everything in his power to keep her safe.

The problem was that the woman was as stubborn as a damned mule. But he was glad that Blythe seemed her former strong, determined self again. Not that he wasn't worried about what she would do next.

Chapter 11

Betsy came out of the shower to find Loretta and Karen sitting on the ends of the bed, glued to the television screen. Her heart kicked up a beat. "What's happened now?" she asked with a sinking feeling.

Loretta grabbed the remote to turn up the volume. A publicity shot of JJ flashed on the screen, then a news commentator was saying that an inside source had confirmed that the body found in the rented sports car convertible was not pop rocker JJ.

"Authorities are asking anyone with information regarding JJ to call the sheriff's department." A number flashed on the screen.

"I don't understand," Betsy said. She knew now why she never watched the news. It depressed her.

"JJ," Loretta said. "She's not dead. She wasn't driving the car that crashed."

"Then who was?" Betsy asked.

Loretta shrugged.

"Then where is JJ?" Betsy asked.

Karen looked over at Loretta. "That's the million-dollar question, isn't it?"

Loretta was already heading for the door. "I need a drink. Call me if you hear anything. I already asked Jett about JJ. He swears he doesn't know where she is. But I wouldn't be surprised if the two of them cooked this up. When I find JJ, she is going to pony up some money for this wasted trip. I swear, that bitch is going down."

As she went out the door, Karen sighed.

"Does she really believe that Jett and JJ cooked up letting some poor young girl die in JJ's car?" Betsy asked. "Is that really what she thinks?"

"Loretta has always had her own way of thinking," Karen said distractedly. "Just as she sees this as JJ owing her."

"What do *you* think about all this?"

Karen seemed surprised that Betsy would ask her. But Karen had always seemed the most sensible one in the band and Betsy said as much.

"Thanks for the vote of confidence, but I have no idea. The police will sort it out. In the meantime, I wish I knew where JJ was."

"You miss her, don't you?"

Karen smiled. "Hard to believe after what she did to all of us, huh."

"She was just offered an opportunity and took it," Betsy said. "I don't blame her. But you were just as good as she was, if not better. I've never understood why Martin chose her and not you."

"I guess he saw something in JJ that I lacked."

"Do you still play and sing?"

"I don't really have the time," Karen said, but Betsy knew it was more than that.

"It hurt us all when the band broke up. Don't you think we could have found another lead singer? I mean, we didn't have to break up the band when JJ left."

Karen smiled as she turned back to her. "We'll never know."

"Loretta says that JJ's leaving was like having the heart ripped out of us because we felt betrayed," Betsy persisted. "Is that how you felt?"

When the door opened and Loretta came in with Jett, Betsy noticed that Karen seemed glad for the interruption. Clearly, she hadn't wanted to talk about JJ anymore. Or how she felt about the girl she considered her sister walking out on her.

"It's all over Twitter," Jett announced. "JJ was seen east of here."

Blythe had some time to think on the way into town. She needed an apartment so she could walk to work. She couldn't keep driving around town in a Chisholm Cattle Company pickup. But she knew that wasn't the real reason she couldn't stay with Logan any longer.

She couldn't put him in any more danger than she already had.

What she'd told Logan had been heartfelt. He had changed everything. She would have kept running, but he made her want to end this so she could get on with her life—and she hoped Logan would be in it.

But until she found out who was after her, she had to put some distance between them. Whoever had put the note on Martin Sanderson's body could have killed her that morning at the Grizzly Club. She figured the only reason they hadn't was that they wanted her running scared still.

She wouldn't let them use Logan Chisholm to do it.

As she drove into the small Western town of Whitehorse, she spotted the local newspaper office. The idea had been brewing all the way into town, but as she pushed open the door to the *Milk River Courier,* she was aware that what she was about to do could be the signing of her death warrant.

"Can I help you?" The young woman who rose from behind the desk had a southern accent and a nice smile.

"Are you a reporter?" Blythe asked.

"Andi Jackson, at your service," she said, motioning to the chair across from her desk.

Blythe saw that the small newspaper office was deserted as she took a seat. "You're a weekly paper? Is it possible to get a story in this week's paper?"

"It would be pushing my deadline, but if it's a story that has to run, I can probably get it in tomorrow's paper," Andi said.

"It is. My name is Jennifer Blythe James, better known as JJ, and until recently everyone thought I was dead."

Andi picked up her notebook and pen and began to write as Blythe told her JJ's story, starting with the small trailer in the middle of the desert, then a band called Tough as Nails and ending with her waitressing at the local café in town.

"This is one heck of a story," Andi said when Blythe had finished. "I'm curious how it's going to end."

Blythe laughed. "So am I." After Andi took her photo, she bought a paper so that she could look for an apartment after work, then she headed for the White-horse Café. The last thing she wanted was to be late for work her first day.

"You aren't going to have to babysit me much longer," Emma said when Logan came through the back door into the kitchen. "Your father has hired someone to keep an eye on me so you can all get back to ranching. The woman is supposed to be here by the weekend."

She glanced at him as he dropped into a chair at the table. "Logan?"

He blinked and looked over at her as if seeing her for the first time that morning. "Sorry, I was lost in thought."

"I can see that." She'd never seen him this distracted and would bet it had something to do with the young woman he'd brought to supper last night.

Having just taken a batch of cranberry muffins from the oven, she put one on a plate for each of them and poured them both a mug of coffee before joining him at the table.

"Okay, let's hear it," she said as she sliced one muffin in half and lathered it with butter.

"It's Blythe," he said with a curse.

She laughed. "Big surprise." Emma took a bite of the muffin. It was warm and wonderful, the rich butter dripping off onto the plate as she took another bite. She really had to quit baking—worse, eating what she baked. "So you've fallen for her."

"No, that is…" He started to swear again but checked himself. "I've never met anyone like her."

"So what's the problem?"

"Someone is trying to kill her."

Emma leaned back in surprise. "It must be something in the water around here," she said, and then turned serious. "Why would anyone want to hurt that beautiful young woman?"

"It's a long story," Logan said with a sigh.

Emma listened, seeing how much this woman had come to mean to him. Chisholm men were born protectors. What they didn't realize sometimes was that they were also attracted to strong women who liked to believe they could protect themselves. Hoyt was still learning that.

"It doesn't sound like there is much you can do if she's set on doing things her way," Emma said. "But you certainly don't have to hang around here babysitting me today. I'll be just fine."

Logan shook his head, grinning across the table at her. "Blythe reminds me a lot of you."

"That's a good thing, right?" she asked with a laugh.

"Stubborn and a woman hard to get a rope on," he joked.

"You Chisholm men. When are you going to learn that you have to let a woman run free if you ever hope to hold on to her?"

"It's a hard lesson," Logan said. "I'm not sure I can do that."

"But then again, you've never been in love before. Love changes everything. Have you told her how you feel?"

"About her determination to stick her neck out and get herself killed?"

"No, Logan, how you feel about *her.*"

"It's too soon."

"Or is it because you're afraid you'll scare her off?" she asked, eyeing him.

He chuckled. "You see through me like a window-pane. You have any more of those muffins? Also, I need to borrow your computer. I have to find out everything I can about who's after Blythe. So far, they don't know where she is. But once they find out…"

After her interview with the newspaper, Blythe hurried to the café to get to work. Within minutes after putting on her apron, she was waiting tables and joking with locals as she refilled coffee cups and slid huge platefuls of food in front of them.

It *was* like riding a bike, she thought.

As she worked, she tried not to glance out the front window at the street or the small city park across from the café. The newspaper article wouldn't come out until tomorrow. Reporter Andi Jackson had told her the Associated Press would pick up the story and it would quickly make every newspaper in the state.

"You realize your story is going to go viral after that," Andi had said. "With communications like they are, everyone in the world will know that JJ is waitressing in Whitehorse, Montana."

That was the plan, Blythe thought.

Still, she couldn't help but feel a little nervous about the repercussions that were to come when Logan found out—not to mention the fact that the story was bound to bring a killer to town.

Right before quitting time, she saw Logan pull up out front. Just the sight of him as he stepped from one of the Chisholm ranch pickups made her heart take off at a gallop. She ached for a future with him. They were just getting to know each other. If she let herself, she could imagine the two of them growing old together in that farmhouse of his, raising kids who Logan would teach to ride horses before they learned to walk, just as he had done.

She could see them all around that long table at the home ranch. She'd never had siblings, let alone lived close to any cousins. She'd always wished for a large family like Logan's and guessed it wouldn't be long before Hoyt and Emma had more grandchildren running around than they could count.

"Hi," she said as she stepped outside, so glad to see him it hurt.

Logan looked into her eyes and she saw the pain in all that blue as he dragged her to him and kissed her. As he drew back, he said, "How was your first day of work?" She could tell it was hard for him to even ask.

"My feet are killing me," she said with a laugh. "How was your day?"

He gave her a look that said he couldn't take any more chitchat. "We need to talk."

Blythe nodded and they walked across the street to the park and took a bench.

"You know how much I want to protect you," he began. "But I can't if you're working here in town."

"I see what your stepmother has been going through waiting for a possible murderer to come after her," she said. "Look what it is doing to your family. I don't want that. If someone wants to kill me badly enough, they will find a way no matter what."

"No, I won't—"

"Worse, if I was with you at the time, then they might kill you, as well." She shook her head. "That isn't happening. That's why I'm getting an apartment here in town, that's why I can't see you—"

"No," he said shooting to his feet and pulling her up with him. He grabbed her shoulders and looked into her eyes. "This is hard enough. If I can't see you... No."

"It's only temporary," she said touched. "I'm sorry. You had no idea what you were getting into when you met me."

"Oh, I had some idea." He let go of her but she could see this was killing him. "What now?"

"Now I find an apartment." She hesitated, knowing what Logan's reaction was going to be when she told him about the newspaper article coming out in tomorrow's paper. "Then when the article comes out tomorrow about JJ being alive and well and waitressing in Whitehorse—"

Logan swore, ripped his Stetson from his head and raked one large hand through his thick blond hair. "You know what bothers me?" He bit off each word, anger cording his neck. "You are filled with so much guilt over leaving behind your former band members that you think you *deserve* this."

She shook her head. "You're wrong. I do regret what I did, but I'm not ready to die. I want to live, really live, for the first time in a long time," she said with passion. "You know why that is? Because of you. I can't wait for the next time I get to make love with you. That's why I'm doing this. I want it over and I don't want you in the cross fire."

He dragged her to him and dropped his mouth to hers for a punishing kiss. "You aren't going to have to wait long for the next time we make love," he said when he pulled back. "Let's find you an apartment. That article doesn't come out until tomorrow, right?"

Sheriff Buford Olson hadn't wanted to like JJ any more than he had Jett Atkins. But the young woman he'd met on her way to her waitress job had impressed him. He couldn't help but like her—and fear for her.

He'd seen the look in her eye. She was planning to use herself as bait. Not that he could blame her for wanting to flush out the killer. He wanted that as badly as she did.

"You'll keep an eye on her," he'd said to Sheriff McCall Crawford.

McCall had nodded. "You think it's one of her former band members?"

"Likely, given what we know. They had motive and opportunity. I'll see what I can find out as far as means and get back to you. The music business sounds more dangerous than law enforcement."

"The nice thing about Whitehorse is that the town is small enough that anyone new stands out like a sore thumb. I'll be waiting to hear from you."

Buford had a lot of time to think on his way back to Flathead. The moment he reached his office, he had a call waiting for him from Jett Akins.

"Is it true?" Jett asked. "Is JJ alive and living in Whitehorse?"

The sheriff shook his head at how fast news traveled. "Where did you get that information?"

"It's all over the internet."

Of course it was. "Under the circumstances, I'm not at liberty to say."

"The circumstances? You don't think I want her dead, do you?"

"It has crossed my mind," Buford said.

"It's these women JJ should be worried about. I just went down to the room where they were staying," Jett said. "They've cleared out."

"Only the Sanderson case is closed, but I can't keep all of you in town any longer."

"That's it?" Jett demanded. "If you knew these women the way I do—"

"I heard that you dated all of them at one time or another. I guess I'm just surprised you aren't the one they want dead," Buford said.

"I'll be leaving town now, *Sheriff*." Jett slammed down the phone in his ear.

Buford hoped that was true. With the news out on the internet, Blythe was already bait—but she might not realize it.

He put in a call to the cell phone number she'd given him. It went straight to voice mail. When he called Logan Chisholm's cell, he answered on the first ring.

The moment Emma saw the sheriff drive up, she knew it was bad news. She stood in the doorway, holding the screen open, afraid to step out on the porch.

Sheriff McCall Crawford climbed out of her patrol SUV. She stopped when she saw Emma watching her, slowing as if dreading what she'd come to tell her.

"Emma," the sheriff said as she mounted the stairs. Not Mrs. Chisholm at least.

"I just made iced tea," Emma said and turned back into the house for the kitchen. She heard McCall behind her. "As I recall, you like my gingersnaps," she said over her shoulder. She wanted to avoid whatever bad news the sheriff had brought as long as possible, since she had a feeling she already knew.

She set about putting a plate of cookies on the table and pouring the tea as the sheriff took a seat at the kitchen table.

"It's about Aggie, isn't it?" Emma said as she put the tea and cookies on the table and dropped into a chair across from McCall. Zane, she noticed, was out by the barn. He was her babysitter today. She told herself the news might turn out to have a silver lining. Maybe it would put an end to this house-arrest life she'd been living.

"We found Aggie," the sheriff said.

"She's dead."

Another nod. "I'm sorry."

"Did you find her in the river?" Emma asked around the lump in her throat. Aggie. She thought of the vibrant, interesting woman, obsessed, yes, but so alive, so filled with a sense of purpose.

"No, not in the river. In Billings." The words fell like stones in the quiet room.

Emma crossed herself, mumbling the Spanish she'd grown up with, the religion Maria and Alonzo had given her.

Neither of them had touched their tea or the cookies.

"I don't understand." That was all she could think to say because she feared she *did* understand.

"She'd apparently fallen ill after going in the river."

Emma raised her gaze from the table to stare at the sheriff with an accusing look she could no longer control. "Don't you mean, after being shot by one of your deputies?"

"She was a wanted criminal who was getting away, though I'm sure the bullet wound added to her deteriorated condition," McCall said without looking away. "She was living in an old motel on the south side of Billings."

Hiding, trying to get well, Emma thought. Her stomach roiled with both grief and anger. "Is that what killed her?"

Now the sheriff looked away. "She was murdered."

"Murdered? Then you know who killed her?"

As McCall finally looked at her again, there was regret in her dark eyes. "After Aggie gave you the photos of the woman she believed was Laura Chisholm, I called in the FBI. They are tracking the woman."

"Without any luck," Emma said.

"We don't know who killed Aggie. She lived in a place where some of the residents had records for violent behavior. One of them could have killed her for a few dollars in her purse. Another woman was also killed in the same building. I wish I had better news."

She scoffed. "How could the news be any worse?"

McCall shook her head as she rose to her feet. "I'm sorry."

Emma looked at the young woman. She wanted to blame her for Aggie's death, blame someone. But if anyone was to blame, it was herself. If she'd gone to McCall and told her she was meeting Aggie…

Water under the bridge now. She studied the sheriff. "When is your baby due?"

McCall's expression softened. "November."

Emma smiled. "Do you know—"

"We want to be surprised." Her smile was strained,

guarded and Emma remembered thinking McCall was pregnant once before, months ago.

"Miscarriage?" Emma said. "I'm sorry. I will keep you and your baby in my prayers."

"Thank you," McCall said, her voice thick with emotion. "I'm sorry about Aggie."

Emma nodded. She couldn't blame the sheriff anymore than she could blame Hoyt. He had called the sheriff when he suspected his wife was up to something involving Aggie that day. Emma would never forgive herself. Aggie had been trying to save her, was no doubt still trying when she was killed. The woman would never give up—that was her downfall as well as her appeal.

Apparently the person who killed her was the same way.

Emma listened to the sheriff leave, then laid her head on her arms on the kitchen table and let the hot tears come. A woman who'd tried to save her was dead and now her murderer was coming for Emma.

If Laura Chisholm had gotten to Aggie, then Emma knew there was little hope for her. Aggie wouldn't have been easily fooled. Laura would find a way to get to her and Emma doubted she would see her coming.

The news got out faster than Blythe had anticipated. Logan had told her it was all over the internet after Sheriff Buford Olson had called to warn him.

"Don't go to work today," Logan had pleaded with her. "Come out to my place. We'll take a long horseback ride up into the mountains."

"Don't tempt me," she'd said.

"Blythe—"

"I have to go back. I'm working a split shift. Maybe I'll see you after work." There was nothing she would have liked better than staying in bed with him. Her heart ached at the thought of giving up a horseback ride with him. Yesterday they'd found her a furnished apartment and made love late into the night.

But Blythe knew the only way she could be free to be with Logan was to end this, one way or another.

Now, at work at the café, there'd been a steady stream of diners since the newspaper article had come out that morning. Most just wanted coffee and pie and to check out this pop rock star who was now waitressing in their town.

Things had finally slowed down when Blythe saw a car pull up out front of the cafe. The car caught her attention because there were so few in this Western town. Pretty much everyone drove trucks.

She'd just served a tableful of ranchers who'd joked with her and still had her smiling, when she saw the woman climb out of the car. A cold chill ran through her. Karen "Caro" Chandler.

Her former best friend from childhood was tall and slim. She wore a cap-sleeved top in a light green with a flowered print skirt and sandals. As she removed a pair of large dark sunglasses, Blythe saw that she was even more beautiful than she'd been when they were girls.

"I'm going to take my break now, if that's all right," she called over her shoulder to the other waitress. Removing her apron, she tossed it on a vacant booth seat and stepped outside.

Karen looked up as Blythe came out the door, her expression softening into a smile. "It's been a long time."

"Too long," Blythe said, and motioned to the park bench across the main street. The sun felt warm and reassuring as they crossed the street. Only a few clouds bobbed along in a clear, blue sky. The air smelling of spring and new things seemed at odds with the conversation Blythe knew they were about to have. The past lay heavy and dark between them.

"So how is waitressing again?" Karen asked. "Remember that greasy spoon where you and I worked in high school? You broke more dishes and glasses than I did. But Huck always forgave you."

"Huck," she said smiling at the memory. "I wonder whatever happened to him?"

"He died a few years ago after rolling his car on the edge of town." Karen nodded at her surprise. "I went back to the desert to take care of Dad. He had cancer."

"I'm sorry." She studied her friend, surprised not that Karen had gone back to take care of her father but that she was stronger than Blythe had ever imagined. When they were girls, Blythe had been the one who made all the decisions about what the two of them did and Karen had let her. She watched Karen brush back a lock of hair and look up toward the warm blue of the sky.

"I know why you're here," Blythe said.

"Do you?" Her former friend looked over at her, their gazes locking.

"I'm sorry. I should never have left the band, left you behind."

Karen laughed. "Is that why you think I'm here?" She shook her head, smiling. "Tough as Nails breaking up was the best thing that ever happened to me. I went to college, met a wonderful man. We live together back east. We have a good life. I'm happy, Blythe. I didn't come here to tell you that you ruined my life. Quite the opposite. After you left, I realized I could do anything I set my mind to, I didn't need you to tell me what to do anymore."

"I'm still sorry. I wish I had kept in touch," she said, hearing bitterness in Karen's voice no matter how much she denied it. "If not to tell me how much you hate me, then why are you here?"

"Luca came to see me before she died," Karen said. "She told me something that I thought you should know. She wrote some songs when she was dating Jett. When they broke up, he took the songs."

That didn't surprise Blythe. "He must not have recorded them or—"

"He did. Right after the two of you signed with Martin. Luca went to Martin. They settled out of court. A couple of the songs were his biggest hits."

"I had no idea," Blythe said, shaking her head.

"Luca felt that she'd been swindled by Martin and Jett. She was going to go public if they didn't pony up more money. The next thing I heard, she'd stepped in front of a bus."

Blythe felt her blood run cold. "You think it wasn't an accident? That someone pushed her?"

Karen nodded. "You were with Jett during the time when he recorded the songs. Do you remember seeing Luca's small blue notebook?"

The chill that ran through her made her shudder. She hugged herself against it, the warm spring sun doing nothing to relieve the icy cold that had settled in her.

"I was afraid that might be the case," Karen said. "Luca had found out that Jett planned to release another of her songs. That is why she was so upset with Martin and Jett. Jett had told her he no longer had the notebook."

He'd lied. No big surprise there. "You think either he or Martin killed her to shut her up."

"If I'm right, then you might be the only one who saw him with that notebook of Luca's songs," Karen said. "Luca's song that he recorded is set to come out next month."

Could this explain the accidents on her road tour? Jett was always around since he'd been closing for her. And he was in Montana. But if anyone had rigged the brakes on the sports car she'd rented, it must have been Martin. Unless Jett had come to town earlier and Martin had let him into the Grizzly Club without anyone knowing it.

She would bet there was a back way out of the club, one only the residents used.

Blythe felt sick. "Thank you for telling me."

Karen shrugged. "You were once like my sister. Whatever happened after that…" She stood. "Good luck, JJ." Her tone said she thought Blythe would need it.

Karen was studying her. "You seem…different."

"I'm not JJ anymore. As far as I'm concerned, she's dead. I'm Blythe again." She'd started going by Blythe in high school because it had sounded more mature, more like the musical star she planned to be. "JJ" had been Martin's idea.

"You do know that there never was going to be a reunion tour of Tough as Nails," Blythe said.

Karen looked amused. "I knew that. I think Betsy

and Loretta did, too. Got to wonder why they came all the way to Montana, don't you."

Blythe could see that Karen was trying to warn her. Jett might not be the only who wanted her dead.

"You going to keep waitressing when this is all over?" Karen asked, sounding skeptical.

"I might. It's honest work and I think I need that right now." She didn't say it, but the next time she picked up a guitar, she hoped it would be to sing a lullaby to one of her children. With Logan Chisholm.

"If you're ever in Whitehorse again…" She realized that Karen didn't seem to be listening. She was staring across the street.

Blythe followed her gaze and saw Logan leaning against his pickup watching the two of them.

"A friend of yours?" Karen asked, turning her gaze back to Blythe. She broke into a grin. "You finally found that cowboy you always said you were going to run away with."

Blythe knew they would never be close again, not like they'd been as kids, but she hoped they stayed in touch. Maybe time would heal the friendship. She sure hoped so. Impulsively, she hugged her former friend.

Karen seemed surprised at first, then hugged her tightly. "Be careful. I hope I get to hear about this cowboy someday."

Blythe glanced at Logan. She'd asked him to stay clear of her. "He's one stubborn cowboy," she said as they started back across the street toward Karen's car.

The truck came out from behind the space between two main drag buildings where there'd been a fire a year ago. Sun glinted off the windshield, the roar of the engine filling the spring air as the driver headed right for the two of them.

Chapter 12

Buford called the airport only to find that none of the four, Jett, Karen, Loretta or Betsy had taken a flight out of town. He was in the process of calling rental-car agencies when Betsy walked into his office.

"There is something I think you should know," she said. She was nervously twisting the end of a bright-colored scarf that hung loosely around her neck.

He motioned her into a chair across from his desk. "What do I need to know?"

"It probably doesn't mean anything, isn't even important," she said haltingly.

"But you're going to tell me so I can be the judge of that, right?"

She nodded solemnly. "Ten years ago I overheard a conversation. I didn't mean to. Everyone thought I'd already left. I was always slower than the rest of them at getting out after a performance."

Buford tried to curb his impatience. "What did you hear?"

"Martin Sanderson. He was making one of the band members an offer," she said.

"JJ." He quickly corrected himself. "I'm sorry, I guess she was Blythe then."

Betsy shook her head. "It was Karen. She was apparently Martin's first choice. I heard him tell her that she had more talent than Blythe and that he could make her a star."

"Karen didn't take the offer," Buford said afraid he saw how this had gone down.

"She said she couldn't do that to her friend. Martin laughed and said, 'Well, she won't feel the same way when I make her the same offer.' Karen said he was wrong. That he didn't know Blythe the way she did."

"I would imagine Karen was upset when she heard that her friend had taken the deal and not looked back," Buford said.

Betsy shook her head. "That's just it. Karen didn't react at all. We all knew she had to be devastated, but she is so good at hiding her true feelings. If anyone hates JJ, it has to be her. She was betrayed worse than any of the rest of us. So you can see why there was no way the band could survive after all that. It was clear that Karen's heart definitely wasn't into it."

Betsy had quit worrying at the end of her scarf. She got to her feet and seemed to hesitate. "Jett said JJ's car had been tampered with and that's what killed that girl who took it."

"Your point?" he asked even though he had a good idea where this was headed.

"Karen's father was a mechanic. She loved to work with him on weekends. She knew all about cars and didn't mind getting her hands dirty. One time, when they were dating, she even fixed Jett's car for him."

Logan had been watching Blythe and another woman he'd never seen before visiting across the street. Was the woman one of the former members of her old band? They had seemed deep in conversation, making him anxious.

When they'd finally stood, hugging before heading across the street, he'd relaxed a little. Whoever the woman was, she apparently didn't mean Blythe any harm.

Then he'd heard the roar of the pickup engine, saw it coming out of the corner of his eye and acted instinctively. Later he would recall rushing out into the street to throw both women out of the way of the speeding truck. Now as he knelt on the ground next to Blythe, his heart pounding, all he could do was pray.

"Blythe! Blythe!" When she opened her eyes and blinked at the bright sunshine, then closed them again, the wave of relief he felt made him weak.

"Blythe," he said, part oath, part thanks for his answered prayer.

"Logan," she said, opened her eyes and smiled up at him.

"Is she all right?" he heard a voice ask behind him.

"She'd better be." There'd been a few moments when she hadn't responded. They'd felt like hours. He'd never been so scared.

She looked around at the small crowd that had gathered. He saw her confusion.

"Do you remember what happened?" he asked.

"Karen?" she said and tried to sit up.

"I'm right here," the woman who'd been with Blythe answered. "I'm fine." She didn't sound fine though. She sounded scared. Her skirt was torn, her top soiled, and like Blythe she'd scraped her elbow and arm when Logan had thrown himself at them, knocking all three of them out of the way of the pickup.

Logan could still hear the roar of the engine, the sound of the tires on the pavement, and see the truck bearing down on the two women crossing the empty street.

"Okay, everybody stand back, please." Sheriff McCall Crawford worked her way through the small crowd as Logan was helping Blythe to her feet. "Someone tell me what happened here."

A shopkeeper told the sheriff what he'd seen. "It appeared the pickup purposely tried to run the two women down."

Blythe leaned into Logan, clearly still shaken. He put his arm around her and tried not to be angry with her, but it was hard not to be. She was determined to risk her life—and push him away. He wasn't having it after this. Whatever he had to do to keep her safe, he was doing it.

"Did anyone see the driver?" McCall asked.

Blythe looked to Karen who shook her head. "The sun was reflecting off the windshield."

"So you couldn't tell if it was a man or a woman?" the sheriff asked.

"No."

"What about you?" McCall asked Logan.

"I heard it coming but I was just trying to get to Blythe before the pickup hit her."

"None of you saw the pickup's license plate, either?" the sheriff asked.

More head shakes.

"It was covered with mud," Logan said. "The pickup was an older model Ford, brown, that's all I can tell you."

She nodded. "I'd suggest you see a doctor," she said to Blythe, who instantly started to argue.

"I agree," Logan spoke up. "She definitely needs her head examined. I'm taking her over to the emergency room now."

"Very funny, Logan," she said under her breath.

"Okay, if you remember anything…" McCall turned to Karen. "I'd like to speak with you if you don't mind."

"We'll be at the emergency room, if you need us," Logan said. "I'll see that Blythe is safe from now on whether she likes it or not."

He'd expected Blythe to argue and was surprised when she didn't. Had it finally sunk in that she was in serious danger?

Blythe glanced around. "Where is Karen?" she asked.

"She left with the sheriff," Logan said.

"I was hoping to at least say goodbye," Blythe said.

"Sorry, but I think she wants to put as much distance between the two of you as she can. Apparently she's having trouble with the idea of someone almost killing her—unlike you."

It wasn't until they reached the hospital that Blythe finally felt her scraped elbow and the ache in her hip where she'd hit the pavement. Logan had refused to leave her side, standing in the corner of the emergency room watching the doctor check her over.

The incident had scared him badly. She could see that he was still worried about her. There was a stubborn set to his jaw that told her he'd meant what he'd said about not leaving her side. The thought warmed her and frightened her. Whoever had tried to run her down today would be back. She was determined that Logan Chisholm not be in the line of fire when that happened.

"No concussion," the doctor said. "I'll have the nurse put something on the scrapes and you are good to go."

As the doctor left, Logan stepped over to her bed. She looked into his handsome face and saw both anger and relief. He'd hurled himself at her and Karen, throwing them out of the way, risking his own life to save hers. Could she love this man any more?

"You saved my life," she said.

He chuckled. "Doesn't that mean you owe me some debt for eternity?"

She knew what was coming. "I hate that you risked your life today because of me. I can't let you keep doing that." He could have been killed today. Karen, too.

"How do you plan to stop me?" he asked, leaning toward her.

She felt her breath catch, her heart a rising thunder in her chest as he leaned down, his lips hovering just a heartbeat away from her own before he kissed her. Her pulse leaped beneath her skin. But when she reached to cup the back of his neck and keep his mouth on hers, he pulled back.

"You are coming home with me or I'm moving into your apartment," he said. "Which is it going to be?"

She could see that there was no changing his mind. "I've missed the ranch and the horses. I've missed you, too." All true. "But Logan—"

"Then it's my place," Logan said, cutting her off.

After the sheriff's visit about Aggie's murder, Hoyt had insisted on staying at Emma's side until the new housekeeper arrived. He took several weapons from his safe and dragged her out to the barn for more target practice.

"I want you to be able to shoot without hesitation," he told her, thrusting a pistol into her hand.

"I can shoot and you already gave me a gun," she said. "That's not what you want me to be able to do."

"No," he agreed meeting her gaze. "I want you to be able to kill if you have to and without a second thought."

Anyone could be taught to shoot a weapon. Killing, well, that was something else.

"What about you?" Emma asked after shooting several pistols and proving that she could hit anything she aimed at.

"I'm not worried about me," he said.

"I am." She looked into his handsome face, saw how much this had aged him. They'd been so happy when they'd first married—before Aggie Wells had come back into his life first with accusations of murder and then with her crazy story about Hoyt's first wife being alive and a killer.

"Can you kill her?" Emma asked him.

His gaze locked with hers. She saw that he wanted to

argue that his first wife was already dead. But maybe even he wasn't so sure now.

"I would do anything to keep you from being hurt. *Anything.*" He pulled her into his arms and held her so tight she couldn't breathe.

He believed he could kill his first wife, his first love, a woman who had broken his heart in so many ways.

But Emma prayed he would never have to look into Laura's eyes and pull the trigger. If anyone had to do it, Emma hoped it wasn't him.

She took the pistol he handed her and aimed at the target on the hay bale and fired. Bull's-eye. But could she put a bullet through another woman's heart?

"So did you see her?"

Buford smiled as his fourteen-year-old granddaughter Amy met him at his front door. "I saw her."

Since the call from the Whitehorse sheriff about an attempt on JJ's life, he'd been distracted with the case. He'd forgotten that this granddaughter knew he'd been to Whitehorse to see her music idol.

"Is she more beautiful in person than even on television?"

"I couldn't say. She's quite attractive." He could tell his granddaughter had hoped for more. "She seems very nice."

Amy rolled her eyes. *"Nice?"*

He didn't know what else to say. "I *liked* her."

That too met with an eye roll. "You like everyone."

If only that were true.

"Can't you even tell me what she looked like? Pretend it's a description of one of your criminals," his granddaughter persisted.

He thought for a moment. "She's tall and slim and has really amazing eyes. The color of…"

"Worn blue jeans?"

He nodded smiling. "She was wearing jeans, a Western shirt, blue I think, and red cowboy boots. Her hair is dark and long and looks natural. And she just learned how to ride a horse."

Amy seemed pleased to hear that. "Did she say anything about when she would be singing again?"

"No. I think it could be a while." If ever. "She's taking a break. Waitressing at a café in Whitehorse."

"That is so cool," Amy exclaimed excitedly. "Can you imagine walking into a café in the middle of Montana and *JJ* was the one who took your order?"

He couldn't. "Are you still listening to Jett Atkins's music?" He was afraid if he told her how much he disliked Jett, it would only make her like the man's music simply out of rebellion.

"I don't like him as well as JJ."

Buford was glad to hear that.

"He really needs a new hit."

"What about that one you played for me?" He'd heard it several times on the alternative radio station since this whole thing started with JJ. He'd been listening to the station realizing it was high time he knew what his granddaughter listened to. "What was the name of that song again?"

"Poor Little Paper Doll." She said it as if she couldn't believe he had forgotten. "That song is really *old*," she said. "It came out in 2002!" The way she said it, 2002 was centuries ago. He supposed it seemed that way to a fourteen-year-old.

"Hasn't he had other hits?" He realized how little he

knew about the music business, just as he'd been told numerous times lately.

"Not really. Especially lately. His songs haven't been very good. I read online that his sales are lagging and his last concert didn't even sell out," she said.

Interesting, he thought. Jett hadn't had a hit for a while and his career was faltering. He said he didn't know why Martin Sanderson had invited him to Montana, but of course he could have been lying about that.

What if Martin was putting some kind of pressure on *him?*

But what could that have to do with JJ?

Buford shook his head. He was too tired to think about it anymore tonight.

"It's funny, the songs that did well for Jett were nothing like the ones he's been singing lately," Amy said thoughtfully as they went to find her grandmother and see what was for supper. "Maybe he's writing his own songs." Apparently seeing that her grandfather had lost interest, she added, "Maybe his songwriter died. Or was *murdered.*" She'd always known how to get Buford's attention.

"What's wrong?" Blythe asked, sitting up in bed to find Logan at the dark window looking out.

"One of the horses got out," he said. "I must not have closed the gate again. Nothing to worry about."

She watched him as he reached for his jeans, pulled them on, then leaned over the bed to give her a kiss.

"I'll be right back."

Blythe lay back down, content and snug under the soft, worn quilt. A cool breeze blew in one of the windows bringing the sweet new smells of the spring night.

She smiled to herself, listening as she heard Logan go down the stairs and out the front door.

Rolling to her side, she placed a hand on his side of the bed. The sheets were still warm from where his naked body had been only minutes before. She breathed in his male scent and pulled his pillow under her head, unable to wipe the smile from her face.

This was a first for her, falling in love like this. She'd thought it would never happen. The men she'd met were more interested in JJ and being seen with her. She'd never met a man like Logan who loved Blythe, the girl she used to be.

A horse whinnied somewhere in the distance. She closed her eyes, wonderfully tired after their lovemaking, and let herself drift.

Logan would be back soon. She couldn't wait to feel his body next to her again, have him put his arms around her and hold her close as if he never wanted to let her go.

She just hoped he was right about them being safer together. She couldn't bear it if something happened to Logan because of her. Just as she couldn't bear being out of his arms.

Logan walked across the starlit yard. No moon tonight, but zillions of stars glittered in a canopy of black velvet. Dew sparkled in the grass, the starlight bathing the pasture in silver.

He had pulled on his jeans and boots, but hadn't bothered with a shirt. The air chilled his skin and he couldn't wait to get back to Blythe. He smiled to himself as he thought of her, but then sobered as he remembered that she was a star.

Maybe she thought she didn't want to go back to it now, but she would. She would miss being up on stage, singing for thousands of screaming fans. Living out here in the middle of Montana certainly paled next to that. Right now, all of this was something new and different—just like him.

She was living her childhood dream of riding off into the sunset on the back of a horse with a cowboy. But that dream would end as the realization of a cowboy's life sunk in. He didn't kid himself that even the fact that he'd fallen in love with her wouldn't change that.

The thought startled him—just as the horse did as it came out of the eerie pale darkness. It was the big bay, and as it thundered past him, he saw that its eyes were wide with fear.

The horse shied away. Something in the darkness had startled the big bay. He'd never seen a rattlesnake near the corral at night, but he supposed it was possible.

Watching where he was walking, he moved closer to the open gate. The barn cast a long dark shadow over most of the corral and the horses inside it.

He heard restless movement. Something definitely had the horses spooked. As he neared the gate, he looked around for the shovel he'd left leaning against the post earlier. If there was a rattler in the corral tonight, the shovel would come in handy. But as he neared the corral, Logan saw with a frown that the shovel wasn't where he'd left it.

Something moved off to his left in the shadowed darkness of the barn and for a moment he thought it was another one of the horses loose.

The blow took him by surprise. He heard a clang rattle through his head, realization a split-second behind the shovel blade striking his skull.

The force of it knocked him forward. He stumbled, his legs crumbling under him as he fell face-first into the dirt.

Buford couldn't sleep. It was this damned case. Slipping out of bed, careful not to wake his wife, he went to his computer. Something his granddaughter had said kept nagging at him.

First he checked to see when Jett's hit song, "Poor Little Paper Doll," came out. Six months after Tough as Nails broke up. Six months after Jett and JJ were "discovered" by Martin Sanderson.

Did that mean something?

He looked at the time line he'd made of the lives of the former members of the band. The only musician whose life changed at that time was Lisa "Luca" Thomas. She'd apparently come into money.

He checked his watch. It was late, but not that late, he told himself. He was afraid this couldn't wait. He called his friend who worked in the U.S. Treasury Department and explained that it was a matter of life and death and there wasn't time to go through "proper" channels.

"Lisa 'Luca' Thomas was employed as a songwriter. Ten years ago? She had a very good year with her songwriting."

"Who paid her the most?"

"Martin Sanderson."

He hung up and called the deputy he'd had working on the backgrounds of his suspects—the former members of the Tough as Nails band as well as Jett Akins. So far, the deputy hadn't come up with anything of real interest, but Buford had told him to keep digging until he did.

"I just put what I found on your desk at the office," the deputy said. "It's a birth certificate."

"Give it to me in a nutshell," Buford snapped.

"Betsy Harper Lee had a baby seven months after the band broke up," the deputy said.

"And I care about this why?"

"At the time the band broke up, according to Jett, who I called to confirm this, he and Betsy were hooking up. She hadn't even met her soon-to-be husband. Jett was the father of the baby Betsy was carrying. I suspected that might be the case when I saw the baby's middle name: Ray, Jett's real name."

"Did Jett know she was pregnant?" Buford asked.

"He did. He came up with all kinds of reasons he couldn't 'do the right thing' ten years ago, but the bottom line was that he left her high and dry because of his career—and he was with JJ by then."

Who would Betsy blame for the father of her baby leaving her? Not Jett—but the woman she believed had stolen him from her: JJ.

Now too wound-up to quit, Buford hung up and called the dispatcher to see if any of the rental agencies had gotten back to him.

"There is a message on your desk. Four different rental agencies called. All four of the names you gave them rented vehicles," the dispatcher said.

"Does it say what kind of cars they rented?" he asked. It did.

Only one had rented a pickup.

* * *

Blythe woke with a start. She hadn't intended to
fall asleep, wanting to wait until Logan returned. The
bed felt cold, the air coming in the window sending
a chill over her bare flesh. She started to pull up the
quilt to cover her shoulders and arms when she heard
what had awakened her.

The phone was ringing downstairs.

She glanced at the clock on the nightstand next to
the bed.

11:10 p.m.?

She blinked in confusion. Logan had gone to check
the horses a little after ten. He hadn't returned from
putting the horse back in the corral?

The phone rang again.

Something was wrong. Hurriedly she sat up and
swung her legs over the side of the bed to reach for Logan's robe. As she hurried out of the room and started
down the stairs, the phone rang again.

"Logan?" She thought he might have come back in
and decided to sleep on the couch for some reason. But
he would have heard the phone, wouldn't he?

The whole house felt empty and cold. Starlight shone
in through the windows, casting the living room in a
pale otherworldly light as she came down the stairs.

As the phone rang again, it took her a moment to
find it. She hadn't even realized that Logan had a landline. Another ring. She realized the sound was coming from the kitchen. From the moonlight spilling in
the window, she saw the phone on the kitchen wall, an
old-fashioned wall mount.

She snatched up the phone. "Hello?"

"JJ?" The voice was gruff and familiar and yet it

took her a moment to place it. She hadn't been sure who might be calling this time of the night—and somehow she'd expected it would be Logan, though that made little sense. He'd only gone out to put the horses back in. Unless there was a phone out in the barn.

"I'm sorry to wake you. Is Logan there?" Sheriff Buford asked. There was an urgency to his tone that sent her heart pounding harder.

"No, I…he went out to check the horses and he hasn't come back. I thought it might be him calling from the barn—"

"Listen to me," the sheriff snapped. "You have to get out of—"

Blythe heard the creak of the old kitchen floor behind her. As she turned, a hand snatched the phone from her and hung it up. She stumbled back as the kitchen light was snapped on, blinding her for an instant, as the last person she'd expected to see stepped from the shadows.

"What are you…" The rest of her words trailed off as she saw the gun.

Chapter 13

"Thought I'd left? Or thought I'd forgiven you?" Karen asked as she leveled the gun at her.

Blythe remembered that bitter edge she'd heard in Karen's voice. She hadn't forgotten or forgiven. "But that truck. It almost hit us both."

Her old friend smiled. "Nice touch, huh. I thought you would appreciate the drama. I certainly lived through enough of yours when we were kids. Remember all the nights you used to crawl in my bedroom window to get away from one of your mother's drunk boyfriends?"

Until one night one of Blythe's mother's boyfriends followed her and threatened to go after Karen if she ever went to her house in the middle of the night again. That's when Blythe had started going to her own bed at night with a knife under the pillow.

"You had to know how much I appreciated that. I don't know what I would have done without you." She thought she heard a sound outside. Logan could be coming in that door at any moment.

"Until you got the chance to make something of yourself and left me behind," Karen snapped.

"I didn't want to. I told Martin I wouldn't go without you."

Karen seemed surprised by that. "What did he say?"

"He told me that he'd already offered you a music contract, but that you'd turned it down. Are you telling me he lied about that?"

"It's true I turned down his offer."

"Karen, why would you do that? Martin told me that you were his first choice because you were the one with all the talent."

Tears welled in her eyes. "Because of you. I couldn't leave you and the band."

Blythe studied her in the harsh glow of the overhead kitchen light. She could see the clock out of the corner of her eye. Logan should be coming back at any moment.

"He won't be coming," Karen said with a smile.

"What did you do to him?" Blythe cried, and took a step toward her.

Karen waved her back with the gun. "Don't worry. I didn't kill him. He's tied up out in the barn. I didn't want him interrupting our reunion. You did plan on the old band doing that reunion tour, didn't you, *JJ?*"

"That was Martin's doing. Not mine. He knew how much you all resented me. I'm sure the twisted bastard was hoping one of you would want to kill me."

"Or maybe he knew all along it would be me," Karen

said. She hadn't let the gun in her hand waver for an instant. There was a determination in her eyes that Blythe remembered from when they were kids.

"I'm going to be someone someday," Karen used to say. "Those people who look down their noses at me now will regret it one day. I want fame and fortune. I want people to recognize me when I walk down the street and say, 'Isn't that her? You know that famous singer.'"

Blythe's dream had been to get out of the desert trailer park and away from her drunk mother's boyfriends. She hadn't dreamed of fame and fortune and yet she'd gotten both.

"You could have had fame and fortune just like you used to say you wanted when we were kids. You turned it down, and not because of me."

Karen started to argue, but Blythe cut her off.

"Martin always said that what I lacked in talent I made up for in guts. He said it was too bad you were just the opposite."

"Don't I look like I have guts?" Karen demanded and took a threatening step toward her. Karen aimed the gun at Blythe's heart. "If you think I won't kill you, you're wrong. I can't bear the thought of you living the life that should have been mine any longer."

"I'm a waitress now, Karen," Blythe snapped. "You want that life, go for it."

The gun blast was deafening in the small kitchen.

Logan woke to the feel of the cold hard ground beneath him and a killer headache. For a moment, he couldn't remember what had happened. If not for the ropes binding him, he might have thought one of the horses had clipped him and he'd hit his head when he went down.

He tried to sit up, straining against the ropes around his wrists and ankles. His head swam at the effort, but as his thoughts cleared, he let out a curse. Blythe.

Whoever had hit him and tied him up was after Blythe.

Rolling to his side, he looked around for something to free himself. In the corner, he spotted an old scythe that he sometimes used to cut weeds behind the barn. He began to work his way over to it, scooting on the cold earth, his mind racing.

He remembered that he'd come out to put the horses back in the pasture. He'd thought he'd left the gate open. It wouldn't have been the first time one of the horses had gotten out. Even when he realized that something was spooking the horses, he thought it must be a rattler.

Never had he thought anyone would come after Blythe out here. His mistake. One he prayed wouldn't cost her her life.

He reached the scythe, knocked it over and positioned it between his wrists as he began to saw. He couldn't believe anyone would want to harm Blythe, certainly not one of her former band members, and yet someone had taken a shovel to the back of his head and left him hog-tied in the barn.

What were they going to do to Blythe?

Not kill her. No, just scare her. Logan desperately wanted to believe that in the end, they wouldn't be able to hurt her. But then he had no concept of the kind of hatred that could bring another person to kill.

Logan sawed through the ropes on his wrist and was

reaching for the scythe to cut the bindings around his ankles when he heard the gunshot. His heart dropped.

Karen smiled as a ceramic container on the kitchen counter exploded, sending shards flying and startling Blythe. "I planned all of this. Hired someone to make it look like someone else from the band had tried to run us down on the street. I know Martin thought I was a coward, that I blamed you because I didn't go for what I wanted ten years ago and instead let you take it from me. Martin told me to my face just before I killed him."

Blythe stared at Karen in shock. "I thought his death was ruled a suicide."

"He said he was going to kill himself when I found him that morning about to write his suicide note," Karen said with a smile. "But we both knew he wouldn't have called me to meet him over at the house unless he lacked the courage to do it. He had the gun pointed at his chest, but I was the one who had to press the trigger. He goaded me into it because he didn't have the guts to do it himself. I was the last person he saw."

"Oh, Karen." She felt sick as she stumbled back against the kitchen table. Her fingers felt the smooth brim of Logan's Stetson and her heart lurched at the thought of him. She prayed Karen was telling the truth and hadn't hurt him.

"You're the one who left the note for me," she said, seeing it all now. "Martin must have told you I was there in another part of the house. All these years. You could have had a career. It didn't have to be either me or you."

"Do you know what makes me the angriest?" Karen said as if Blythe hadn't spoken. "You had it all and you were going to throw it away. Martin told me how you didn't appreciate it. You had everything I'd dreamed of and yet it meant nothing to you."

"Karen, that's not—"

"Don't bother to lie. You took what was mine." Her face twisted in a mask of fury. "Martin was right. You don't deserve to live."

Blythe had only a split second to react as Karen brought the gun up and squeezed the trigger. The Stetson brim was already in the fingers of her right hand. She drew it from behind her and hurled the hat at Karen as she dived for the floor.

Logan hurriedly cut through the ropes. As he stumbled to his feet, he felt the effects of the blow to his head. He could barely breathe, his fear was so great, but it was the dizziness that made him grab hold of the barn wall for a moment. His vision clearing, he raced toward his pickup and the shotgun that hung in the rack in the back window.

Two gunshots. His heart was in his throat as he saw that the kitchen light was on. But he saw no one as he quietly opened his pickup door and took down his shotgun. From behind the seat, he found the box of shells and popped one in each side of the double barrels. Snapping it shut, he headed for the front door.

He knew he couldn't go in blasting. If Blythe wasn't already dead—

The thought clutched at his heart. He'd brought her out here so he could protect her. If he'd gotten her killed—

He eased open the front door and instantly heard what sounded like a scuffle just inside.

* * *

Blythe wasn't sure if she'd been hit or not. She felt the hard floor as she hit her already scraped elbow. But even that pain didn't register at first as she knocked Karen's feet out from under her.

Karen came down hard next to her. A loud "oof!" came out of her as she hit the floor. Blythe saw that there was a red welt on Karen's cheek where the Stetson brim must have hit her.

Blythe grabbed for the gun, but Karen reacted faster than she'd expected. She kicked out at Blythe, driving her back as she brought up the gun and aimed it at her head.

As Karen scrambled to her feet, Blythe slowly got to hers.

"I'm sorry this is how it has to end," Blythe said as she saw the front door slowly swing open behind Karen. "I never wanted to hurt you. You were like a sister to me. I missed you so much. I can't tell you how many times I wanted to pick up the phone and call you."

"Why didn't you?" Karen demanded, sounding close to tears. Her arm was bleeding from where she'd gotten skinned-up earlier on the main drag in Whitehorse. She must have hit it when she fell, Blythe thought as she tried to think about anything but Logan.

He had slipped in through the front door, a shotgun in his hands, and was now moving up behind Karen. He motioned for her to keep talking.

"I didn't think you would want to hear from me after the band broke up," she said. "I blamed myself for leaving it and leaving you. I guess I also didn't believe Martin that you'd turned down an offer to do what I was doing. I thought he'd lied. It wouldn't have been the first time."

Logan was now right behind Karen, practically breathing down her neck. She was crying, big fat tears running down her face.

"He was right, you know?" Karen said and made a swipe at her tears with her free hand. "I was afraid that I wouldn't be good enough to make it. I hoped you would fail but when you didn't…" She seemed to get hold of herself, inhaling and letting out a long sigh. "It's too late now. I've burned too many bridges. This has to end here. You and me. Just as it always should have been."

Something in Karen's gaze suddenly changed. Blythe saw Logan raise the shotgun and cried out to warn him as Karen suddenly spun around.

Blythe felt her legs give under her. She dropped to her knees as she watched Logan bring the butt of the shotgun down on the side of Karen's head. As she crumbled like a ragdoll, she managed to get off another shot. It whizzed past Logan, missing him only by inches, before shattering something in the living room.

In the distance, she heard the sound of sirens and remembered the call from Sheriff Buford Olson earlier. He must have called the local sheriff, McCall Crawford, for moments later the ranch yard filled with flashing lights and the sound of doors slamming and running feet on the porch steps.

Blythe buried her face in Logan's shoulder as he dropped to his knees beside her. His breath was ragged, his heart a drum in his chest as he dragged her to him.

She heard his voice break with emotion as he thanked God that she was alive.

Then he lifted her face to his and told her he loved her.

Epilogue

"If I could have your attention please." Logan rose from his chair at the long table in the dining room of the main house at Chisholm ranch. He touched his knife to his wineglass again. A hush fell over the room as all eyes turned in his direction.

Blythe felt her heart kick up a beat as Logan smiled down at her. She wanted to pinch herself. So much had happened since that night in the kitchen. Everything about JJ and the past had come out. Logan's family had been so supportive, just the memory brought tears to her eyes.

They'd spent the rest of that night giving their statements to the sheriff, having the doctor check Logan over to make sure he didn't have a concussion and filling his family in on JJ and everything else that had happened.

Sheriff Buford Olson had picked up Loretta and charged her with attempted murder after discovering that she'd rented the pickup and had been the driver in the near hit-and-run. Karen had paid Loretta to do it, but Loretta told Buford that she'd been happy to. In fact, she'd done her best to hit both of them.

Karen had hired herself a good lawyer. When Blythe had tried to visit her in jail, Karen had refused to see her. As she'd left the sheriff's department, she didn't look back. She was through blaming herself for the events of the past.

Before he died, Martin Sanderson had also released Jett from his contract, but Jett was quickly finding out that no other recording studio was interested. On top of that, Betsy had produced a sworn affidavit from their deceased band member Lisa "Luca" Thomas, stating that Jett had stolen songs from her and what she'd been paid for them—after he'd recorded the songs as his own. Her estate was suing Jett for full disclosure.

That had pretty much driven a stake through the last of his singing career.

Blythe had been glad to see that Betsy had more backbone than any of them had seen before. She'd known that Betsy was pregnant all those years ago before the band broke up. But if her oldest son was Jett's, then it was a secret Betsy intended to take to her grave.

A few days ago, Blythe had been sitting on the porch in the shade after a long horseback ride with Logan when he joined her.

"I love you," he said. Blythe started to speak, but he stopped her.

"You don't have to say anything. I know that staying here, on this ranch, in the middle of nowhere is the last thing in the world you want to do."

"Logan—"

He touched a finger to her lips. "Let me finish. I didn't tell you I love you to try to get you to stay. I just wanted you to know that if you ever need to get away from your life again, I'll be here."

She smiled and shook her head. "I'm not going to want to escape my life again. All of this has helped me know what I want to do with the rest of it." She touched his handsome face, cupping his strong jaw with her palm. "I love you, Logan Chisholm, and there is no place I want to be other than right here with you."

He'd stared at her in surprise. "What about your career—"

"Martin freed me from my contract, so I do still have my singing career if I wanted it. But since climbing on the back of your motorcycle that day over in the Flathead, I've known that the only singing I want to do is to my babies. You do want children, don't you?"

"There's something I need to ask this woman," Logan said now as he reached down and took Blythe's hand. "Jennifer Blythe James, would you be my wife?"

Blythe felt tears blur her eyes as she looked around the table and saw all the smiling welcoming faces. Then she turned her face up to Logan. "There is nothing I would love more," she said.

He dragged her to her feet and into his arms. She leaned into him, felt his strength and that of his family around them, all the things a good marriage needed.

The room burst with applause and cheers around them as Logan kissed her. Blythe could see their children running through this big house, all the holidays and birthdays, all the cousins, aunts and uncles.

She'd dreamed of a big family, but the Chisholms were bigger and more loving than any she had ever dreamed possible.

When Logan finally released her, she found herself hugged by everyone in the room. Emma was last. She'd cupped Blythe's shoulders in her hands and just looked at her for a long moment.

"You are going to make the most beautiful bride and such a good wife to our Logan," she said, her voice breaking with emotion. "Welcome to the family." Emma pulled her into a hug.

Through her tears, Blythe saw her future husband standing nearby looking at her as if he would always see her as she was now. She smiled back, picturing getting old with this man. Yes, after all the fame and fortune, this was exactly where she wanted to be.

Her name was now Cynthia Crowley. She'd picked the name out of thin air—just as she did most of her names.

She thought of it as reinventing herself. She cut her hair, dyed it, got different colored contact lenses, changed her makeup, her address, became the woman she imagined Cynthia Crowley was. A widow with no family and no real means of support.

Laura had first discovered in high school drama class that she could don a disguise like an outer shell. She'd loved acting and she was good at it. Everyone said she seemed to transform into her character. The truth was, her characters had felt more real to her than whoever she'd been before she pulled on their skin.

She liked to think of herself as a chameleon. Or a snake that was forever shedding its skin. She had changed character so many times that some days she could hardly remember that young woman who'd married Hoyt Chisholm. Laura suspected though that Mrs. Laura Chisholm had been as big a fake as Cynthia Crowley was now.

Women did that when they married for life. They became who their husbands *thought* they had married. That's what she had done with Hoyt. She'd played the role of his wife. At least for a while.

It was no wonder that her life had led her to the special effects department of several movie studios in California. It was amazing how the new products could transform an actor. She especially loved a type of substance that reminded her of the glue she'd used in grade school. As a special effects makeup artist, she had worked with actors to make them look old and wrinkled or badly scarred.

The work was rewarding. She loved what she did and often experimented with her own disguises. But ultimately, there was only one constant in her life. Hoyt Chisholm.

Laura remembered the first time she'd seen Hoyt. She'd known then that she would love him until the day she died. She'd also known that he would never love her as much as she loved him. It had broken her heart every moment she'd been with him. That was why she hadn't been able to stay. It had been too painful knowing that one day he would see the real her and hate her.

She was tortured by the way other women had looked at him. It had been impossible not to imagine him with one of them instead of her. Hoyt would become angry when she'd voice her fears and she'd feel another piece of her heart gouged away by his lack of understanding.

Once he'd decided to adopt the boys, she'd lost more of him. He'd actually thought the boys would bring the two of them closer, but when she'd seen his love for babies that weren't even his own blood, she'd felt herself losing more and more of him. He'd tried to make it up to her, trying so hard it made her hurt even worse. She'd seen him start to pull away from her and knew she had to escape before it got any worse.

Divorce was out of the question. She would always be his only wife till death parted them. She could have warned him not to ever remarry before she faked her death that day on Fort Peck Reservoir. But Hoyt wouldn't have understood. You had to love someone so much it hurt to understand.

She'd known he would remarry. She'd thought he would have to wait seven years to have her declared dead. But he'd found a way around it, marrying that bitch Tasha. Unlike her, Tasha had shared Hoyt's love of horses. Oh, the horrible pain of watching the two of them together, until one day she couldn't take it any longer and had rigged Tasha's saddle.

After that, she'd hoped Hoyt wouldn't marry again. But Hoyt hadn't been able to resist the young woman who'd been helping take care of his boys. Krystal appealed to Hoyt's need to protect a woman in trouble. He would have continued to try to save Krystal if Laura hadn't helped him by getting rid of her for good.

From a safe distance, she had watched him raise the boys alone, all six of them, and build an empire. She'd been proud of him, had actually loved him more.

Then Emma had come along.

Laura shook her head. Just the thought made her hands ball into fists, her jaw tightening, her heart on fire.

Hoyt was in love. Or so he thought. She knew the power of love, but it was a weak emotion compared to hate. Hate, now there was something with substance, something you could feel deep in your bone marrow, something to live for.

Laura lived now for only one thing. To see Emma Chisholm dead and gone. But this time she thought Hoyt might have to go, as well. Maybe his sons and their fiancées too. Maybe it was time to finally end this pain once and for all. If only Hoyt had loved her and only her.

As she parked her car and got out, it looked as if they were having a party, but she knew Emma made a big deal out of suppers at the ranch. Everyone was here. Perfect.

She stood for a moment, looking at the huge house all ablaze with lights, remembering when it had been hers and Hoyt's.

Then she made her way up to the front door and rang the doorbell. It would be her house again in a few moments, she thought with a crooked smile.

When the doorbell rang, everyone turned in surprise toward the front door.

"Are you expecting someone?" Emma asked her husband.

Hoyt shook his head. "Unless it's the live-in housekeeper. She wasn't supposed to be here until tomorrow though. I'll go see."

Emma asked her future daughters-in-law to serve dessert and went into the living room. Hoyt was already at the door, opening it as the bell rang again.

Standing back, Emma waited. She wondered what this woman Hoyt had hired to babysit her would be like. Dreaded, was more like it. Older, he'd said. Experienced, he'd said.

Emma feared she would be dull as dirt, when what she needed was to kick up her heels after everything she'd been through since marrying Hoyt.

But she wasn't going to complain. If the woman wasn't any fun, then Emma would find a way to sneak away from her.

Bracing herself, Emma watched Hoyt open the door. He hadn't turned on the porch light so she couldn't see the woman standing on their doorstep clearly.

"Come on in, Cynthia," Hoyt said. "We expected you tomorrow, but tonight is fine. You're just in time for dessert."

"Call me Mrs. Crowley," the woman said in a low hoarse voice. She spoke strangely as if out of one side of her mouth. Had the woman had a stroke?

And as she stepped into the light, Emma saw that her face was badly scarred on one side as if she'd been burned in a fire.

"Whatever you prefer," Hoyt said and turned to see Emma standing at some distance behind him. "Mrs. Crowley, I'd like you to meet my wife, Emma."

The woman looked up then and Emma felt a chill race through her. One of the woman's eyes was a dark brown. The other one on the side that had been burned was completely white and sightless.

"I know I don't look like much," the woman said in her hoarse voice. "But I'm a hard worker."

"I'm sure you are," Emma said stepping to her to take her hand. "Welcome to Chisholm ranch."

The woman's grip was strong. "Thank you, Mrs. Chisholm."

She hated that the woman was hard to look at because of her injury, but she knew over time, they would all adapt to it, just as Cynthia Crowley had herself.

"Please call me Emma," she said warmly.

"Don't you worry, Emma. I am much stronger than I look. Before long, I promise you'll be surprised at what I'm capable of doing."

* * * * *

USA TODAY bestselling author **Barb Han** lives in north Texas with her very own hero-worthy husband, three beautiful children, a spunky golden retriever/ standard poodle mix and too many books in her to-read pile. In her downtime, she plays video games and spends much of her time on or around a basketball court. She loves interacting with readers and is grateful for their support. You can reach her at barbhan.com.

Books by Barb Han

Harlequin Intrigue

An O'Connor Family Mystery

Texas Kidnapping
Texas Target

Rushing Creek Crime Spree

What She Did
What She Knew
What She Saw

Crisis: Cattle Barge

Kidnapped at Christmas
Murder and Mistletoe
Bulletproof Christmas

Visit the Author Profile page at Harlequin.com for more titles.

STOCKYARD SNATCHING

Barb Han

My deepest thanks to Allison Lyons.
It's hard to believe this is already our 10th book
together! Working with you is a dream come true
and I'm so very grateful. Special nod to Jill Marsal
for your unwavering support and guidance
(and brilliance!).

My love to Brandon, Jacob and Tori.
I'm so proud of each one of you. You're bright,
talented and have the best quirks!

To Amelia Rae, you stole our hearts a year ago.
Happy 1st birthday!

And to you, Babe. I can't even imagine
being on this journey without you.
All my love. All my life.

Chapter 1

It was a bitterly cold early October morning. The temperature gauge on Dallas O'Brien's dashboard read 17 degrees, beneath a gray sky thick with clouds.

As it turned out, the Lone Star State had a temper and its tantrums came in the form of cold snaps that made him miss having a winter beard. Dallas hated cold.

Yesterday, the sun had been out and he had been in short sleeves. Texas weather—like life—could turn on a dime.

Another frigid breeze blasted through Dallas, piercing his coat as he slid out of the driver's seat and then closed the door of his pickup. He flipped up the corners of his collar. Since there was no traffic, he'd made it to the supply store in record time. Normally the place would be open, but Jessie had been running late ever since his wife gave birth to twins early last month.

A car tooled around the back of the building and across the parking lot. Was that Kate Williams, the proud owner of the soup kitchen, The Food Project? Dallas hadn't had a chance to meet her yet, with everything going on at the ranch after his parents' deaths.

A female came out of the driver's side, rounded the car and moved to the rear passenger door. From this distance, Dallas estimated she wasn't an inch more than five and a half feet tall. He couldn't see much of her figure through her thick, buttoned-to-the-collar, navy blue peacoat. Her cable-knit scarf looked more like an afghan wrapped around her neck. He suppressed a laugh. Apparently, she didn't do cold any better than Dallas.

From what little he could see of her legs, she had on blue jeans. Furry brown boots rose above her calves. She wore expensive clothing for someone who owned a soup kitchen. And apparently—Dallas glanced at his watch—that process began at five thirty in the morning.

This had to be her, he reasoned, as she pulled a baby out of the backseat, bundled from head to toe in what looked like a fitted blue quilt. Blue.

A boy?

Didn't that twist up Dallas's insides?

First, his ex Susan Hanover had dropped the bomb that he was going to be a father. Then she'd pulled a disappearing act. And even the best private investigator money could buy hadn't been able to locate her or the baby since.

Knowing Susan, she'd been lying to trap him into a wedding ring. Dallas's finger itched thinking about it.

With her and the baby gone, all he had left were questions—questions that kept him tossing and turning most nights.

What if she'd been lying? What if she hadn't? What if Dallas had a child out there somewhere? What if his child needed him?

Dallas would never be able to rest until he had answers.

Walking away from a child wasn't something an O'Brien could ever do. Dallas had already lost his parents, and family meant everything to him.

As Ms. Williams closed the door to her vehicle, shivering in the cold, a male figure emerged from around the side of her building. The guy had on a hoodie and his face was angled toward the ground. His clothes were dirty, dark and layered. He was either homeless or trying to look the part.

The guy glanced around nervously as he approached Ms. Williams.

Didn't that get Dallas's radar jacked up to full alert? He strained to get a better view. *Come on. Look up.*

All this guy would have to do would be to ask Ms. Williams a question to distract her—say, what time the place opened. She would answer; he would rob her and then run. There were plenty of places to disappear downtown or in the neighborhood near the stockyard.

It would be a perfect crime, because not only was she holding a baby, but her thick clothing would weigh her down, making it impossible for her to catch him.

Well, a perfect crime if Dallas wasn't right there watching.

Then again, this really could be a man in need of a meal. Experience had taught Dallas not to jump the gun when it came to people. There was no shortage of homeless, even in a small town like Bluff, Texas.

The times he had driven by this location early in the morning and found the line of needy individuals stretched around the block were too many to count. He was pretty certain Ms. Williams's neighbors on Main Street didn't appreciate her clientele. None of them would be wandering through the stores after a meal to buy handmade jewelry or quaint Texas souvenirs. These businesses were important to the local economy.

Just then, the hooded figure lifted his head and made a grab for the baby.

This wasn't a robbery; it was a kidnapping.

Dallas spewed curse words as he ran full throttle toward them. "Stop right there!" he shouted.

Ms. Williams fought back and her attacker shifted position, ensuring she was between him and Dallas.

The baby cried, which seemed to agitate the attacker. Ms. Williams kicked the guy where no man wanted the tip of a boot. He coughed, then cursed as he seemed to catch sight of Dallas out of the corner of his eye.

The man shouted as he struggled to take the baby out of Ms. Williams's arms. "Don't come any closer!" His voice was agitated and Dallas didn't recognize it. Must not be someone local. The guy forced the woman back a few steps with him, a knife to her throat. "I didn't want to do it like this, but now she's coming with me."

The baby wailed and Dallas came to a stop.

This situation had gone sour in a heartbeat.

To make matters worse, all Dallas could see clearly of Ms. Williams was a set of terrified blue eyes staring at him. She had that desperate-mother look that said she'd do anything to save her son. Dallas's heart squeezed as she held tight to her baby with the determination only a loving mom could possess.

He hoped like hell she wouldn't do anything stupid.

Tires squealed from behind the building and Dallas instantly wished it would be his best friend, Sheriff Tommy Johnson. No way would Tommy be dumb enough to come roaring up, however. His friend was smarter than that and a better lawman.

A vehicle rounded the corner and lurched to a stop nearby. The white minivan's sliding door opened.

The attacker broke eye contact to look. If Dallas had a shot at taking the guy down, he'd grab it.

"Toss your keys to me," the kidnapper shouted to him.

Dallas dug a set from his pocket and pitched them forward.

If he didn't make a move soon, this jerk would disappear into that van with mother and baby. She'd most likely be killed and her body dumped before they left the county. Dallas had read about vicious illegal adoption rings in the area and stories of mothers being killed for their infants.

Between the hoodie pulled over the thug's forehead and the turtleneck covering his jaw, Dallas couldn't get a good look at his face. The guy glanced away again, as if calculating the odds of getting inside the vehicle before Dallas could catch him. Then he bent to grab the keys.

It was now or never.

Dallas lunged toward his target and knocked the guy's arm away from Kate's throat. The sheer amount of fabric she had wrapped around her neck made certain the blade wouldn't get anywhere near her skin. For the first time in his life, Dallas thanked the cold weather.

Breaking free, Ms. Williams bolted toward her car, while trying to soothe the crying infant.

In the bustle, the attacker broke out of Dallas's grip and darted toward the vehicle. Damn. No plates.

"The sheriff is on his way," Dallas said in desperation, knowing full well his target was about to hop into that van and disappear.

Just as expected, the guy hurled himself in the open door and, without waiting for it to close, shouted at the driver to go. On cue, the van swerved, then sped away.

Dallas muttered a curse. Pulling out his cell, he told Ms. Williams to stay put. Even though his pickup wasn't far, he couldn't leave her to give chase. No way would he risk this guy circling back or sending others to finish the job. Dallas would have to stay with her to ensure her safety.

At least this morning wasn't a total bust. The baby was safe in his mother's arms. Dallas could call his friend the sheriff, who would track down the minivan while Dallas guarded Ms. Williams.

"Where are you?" he asked as soon as Tommy picked up.

"A couple of blocks from Main Street," the lawman replied. "Why? You okay?"

"I'm in the back parking lot of the soup kitchen and a man just tried to abduct Ms. Williams's baby. There's a white Mazda minivan heading in your direction. He hopped inside it before I could get to him. No tags in front," Dallas reported, noticing for the first time that he was practically panting from adrenaline. He took a deep breath and then finished relaying the details of what had just gone down.

"Is there a high point you can get to for a visual on the minivan?" Tommy asked.

Dallas kept an eye on Ms. Williams as he climbed on top of the closed Dumpster to see if he could spot the vehicle. She had managed to settle the baby. Dallas was certain her hands would be shaking from her own adrenaline, and he was grateful for the few extra minutes he'd get while she fumbled with securing her son in the car seat. The panicked look on her face said she'd get as far away as possible the second she could.

"No. I don't see him," Dallas said.

"I'm on Main now. A couple of blocks from your location, but I don't see anyone on the street." Tommy asked Dallas to stand by while he gave his deputies a description of the vehicle. "I'm sending someone over to you just in case the guy is on his way back or sends someone else."

"Call me back when you know anything. I have to check on Ms. Williams and make sure she doesn't do anything stupid," Dallas said, knowing full well that her eyes would haunt him if he didn't ensure she was okay. It would be a long time before he shook off the image of those frightened sky blues, and he had to admit to being a little interested to see what the rest of her face looked like. He told himself it was protective instinct mixed with curiosity and nothing more.

Besides, she'd been as blindsided by all this as he had. He hopped down and jogged toward her sedan. "Ma'am."

She spun around with a gasp. "Kate. It's Kate."

He brought his hand up, palm out, to help communicate the idea that he wasn't there to hurt her.

"I'm Dallas O'Brien." He offered a handshake. She was most likely still in shock, and from the look of her wild eyes, she was in full get-the-heck-out-of-Dodge mode. "The sheriff is sending someone over to talk to us."

She stood there, frozen, for several seconds, as if her mind might be clicking through options. She didn't seem to realize there was only one: talk to Dallas.

"Do you know who that was?" he asked, figuring he already knew the answer. But he wanted to get her talking.

"No. I've never seen him before in my life." Her breath was visible in the cold air as she spoke, and even though she had on a thick layer of clothes, she was shivering. That, too, was most likely caused by residual adrenaline.

"First of all, I want to make sure you and your baby are safe. Can we go inside the building?" Dallas's own adrenaline surge was wearing off and he was starting to feel the biting wind again. He'd stay with her until law enforcement arrived and then he'd get supplies and head back to the ranch.

"Okay. Yes. Sure. I was going in anyway before—" She stopped midsentence, as if she couldn't bring herself to finish.

Then another round of panic seemed to set in.

"No. Never mind. We have to go somewhere else," she insisted, her gaze darting from left to right.

"He's gone. They won't be back, especially not while I'm here," Dallas stated.

"You can't know that for certain," she said quickly.

"Kate, I can assure you—"

"No. You can't. We can talk, but we have to do it somewhere else." She glanced about, her terror and desperation mounting.

Dallas's cell phone buzzed. He fished it from his coat pocket and checked the screen. "This call is from the sheriff. I need to answer."

She nodded.

"Give me some good news," Dallas said into the phone.

"Wish I could. Seems your white Mazda minivan is just as slippery as your suspect. There's no sign of either anywhere. We have no plans to give up searching. You'll be the first to know when we locate him," Tommy said with a frustrated sigh.

Dallas thanked his friend for the update and then ended the call, cursing under his breath.

An expectant victim stared at him, needing reassurance.

He shook his head.

"I have to get out of here before they come back," she said, making a move toward the driver's side of her sedan.

"Hold on," Dallas cautioned. "What makes you so sure he'll try again?"

Chapter 2

"I feel too exposed here. Can we go somewhere besides my soup kitchen? I need to get away from this place," Kate blurted out. It was then she realized that she'd been holding her breath. She exhaled, trying to calm her rapid pulse.

"A deputy is on his way," the handsome cowboy said, and his name finally sank in. Dallas O'Brien. She knew that name from somewhere. But where?

Her mind raced. She was still shocked that anyone would try to rip her baby from her arms in the middle of town. She'd waited so long for him, had been through hell and back. What kind of horrible person would try to take him away?

Tears threatened, but Kate forced herself to hold them at bay.

"My son will need to eat soon and I'd rather not

feed him in the parking lot, whether a deputy is coming or not," she said, glancing from Dallas to Jackson.

The cowboy looked around and then checked his watch. "Fine. We're going to the sheriff's office to give statements, then," he said.

Jackson would be safe there, so she nodded.

"I don't have a child safety seat in my truck, so we'll have to take your car," he added, his voice sturdy as steel.

As calming as his presence was, her body still shook from fear of that man coming back and the horror of him trying to pry Jackson out of her arms.

"You gave him your keys," she reminded Dallas, wasting no time slipping into the driver's seat, while he took the passenger side of her sedan.

"Those? That'll get him into my old post office box," he said with a wry grin. It was the first time she really noticed Dallas's good looks. He had a strong, square jaw and intelligent dark eyes.

"I'd like to go home," Kate said as she turned the ignition. "Can the deputy meet us there?"

"Too risky," Dallas said.

It took a second for her to realize that he meant the men might know where she lived.

Could they?

Being single and living alone, she'd taken great pains to ensure her personal information remained private. Then again, with the internet these days, it seemed there was no real privacy left, and most people in the small town knew each other anyway. All a determined bad guy would have to do was ask around and he'd be able to figure out where she lived.

"All of Jackson's supplies are there, except what's

inside the diaper bag in the backseat," she said as she pulled onto Main from the alley.

Dallas surveyed the area and she realized that with her driving, he would be able to keep watch for the minivan in case it returned. She racked her brain, trying to figure out how she knew him.

"We can pick up new diapers if need be. I don't want to go to your place until we know it's safe. For now, take a right at the next stoplight," Dallas said. He sent a text and she assumed he was telling the sheriff about their change in plans.

Normally, being told what to do was like fingernails on a chalkboard to Kate. In this case, she decided it was better to do as Dallas said. At least he was strong and capable. She already knew he could handle himself in a fight, and he had just saved her and Jackson, so she knew she could trust him.

"Three blocks ahead, take another right, then a left at the stop sign," he instructed.

She did. The horror of what had just happened was finally sinking in and it dawned on her how lucky she'd been that someone was there to help.

"I owe you an apology for being rude to you. Thank you for stepping in to save my son," she said. "You didn't have to get involved."

"You're welcome," Dallas replied. "I'm just glad I was there to help. I don't normally go to the supply store on Wednesdays."

"Your change of plans probably just saved Jackson's life." She shivered at the thought of what might've happened if this cowboy hadn't been there to intervene. "I know it saved mine."

Reality was setting in, which also made her realize there was no one to open the kitchen this morning. She needed to call her assistant director or dozens of people would go hungry.

"I have to make sure the kitchen opens on time. Is it okay if I make a quick call before we go inside?" She parked in the lot of the sheriff's office and gripped the steering wheel. "A lot of people are counting on me for a meal."

Dallas nodded, while staring at the screen of his cell. "Make an excuse as to why you can't do it yourself, and put the call on speaker. I don't want you to give away what happened yet. Got it?"

She shot him a sideways glance. "Why?"

"That was a planned attack. Those men knew exactly when and where you'd be alone. The sheriff will want to know if someone close to you gave them that information, and we have to assume it could've been anyone, even people you trust."

An icy chill ran down her spine. "You think one of my employees might've supplied that?" she asked, not bothering to mask her shock. Who would want to hurt Jackson or her? He was just a baby. Her mind could scarcely wrap around the fact that someone had tried to take him in the first place. Panic flooded her at the memory. "Who would plan something like this?"

"The sheriff will help find the answer to that question," Dallas said, his voice a study in composure, whereas she was falling apart.

"None of this seems real," she said, bile rising, burning her throat. "I think I might be sick."

"Take a few deep breaths." His voice was like calm, soothing water pouring over her.

She did as he suggested.

"Better?" he asked.

"Yes." She apologized again.

"Don't be sorry for wanting to protect your child," Dallas said. And there was an underlying note in his tone she couldn't easily identify. Was he a father?

"You have every right to be upset," he said.

"It's just that I moved here for a safe environment." And now it felt as if everything in her life was unraveling. Again.

"Who are you going to call to open the kitchen?" Dallas asked.

Oh, right. She'd gotten distracted once more. Her mind was spinning in a thousand directions. "Allen Lentz. He's my second in command and my right hand."

Her phone weighed almost nothing and yet shook as she held it. She paused. "You don't think…?"

"Get him on speaker." There was a low rumble to Dallas O'Brien's voice now, a deep baritone that sent a different kind of shiver racing down her spine—one that was unwelcome and inappropriate given the circumstances.

Her rescuer's name seemed so familiar and she couldn't figure out why. Wait a minute. Didn't his family own the Cattlemen Crime Club? She'd received an invitation to a Halloween Bash in a few weeks, which was a charity fund-raiser, and realized that she'd seen his family name on the invite.

In fact, her kitchen was one of the beneficiaries of his family's generosity. She hadn't met any of the O'Briens yet. She'd read that they'd lost their parents in an accident a few weeks ago.

So far, she'd dealt with office staff, even though

she'd been told that the O'Briens personally visited every one of the charities they supported.

She hadn't expected Dallas O'Brien to be this intense, down-to-earth or staggeringly handsome. Not that she could think of a good reason why not. Maybe since he'd grown up with money she'd expected someone entitled or spoiled.

And yet now wasn't the time to think about how off her perception had been or that her pulse kicked up a few notches when he was close. She chalked her adrenaline rush up to the morning's events and closed the door on that topic.

Lack of sleep was beginning to distort her brain. No one had prepared her for the fact that she'd worry so much or rest so little once the baby arrived. No way would she admit defeat to her parents, either. They'd been clear about how much disdain they had for her decision to have a baby alone. Her mother had been mortified when she found out Kate was getting a divorce, so adopting a baby by herself was right up there on the list of ways she'd let her mother down.

Kate had expected her mom to come around once she met Jackson, but was still waiting for that day to happen.

This battle was hers to fight alone.

And none of that mattered when she held her little guy in her arms. No matter how tired she might be or how distanced she was from her family, she wouldn't trade the world for the baby of her heart.

"Hey, what's going on?" Allen asked, sounding surprisingly alert for five fifty in the morning. The phone must've startled him.

"I need your help. Can you open the kitchen for

me?" she asked, trying to think up a reasonable excuse to sell him. Then she went with the tried-and-true. "Jackson kept me up all night again."

"Oh, poor baby. And I'm talking about you," Allen said with a laugh. He yawned, and she heard the sound clearly through the phone. "His days and nights still confused?"

"Yes, and I have the bags under my eyes to prove it," she said, hating that she had to lie to cover what had really happened. Allen had been nothing but a good employee and friend, and she hated deception.

"No problem. I'll throw on some clothes and head over," he said.

"You're a lifesaver, Allen."

"Don't I know it," he quipped. There was a rustling noise as if he was tossing off his covers and getting out of bed.

"I'll owe you big-time for this one," Kate said.

"Good. Then get a babysitter for Friday night and let me take you out to dinner." He didn't miss a beat.

Out of the corner of her eye, Kate saw Dallas's jaw muscle clench. She couldn't tell if his reaction was good or bad.

"I don't know if I'll be in today," Kate said awkwardly. She quickly glanced at Dallas, realizing that she needed to redirect the conversation with Allen. "The Patsy family's donation should hit the bank today. Would you mind watching for it and letting me know when it arrives?"

"Got it," he said. "And don't think I didn't notice that you changed the subject."

"We've already gone over this, Allen. He's too little to leave with a sitter," Kate said quietly into the phone.

Her cheeks heated as she talked about her lack of a life in front of a complete stranger, and especially one as good-looking as Dallas.

"That excuse doesn't fly with me and you know it," Allen said flatly.

Kate had no response.

"Fine. At least take me as your date to the Hackney party next weekend," he offered.

"I'm skipping that one, too. Can we talk about it later? I'm too tired to think beyond today," she said, then managed to end the call without any more embarrassing revelations about her life. The truth was her perspective had changed the instant Jackson had been placed in her arms. There was no man worth leaving her baby for, even for a night.

"Is he usually so…friendly?" Dallas asked.

"I stay out of my employees' personal lives," she said, hating the suspicion in Dallas's voice. "There's no way Allen would do anything to hurt me or Jackson."

"I take it there's no Mr. Williams to notify?" Dallas asked.

Clearly, he'd picked up on the fact that she was single. She'd listened intently for condemnation in his tone and was surprised she didn't find a hint. She'd expected to and more after cashing out her interests in the tech company she and her brother had started together and moving to a small town. If her own family couldn't get behind her choices, how could strangers?

"No. There isn't. Is that a problem?" she asked a little too sharply. Missing sleep didn't bring out the best in her, and she'd been only half lying about not sleeping last night due to Jackson's schedule or lack thereof. At his age, he took a bottle every four hours, day and night.

"Not for me personally. The sheriff will want to know, and I'm taking notes to speed along the process once we go inside." Dallas motioned toward the small notepad he'd taken out of his pocket.

"Oh. Right." As soon as Jackson was old enough to take care of himself—like, age eighteen—Kate planned to stay in bed an entire weekend. Maybe then she'd think clearly again. Heck, give her a hotel and room service and she'd stay there a whole week.

"Where's the father?" Dallas asked, still with no hint of disapproval in his voice.

"Out of the picture."

There was a beat of silence. "Ready to go inside and talk?" he asked at last, his brow arched.

"Yes. I'll just get Jackson from the backseat," she said defensively. There was no reason to be on guard, she reminded herself. Besides, what would she care if a stranger judged her?

Dallas stood next to her, holding the car door open. She thanked him as she pulled Jackson close to her chest. Just the thought of anything happening to her son...

She couldn't even go there.

"Can I help with the diaper bag?" Dallas held out his hand, still no hint of condemnation in his tone.

"You must have children." Kate managed to ease it off her shoulder without disturbing the baby, who was thankfully asleep again. Her nerves were settling down enough for her hands to finally stop shaking.

"Not me," he said, sounding a little defensive. What was that all about?

Kate figured the man's family status was none of her business. She was just grateful that Jackson was still asleep.

Thank the stars for car rides. They were the only way she could get her son down for a nap some days. It probably didn't hurt that he'd been awake most of the night. He'd been born with his days and nights mixed up.

Family man or not, Kate's life would be very different right now if Dallas hadn't been there. Tears threatened to release along with all the emotions she'd been holding in.

Or maybe it was the fact that she felt safe with Dallas, which was a curious thought given that he was a stranger.

This wasn't the time or place to worry about either. Kate needed to pull on all the strength she had for Jackson. He needed his mother to keep it together.

"I can't thank you enough," she said, knowing that she wouldn't be holding her baby right now if not for this man. "Not just for carrying a diaper bag, but for everything you did for us this morning."

Dallas nodded. He was tall, easily more than six foot. Maybe six foot two? He had enough muscles for her to know he put in serious time at the gym or on the ranch owned by him and his family. His hair was blacker than the sky on any clear night she'd seen. There was an intensity to him, too, and she had no doubt the man was good at whatever he put his mind to.

She told herself that the only reason she noticed was because they'd been in danger and he'd just saved her son's life.

* * *

Dallas walked Kate into the sheriff's office and instructed her to take a seat anywhere she'd be comfortable.

Looking at the baby stirred up all kinds of feelings in him that he wasn't ready to deal with. Not until he knew for sure one way or the other about his own parenthood status. Being in limbo was the absolute worst feeling, apart from knowing that he was in no way ready to be a father.

And yet a part of him wondered what it would be like to have a little rug rat running around the ranch. He chalked the feeling up to missing his parents. Losing them so unexpectedly had delivered a blow to the family and left a hole that couldn't be filled. And then there was Dallas's guilt over not being available to help them out when they'd called. He'd been halfway to New Mexico with an unexpected problem in one of his warehouses.

His gut twisted as he thought about it. If he'd turned around his truck and come back like they'd asked, they'd still be alive.

Dallas needed to redirect his thoughts or his guilt would consume him again. An update from his private investigator, Wayne Morton, was overdue. When Morton had last made contact, three days ago, he'd believed he was on a trail that might lead to Susan's whereabouts. He'd been plenty busy at the ranch, trying to get his arms around the family business.

"Can I get anything for you or the baby?" Dallas asked Kate, needing a strong cup of coffee.

"Something warm would be nice," she said, wedging the sleeping baby safely in a chair.

Dallas nodded before making his exit as she began peeling off her scarf and layers of outerwear.

A few minutes later he returned with two steaming cups of brew. He hesitated at the door once he got a good look at her, and his pulse thumped. Calling her five and a half feet tall earlier had been generous. The only reason she seemed that height was the heeled boots she wore. Without them, she'd be five foot three at the most. She had on fitted jeans that hugged her curves and a deep blue sweater that highlighted her eyes—eyes that would challenge even the perfect blue sky of a gorgeous spring day. Her shiny blond hair was pulled off her face into a ponytail.

"Wasn't sure how you took yours, so I brought cream and sugar," he said, setting both cups on the side table near where she stood. He emptied his coat pocket of cream and sugar packets, ignoring his rapid heartbeat.

She thanked him before mixing the condiments into her cup.

The baby moved as she sat down next to him and she immediately scooped him up and brought him to her chest.

The infant wound up for a good cry, unleashed one, and Kate's stress levels appeared to hit the roof.

"He's got a healthy set of lungs," Dallas offered, trying to ease her tension.

"He's probably hungry. Is there a place where I can warm a bottle?" she asked, distress written in the wrinkle across her forehead.

Abigail, Tommy's secretary, appeared in the doorway before Dallas could answer. She'd been with the sheriff's office long before Tommy arrived and had become invaluable to him in the five years since he'd taken the job. She threatened to retire every year, and every year he made an offer she couldn't refuse.

"I can take care of that for you," she said. "Where's the bottle?"

"In there," Kate said, attempting to handle the baby and make a move for the diaper bag next to her. She couldn't quite manage it and started to tear up as Abigail shooed her away, scooping the bag off the floor.

"Thank you," Kate said, glancing from Abigail to Dallas.

"Don't be silly." The older woman just smiled. "You've been through a lot this morning." She motioned toward Jackson. "It'll get easier with him. The first few months are always the most difficult with a new baby."

Dallas felt as out of place in the conversation as catfish bait in a tilapia pond. And then a thought struck him. If he was a father—and he wasn't anywhere near ready to admit to the possibility just yet—he'd need to learn about diaper bags and 3:00 a.m. feedings. Kate's employee had taken her up-all-night excuse far too easily, which meant it happened enough for her to be able to know using it wouldn't be questioned.

Speaking of which, Allen seemed to know way too much about Kate's personal life, which could mean that the office employees were close, and it was clear he wanted more than a professional relationship with her. The guy was a little too cozy with his boss and Dallas didn't like it. She obviously refused his advances. A thought struck. Could that be enough for him to want to punish her by removing the only obstacle between them—her child?

He was probably reaching for a simple explanation. Even so, it was a question Dallas intended to bounce around with Tommy.

Dallas made a mental note to ask Kate more about her relationship with Allen as soon as the baby was calm again, which happened a few seconds after Abigail returned with a warmed bottle and he began feeding.

The look of panic didn't leave Kate's face entirely during the baby's meal, but she gazed lovingly at her son.

Dallas had questions and needed answers, the quicker the better. However, it didn't feel right interrupting mother and son during what looked to be a bonding moment.

But then, not being a father himself, what the hell did he know about it?

Sipping his coffee, he waited for Kate to speak first. It didn't take long. Another few minutes and she finally said, "I want to apologize about my behavior this morning. I'm not normally so...frazzled."

"You're doing better than you think," he said, offering reassurance.

"Am I?" she asked. "Because I feel like I'm all over the place emotionally."

"Trust me. You're doing fine."

Her shoulders relaxed a little and that made Dallas smile.

"I do have a question for you, though," he said.

She nodded.

"How well do you know your employees?" he asked, ignoring the most probable reason Allen's attraction grated on him so much. Dallas liked her, too.

"Some more than others, I guess." She shrugged. "We're a small office, so we talk."

The baby finished his bottle and she placed a cloth napkin over her shoulder before laying him across it and patting his back.

"What does that do?" Dallas's curiosity about babies was getting the best of him. His stress was also growing with every passing day that Morton didn't return his texts.

"Gets the gas out of his stomach. Believe me, you want it out. If you don't he can cramp up and become miserable." She frowned.

"And when he's miserable, you're miserable."

"Exactly," she said, her tone wistful. A tear escaped, rolling down her cheek. She wiped it away and quickly apologized. "This whole parenting thing has been much harder than I expected."

"Whoever did this to you and left should be castrated," Dallas said. And he figured he was a hypocrite with that coming out of his mouth, given that he might have done the same to another woman. However, he had very strong feelings about the kind of man who didn't mind making a baby, but couldn't be bothered to stick around to be a father to the child. The operative word in his situation was that he might have *unwittingly* done that to someone. And he had no proof that Susan had actually been pregnant with his child, given that she'd disappeared when he'd offered to bring up the baby separately, instead of agreeing to her suggestion that they immediately marry. Her call had come out of the blue, months after they'd parted ways.

His gaze didn't budge from Kate. He expected some

kind of reaction from her. All he saw was genuine embarrassment.

"Oh, I have no one to blame. I did it to myself," she said.

"I may not be an expert on babies, but I do know how they're made. And I'm fairly certain there has to be a partner." It was Dallas's turn to shoot her a confused look.

"Adoption," she said.

He gave her another.

"Surely you've heard of adopting a baby?" she asked tartly.

"Of course I have. I just didn't know that was your circumstance," he said stupidly.

Looking closer at the baby, Dallas couldn't help but notice the boy had dark curly hair.

Not unlike his own.

Chapter 3

Kate recognized the sheriff as soon as he stepped inside his office. Not only had she seen him around town, he'd stopped by the kitchen to welcome her when she'd first opened her doors.

He was close to Dallas O'Brien's height, so at least six feet tall. His hair was light brown and his eyes matched the shade almost perfectly.

She was relieved for the interruption, after sharing the news about Jackson being adopted, and especially after Dallas's reaction, which made no sense to her. He seemed fine with her being a single parent, but lost his ability to speak once she'd mentioned the adoption. What was up with that?

The sheriff acknowledged Dallas first and then offered a handshake to Kate.

Dallas relayed the morning's events succinctly and

Kate's heart squeezed at hearing the words, knowing how close she'd been to losing her son. She reminded herself that she had Dallas to thank for thwarting the kidnapping attempt.

If he hadn't been there...

She shivered, deflecting the chill gripping her spine.

"Most kidnappings involve family. Sounds like that isn't the case here," the sheriff said. "We can't rule out the birth parents. What's your relationship with them?"

"None," Kate responded. She hadn't thought about the possibility that Jackson's biological parents could've changed their minds. "The adoption was closed, records sealed, based on the mother's request."

"I'll make contact with the agency to see if I can get any additional information from them. I wouldn't count on it without a court order, though," Tommy warned. "What's the name?"

"Safe Haven," she stated.

Tommy nodded. "Good. I know who they are."

Kate held tighter to Jackson. Could the kidnapper have been the birth father? If an investigation was opened, could the birth mother change her mind and take her son away?

"Can you give a description of the man from this morning?" Tommy asked.

"Everything happened so fast. All I can remember is that he was wearing a hoodie and a high turtleneck. He was medium height and had these beady dark eyes against olive skin. It didn't look like he'd shaved in a few days. That's about all I can remember," she said.

"It's a start," Tommy said, and his words were reassuring.

He turned to Dallas with that same questioning look.

"He was young and I didn't recognize his voice, so I don't think he's from around here," Dallas added.

"Is it possible that he's the father? If he's not local, then maybe he just found out about the baby and tracked us down," Kate said, fear racing through her at the thought.

"We can't rule it out, but that's just one of many possibilities," Tommy said. "What about your neighbors on Main? I heard some of them weren't too thrilled when you moved in."

"That's the truth," she said.

"Someone might have tried to scare you enough to get you to close shop and leave town. That's a best-case scenario, as far as I'm concerned, because it would mean they never intended to hurt you or the baby. I need a list of names of family, friends, anyone who you've had a disagreement with, and your employees."

The last part caught her off guard. *Employees?*

That had been Dallas's first suspicion, too.

"Sheriff Johnson, you don't seriously think one of my people could be involved, do you?" she asked, not able to fathom the possibility that one of her own could've turned on her.

"Please, call me Tommy," he said. "And I have to search for all possible connections to the guy we're looking for. You'd be surprised what you find out about the people you think you know best."

In his line of work, she could only imagine how true that statement was. How horrible that anyone she trusted might've been involved.

No, it had to be a stranger.

"I have received threats from some of my business neighbors," she said.

"Tell me more about those," Tommy said, leaning forward.

"A few of the other tenants got together to file a complaint with my landlord. They said they didn't think Main was the appropriate place for a soup kitchen," she explained.

"And what was his response?" Tommy asked.

"He didn't do anything. Said as long as my rent was paid on time and I wasn't doing anything illegal, it wasn't anyone else's concern," she said.

"I'll send one of my deputies to canvass the other tenants and see what he can find out. We'll cover all bases with our investigation." Tommy glanced up from his pad. "How long ago did they make the complaint?"

"Right after we first moved in, so about six months ago," she said.

"Anyone make a formal complaint since?"

She shook her head.

"What about direct threats?" Tommy asked.

"Walter Higgins threatened to force me out of town," she said. "But that was a while ago."

"The town needs your services," Dallas said through clenched teeth. "What kind of jerks complain about a person doing something good for others?"

Jackson stirred at the sound of the loud voice and Kate had to find his binky to pacify him. She shuffled through the diaper bag and came up with it. Jackson settled down as soon as the offering was in his mouth.

"Sorry," Dallas said with an apologetic glance.

"It takes all kinds," Tommy agreed. "I'm guessing they figured it would hurt their business. We'll know more once my deputy speaks to them."

"It's not like people hang around after they eat. There's no loitering allowed downtown," Kate said.

"It's a big escalation to go from complaining to your landlord to a personal attack like this on your son." Based on the sheriff's tone, her neighbors weren't serious suspects. Tommy fired off a text before returning his gaze to Kate. "Now tell me more about your people."

"We have a small office staff," she conceded. "Allen Lentz is my second in command and takes care of everything when I'm not around. Other than that, there are about a dozen cooks and food service workers. Only one is on payroll. The others are volunteers."

Dallas's posture tensed when she mentioned Allen.

Kate registered the subtle change and moved on. She rattled off a few more names and job descriptions.

The sheriff nodded and jotted a few notes on his palm-sized notebook.

"And then there's Randy Ruiz. He keeps the place running on our tight budget. He's our general handyman, muscle and overall miracle worker. Anything heavy needs lifting, he's our guy. He's been especially helpful and dependable in the six months he's been with us." Despite Randy's past, she knew full well that he would never hurt her or Jackson.

Dallas seemed to perk up and she was afraid she'd tried to sell Randy a little too hard. True, she could be a little overprotective of him. He'd had a hard road and she wanted to see him succeed.

"Tabitha Farmer does all our administrative work," Kate added quickly, to keep the conversation moving. "Her official title is volunteer coordinator."

"How close are you with donors?" Tommy asked.

Thinking about the possibility that anyone in her circle could have arranged to have her child kidnapped was enough to turn Kate's stomach. She clasped him closer.

For Jackson's sake, she had to consider what Dallas and the sheriff were saying no matter how much she hated to view her friends and acquaintances with a new lens.

Maybe she was being naive, but she'd been careful to fill her life with genuine people since moving to Bluff from the city. "I maintain a professional distance. However, I do get invited to personal events like weddings and lake house parties."

"And what do you do with your son during these outings?" Dallas interjected, no doubt remembering her conversation with Allen earlier.

"I don't usually go. But I used Allen once," she replied.

"Allen?" Dallas looked up from intensely staring into his cup of coffee.

"We're like a family at the kitchen, and we take care of each other," she said defensively.

Dallas's cocked eyebrow didn't sit well with her. She could feel herself getting more and more defensive.

"Despite what you may be thinking about my employees, they really are a group of decent people," she stated, making eye contact with him—a mistake she was going to regret, given how much her body reacted to the handsome cowboy.

"In my experience, that doesn't always prove the truth," he said, holding her gaze. "When did Allen babysit for you?"

"It's been a while. I used Tabitha one other time recently."

"There a reason for that?" Dallas asked, lifting one dark eyebrow.

"Yes, but it doesn't mean anything," she said quickly. Then she sighed. "Okay, I thought Allen was getting a little too…involved with me and Jackson, so I thought it would be best to use Tabitha instead. He's made it clear that he'd like to date." She involuntarily shivered at the thought of going out with anyone, much less someone from work. "And I'm just not ready for that."

She'd probably emphasized that last bit a little too much, but what did she care if they knew she wasn't in the mood to spend time with a man, any man.

"How old is your son?" Tommy asked, after a few uncomfortable seconds had passed.

"Jackson? He's almost three months old." Kate gently patted her baby on the back, noticing something stir in Dallas's eyes.

"What about friends and family?" Tommy asked, his gaze moving from her to his friend. "Anyone in the area?"

"I didn't know anyone when I moved here, and everything about preparing for the baby was harder than I expected, so, yes, I bonded with my employees."

"You don't have family in this part of Texas?" Tommy asked.

"It's just me and Jackson." She shook her head. "My brother and I are close, but he lives in Richardson, which is a suburb of Dallas. He works nonstop. We started a tech company together after college and made enough to do okay. I sold my interest in the business to have a baby, and now he's running it alone."

"Forgive this question…" Tommy hesitated before continuing, "But how did your brother take the news about you leaving the business the two of you started?"

"Carter? He was fine with my decision. He knew how much I wanted to start a family," she said defensively, a red rash crawling up her neck. And if he hadn't been the most enthusiastic about her choice at first, he'd come around.

"Again, I'm sorry. I had to ask," the sheriff murmured, taking a seat across from her in the sitting area of the office.

"Mind if I ask why you decided to move to Bluff?" Dallas asked.

"There was a need for a soup kitchen, and it's one of the most family-friendly towns in Texas three years running, according to the internet," she said with a shrug. "I thought it would be a good place to bring up a baby."

"Even without family here?" Tommy asked.

"My parents didn't approve of my decision to have a child alone." She didn't really want to go down that road again, explaining the quirks of her family to a stranger. The one where her mother had flipped out and pretended to have a heart attack in order to alter Kate's course.

She glanced at Dallas, ready to defend herself to him, and was surprised by the look of sympathy she got instead.

"I guess I don't understand that particular brand of thinking. It's my personal belief that families should stick together even if they don't agree with each other's decisions," Dallas said, his steely voice sliding right through her.

The sincerity in those words nearly brought her to tears.

Why did it suddenly matter so much what a stranger thought about her or her family?

Dallas noticed Kate's emotional reaction to what he'd said about family. If she really was at odds with hers then they couldn't rule them out as suspects.

"If you'll excuse us, I'd like to speak to the sheriff in the hallway for a minute," he said to her.

"Do we have to wait around? Can we go home now?" she asked, clearly rattled from their conversation.

"I don't think it's safe," Dallas said, before Tommy could answer. "This attack was ambush-style and planned."

His friend was already nodding in agreement. "The kidnapper had a knife and a getaway vehicle," he added. "This indicates premeditation. I'll need to run this scenario through the database and see if there are similar incidents out there. In the meantime, I'd like to send a deputy to your house to take a look around."

Kate gasped and the baby stirred. She immediately went into action, soothing the infant in her arms. He was such a tiny thing and looked so fragile.

"You think they know where I live?" she asked when the baby had settled into the crook of her arm.

"It's a possibility we can't ignore, and I'd rather be safe than sorry," Tommy said.

"Can I see you in the hallway?" Dallas asked Tommy as his friend rose to his feet. Dallas's protective instincts were kicking into high gear.

"If you're going into the hall to discuss my case, I

have a right to know what's being said." Kate's gaze held steady with determination.

Dallas paused at the doorjamb. He couldn't deny that she was right, and yet he wanted to protect her and the baby from hearing what he needed to ask Tommy next.

"Whatever it is, I deserve to hear it," she insisted.

A deep sigh pushed out of his lungs as he turned toward her and stepped back inside, motioning for Tommy to do the same. "The person who did this could be someone who sees Jackson as in the way of being with you," Dallas said, and it seemed to dawn on her that he was talking about Allen.

"Is that why you zeroed in on Allen when I called him earlier?" she asked Dallas pointedly.

"Yes," he answered truthfully.

"We won't stop searching for whoever is behind this," Tommy interjected. "And we're considering all possibilities."

She sat there for a long moment. "What about those other possibilities, Sheriff?" she finally asked.

"It could be that someone wants revenge against you. It's obvious that your child is very important to you and that snatching him would be one way to hurt you," Tommy said. "Or a teen mom has changed her mind about giving up her child. She might've figured out who you were and told the father."

"The adoption was sealed based on the mother's request. However, I made sure of it to avoid that very circumstance. How on earth would she know where Jackson is?" Kate asked.

"You can find out anything with enough money or computer hacking skills," Dallas answered, even though he knew firsthand either option could take time.

And in this case, maybe it had. Jackson was nearly three months old, so that would give someone plenty of time to find the two of them. Grease the right wheels and boom.

"I have to think that if this was a teen mother, then she'd be destitute. Wouldn't she? If she had money or family support, would she really be giving up her baby in the first place?" Kate asked.

Good points.

"How well did you vet this adoption agency before you used them?" Dallas asked.

"They're legitimate, from everything I could tell. I hired a lawyer to oversee things on my end and make sure everything was legal," Kate stated.

"I'll need the name of your lawyer," Tommy said.

"William Seaver."

"Is he someone you knew or was that the first time you'd dealt with him?" Tommy asked.

"My brother connected us. He'd heard of Seaver through a mutual friend. I'm sure he checked him out first," Kate replied.

"I'll run his name and see if we come up with anything in the database," Tommy offered. "We'll be able to narrow down the possibilities once I get all this information into the system and talk to a few people. Also, I'd like to send someone to take a look at your work computers. I need permission from you in order to do that."

Kate gave her consent even though she seemed reluctant. Her reaction was understandable given the circumstances. Dallas would feel the same way if someone wanted to dig around in the ranch's books.

Tommy called for Abigail.

The older woman appeared a moment later and he asked her to send someone to Kate's house to look for anything suspicious, and after that to run information through the database to see if she got a hit on any similar crimes.

As soon as she left, Dallas turned to Kate. "That's everything I wanted to ask or say about your case. If you'll excuse us, I need to discuss a personal matter with the sheriff."

Dallas motioned for his friend to follow him down the hall and into the kitchenette.

"I'm sorry we lost the guy earlier," Tommy said once they were out of earshot. "If we'd caught him, this nightmare could be over for her."

"Whoever it was seems to know how to disappear pretty darn quick," Dallas commented.

"It's difficult to hide something that weighs more than four thousand pounds," Tommy agreed, obviously referring to the minivan.

"You think this whole thing might've been a setup to scare her out of town?" Dallas asked, unsure of how to approach the subject of his possible fatherhood to his friend.

"I thought about that, as well," he admitted. "It's too early to rule anything out even though it's not likely. I'm anxious to see if we find similar crimes in the database. And, of course, we'll look at her personal circles."

Dallas leaned against the counter and folded his arms across his chest. "I've been looking into adoption agencies myself lately."

"Come again?" Tommy's eyebrows arched and Dallas couldn't blame his friend for the surprised glance he shot him. "I know you're not looking to adopt."

"You remember Susan," Dallas began, uneasy about bringing this up. Susan had grown up in Bluff, so Tommy knew her well.

"So glad you finally saw through her and moved on." His friend rolled his eyes. "She was a head case."

Dallas couldn't argue. His judgment had slipped on that one. As soon as he'd figured her out, he'd broken it off. "She might be more than that. She might be the mother of my child."

The possibility that Dallas could be that careless had never occurred to his friend, a fact made clear by the shock on his face. "There's no way you could've done that!" he declared. "Have you considered the possibility that she's lying?"

"Of course I have," Dallas retorted.

"If this is true, and I'm not convinced it is, where is she? And why didn't you come to me before?" Tommy asked.

"Those are good questions," Dallas admitted. "As far as where she went, I'm looking to find an answer. She disappeared from New Mexico and not even her family here in Bluff has seen her since. We both know that she loved it here. Why wouldn't she come back?"

"She didn't say anything to you before she left?" Tommy folded his arms, his forehead wrinkled in disbelief.

"And I didn't get a chance to ask where she was headed before she disappeared."

"What makes you think she used an adoption agency?" Tommy said, after carefully considering the bomb that had just been dropped. "And why *didn't* you come to me sooner?"

"She told me she was pregnant and said we should

get married right away," Dallas said. "I told her to hold on. That I would be there for my child, but that didn't mean we needed to make a mistake."

"That probably went over as well as a cow patty in the pool." His friend grunted. "She seemed bent on signing her name 'O'Brien' from when we were kids."

Dallas had been an idiot not to see through her quicker.

"But that still doesn't answer my question of why you didn't come to me right away," Tommy said.

"I needed answers. You have to follow the letter of the law," Dallas said honestly. "I wanted someone who could see those lines as blurry."

Tommy took a sip of his coffee. "That the only reason?"

"I knew you'd want to help, and you have a lot of restrictions. I wanted fast answers and I wasn't even sure there'd be anything to discuss," Dallas said. "Plus I didn't want to tell anyone until I was sure."

"Didn't you suspect she was seeing someone else?" his friend asked.

Dallas nodded. "I'm certain she was. I figured she was making a bid for my money when she played the pregnancy card with me."

"She probably was." Tommy grimaced. "Which was a good reason for her to disappear when you refused to marry her. She couldn't get caught in her lies."

"I thought of that, too. There's another thing. I used protection, but it's more than that. We didn't exactly… It's not like…" Hell, this was awkward. Dallas didn't make a habit out of talking about his sex life with anyone, not even his best friend. "There was only the one time with Susan and me. Afterward, she got clingy and tried to move into my place. Started trying to rearrange furniture. I caught her in lie after lie and broke it off clean after I witnessed her in the parking lot with that other guy, looking cozy. I'd suspected she was seeing someone else and she got all cagey when I confronted her and asked her to leave. I couldn't prove my suspicion, though. But when she called a few months later and said she was pregnant with my child, I didn't believe her."

"I can't blame you there," Tommy said. "I wouldn't have bought it, either."

"But I can't turn my back until I know for sure." If what Susan said was true, then he'd already messed up what he considered to be the most important job in life—fatherhood.

Dallas had known Susan could be dishonest, and that was the reason he'd broken it off with her. He couldn't love someone he couldn't trust. But he never imagined she'd lie about something this important.

"If there was another guy involved, and I believe you when you say there was, then he could be the father of her child." Tommy sipped his coffee, contemplating what he had just learned.

"You know I can't walk away until I know one way or the other," Dallas said. "This isn't something I can leave to chance."

"And there was that one time," his friend finally said, his forehead pinched with concentration. "So, there is a possibility."

"If I'm honest…yes."

"But it's next to impossible. I know you. There's no way you would risk a pregnancy unless you were one hundred percent sure about a relationship staying together," he stated.

Dallas nodded.

And then it seemed to dawn on Tommy. "But she could've sabotaged your efforts."

"Right."

"Well, damn." His friend's expression changed to one of pity. "I'm sorry to hear this might've happened. Any idea how old the baby would be now?"

"According to my calculations…about three months old." And that was most likely the reason Kate's case hit him so hard. If he had a son, the boy would be around the same age as Jackson.

"Any idea where Susan and the baby may be? It'd be easy enough to get a paternity test once you find them."

Tommy said the exact thing Dallas was thinking.

"I don't know. Neither does the man I hired to find them. She literally disappeared." Ever since hearing about a possible pregnancy with Susan, Dallas had found his world tipped on its axis and he didn't exactly feel like himself.

"There might not even be a baby," Tommy said.

Dallas's phone buzzed. He fished it out of his pocket and then checked the screen. "Susan had a boy," he said, focusing on the message from his private investigator's assistant, Stacy Miller. "And Morton was able to link her to an adoption agency."

Tommy rubbed his chin, deep in thought.

Yeah, Dallas felt the same way right about now. Especially when the next text came through, and he learned the adoption agency was named Safe Haven.

Chapter 4

"I'd say that's a strange coincidence, but I know Safe Haven is the biggest agency in the area, so I guess I'm not too surprised to hear their name again," Tommy said. "And just because Susan had a baby doesn't mean it's yours."

"That kid in there is around the age Susan's baby would be," Dallas supplied.

"Doesn't mean he's Susan's," Tommy said. "Odds are against it."

"I know." Dallas nodded, still trying to digest the news. His plans to help Kate Williams get settled with the sheriff and then head back to the ranch to start a busy day exploded. They had a record number of bred heifers and there'd be a calf-boom early next year that everyone was preparing for. But nothing was more important than this investigation.

"In fact, I'm inclined to think that's the closest thing we have to proof that the baby isn't yours."

Dallas made a move to speak, but his friend raised his hand to stop him. "Hear me out. If Susan was telling the truth and the baby was yours, she would stick around for a DNA test. If she couldn't have your last name, then at least her son would, and he'd have everything that comes with being an O'Brien, which is what we all know she's always wanted anyway."

Dallas thought about those words for a long moment. "I see your point."

"And I'm right."

"Either way, if she used Safe Haven, then everything should be legit, right?" Dallas asked, hoping he'd be able to gain traction and get answers now that a child had been confirmed and he had the name of an adoption agency. His investigator was making good progress.

"They've been investigated before and came up clean." Tommy took another sip of his coffee. "That doesn't mean they are. They could be running an off-the-books program for nontraditional families. Kate's case gives me reason to dig into their records. I'll make a request for access to their files and see how willing they are to cooperate."

"Will you keep me posted on your progress?" Dallas asked, knowing he was asking a lot of his friend.

Tommy nodded. "I'll give you as much information as I legally can."

"As far as Susan goes, you're the only one who knows, and I'd appreciate keeping it between us for now."

"You haven't told anyone in the family?" Tommy asked in surprise.

"Everyone's had enough to deal with since Mom and Pop…" Dallas didn't finish his sentence. He didn't have to. Tommy knew.

"If you have a child, and I'd bet my life you don't, we'll find him," Tommy said, and his words were meant to be reassuring.

He was the only person apart from Dallas's brothers who would know just how much the prospect would gnaw at him. And if his brothers knew, they'd all want to be involved, but Dallas didn't want to sound the alarm just yet. There might not be anything to discuss, and he didn't like getting everyone riled up without cause.

Another text came through on his phone.

"Looks like my guy left to investigate Safe Haven last night and hasn't checked in for work this morning," Dallas murmured. "His assistant said he's always the first one in the office. She's been texting and calling him and he isn't responding."

"We need to talk to her," Tommy said. "You know I'm going to offer my help investigating Susan's disappearance. She's originally from here and that makes her my business."

"And I'll take it," Dallas declared. He wouldn't rely solely on Tommy, because his friend was bound by laws. Dallas saw them more as guidelines when it came to finding out the truth. "We can work both cases and share information. As far as Kate's goes, I'm not sure I like Allen Lentz."

The sheriff leaned against the counter with a questioning look on his face.

"He sounded possessive of her when she called him this morning, and I got the impression he sees the kid as an obstacle to dating her," Dallas explained. The news that Susan had had a boy was still spinning around in the back of his mind.

"I'll have one of my deputies bring him in for questioning this morning," Tommy said. "See if I can get a feel for the guy."

"I'd be interested to hear your take on him," Dallas stated. "I told her not to clue him in to what had happened this morning when she phoned him to open the kitchen for her. And I asked her to put him on speaker so I could hear his voice."

"What was your impression of how he sounded?"

"I didn't like the guy one bit." Dallas would keep the part about feeling a twinge of jealousy to himself.

"Wanting the kid out of the way would give him motive," Tommy said. "I'll run a background check on him when I bring him in. See if there's anything there."

Tommy's phone buzzed. "This is my deputy," he said, after glancing at the screen.

Dallas motioned for them to return to Kate as his friend answered the call.

She was cradling the baby and Dallas got another glimpse of the little boy's black curly hair—hair that looked a lot like his own—as they walked into the office. Dallas wasn't quite ready to accept that possibility completely as he moved closer to get a better look at Jackson. There was no way that Kate's son could be Susan's baby.

Right?

Tommy was right. All of this would be way too much of a coincidence. The adoption agency was large and there had to be dozens of dark-haired baby boys who had been adopted around the same time. Not that logic mattered at a time like this.

Plus, Dallas hadn't considered the fact that if Susan had had his baby, then wouldn't she sue him for support? Or blackmail him to keep the news out of the press?

Until he could be certain, would Dallas look at every boy around Jackson's age with the same question: Could the child be his?

Not knowing would be mental torture at its worst. Every dark-haired boy he came across would get Dallas's mind spinning with possibilities. What-ifs. Was he getting a glimpse of the torment he'd endure for the rest of his life if he couldn't find Susan?

Morton had confirmed there'd been a child, which didn't necessarily mean Dallas was a father. And Morton had been able to link Susan to Safe Haven Adoption Agency. Dallas had every reason to believe that his PI would figure out the rest and Dallas would get his answers very soon. Being in limbo, not knowing, would eat what was left of his stomach lining.

Kate was watching him with a keen eye as Tommy entered the room.

"Can I go home now?" she asked, cradling Jackson tighter.

"This might sound like an odd question, but do you close and lock your doors when you leave your house?" Tommy asked.

"Yes. Of course. I'm a single woman who lives alone with a baby, and I wouldn't dream of leaving myself vulnerable like that," she said, and her cheeks flushed.

Embarrassment?

Dallas noted the emotion as his friend moved on. "Well, then, your place has been broken into," Tommy said.

"What happened?" Kate's face paled.

Dallas's first thought was Allen. But wouldn't he already have access to her house?

Not if she never let him inside. Maybe the date bit was a ruse to get into her home.

"The back door was ajar and the lock had been tampered with. My deputy on the scene said that nothing obvious is missing inside. All the pictures are on the walls and the place is neat." Tommy listened and then said a few "uh-huh"s into the phone.

"Do you have a home computer?" he asked Kate.

"A laptop on my desk," she answered.

Tommy repeated the information to his deputy and then frowned.

So, someone took her laptop?

"Are you sure it was on your desk the last time you saw it?" Tommy asked.

"Certain. Why? Is it gone?"

He nodded. "The cable is still there."

That same look of fear and disbelief filled her blue eyes.

"Can you think of anything on your hard drive someone would want?" Tommy asked. He also asked about work files, but Dallas figured whoever broke into her house wasn't going after those. This had to be personal, especially after the failed kidnapping attempt.

If someone was trying to scare her, then he was doing a great job of it, based on her expression.

"No. Nothing. I keep all my work stuff at the office. I vowed not to work at home ever again once I left the corporate scene. I have a manila file folder in the drawer, right-hand side, about Jackson's adoption," she added, holding tighter to her baby. "Is it missing?"

Once again Tommy relayed the information and then waited. "There's nothing labeled Safe Haven or Adoption," he said at last.

"Then that's it," she murmured, almost too quietly to hear.

Tommy thanked his deputy and ended the call. "How did you get connected with Safe Haven?"

"Through my lawyer. He was the one who arranged everything," she said, and based on her expression, Dallas figured her brain was most likely clicking through possibilities.

He made a mental note that they needed to speak to her brother, and the rest of her family, as well. Dallas didn't like to think that her family wouldn't be 100 percent supportive of her choices, but he wasn't stupid. He couldn't fathom it, but if her mother was really against the adoption, then she could be trying to interfere by shaking Kate up. Maybe even hoping that she'd realize she'd made a mistake.

If that were true, then Kate's mother hadn't seen the woman holding Jackson.

A family intervention, albeit misguided, would be so much better than the other options Kate faced. Such as an employee's fixation or the fact that this could've been a shady adoption gone bad for Safe Haven.

Kate held on to Jackson as if he'd drop off a canyon wall if she let go. She'd walked away from the only life she'd ever known to have a chance at a family. Her husband, Robert Bass, had filed for divorce within weeks of learning that she had a 4 percent chance of ever getting pregnant. Four percent.

Half the reason she'd worked so hard at the start-up was so she could sell her interests when she became pregnant and be home with the baby. And then suddenly that wasn't going to be an option, ever.

At thirty-three, she'd had everything she thought she wanted, a nice house, a Suburban and a husband. She'd believed she was on the track to happiness, and it was easy to ignore shortcomings in her marriage to Robert considering how much time she spent at the office. He worked all the time, too.

Within weeks of learning the devastating news, her entire life had turned upside down, and all she could do was kick herself for not seeing it coming earlier. All those times Robert had decided to stay late at the office even when she'd made special arrangements to leave early… And she'd been too busy to really notice how frequent his ski trips had become—ski trips she later realized hadn't been with his best friend, but with his coworker Olivia Gail.

In fact, he'd been on the road more than he was home and Kate felt like an idiot for thinking he was working hard to secure a future for their family, too.

Whatever love had been between them had died long before she'd been willing to acknowledge it. Or had she kept herself too busy to notice? Too busy to face the reality of the loneliness that had become her life?

She'd been trapped with a husband who cared for her but didn't love her. And the worst part was that she'd kept convincing herself that they'd be able to get back what they'd had in the early days of their relationship as soon as she had more time or had a baby. How crazy was it to think a child would somehow make things better, make them a family?

To make matters worse, Kate Williams didn't give up. Hard work and staying the course had made her business a success. It had gotten her through a difficult childhood with a mother who was bent on controlling her. Was her mother's lack of real love the reason Kate had fallen for Robert in the first place? Was she seeking approval from someone who would never give it?

Robert had been all about keeping his tee time and staying on track with his future career plans. He even seemed content to have a family with Kate though he no longer loved her.

And then when the disappointing news had come that having a baby would be next to impossible, he'd started traveling even more. He'd lost interest in her sexually.

Kate had reasoned that he needed time to process the news, as she did. It was a bomb she'd never expected to be dropped on her, especially not when her biological clock wouldn't expire for years.

Robert's decision to give up on the marriage shouldn't have come as a complete shock. Except that she'd ignored or made excuses for every single one of the signs that it was coming.

Given the amount of time he had spent calculating return on investment with his stock portfolio, she should've realized he'd cut his losses with her when she was no longer a good deal. Apparently, she hadn't been worth the risk. It had taken Robert about six weeks to divest himself of her.

Kate had signed the divorce papers and then made a life-changing decision.

She was going to have a family anyway.

When she'd told Carter, her brother, he'd scoffed at the idea, initially telling her to take a long vacation instead. Then he'd reminded her how much she'd be hurting their mother, as if Charlotte Williams hadn't already made her position clear throughout the whole divorce. Chip and Charlotte had been the perfect parents, to hear her mother talk about their life.

Kate had been clear on what she wanted, and being a mother had more to do with love than DNA, so she'd decided to adopt.

Carter came to his senses, apologized and then located the best adoption attorney he could find.

Not long after, Kate had sold her interests in the company and moved to Bluff.

Life might have thrown her a twist, but that didn't mean she had to roll over and take it.

The move had given her a new lease on life. Becoming Jackson's mother was the greatest joy she'd experienced. And, dammit, no one would take that or him away from her.

A voice she immediately recognized as Allen's boomed from the other room.

Kate popped to her feet. "Why's he here?" she asked, glancing from Tommy to Dallas.

"I'll be interviewing everyone on your staff," the sheriff said, drawing her gaze back to him. "Would your family members be willing to come down and speak to us, as well?"

"My family?" she echoed, as Allen walked into the office.

"What's going on?" he asked, concern widening his eyes as he zeroed in on Kate and the baby.

Dallas stepped in front of her, blocking his path.

"Did something happen?" Allen shouted over him. "Are you okay?"

"I'm fine now," she said, hating that her employees would be worried.

"Will someone please tell me what's going on?" Allen begged, and there was desperation in his voice as he was being hauled away.

Dallas positioned himself near the two-way mirror on the other side of the interview room. His cup of coffee had long ago gone cold, but holding on to it gave him something to do with his hands.

"Miss Williams authorized my department to take a look at your computer," Tommy said to Allen.

"So what?" The confusion on the guy's face was either an award-worthy acting job or he really didn't have a clue.

"Would you agree to give one of my deputies access to your house?" Tommy asked. He knew full well that an innocent guy would have nothing to hide.

"Not until you tell me what this is about," Allen retorted.

Fair enough.

"We're looking for information that will aid an ongoing investigation," Tommy hedged.

"One that involves my boss." It wasn't a question.

The lawman nodded.

"Look, I would do anything to help Kate. She's like family to me," Allen said. "But I have no idea what's going on."

So asking out a family member was okay in Allen's book? Dallas covered up his cough.

"And I'm not sure how invading my privacy will accomplish your mission, so I'm afraid you'll have to tell me a little bit more about what you think you'll find," Allen added.

Dallas had been sure this guy was guilty as sin, but something was gnawing at him and he couldn't figure out what. He might be covering for a crush he had on his boss and didn't want to be embarrassed any further.

Based on his actions so far, Allen was coming across as a concerned friend. But then, he might just be that good at acting.

Dallas returned to Tommy's office, where Kate waited.

"How long has Allen worked for you?" he asked.

"He was my first hire," she said, looking as if she was about to be sick. "So, about six months now."

"Do want water or something else to drink?" Dallas asked.

She shook her head and mumbled that she was fine.

Tommy walked in.

"How would you characterize your relationship with Allen Lentz?" he asked Kate.

"Professional," she retorted.

"I had to ask." Tommy brought his hand up defensively.

"But he wasn't kidding about our office being like a family. Do you really think he broke into my house and stole my laptop and adoption files?" she asked Tommy, looking as if she was trying to let that possibility sink in.

"Not completely, no," he answered. "It doesn't mean he's not involved, though. The kidnapping attempt could've been a distraction while the burglar got what he really wanted."

Kate pinched the bridge of her nose as though staving off a headache.

Tommy's cell buzzed. He glanced at the screen. "If you'll excuse me."

Kate nodded as Tommy hurried out of the room.

Dallas didn't say that none of this added up quite in the way he wanted it to. All her employees would know that she was already at the soup kitchen. If someone wanted her laptop and adoption files, all he had to do was break in while she was gone. But it was clear that her adoption was at the center of the kidnapping attempt. Could someone be trying to erase the paperwork trail? "Do you ever go back to your place after leaving for work?"

"Not unless I've forgotten something for Jackson," she said.

"Do you normally take him to work with you?" Dallas asked.

"Yes. And then Mrs. Zilker picks him up, although sometimes she sticks around the office for a while," Kate stated. "Oh, no. I forgot to let her know I don't need her today."

"Then someone could've been trying to make sure you didn't go back home," Dallas said.

"I hope that's all it is and not the fact that someone wants to take Jackson away from me." Kate clutched him closer, as if daring anyone to try.

"If Allen will agree to let a deputy search his house, then that'll go a long way toward clearing him," Dallas said.

"I hope he does so we can cross him off the suspect

list," she said, and she sounded as if she really didn't want her friend to be involved, more than that she was convinced he wasn't.

Tommy entered the room with a stark expression.

Dallas didn't like the look on his friend's face.

"What is it?" he asked.

"A vehicle registered to Wayne Morton was found abandoned off of Farm Road 23," Tommy said, a look of apology in his eyes. "They found blood spatter but no sign of a body."

"I'm guessing there's no other indication of Morton anywhere?" Dallas asked. But he already knew the answer to that question and an ominous feeling settled over him. Between the blood spatter and the fact that Morton hadn't checked in with his assistant this morning, Dallas feared the worst. "We need to talk to Stacy to find out what she knows about his itinerary."

"No. I need to talk to his assistant," Tommy said. "I can send a deputy to Morton's office."

"Might be best if I speak to her personally. She might open up to me more than a stranger," Dallas suggested. He felt guilt settle heavy on his shoulders, knowing that if anything had happened to Morton it could be his fault. History would be repeating itself. He muttered a curse too low for anyone else to hear.

"Does this have anything to do with my case?" Kate asked. "Because if it does, I'd like to go with you."

"No," Dallas said. "You should stay here in the sheriff's office just to be safe."

He hadn't anticipated the uncomfortable feeling he got in his gut at the thought of leaving her. She'd be in good hands with Tommy and yet he felt the need to stick around and watch over her. He told himself that it was all protective instinct and had nothing to do with the sizzle of attraction he felt when she was near.

"Hold on a sec. Did Lentz give you permission to search his place?" Dallas asked Tommy, figuring it would be good to rule out one suspect.

His friend said, "No."

"Are you done questioning him?" Dallas pressed.

Tommy frowned. "He lawyered up."

Chapter 5

"Deputy Lopez just briefed me on the computer search at the soup kitchen," Tommy said to Dallas. "Turns out that Allen Lentz has an unusual amount of pictures of Ms. Williams on cloud storage that we accessed via his computer."

Dallas didn't like the sound of that.

"He takes all the office party photos." Kate jumped to Lentz's defense.

Abigail knocked on the door to Tommy's office and all eyes focused on her. "There have been six other kidnappings in the past three weeks in Texas, all boys, all adopted and all at gunpoint."

"He used a knife with me," Kate stated, shivering at the thought that it could've been worse.

"The first infant was found three days later in a car seat on the steps of his day care center," she said. "The second and third were found several days after their disappearances, under similar circumstances."

"Three are still missing?" Tommy asked.

His secretary nodded. "The three most recent ones."

"Was there a ransom demand in any of the cases?" Tommy asked.

"Not once," she stated.

"Have Deputy Solomon check into the incidences to see if we can find a link to Safe Haven," Tommy said.

Kate perked up. "That means Allen is innocent, right?"

The sheriff looked from Dallas to her apologetically. "Not necessarily. He could be mimicking other kidnappings to distract attention away from him. The MO was different with you and I can't rule anyone out until I know why."

"To be clear, someone is taking babies who are the same sex and around the same age with no ransom demand and then making sure they're found a couple of days later?" Dallas asked Tommy.

"I'm inclined to draw the same conclusion," Tommy said. "The kidnappers are looking for a specific child."

Abigail moved to Kate, motioning toward Jackson. "Let me take him in the other room where he can sleep peacefully."

Kate stilled.

"I'll take good care of him. Don't you worry," Abigail assured her. "He's in good hands with me."

"Thank you." She handed over her sleeping baby. "So the pictures you found on Allen's computer aren't office pictures, are they?" she said, sinking back into the chair.

"No, ma'am." Tommy waved her and Dallas over

to his desk and then pulled up a file on his computer, positioning the monitor for all three of them to see.

One by one, pictures of Kate filled the screen.

"These were taken in my house," she said, shock evident in her voice.

"Actually, from outside your house, like through a window," Dallas observed.

"He's been watching me?" Her hand covered her mouth as she gasped. "Pictures of me sleeping?"

The questions were rhetorical, and the hurt and disbelief audible in them was like a punch to Dallas's gut.

He reached out to comfort her, not expecting her to spin around into his arms and bury her face in his chest.

This close, he felt her body trembling. A curse tore from his lips as he pulled her nearer, ignoring how soft her skin was or how well she fitted in his arms. His attraction to her was going to be a problem if he didn't keep it in check.

"Sheriff, can I see you in the hallway for a moment?" Deputy Lopez peeked inside the door.

Tommy agreed and then shot a warning look toward Dallas. He was telling him not to get too close to the victim, and Dallas couldn't ignore the fact that it was sound advice.

He had moved past logic and gone straight to primal instinct the second her body pressed to his.

But he wasn't stupid enough to confuse this for anything more than what it was for her—comfort from a stranger.

The sudden urge to lift her chin and capture her mouth with his wasn't logical, either. But Dallas couldn't regret it the instant her pink lips pressed against his.

Her arms came up to his chest, her palms flat against his pecs.

As if they both suddenly realized where they were and that someone could walk through that door at any second, they pulled back, hearts pounding in rhythm.

Chemistry sizzled between them, charging the air.

Tommy walked in and his tense expression signaled more bad news.

"Two things," he stated. "First, Morton's body has been found floating in the lake on the Hatches' property. He'd been fatally shot, but the perp tied a bag of heavy rocks around his midsection."

"Amateurs?" Dallas asked.

"It would appear so," Tommy agreed. "And it looks like they did this on the spur of the moment, using whatever they could find."

"What else?" Dallas was trying to digest this news. He was the one who'd gotten Morton involved in this case and now the PI was dead. Guilt sat heavy on his chest as he tried to take a breath.

"The other news—" he glanced from Dallas to Kate "—is that more pictures were found at Lentz's place. A lot of them."

"And that would confirm his fixation on Kate," Dallas said, which was the logical assumption. But he had a gnawing feeling that the guy was innocent. Dallas wanted him to be guilty. That would tie this whole troubling case up with a bow. Lentz would be arrested. Kate and Jackson would be safe. Problem solved.

And yet Dallas worried this was more complicated. Babies were going missing. Investigating Safe

Haven had most likely cost Morton his life. Anger pierced Dallas, leaving a huge hole in his chest.

Kate took a step back, grabbing the desk to steady herself. "What kind of pictures?"

"Just like the ones you saw earlier," Tommy said. "And there were ones with markings across Jackson's face."

Kate gasped again, looking stunned. "I can't believe Allen would do something like that. I know I saw the photos with my own eyes, but it doesn't make any sense."

As much as Dallas didn't like the guy, part of him agreed with Kate. This was too easy. "Does Allen have any enemies? Did he get into a fight with anyone lately?"

Someone could be setting up Lentz. But who? And why?

Her lips pressed together and Dallas forced himself not to stare. Thinking about that kiss was inappropriate as hell and yet there it was anyway.

"The baby keeps me busy. I don't really socialize with anyone outside of work, so I couldn't say for sure about his personal life." She shot an apologetic look toward Tommy. "He didn't talk about having any arguments and no one's been around the soup kitchen."

"Kate!" The anguish in Allen's voice shattered the silence in the hallway. "Let me talk to Kate. Those aren't my pictures. I don't know where they came from. I'm being set up."

Dallas heard one of the deputies shuffling Lentz down the hall, most likely to a jail cell.

"I would never do something like this. I love Jackson," the man shouted, and it visibly shook Kate.

She glanced around the room. "I honestly don't know what to say. I have no idea who would do this to him, and even though those pictures completely creep me out, I still can't believe he would do something like this."

Dallas rubbed his chin. "It would have to be someone with access to his computer at work and at his home."

Kate gripped the desk. "There's one person I can think of who would have access to both, but there's no way he would do anything like this."

Dallas nodded, urging her to keep talking.

"My handyman, Randy Ruiz," she finally said and then bit her bottom lip.

"I'll check him out." Tommy typed the name into the system. "We ran Lentz earlier and his background check came up clean, by the way."

"And Ruiz?" Dallas asked.

"He has a record," Tommy noted, staring at his computer screen.

"I know. I knew that when I hired him. But that was a long time ago, and good people deserve a second chance," Kate said. "He's never been so much as late to work, let alone missed a day. He has a wonderful family."

And a rap sheet, Dallas thought.

Tommy locked gazes with him. "Ruiz has a history of burglary."

"So he would know how to get in and out of a house without anyone seeing him," Dallas confirmed.

"He wouldn't have had to. Allen gave him a copy of his keys so he could fix a leaky pipe in his downstairs bathroom," Kate declared.

Dallas could only imagine how difficult it must be to have to think about the possibility that people she trusted would do something to hurt her. The employees at the ranch were more family than most of Dallas's cousins.

"We need to bring in Ruiz for questioning," Tommy said.

"I'm so sorry this is happening, Randy," Kate said to her employee as he was led into the sheriff's office.

"Someone tried to hurt you and little Jackson?" Randy asked, concern lines bracketing his mouth.

"Yes. This morning," she said.

"That's why you weren't at work today?"

She nodded.

"Mrs. Zilker was worried. Allen told her everything was fine and to take the day off," Randy said.

Dallas couldn't help but notice the prison tattoos on the handyman's arms when he took off his jacket. The guy was a five-foot-nine wall of solid muscle. He had clean-cut dark hair and a trim mustache. His genuine worry made him seem far less threatening. And even though his job could have him snaking out a toilet at a moment's notice, his jeans looked new and had been pressed. He definitely fit the bill of someone who cared about doing a good job.

Kate nodded. "I told the sheriff how much you love your job and what an exemplary employee you are," she said to Randy. "I'm so sorry you have to come here and answer questions."

"I'm not," he said emphatically. "If this helps them find the guy who tried to kidnap Jackson, then I want to do everything I can to help."

Kate thanked him.

Based on his serious expression, he meant every word. And that pretty much ruled him out as a suspect, because with his record, Dallas would've thought he'd be offended. His genuine lack of self-concern said he would jump through any hoop if it meant figuring out who was trying to hurt Kate.

But the interview wasn't a total loss. They'd ruled someone out and it was possible that Randy had seen or heard something that could help them figure out if anyone else in the office was involved.

Tommy shot a sideways glance toward Dallas and he immediately knew that his friend thought the same thing.

"I heard about what happened to Allen," Randy said, shaking his head, his slight Hispanic accent barely noticeable.

Interesting word choices, Dallas noted.

"I made mistakes in the past, but I'm a family man now," he said to the sheriff. "Don't waste your time looking at me."

"All I need is for you to answer a few questions so we can figure out who did this," Tommy replied, a hint of admiration in his eyes.

"Allen's a good guy," Randy said. "He would never do anything to hurt Miss Kate or her baby."

Dallas believed that to be true, too. It was almost too easy to pin this on Lentz. And that made Dallas believe that the guy might have been set up.

"How long did it take Deputy Lopez to find the pictures on Lentz's computer?" Dallas asked Tommy.

"Not long. Why?" his friend asked.

"How good is Allen with computers?" Dallas asked

Randy, and Tommy's nod of approval said he'd figured out where Dallas was going with this.

"That man knows his way around them for sure. He helps me all the time with the one I have at home for my kids," the handyman said.

Dallas turned to Kate. He needed a reason to rule out Lentz. "How would you classify Allen's computer skills?"

"Very competent," she said, and then it must've dawned on her. "And you're thinking why wouldn't he have password protected those files, aren't you?"

"That's exactly what I'm thinking," he agreed. "I'm sure the deputies could've gotten to those files, given enough time, even if they'd been buried. But it was easy."

"Too easy," Tommy said, "because they weren't hidden at all."

"And then at Allen's house they happen to find even more damning evidence," Dallas said.

Kate was already rocking her head. "The black bars across Jackson's face."

"Let's take a closer look at some of those pics and see if we can get a clue." Tommy moved to his computer and his fingers went to work on the keyboard.

"If not Allen, then who took the pictures?" she wondered.

"Great question," Dallas said.

Tommy clicked through the pictures once again, slowly this time.

"What are you looking for?" Dallas asked.

"Clues to when these pictures were taken. I'm trying to piece together a timeline. It'll take a while to have all the evidence analyzed, but maybe we can figure out a window and then narrow down the possibilities. Kate, can you identify when you wore those pajamas?"

"Hard to tell. I wear something like those most nights." A red blush crawled up her neck to her cheeks.

Randy's gaze immediately dropped to the floor, as if to spare her further embarrassment.

"I can clear the room if you'd be more comfortable doing this alone," Tommy said to her.

"No. It's fine," she said. The red blush on her cheeks belied her words. "I always wear an oversize T-shirt. I rotate between a couple, so that could be any night."

She studied the new picture on the screen. "This one was recent." She pointed to a mug on the side table next to her bed. "I just started drinking tea within the last two weeks."

"Good," Tommy said. "Could most of these pictures have been taken within that time frame?"

"Let's see," she said, studying each one as more flashed across the screen. "Yes. All of them could."

"So, someone gets happy with a camera in the past two weeks and then tries to snatch Jackson, all while pointing the finger at Allen to distract attention from the real person behind this." Dallas summed it up. On a larger scale, baby boys around Jackson's age were being kidnapped and released.

"And then we have the issue of Kate's kidnapping attempt being slightly different than the others," Tommy said, and that was exactly Dallas's next thought. Jackson's kidnapper had used a knife. And someone had broken into her house and stolen her adoption files.

"Were there break-ins at the other houses?" Dallas asked.

Tommy said there weren't.

"I should go." He needed to get over and talk to Stacy, to see what else she knew about Morton.

"I know what you're thinking. I'm coming with you," Tommy said.

"I might get more out of Stacy if I'm on my own," Dallas pointed out. "And I need to follow up with Safe Haven."

"This is a murder investigation, Dallas. I'm going with you or you're not going at all." The lawman's tone left no room for argument.

"I'm coming, too," Kate said. Her eyes fixed on Dallas and all he could see was that same determination he'd noted earlier when someone had been trying to snatch her baby from her arms.

"Absolutely not." He didn't have to think about the answer to that one.

"If this involves Jackson, then I'm coming, and you can't stop me," she said emphatically.

"I don't know if it does or not yet." If someone at the adoption agency was involved in Morton's murder and that same person was after Jackson, the last thing Dallas intended to do was put Kate in harm's way.

"That's the place I adopted him and my files are missing from home," she said. "I have to believe that's not a coincidence."

Maybe not.

"It might be best for you to stay put," Dallas countered. The thought that this could be one of her neighbors died on the vine.

"I don't have to ask your permission. I can go with or without you." She stood her ground. "I have a relationship with them and I have every right to request my file and talk to the people there who were involved in my case."

Dallas blew out a frustrated breath, suspecting that if she went in alone she could be walking into danger. A perp could be watching the place, seeing who came and went to get information.

"Both of you need to calm down," Tommy said. "I don't want either one of you going without me, especially if they're responsible for a murder. You'd be putting yourself in unnecessary danger."

Tommy was right about one thing. Kate had no business investigating Safe Haven, given what had happened to Morton after he'd started going down that route.

"A man is dead because of me," Dallas said to his friend.

"He was a professional and he knew the risks his job carried," the lawman said soberly.

"I hired him and he was there because of me. I'm responsible for him," Dallas countered, realizing he was arguing with the one man who'd understand taking risks on his job.

"Does this mean Allen is in the clear?" Randy asked.

"It does for now," the sheriff said.

"Good. Then I can give him a ride home."

"Not yet," Tommy said. "I have a few more questions for him, so I want him to stick around."

Dallas stood and thanked the handyman, offering a handshake.

"I know this is asking a lot," Kate interjected, "but could you go back to the office? I have no idea when I'll be able to return, and I want to make sure people are being fed."

"Of course," Randy said. "We'll keep things running until you can come back."

"Thank you!" Kate rose to her feet and gave him a hug. "I'm so sorry that this is happening and I hope you know how much I trust you and the rest of the staff."

"Don't worry about us or the soup kitchen." Randy looked her in the eye. "We're all adults. We can handle this. Just take care of yourself and little Jackson and leave the rest up to us."

Dallas could feel the sense of family in the room. He would know, because he had five brothers who would be saying the same things had they known what was going on.

Which reminded him that he needed to fill them in on his situation with Susan. Just not yet.

With Morton's death, Dallas also realized that Susan could have gotten involved with the wrong people and ended up in over her head. The two of them as a couple didn't work, but he had some residual feelings for her. She was someone he'd dated and at one time had wanted to get to know better. They'd grown up in the same town and had known each other for years. Dallas didn't wish this on anyone and especially not Susan. Baby drama aside, he hoped that she hadn't done something to put herself at risk.

For her sake as much as his, Dallas needed to know what had happened to her and the baby she'd given birth to.

As he started toward the door, he realized that he had no means of transportation. He also realized he had a shadow. Kate was buttoning up her coat as she followed him.

He stopped and she had to put on the brakes in order

to avoid walking straight into him. Her flat palms on his back brought a jolt of electricity.

Dallas turned around quickly and Kate took a step back. "My pickup is at the supply store parking lot. Can you take me to it?"

"For the record, I don't like either one of you anywhere near the attempted kidnapping site or Safe Haven," Tommy interjected.

Dallas shot his friend a telling look. "I'm going to talk to Stacy first."

"While you do that, I'll investigate the crime scene," the sheriff conceded. "Keep me posted on what you find out from her and let her know that I'll be stopping by her office for a statement later today."

Kate hated the thought of being separated from Jackson, to the point her heart hurt. If leaving to find answers wasn't a trade-off for his ultimate safety, then she wouldn't be able to go, not even knowing he'd be with someone as competent as Abigail. His security had to be the priority.

For a second, Kate considered calling her babysitter, but after this morning's kidnapping attempt there was no way she would risk putting Mrs. Zilker in danger.

Abigail stopped at the doorway, Jackson resting peacefully in her arms. "Walter Higgins is refusing to answer questions without an attorney present."

"He's always been a stubborn one." Tommy shook his head and shrugged. "We'll give it to him his way. Send Deputy Lopez to pick him up and bring him in. I doubt he'll be useful given the turn of events, but I'd like him to know that we're aware of his antics with Ms. Williams."

"Yes, sir."

"Any news about the other incidences?" the sheriff asked.

Her gaze bounced from Kate to him, making the hair on Kate's arms stand on end. "So far, we've been able to make contact with one of the families."

"And?" Tommy asked.

"They adopted their son from Safe Haven almost three months ago," Abigail stated, with an apologetic glance toward Kate.

Kate struggled to breathe as anxiety caused her chest to squeeze.

"Any other obvious connections to our current case?" he continued.

"Other than the fact they've all occurred between Houston and San Antonio?" Abigail asked.

Tommy nodded.

"That's all I have so far," she replied. "We'll know more as we hear back from the other families."

Kate stepped forward and kissed Jackson, praying this would not be the last time she saw him. Then she walked out the door and toward her car.

"We need to switch to my pickup at some point today," Dallas said, once they were in the parking lot.

"Hold on a second. I have a few questions before we leave." She stopped cold. She'd been so distracted by her own problems, she hadn't stopped to really think about everything she'd heard at the sheriff's office.

Dallas turned around and faced her.

"What is your connection to Safe Haven?" she asked.

"I've been helping a close friend figure out if he's a father or not," he said, and something told her there was more to that story than he was sharing. "He wants to keep his identity out of the papers, so he asked me to help. I hired Morton to investigate and you know the rest from there."

Kate tossed him her keys. No way could she concentrate on driving in her current state.

"My adoption was legal," she said, once she was buckled in. "I followed all the right channels."

Kate pressed her fingers to her temples to stave off the headache threatening.

Dallas glanced at her and then quickly focused on the road again. "When was the last time you ate?"

"Last night, I think," she said. "Guess I shouldn't have had that cup of coffee on an empty stomach. I feel nauseous."

Dallas cut right.

"Where are you going?" she asked.

"Somewhere I can get you something to eat," he said in a don't-argue-with-me tone.

So she didn't. There wouldn't be a point, and Kate didn't have the energy anyway. She'd drained herself putting up enough of a fight to go with him.

"What about your truck?"

"We'll swing by and pick it up after I get food in you."

She expected Dallas to pull into the first fast-food drive-through they saw, but there were none on the route he chose. After a good twenty minutes, she started to ask where he was taking her and then saw the sign for his family's ranch, Cattlemen Crime Club.

"Why are we here?" she asked. Wasn't this too far out of the way?

"Because I need to know that you'll be safe while I

feed you," Dallas said, pulling up to the first gate and entering a code. A security officer waved as Dallas passed through the second checkpoint.

"I still think these guys are after Jackson, not me," she countered. "But I won't argue, since we're already here."

Kate didn't want to admit to being curious about Dallas. In fact, she wanted to know more about him, and that was a surprise given that she didn't think it would be possible for her to be interested in another man so soon after Robert.

Interest wasn't necessarily the word she'd use to describe what she was feeling for Dallas. Attraction? Sizzle? She felt those in spades. Neither seemed appropriate under the circumstances. But there was something about the strong cowboy that pulled her toward him. Something she'd never felt with another man. Not even with Robert. And she wasn't sure how to begin to process that. Kate had loved Robert…hadn't she?

She'd been married to the man and yet she hadn't felt this strong of a pull toward him. There was something about the cowboy that caused goose bumps on her arms every time he was near. So much more than sexual attraction.

And even in all the craziness, she couldn't ignore the heat of that kiss.

Chapter 6

To say the ranch was impressive was like saying Bill Gates had done okay for himself.

The land itself was stunning even though the cold front had stripped trees of their foliage, scattering orange and brown leaves across the front lawn.

The main building was especially striking. It was an imposing two stories with white siding and black shutters bracketing the windows. Grand white columns with orange and black ribbons adorned the expansive porch filled with black, orange and white pumpkins. Large pots of yellow and orange gerbera daisies led up the couple of stairs to the veranda, where pairs of white rocking chairs grouped together on both sides. The dark silhouette of a witch loomed in the top right window. Kate counted fourteen in all, including a set of French doors on the second floor complete with a quaint terrace. When she thought of a Texas ranch, this was exactly the kind of picture that would've come to mind.

The place was alive with charm and a very big part of her wished this for Jackson. Given the strain on her family since the divorce and the adoption, she didn't expect to go home for the holidays this year.

In fact, that was the last fight she and her mother had had.

If her mom couldn't support her decision and accept Jackson, then Kate had no intention of visiting at Halloween, Thanksgiving or anytime. Jackson was just as much a part of the family as she was, so rejecting him was no different than rejecting her.

Thinking about the fight still made her sad and she wished her mother understood. But her mom had been clear. Kate had been clear. And neither seemed ready to budge.

And right now, Kate had bigger problems than disagreeing with her mother over her adoption.

"Do you live here?" Kate asked, wiping away a sneaky tear while trying to take in all the warmth and grandeur of the place.

"I do now but not in this building. This was my parents' home. They opened up a wing for club guests and there are offices on the other side. My brothers and I each have our own hacienda at various places on the land," he said. "Our parents built them in hopes we'd stay on after college."

"Your parents don't live here anymore?" she asked, unable to imagine leaving such a beautiful home.

Dallas shook his head, and seeing the look on his

face, a mix of sorrow and reverence, she regretted the question.

"They died a few weeks ago." He said the words quietly, but the anguish in his voice nearly robbed her of breath.

She exhaled and said, "I'm so sorry."

He put the car in Park, cut the engine and stared out the front window for a few seconds. "Let's get some food in you," he finally said. Then he opened the door and exited the car.

Before she could get her seat belt off, Dallas was opening her door and holding out his hand. She was greeted by a chocolate Lab.

"Who's this guy?" she asked, patting him on the head.

"That's Denali. Been in the family fourteen years," Dallas said.

"He's beautiful." She took his outstretched hand, ignoring the sensual shivers vibrating up her arm from the point of contact. What could she say? Dallas was strong, handsome. The cowboy had shown up just in time to save her and her son from a terrible fate. So she couldn't deny a powerful attraction.

He was also a complete stranger, a little voice reminded her—a voice that repeated those words louder, a warning from the logical side of her brain.

Maybe if she had taken more time to get to know Robert before she'd jumped into a relationship and marriage, things might've turned out differently, that same annoying voice warned.

Instead, she'd allowed herself to be influenced by his easy charm and good looks. She'd gone against her better judgment after a couple of months of dating when he'd handed her a glass of wine and asked if she wanted to "get hitched and make babies."

Looking back, a piece of her, the logical side, had known all along that she didn't know Robert well enough to make a lifelong commitment. She'd been young and had given in to impulse.

And when things didn't go as planned, he'd bolted.

Not that she could really blame him for wanting out when she couldn't make the last part happen. He'd been clear that babies had been part of the deal all along. And his attention had wandered after that. Or maybe even before. Kate couldn't be sure. All she knew for certain was the information in the texts that she'd seen once she'd figured out he was having an affair. Even though she should've read the signs long before, and maybe a little part of her knew, there was still something about discovering proof of his lies—seeing them right there in front of her—that had knocked the wind out of her.

Logically, she knew all men were not Robert. But her heart, the part of her that withstood reason, knew she'd never be able to completely trust a man or a relationship again. She'd always question her judgment when it came to them now.

Dallas held the front door open for her as she forced her thoughts to the present. One step at a time, she entered the O'Brien home. The inside was even more breathtaking than the outside, if that was possible.

"Did you grow up here?" She imagined him and his brothers chasing each other up one side and down the other of the twin staircases in the foyer.

"Yes, ma'am," Dallas said, and there was something

about his deep baritone that sent sensual shivers racing down her back.

"It must've been a wonderful childhood," she said and then chided herself for saying it out loud. She, of all people, should know that looks could be deceiving when it came to families. Maybe her perfect-on-the-outside relationship with Robert had been easy to fake, given that she'd grown up in a similar situation. Oh, the holiday cards her mother had insisted on posing for and sending out had painted a different picture. In those, they'd looked like the ideal family, complete with the requisite perfect boy and girl. What couldn't be seen in those paper faces and forced smiles was the constant bickering between her parents. Or how much her mom had needed both her children to be perfect in every way.

Kate could still see the disappointment in her mother's eyes when she'd brought home a C in Lit or when her SAT scores didn't quite measure up to expectations.

Their relationship had really started to fragment when Kate left for college and declared that she wanted to study computers instead of interior design. Her mom had thrown another fit, saying that career field was unfeminine.

Even when Kate and Carter had created a successful tech business together, their mother hadn't changed her position. She'd mostly been impressed with Carter and had insinuated that he'd carried Kate.

In selling her share, she'd done well enough to buy a house in Bluff, finance an adoption and provide the seed money to start The Food Project. And she'd still managed to save enough money for Jackson to study whatever he wanted in college.

"It was," Dallas said, bringing her out of her reverie. And she realized he'd been studying her reaction all along.

"So you spent your whole life here?" Kate asked, following him down the hall and into an impressive kitchen, the chocolate Lab at her heels.

There were batches of cookies in various stages of cooking. The place smelled like warmth and fall and everything wonderful. "Is that hot apple cider mulling on the stove?"

Dallas nodded and gave a half smile. "Janis goes all out this time of year through New Year's. She keeps this place running and has been helping my family most of my life. Would you like some cider?"

An older woman padded in from the hallway. "Dallas O'Brien, what are you doing in my kitchen this late? I expected you two hours ago for lunch," she said.

"Janis, I'd like you to meet Kate." He motioned toward her.

Janis wasn't tall, had to be right at five foot or a little more. She was round and grandmotherly with soft features.

Kate held out her hand. "Nice to meet you."

"My apologies for being so rude. I didn't realize Dallas had company," Janis said, shaking Kate's hand heartily. She had on a witch hat and her face was painted green.

Janis must've caught Kate's once-over because she added, "And forgive this old outfit. I just delivered cookies to The Learning Bridge Preschool for Special Children."

"You look—"

"Silly to anyone standing over three feet tall," Janis said drolly, cutting Kate off.

"I was going to say 'as adorable as a witch.'"

The woman grinned from ear to ear.

Kate wasn't trying to score brownie points with the comment, but it seemed that she had.

"Well, then, can I get you something to eat? I made a special Italian sausage soup this morning," Janis said. "Can't believe how cold it is this early in the season. Then again, I shouldn't be surprised given how unpredictable Texas weather can be."

"That sounds like heaven." Kate smiled. She couldn't help but like pretty much everything about the O'Brien house. She could imagine the look on Jackson's face when he was older, running through halls like these, surrounded by family.

Her heart squeezed, because Jackson would never have that. But he had her and Carter, and they would have to be enough, she told herself. Or maybe just her, that irritating little voice said, because Carter hadn't been out to meet his nephew yet, either.

"There's a formal eating space in the other room, but this is where my brothers and I prefer to hang out." Dallas motioned toward the oversize wood table in the kitchen. "Janis would tease us and say it's because we weren't taught enough manners to sit in the other room."

"This is perfect. Closer to the source," Kate said.

"Where is everybody?" Dallas inquired.

"After lunch, they all took off outside. A few of the boys headed to the barn. Austin said he would be running fences if anyone needed him," Janis added, bringing two steaming bowls of soup to the table.

"He's been doing that a lot lately," Dallas noted thoughtfully, almost as if talking to himself. "I'll check on him later." He walked over to the stove.

"Running fences?" Kate asked.

"We have livestock on the property, so every foot of fence has to be routinely checked," he explained.

The hearty soup smelled amazing and Kate figured it was about the only thing she would be able to get down. Even though she knew she should eat, it was the last thing on her mind, since her nerves were fried and her stomach was tied in knots.

Dallas brought her a cup of apple cider and it smelled even more delicious. But nothing was as appealing as Dallas when he hesitated near her. His scent was a powerful mix of virile male and the great outdoors, and it affected her in ways she didn't want to think about right then.

"This food is amazing." She couldn't allow herself to get too carried away in the moment because the horrible events of the day were constant in her thoughts, and being separated from Jackson even though he was safe at the sheriff's office was another reminder of their present danger. Her son being secure was the most important thing, and she needed to get back to him as soon as possible.

The best way to do that would be to figure out what was going on and stop it, she reminded herself.

"Janis is the best cook in Collier County," Dallas was saying, and the older woman smiled.

"Did you make contact with Stacy to let her know we're coming?" Kate asked a moment later, focusing on the problem at hand.

"I'll do that now." Dallas took a seat across the table

from her, fished his phone from his front pocket and then sent a text.

The soup tasted every bit as good as it smelled and eased her queasy stomach instantly.

Janis brought over a plate of fresh bread before asking Dallas to keep an eye on the timer for the latest batch of cookies while she changed into regular clothes.

"Earlier, you gave the impression you'd moved back to the ranch. Where did you live before?" Kate asked him.

"I had a logistics business based in New Mexico," he explained.

"I've been to Taos to ski," she offered.

"Up the mountain is too cold for my blood." Dallas laughed and the sound of his voice filled the room. "But then, I figure you know a thing or two about that, given the way you were dressed this morning."

"There's no substitute for sunshine and Texas summers," Kate said. "Why did you move back?"

"There were a lot of reasons to come home, but the main one was to run the ranch with my brothers," Dallas said. His business in New Mexico was booming and he'd built a life there, but no sacrifice was too great for his family, and he'd always known that he'd return to the ranch full-time at some point. This land was where his heart belonged.

"I'm sorry again about your parents." Kate must've realized the real reason he'd returned.

"We inherited the place along with an aunt and uncle, and I guess it just felt right to keep ownership in the family. Between the cattle ranch and rifle club, this place is more than a full-time job and it takes all of us pitching in to keep it going. Especially now. We're still getting our arms around the business, while a few of us are in the process of selling off our other interests."

"How many brothers did you say you have?" Kate asked, taking another spoonful of soup. The little moan of pleasure in her throat made him think of their kiss—a kiss that wasn't far from his thoughts, no matter how little business it had being there.

"Five, so there are six of us total. One is still living in Colorado, but the others are settling their affairs and/or living here. The youngest two are twins," he said. Dallas wasn't much of a talker usually, but conversation with Kate came easy.

"Twins?" she gasped. "My hands are full with one baby."

Dallas couldn't hold back a chuckle. "Tommy practically grew up in this house, too. He came to live with his uncle, Chill Johnson, who's been a ranch hand since longer than I can remember. So he makes a solid seven boys."

The bewildered look in Kate's eyes was amusing. "I can't even imagine having that many kids around. Taking care of Jackson is keeping me busier than I ever thought possible." She glanced about. "Then again, it's just me and Jackson."

Something flashed in her eyes that Dallas couldn't quite put his finger on.

"Despite having plenty of help around, Mom insisted on taking care of us herself," he said. "She was an original DIY type."

"Then she really was an amazing woman," Kate declared.

"Pop helped out a lot," Dallas added. "Being the

oldest, so did I. They were forced to hire more help around the ranch, especially as they got older and we moved on to make our own way in life."

The look of admiration in Kate's eyes shouldn't make Dallas feel proud. But he didn't want to spend any more time talking about himself.

He wanted to learn more about Kate Williams.

Before he could ask a question, she'd devoured the contents of her bowl, drained her cider and made a move to stand.

"We should head to your detective agency," she said, and that look of determination was back. That was most likely a good thing, because Dallas didn't need to go down that path, didn't need to go to the place where he was getting to know her better and learning about all the little ticks that made her unique. Especially if Susan's baby turned out to be Jackson.

As he walked her to the front door, Janis met them in the hallway.

"I almost forgot to tell you that your uncle Ezra was around looking for you this morning," she said. "He and his sister are at it again, and I think Ezra was jockeying for support. He said that he didn't want to trouble you, but when one of your brothers shot down his idea he felt he needed to get another opinion."

"If he's still angling to get an invite for the McCabe family to the bash then he's barking up the wrong tree." Hollister McCabe and Dallas's father had been at odds for years. McCabe had been trying to buy fifty acres from Pop, and when Dallas's dad had refused, the other rancher had tried to strong-arm a local politician to force the issue. That hadn't gone over well with the self-made, independent-minded senior O'Brien.

And Dallas had never trusted the McCabe family. Especially since Faith McCabe was one of Susan's best friends. That should've been enough of a red flag for him. Maybe it was the fact that he'd missed home that had drawn him to date Susan in the first place. Susan had always loved Bluff, so it was even more of a surprise that she'd come to New Mexico. Tommy had balked when Dallas had told his friend about who had shown up to a job interview at D.O. Logistics, the successful company Dallas had founded. He'd said that he shouldn't be too surprised given how much she'd been talking about missing Dallas around town.

"I believe that was one of Ezra's complaints," Janis said, snapping his mind to the current conversation. "But he's always got something up his sleeve."

Knowing Ezra, that was the tip of the iceberg. He'd been making a play for more control over the family business since before Pop's death—a business Pop had begun and made a success on his own. In the weeks since his death, Ezra's efforts had doubled.

Pop had included his siblings, giving them a combined 5 percent of the company in order to help them be more independent in their older years. Pop was a tough businessman, but his heart was gold, and even though he'd disagreed with his brother and sister on most counts, he'd felt a responsibility to take care of family.

Dallas could relate to the emotion, being the oldest of the O'Brien siblings, and was grateful that his brothers shared the same work ethic as he did and he wouldn't have to carry them.

"Gearing up for the holiday season always brings

out the best in those two, doesn't it," he said to Janis, shaking his head.

"I don't know why they have to act up around the biggest parties of the year." She nodded and took in a slow breath.

"How's planning going for the Halloween Bash?" Dallas asked.

"Good. Busy. You know how it is around this time. You'd think with all we have going on that he'd relax." She paused and then added, "But no. He's always scheming. Families can be *interesting* sometimes."

"That's a good word for it," Dallas agreed. Janis had become as much a part of the O'Brien clan as anyone in her decades of service.

"Will you be back in time for supper?" she asked.

"Not exactly sure. Don't hold it up on my account, though. Also, I need to let the others know I have a situation to deal with and I might need their assistance. Do you mind helping with that?" Dallas asked.

"Consider it done."

"Hold on." He moved to his father's gun cabinet and pulled out his favorite, a .25 caliber, put on a shoulder holster and secured the weapon underneath his coat.

He returned, thanked Janis and then placed his hand on the small of Kate's back to usher her out the front door. It was too much to ignore the heat rippling through him from the contact, even though she wore a coat, so he accepted it.

There was no use denying the fact that Kate was a beautiful woman. Dallas needed to leave it at that. Because not keeping his feelings in check would just complicate an already crazy situation. Hormones had no place in the equation. He'd already decided to offer her and Jackson a place to stay on the ranch. There was plenty of room in his hacienda, and Tommy would be hard-pressed to find anywhere for them with better security.

And Dallas didn't need to create an unnecessary distraction because of the feelings he was developing for Kate. *Feelings? This soon?*

He wasn't going to touch that one.

Besides, having her and the baby stay with him had everything to do with offering a safe place for the mother and child. State-of-the-art security was a necessity on the ranch, given that this part of south-central Texas was known for poachers. Other than being some of the worst scum on earth, poachers presented a danger to their clients and the hunting expeditions offered by the Cattlemen Crime Club.

Kate was quiet on the ride over. Dallas exited the sedan and she followed suit. He'd caught a glimpse of her, of the questions she had. At least for now she seemed to think better of asking.

"Mr. O'Brien, how can I help you?" Stacy peeked out the door. The petite brunette wore business attire that highlighted her curves. Based on her puffy eyes, Dallas guessed she'd been crying all day.

"I'm here to talk to you about Wayne and the case he was investigating," Dallas said.

"Of course you are. Come in. I'm sorry. My mind's not right. Not since learning about Wayne this morning from the deputy." She froze, embarrassment crossing her features, and then corrected herself. "Mr. Morton. It's all such a shock."

Based on the woman's general demeanor, it occurred

to Dallas that she and Morton might have had more than a working relationship. Given the circumstances, he wasn't surprised that she looked in such bad shape.

"This is my friend Kate Williams," Dallas said.

"Please, come in," Stacy said. "It's nice to meet you."

She and Kate shook hands as she invited them inside.

"Has anyone else been here to speak to you?" Dallas asked, instinctively positioning himself between Kate and the door.

"Just the appointments Wayne—Mr. Morton—already had on the books," Stacy said, blowing her nose into a wrinkled handkerchief. "Excuse me. I'm sorry, but I'm just a mess. He was a good guy, you know, and I can't believe he's gone."

"No need to apologize," Dallas said quickly, guilt settling on his shoulders yet again. He knew full well that Morton would still be alive were it not for Safe Haven and Dallas's case. "I couldn't be sorrier this happened."

"It's not like his job doesn't bring with it a certain amount of danger," she continued, as more tears rolled down her cheeks. "He's licensed to carry."

Dallas knew that meant Morton had been armed.

"And he went to the gun range all the time to keep his skills sharp," she said with a hiccup. "I just can't believe someone would get to him first like that."

"It shouldn't have happened. Other than working on my case, has there been anything unusual going on lately with Wayne? Has he been keeping any late nights or other appointments off the books?" Dallas asked, knowing Safe Haven was the reason Morton was dead, but wishing for another explanation.

"No. Not that I can think of anyway, but then, you know Wayne." She seemed to drop the front of being strictly professional with her boss. "He took on extra assignments all the time, which didn't mean I'd know about them."

Any hope, however small, that this wasn't Dallas's fault was slowly dying.

More tears spilled out of Stacy's eyes and she looked like she needed to sit down.

Dallas urged her toward one of the seats in the lounge area of Morton's expansive office. She perched on the arm of a leather chair as Kate took a seat near her on the matching sofa.

"First of all, I want to say that I'm really sorry about Wayne," Kate said sympathetically, leaning toward her. "I can only imagine the pain you must be feeling right now."

The gesture must've created an intimacy between the two because Stacy leaned forward, too, and her tense shoulders relaxed a bit.

"I just keep expecting him to walk through that door," she said, looking away. "It hasn't really hit yet that he's not going to, ever again."

"It's unfair to have something unthinkable happen to someone you love," Kate continued. "My son was almost abducted this morning and we're here because we think the cases might be connected."

Kate was taking a long shot, but Dallas understood why she'd need to try.

"Where are my manners?" the other woman asked,

looking noticeably uncomfortable. "Can I get either of you something to drink?"

"No, thank you," Kate said.

"Can you tell me what's been going on the past few days? Maybe a timeline of his activities would help," Dallas said.

"He's been acting weird ever since he started investigating that adoption agency for—" Stacy glanced from Dallas to Kate "—you."

"How long ago did he fit the pieces together of Susan and Safe Haven?" he asked, as Kate crossed her legs and folded her arms. Everything about her body language said she was closing up on him.

He shouldn't be surprised. They knew very little about each other aside from facts pertaining to her case. Circumstances had thrown them together and they'd been through more this morning than most people would in a year. There was an undeniable pull, an attraction, between them, but that was where it ended. Where it had to end. As soon as she and Jackson were safe, Kate and Dallas would return to their respective lives.

"Let's see…" Stacy leaned back and thrummed her manicured fingernails on her thigh. "It had to be recently, because he decided to make an official visit this morning and he never does that before he thoroughly checks out a place. Normally, he gives me names—" she paused long enough to glance between Kate and Dallas "—just in case things go sour. This time, he only gave me the address where he was going. He didn't even tell me the name of the agency. I had to look it up on the internet when he didn't come home after checking the place out last night. Then I called the sheriff's office and spoke to a deputy. Not long after, they found his car."

Dallas figured all the secrecy was due to the fact he'd paid Morton extra in order to keep the information private. The last thing Dallas needed was for a news outlet to get wind of what was going on. Not that he gave a damn about his own reputation. People had a way of making up their own minds with or without actual facts. He was trying to keep Susan's name out of the papers, as well as that of the family business. The amount of false leads news like this could generate would make it next to impossible for Tommy to sort out fact from fiction and would add too much weight to the investigation. A whole lot of people would likely come out of the woodwork to get their hands on O'Brien money if they thought a reward was involved.

"Any idea about the trail leading up to Safe Haven? Who Wayne might have contacted in order to get that information in the first place?" Dallas asked, hoping for a miracle.

"Those are great questions," Stacy said, looking flustered. "He usually runs everything past me, but he was keeping this one close to the vest. He does that with special clients, so I didn't think to ask more. Believe me, I've been kicking myself all day over it."

"You couldn't have known this would happen," Kate said sympathetically.

The woman smiled weakly.

"Does he keep a file on his more discreet clients in the office anywhere?" Dallas pressed. Tommy wouldn't like that he had asked the question, but this was starting to feel like a complete dead end. For the sheriff to get the records, he'd have to get a court order, which would take time. Dallas didn't have that luxury. He had a woman and child being targeted, no answers, and his own personal agenda to explore. If investigating Safe Haven was responsible for Morton's murder, then they could also be the reason Susan hadn't turned up.

Dallas was still trying to figure out why the kidnappers would change their MO, using a knife instead of a gun when they'd targeted Jackson. If it was the same group, that didn't make sense.

Stacy was too distraught to think clearly, which was understandable under the circumstances.

And now Kate had locked up on him, too.

Dallas was cursing under his breath just as the door to Morton's office flew open and two men burst in.

Stacy jumped to her feet and ran toward them, blocking Dallas's view. "The office is closed. You need an appointment to come in here."

The entrance to the private bathroom was about six steps away. If he could get Kate inside and lock the door, then he could face down the pair of men threatening Stacy.

Just as Dallas made it to the door, Stacy shouted, *"Go!"*

Chapter 7

Before Dallas could react, a bullet cracked through the air, and a split second later Stacy let out a yelp. Another bullet pinged into the wood not a foot from Dallas's head. He ducked and shoved Kate into the bathroom, falling on top of her. He performed a quick check to see if either one of them had been hit, needing to get her to safety so he could return to Stacy.

The guys in the other room had no intention of allowing him or Kate to walk out of here alive. They hadn't come for Stacy, so her best chance at survival was if he and Kate got the hell out of Dodge.

Dallas closed and locked the door.

The office was on the second floor, which could present a problem getting out the window. Land the wrong way, break an ankle and it was game over.

"Where is he?" one of the men asked.

"I don't see him," the other replied.

The first man cursed.

As Dallas moved to the small box window, he quickly scanned himself and Kate again for signs of blood, relieved when he saw none. From his experience with guns, he knew that bullets didn't travel in a straight line. They rose after exiting the barrel and then started dropping. Aiming a fraction of an inch off could make a decent marksman miss his target even at fairly close range.

Dallas opened the window and checked below. A row of bushes would help break Kate's fall.

He stepped aside, allowing her enough room to climb into the small space. She'd fit through it just fine, but Dallas was much bulkier. He'd have a difficult time getting through that tiny opening.

"Take your coat off," he said.

She pushed it through the window and let it drop to the ground.

"Run as soon as you get down there. Don't wait for me, okay?" he said, boosting her up to the window ledge.

She hesitated, which meant she must've realized what he already knew—he'd be trapped if he couldn't squeeze through. He knew she was about to put up an argument. He couldn't let her. She had a child depending on her and she had to make it to safety.

So he hoisted her up and through before she could protest, hoping that she'd call Tommy as soon as she was in the clear.

On closer inspection, the window was definitely too small for him to climb through, so he decided to create a diversion to keep the men engaged upstairs while Kate escaped.

The knob jiggled and then it sounded like someone was taking a hammer to the door followed by a male-sounding grunt.

"We're coming out. Get down on the floor," he shouted, pulling the .25 caliber from his holster. He fired a shot at the panel.

A few bullets pinged around him, so he dropped to the tiles. Scuffling noises in the other room gave him the impression the guys might be leaving. That couldn't be good. Then again, it could be a ploy to draw him out.

"Stacy," he shouted and then quickly changed position so they couldn't target him based on his voice.

Dallas palmed his phone and dialed 911. He immediately requested police and an ambulance and then ended the call.

Next, he moved to the window to check on Kate. His chest almost went into spasm as he realized what could've happened to her. He pushed his head through the opening and scanned the row of boxwoods below, releasing a relieved breath when he didn't see her.

Surveying the area between buildings revealed no signs of her, either.

Good.

He'd have to take a risk in order to check on Stacy. She might be hurt and there was no way he'd leave her bleeding out when he could help.

Dallas listened at the door for what felt an eternity, but was more likely a minute. There were no sounds coming from the other room. He muttered a string of swearwords, took a deep breath and then opened the door a crack.

He couldn't get a visual on anyone, so he opened the door a little more.

Footsteps shuffled on the wooden stairs leading down to the street.

As soon as he realized the men were gone, Dallas bolted toward Stacy, who was on the floor curled in a ball. Not moving.

"Stacy." He repeated her name as he dropped to his knees beside her. Red soaked her shirt by her right shoulder. He felt for a pulse and got one.

"Hang in there, Stacy," he said. "Help is on the way."

Dallas could already hear sirens, and relief washed over him when her eyes fluttered open.

More footsteps sounded, growing louder. Could the men be returning to finish the job with Dallas?

They'd been looking for someone. A man?

He pointed his gun at the door, with every intention of firing on anyone who walked through it. He couldn't leave Stacy alone, especially when she gripped his hand. He was her lifeline right now and he knew it.

The door burst open as Dallas's finger hovered over the trigger, ready to fire.

"Dallas," Kate said, her chest heaving from running. "Oh, my gosh. Is she okay?"

"Get inside and shut the door behind you," Dallas growled, lowering his pistol. He knew the door locked from prior visits to Morton's office. "Shove the back of that chair against the knob. Let only the law or an EMT cross that threshold."

Kate did.

Dallas cradled the wounded woman's head and neck in his free hand. "Stay with me, Stacy," he said. "Help is almost here."

"I loved him," she said, and the words were difficult to make out.

"I know you did. And he loved you, too," Dallas replied, trying to comfort her. He was never more thankful than when an emergency team showed up and went to work on her.

The gunshot wound in her shoulder was deep and she'd lost a lot of blood. As the EMT strapped her to a gurney and another placed an oxygen mask over her nose and mouth, Dallas heard them reassure her that she was going to be fine.

And Dallas finally exhaled. He palmed his phone and called Tommy with a quick explanation of what had just gone down.

The lawman agreed to take their statements personally and said he'd let the deputy who was about to arrive on the scene know the details. "Do not visit Safe Haven."

Dallas contemplated his friend's suggestion. Tommy was right. "I won't. I'm bringing Kate to the station."

"Good," Tommy said, ending the call.

"Let's get out of here," Dallas said to Kate.

She didn't utter a word as they made their way back to her vehicle, and he suspected she was in shock.

"I'm driving to my truck first," he stated, as he fired up the engine. "And then I'm going to drop you off at the sheriff's office, where you'll be safe."

"That was horrible," Kate murmured, obviously still stunned and trying to process everything that had just happened.

"I'm sorry. I shouldn't have brought you here." Dallas half expected her to curse him out for putting her in danger.

"It's not your fault, and I can't go back to the station until we figure this out," she said. "So where are we heading next?"

"We have no idea where those men could be or why they left," he said. "You're going back to the sheriff's office."

Gripping the steering wheel, Dallas noticed the blood on his hands. Anger surged through him that he hadn't been able to stop Stacy from being shot. No way would he put Kate in further danger. She could argue all she wanted, but he was taking her back to Tommy.

Then Dallas had to fill his brothers in on the situation, so he could hide her at the ranch.

He had every intention of helping Kate and Jackson, so he needed to have a family meeting to figure out how best to proceed. It wouldn't be fair to put at risk anyone who wasn't comfortable with that.

And Dallas might have a target on his own back now that he'd stirred up an investigation into Safe Haven. That would bring more heat to the ranch—heat that he had no doubt they'd be able to handle.

His cell buzzed. Dallas took one hand off the wheel to fish it out of his pocket.

"Would you mind answering that and putting the call on speaker?" He handed his phone to Kate.

She took it and did as he asked.

"This is Dallas and you're on speaker with me and Kate," he said.

"Where are you?" Tommy asked, and Dallas immediately picked up on the underlying panic in his friend's calm tone.

"Heading toward Main to get my pickup. Why?" Dallas asked, an ominous feeling settling over him.

"Someone just tried to break into my office," the sheriff said. "Jackson is okay. He didn't get to him."

Kate gasped. Dallas didn't need to look at her to know her eyes were wild, just like they'd been earlier that morning.

"What happened?" he asked, glancing at her before making the next left. His pickup could wait. Based on Kate's tense expression, she needed to get to her son and see for herself that he wasn't harmed.

"He's safe," Tommy reiterated. "I have him in protective custody and I promise no one will get to him on my watch."

The desperate look Kate gave Dallas sent a lead fireball swirling through him.

"We're on our way," Dallas said. "Did you find anything at the Morton crime scene?"

"Nothing yet. It'll take a while to process and it could be days or weeks before we get anything back from analysis," Tommy said truthfully.

Kate had had so many other questions—questions about the man sitting in the driver's seat beside her—all of which died on her tongue the second she'd heard that Jackson was in danger.

Dallas couldn't drive fast enough to get her to the station so she could see her son. Her brain was spinning and her heart beat furiously, but more than anything her body ached to hold her baby.

Dallas thanked the sheriff and asked her to end the call.

Whoever was after them had proved at Morton's office just how dangerous they could be. People were being shot right before her eyes, not to mention turning up dead. She and Dallas had barely survived another blitz-like attack, this time with guns.

The thought of men like that being after her baby was almost too much to process at once. It was surreal.

She remembered them asking if "he" was there. Did they mean Jackson? If so, they must've realized he wasn't with her.

Nothing could happen to her little boy. He was more than her son; he'd been her heart from the moment the adoption liaison had placed him in her arms. The thought of anyone trying to take him away from her, especially after how hard she'd fought to get him, was enough to boil her blood.

"Why would they want to harm an innocent little baby?" she fumed.

"They don't. I know how bad things look right now, but even if they got to Jackson, and they won't, they wouldn't hurt him."

"How can you be so sure? People are being shot, killed," she countered.

"Think about it. Hurting him doesn't make sense. A few of the other babies have been returned. My guess is that someone is looking for their child, a child they very much want," Dallas said.

He was right.

Logic was beginning to take hold.

And yet that didn't stop her blood from scorching.

"A stray bullet could've killed him," she said.

Dallas agreed.

"How much longer until we get there?" She didn't recognize any of the streets yet. Not that she'd been anywhere aside from home and downtown at the soup kitchen in the six months she'd been in Bluff. There had been a couple of donor parties, but most of them were lined up in the future. The Halloween Bash at the ranch that she'd been invited to was next on the agenda, but the last thing she could think about was a party.

"I'm taking a back road, so I can make sure we aren't being followed, and because this should shave off a few minutes." He floored the gas pedal, pushing her car to its limit. "We'll be there in five."

"I'm scared," she said, hating how weak her voice sounded.

"I know," he murmured—all he had to say to make her feel she wasn't alone. "Jackson is in good hands."

"They tried to…"

She couldn't finish, couldn't face the harsh reality that someone was this determined to find her son and take him away from her.

"We know whoever is behind this is capable of horrendous acts," Dallas said. "But they wouldn't hurt Jackson even if they could get to him, which they can't and they won't."

"You said it before and you're right," she admitted, and it brought a little relief. Still, the idea that Jackson could be taken away and she might never see him again, when he was the very thing that had breathed life into her, was unthinkable.

Kate might not have been deemed "medically desirable" by nature—wasn't that the phrase the infertility specialist had used?—but she was born to be a mother. She'd stayed awake the entire first night with Jackson while he'd slept in her arms. And it hadn't mattered to her heart one bit that she hadn't been the one to deliver him—Jackson was her son in every way that mattered.

Being a mother was the greatest joy.

And no one—no one—got to take that away from her.

Dallas pulled into the parking lot of the sheriff's office. His set jaw said he was on a mission, too. And it was so nice that someone had her back for a change. Carter had been her lifeline before, but even he'd had his doubts about her plans, and she never saw her brother since leaving the business.

She also knew that Dallas had questions of his own about Safe Haven. Supposedly for a friend but she wondered if that was true. No matter how many times she'd thought about the kiss they'd shared this morning, she was keenly aware of the fact that this man had secrets.

As soon as the car stopped, Kate unbuckled her seat belt.

"Hold on there," Dallas warned. "Someone might be waiting out here."

That could very well be true, but she was determined to see her son.

She practically flew through the door, Dallas was a step behind, and all eyes jumped to her.

"I'm sorry." She held up a hand. "I didn't mean to startle anyone. I'm looking for my son."

At that moment, she heard Jackson cry from somewhere down the hall and she moved toward the sweet sound of her baby.

Abigail met her halfway and handed Jackson over, and then Dallas was suddenly by her side, just as Tommy appeared from his office.

"Hold on. I need to call my brothers," he said, stepping inside a room while digging out his cell.

He returned a few minutes later with a nod.

"I need to get him out of here," Kate said. "And to someplace safe."

"You can't take him home." The sheriff didn't sound like he was disagreeing so much as ruling out possibilities.

"She can take him to my place," Dallas said. "I just had a quick conversation with my brothers about it. They don't have a problem with the arrangement."

Tommy looked to be seriously contemplating the idea.

"I don't want to put your family at risk," Kate argued.

"I can put you in a safe house but it might take a little time," the lawman said. "You'd be welcome to stay here in the office in the meantime."

"My place is better," Dallas protested as he shifted his weight. "You already know how tight security is."

"I advised you on every aspect of it," Tommy agreed. "But—"

Dallas's hand came up. "It's perfect and you know it. There's no safer place in Bluff right now. My family is fine with the risk."

Kate hesitated, trying to think if she had another option. She could go to her brother's house, but it was nearly a four-hour drive and he had no security. Also, she might be placing him in danger. Ditto for her parents' home. She couldn't risk her family, and honestly, she'd have so much explaining to do it wasn't worth the effort.

No, if these guys were bold enough to strike at the sheriff's office, then they would stop at nothing to get to Jackson.

At least for now, she had no other options but to stay with Dallas until a proper safe house could be set up. Jackson's security was the most important thing to her and had to take precedence over her internal battle about whether or not spending time with the strong and secretive cowboy was a good idea for her personally.

"I'm all for any place we can keep Jackson safe," she said to the sheriff. "If you think this is a good idea."

Tommy nodded.

"Then let's go back to the ranch," she said.

The sheriff shot a look toward Dallas that Kate couldn't get a good read on. What was up with that?

She didn't care. The only thing she was focused on at this point was her son. And ensuring that he didn't end up in the hands of very bad men. She held him tighter to her chest and he quieted at the sound of her voice as she whispered comforting words.

"Allen can go now, right?" she asked Tommy. "If the attacks are still happening while he's locked up, then he can't be involved."

"A deputy is already processing his paperwork," the sheriff said.

"It's been a very long day and I'd like to get out of here," she said to Dallas. Then she turned toward Tommy. "Are you okay with us leaving?"

"Go. Get some rest. We're trying to track down your lawyer to bring him in for questioning. So far, he isn't answering our calls." Tommy paused. "Also, you should know that we're planning to send a deputy to talk to your family members."

"My family?" she echoed, not able to hide her shock.

"It's routine in cases like this," he said. "We take the 'no stone left unturned' approach to investigations."

Oh. Kate tried to process that, but it was all too much and she was experiencing information overload.

She needed a few quiet hours to focus on feeding Jackson and allow everything that had happened that day to sink in. Even though it was only four o'clock in the afternoon, she was exhausted. A warm shower and comfortable pajamas sounded like pure heaven to her right then.

"And it might be better if they don't know we're coming," Tommy said, and the implication hit her square in the chest.

"Surely you don't think…" No way could her family be involved. She held on to Jackson tighter. They had their differences about the adoption, but they were still family.

"I won't take anything for granted," the lawman said.

Dallas's strong hand closed around her bent elbow, sending all kinds of heat through her arm. Heat that had no business fizzing through her body and settling between her thighs.

Dallas O'Brien was a complete stranger, and since that scenario had worked out so well the first time she'd broken her rules for someone, she decided no amount of chemistry was worth falling down another rabbit hole like that. But she wasn't fool enough to refuse his help.

He urged her toward the door and then to the car, surveying the area as they walked out.

She buckled Jackson into his seat and slid next to him in the back.

A few seconds later they were on the road again, but this time Dallas drove the speed limit and she appreciated the extra care he was taking with her son in the car.

If Dallas O'Brien was a father, and she figured that

had to be the real reason he was investigating Safe Haven, then he was going to be a great one. He already had all the protective instincts down.

She could only imagine what horrible circumstance had brought him the need to hire a private investigator, but decided not to let her imagination run wild. Especially when she kept circling back to that kiss and the fizz of chemistry that continued to crackle between them.

Because another thought quickly followed. How could a man who obviously loved his family so much allow his own child to be adopted? The question helped her see how precious little she knew about the magnetic cowboy. And even if she could risk the attraction on her own behalf, she'd never be able to go down that road now that she had a baby.

"Is there anything Tommy should know about your family?" Dallas asked, his voice a low rumble that set butterflies free in her stomach.

"You already know they don't support my decision to bring up a child alone," she said softly. "Our relationship has been strained since my divorce, and my mother sees *this*—" she motioned toward Jackson "—as me adding insult to injury."

In the rearview mirror, she could see Dallas's eyebrows spike. She could also see how his thick dark eyelashes framed his dark brown eyes, and her heart stirred in a way she'd never experienced.

She ignored that, too.

Besides, they'd dodged bullets and he'd saved her son. Of course she'd feel a certain amount of admiration and respect because of that, and a draw to his strength. That was normal in such a situation, right?

"I'm sorry about your folks. Everyone should have love and support from their family, even if they don't agree with your choices."

"My mom has never been the type to give up that kind of control," Kate said, trying to make a joke, but recognizing that the words came out carrying the pain she felt instead. "Sorry—you don't want to hear about this."

"I do," Dallas said so quickly she thought he meant it.

Why would he care about her family drama?

Kate didn't talk about it with anyone. She figured she'd have to explain to Jackson one day why he didn't have grandparents, but life for her was a "take one day at a time" commitment at the moment.

"That must be hard," Dallas said.

And lonely, she added in her head. Thank the stars for the relationship she had with Carter, barren as it was now that she didn't see him on a daily basis.

Speaking of which, she needed to call her brother as soon as Tommy gave her clearance.

Carter and she had forged a tight bond that had felt strained since Kate had said she was leaving the business they'd started. He had said he understood, but she knew down deep he'd been hurt by her decision.

"My brother and I were close growing up, and that helped," she said, trying to gain control of her emotions before she started crying. Even though she knew that her mother's rejection wasn't her fault, it still stung.

"Brothers can be a blessing and a curse," Dallas said, sounding like he was half joking.

She was grateful he seemed to take the cue that she needed a lighter mood. There was so much going on around them and she felt so out of control that she needed levity to help her get a handle on her emotions.

"That's the truth," she agreed, thinking about all those times her younger brother had annoyed her over the years.

She glanced down at Jackson. He was her sanity in this crazy, mixed-up world. He made her see that life was bigger than just her and her problems.

"I used to be so angry at my parents," she said, finding love refilling her well, as it did every time she looked at her son.

"What changed?"

"Him."

The surprised look on Dallas's face caught her off guard. Because there was something else there in his expression. It was so familiar and yet she couldn't quite put it into words. "Can I ask a personal question?" Kate murmured.

He nodded.

"Was Susan your girlfriend?"

"Yes. A while back," he admitted. He took a hard right turn and there was a security gate with a guard.

"And the baby you're investigating… Is that for you or a friend?" Kate didn't look at him.

"Me," he said so quietly that she almost didn't hear him.

"Where are we?" she asked, not recognizing the wooded area. Hadn't there been another layer of security earlier?

"This is the west end of the ranch property," he answered, as he was waved in by security.

When Dallas had told her he owned a hacienda on

the ranch, she wasn't sure what she'd expected. A large shed? A tiny log cabin?

Certainly not this.

The gorgeous Spanish-style architecture was about the last thing she would have imagined.

He'd explained that each of his brothers had a place on various sites on the land. His sat near the west end so he could take advantage of the sunset.

"This whole property must be enormous," she said, eyes wide.

"Pop added acreage over the years," Dallas said as he parked in the three-car garage.

There was a vintage El Camino, completely restored, in the second.

"That belong to you, as well?" She hadn't thought about the fact that Dallas might not live alone.

"I like to work on cars in my spare time," he said, holding her door open. "That is, I did when I *used* to have free time."

She let him take the diaper bag as she unhooked Jackson, and then she followed Dallas into the house.

The kitchen was massive and had all gourmet appliances. There was an island in the center with enough room for four bar chairs.

"Is the ranch keeping you too busy to pursue your hobbies?" she asked.

"That and trying to transition my old business to the new owner," he said.

"Why sell? Why not hire someone to run the other business for you and keep it?" she asked.

"Didn't think I could do justice to either place that way." Dallas's tone was matter-of-fact. "If I'm involved in something then that's what I want to be able to put all my attention into, and not just write my name on an office door for show. A man's name, his reputation and his word are all he really has in life."

"Powerful thought," she said, trying not to admire this handsome stranger any more than she already did. Those were the kinds of principles she hoped to instill in her son.

Dallas stood there, his gaze meeting hers, and it felt like the world stopped for just that brief moment.

And that was dangerous.

Kate threw her shoulders back. "Is there somewhere I can give Jackson a bath?"

"Let me give you a quick tour so you'll know where everything is," he said. "My brothers arranged for you to have supplies waiting."

She nodded, afraid to speak. Afraid her voice would give away her emotions.

The rest of the house's decor was simple, clean and comfortable looking.

"A crib was delivered from the main house. They keep a few on hand up there for overnight guests." He stopped in the middle of the living room. "If you need to reach out to your employees, I'd rather not alert anyone to the fact that you're here. The fewer people who know where you and Jackson are, the better."

"I know I already asked, but are you sure this is a good idea?"

"The security staff knows we have a special guest and that you're staying at my place. They'll tell maintenance what they need to know to stay safe, so no one's in the dark. But it'll be best to keep your identity as quiet as possible," Dallas said, showing her the bathroom attached to her guest suite. "Is there anything else I can do?"

"Once I'm able to put Jackson down, I'd love clean clothes to change into after a hot shower."

A dark shadow passed through Dallas's eyes.

"What's wrong?"

"I don't want to think about you naked in the shower," he grumbled. Then he said something about making a fresh pot of coffee and walked out of the room.

Kate smiled in spite of herself. She didn't want to like the handsome cowboy any more than she already did. Her heart still hadn't recovered from its last disappointment.

And an attraction like the one she felt for the cowboy could be far more threatening than anything she'd experienced with Robert.

Adding to her confusion was the fact that Dallas O'Brien had secrets.

Chapter 8

He had tried not to watch too intently as Kate fed Jackson his bottle. But Dallas couldn't help his natural curiosity now that the seal had been broken on that subject and the possibility he was a father grew a fraction of an inch.

"Mind keeping an eye on him while I clean up?" Kate asked and then laughed at Dallas's startled reaction.

Dallas couldn't say he'd had a stunning track record watching his brothers. Colin had broken his arm twice in one year on the tire swing Pop had set up on the old oak in the yard. Both the twins, Ryder and Joshua, had endured broken bones more than once on Dallas's watch, while climbing trees, and then there was the time Tyler had rolled around in poison ivy. And forget about Austin. That kid had had Pop joking that he needed a physician on staff for all the sprained ankles and banged-up body parts over the years.

"You sure about this? I'm not exactly qualified to take care of a baby," Dallas said, eyeing the sleeping infant.

The little boy looked so peaceful and innocent.

And Dallas figured that would last until Kate turned on the water in the shower.

"I think you'll be okay while he's out. He's a heavy sleeper," she said. "Or I could just take him in the bathroom with me and open the shower curtain to keep an eye on him, if you're not comfortable."

"No, don't do that," Dallas said, figuring he might need to know how to take care of a baby sooner than he'd anticipated. If Susan's child was his, these were skills he was going to need. And Jackson really did seem like a good baby. "I'll be okay."

"Are you sure?"

"Positive," Dallas said with more confidence than he felt.

"I'm just in the next room showering if you need me," she said, and he shot her a warning look about mentioning the shower again.

The last thing he needed while he was caring for a baby was the image of her naked in his mind.

His nerves were already on edge and even seeing the baby sleeping so peacefully in his Pack 'n Play didn't help settle them.

"Just go before you put any more images in my mind I can't erase," Dallas said to Kate.

One corner of her lip turned up in a smile and it was sexy as hell.

Watching a sleeping baby had to be the easiest gig

ever, he told himself. And yet he could feel his own heartbeat pounding at the base of his throat. His mouth was dry, too. He hadn't felt this awkward and out of place since he'd asked Miranda Sabot to be his girl-friend in seventh grade.

Jackson half smiled in his sleep and it nearly melted Dallas's heart. There was a whole lot of cuteness going on in that baby basket.

There was a knock at the door. Thankfully, the dis-turbance didn't wake the baby.

Dallas welcomed the delivery from Sawyer Miles, one of the security team members who worked for Gideon Fisher. He thanked him and brought the box into the kitchen.

The pj's were folded on top, so he took those and placed them on the bed in the guest room. Next, he put the food containers in the fridge for later. Dallas returned to the living room and eased onto the chair next to the little boy.

All Jackson had to do was fist his little hand or make a sucking noise for Dallas to jump to attention. Was this what parenting was like all the time? He felt like someone had set his nervous system on high alert. It was fine for a few minutes, but this would be exhaust-ing day and night.

He'd seen that same look of panic on Kate's face more than once in the past twelve hours, and for good reason.

Being alone with a baby was scarier than coming face-to-face with a rabid dog in a dark alley.

Jackson made a noise and Dallas jumped to his feet. He stared down at the Pack 'n Play with more inten-sity than if there was a bomb ready to explode inside.

The little guy must be dreaming, because he was making faces. Cute faces. And they spread warmth all through Dallas, which caught him completely off guard. He didn't expect to feel so much for a baby who probably wasn't even his.

The door to the guest room opened and Dallas heard Kate padding down the hall.

He swallowed his emotions.

"Going outside to get some fresh air. Jackson's fine," he said, before she entered the room.

Dallas moved to the back door and walked outside.

The past half hour had been nerve-racking, to say the least. A whole host of emotions Dallas wasn't ready to acknowledge had flooded him. If he was a father, would he be awful at it?

He told himself that knowing Kate was in the shower had him on edge. But it was more than that and he knew it. Being on the ranch had always centered him, no matter how crazy the world around him became. Not this time. His life had spun out of control fast. And he felt nothing but restless.

Distancing himself from Kate and the baby would provide much-needed perspective, he told himself as he tried to regain footing on that slippery slope.

The truth was he liked having Kate and Jackson in his home, way more than he'd expected or should allow. And that caught him off guard. He chalked the sentiment up to facing the first holiday season without his parents.

Then there was the issue of what had happened to Susan and her baby. Dallas hoped both were doing fine. He hadn't thought about babies much before being told that he might be a father. He'd been too focused on making a name for himself, striking out on his own. Not that his last name was a curse, by any means; Dallas had never thought of "O'Brien" as anything but a blessing.

But being a man, he'd needed to make his own mark on the world. Having come from a close family with a man like Pop at the helm had made Dallas want to do his father and himself proud.

Instead, he'd let him down in the worst possible way.

Dallas had always known he'd eventually come back to the land he loved so much and step into his legacy. That was all supposed to happen far off in the future, however.

His parents weren't supposed to die. And it sure as hell wasn't supposed to be his fault.

If they'd only listened to him when he'd said he could arrange to have the unsold art pieces taken back to the art gallery in the morning, instead of insisting on returning them that evening. Then Pop wouldn't have had that heart attack while driving, and both would still be alive.

He couldn't help but wonder if his father would think of him as a disappointment now. Sure, Dallas had been successful in business, but his personal life had always been more important to Pop. Dallas had failed his parents. And he couldn't help but think he'd failed Susan in some way, too.

Not knowing what had happened to her and her baby gnawed at him.

Then there was the news about Morton's death. So much was going on, and Dallas decided that half the reason his attraction to Kate was so strong was that, on a primal level, he needed comfort, proof life could still be good.

He tapped his boot on the paved patio as he gripped the railing. Even the evening chill couldn't snap him out of the dark mood he was in.

He could blame his missteps on working too much, or on his emotional state, but the truth of the matter was he should've known better.

Now Susan might be dead, and he couldn't ignore the weight of that thought or how awful it made him feel.

If he'd told her they could get married, would she be okay?

Maybe he should've strung her along until the baby was born, and all he'd have had to do was swipe a pacifier and send it to the lab for DNA testing. Susan would have never had to know and wouldn't have been in such a desperate state.

Then he'd know for certain if the child was his. He could've arranged help for Susan, and not just with the baby. She needed counseling or something to help get her mind straight.

Dallas stabbed his fingers in his hair as the wind blew a chill right through him.

So many mistakes. So many questions. So many lives hanging in the balance.

He caught a glimpse of one of his brothers out of the corner of his eye.

"Hey," Tyler said. A shotgun rested on his forearm as he approached.

"What are you doing out here?" Dallas asked, before he hugged him.

"We're taking voluntary shifts, walking sections of

the property," Tyler replied. "Haven't seen anything suspicious so far."

"Thank you for everything," Dallas said.

"What are you doing out here all by yourself?" Tyler asked.

"Thinking."

"You figure anything out yet?" he said with a half smile. He always knew when to make a joke to lighten the tension.

"Pie is better in my mouth than on paper," Dallas quipped.

"A math joke." Tyler chuckled. "I like it." His expression became solemn. "Seriously, is there something on your mind you want to talk about?"

"Nah. I got this under control," Dallas said. He did want to talk, but surprisingly, not with one of his brothers. He wanted to talk to Kate.

"You always did carry the weight of the world on your shoulders, big brother," Tyler said. "We're here to help if you want to spread some of that around."

"And you know how much I appreciate it," Dallas answered.

They stood in comfortable silence for a little while longer, neither feeling the need to fill the air between them.

"It's going to be different this year," Tyler finally said with a sigh. He didn't need to elaborate for Dallas to know he was talking about the upcoming holidays.

"Yeah."

"Won't be the same without her holiday goose and all the trimmings at Christmas supper," Tyler murmured.

"Nope." None of the boys had accused Dallas of

being responsible for their parents' deaths and none would. He held on to that guilt all on his own.

"You heard anything from Tommy lately about possible involvement from another vehicle?" Tyler asked.

"Nothing new." Dallas rubbed his chin and looked toward the setting sun.

"I get angry thinking about it," his brother admitted.

Dallas nodded and patted him on the shoulder. "Heard Uncle Ezra has been talking to the rest of the family about letting him take over the gala," he said at last.

"You know him—always blowing smoke," Tyler said. "He couldn't handle it alone anyway, and I don't know why he wants his hand in everything."

"Have you spoken to Aunt Bea lately?"

"Heard it through the grapevine that Uncle Ezra has been trying to get her to sell her interests in the ranch to him," Tyler said. "And he's been cozying up with the McCabes, which I don't like one bit."

"Neither do I. That family has been nothing but trouble over the years, and just because Pop is gone doesn't mean I'd betray his memory by bringing them anywhere near the ranch, let alone the gala." Dallas swung his right leg up and placed his foot on the wooden rail off the decking, then rested his elbow on his knee.

"Isn't that the truth," Tyler said. "Uncle Ezra needs to check his loyalty. He wouldn't have anything without Pop's goodwill."

"Unfortunately, not everyone is as grateful as Aunt Bea," Dallas said. "Plus, together they only own five percent of the company. What does he hope to gain by forcing her out?"

Tyler shrugged. "He's making a move for something. We'd better keep an eye on him. Harmless as he seems, we don't know what he's really up to, and I just don't trust him. I don't think Mom ever did, either."

"Good point. She was adept at covering up in front of Pop, but I saw it, too."

The back door opened as the sun disappeared on the horizon.

"Everything okay out here?" Kate asked.

"I better get back to the main house," Tyler said to Dallas.

"Check in if anything changes," he replied, then introduced his brother to Kate.

"Evening, ma'am." Tyler tipped his gray Stetson before disappearing the way he'd come.

"I didn't mean to make your brother feel like he had to leave," Kate said.

"You didn't," Dallas assured her.

"I made coffee in case you want more," she told him, stepping onto the patio and shivering.

"It's cold out here. We can talk without freezing inside." Dallas glanced around, aware that there could be eyes watching them from anywhere in the trees.

This time of year, the sun went down before six o'clock.

"Where's Jackson?" he asked.

"Sleeping in the other room." As Kate walked past him, Dallas could smell the wild cherry blossom shampoo Janis kept stocked, and it reminded him of a warm, sunny Texas afternoon. There wasn't much better than that. "It's been a long day and I'm glad he doesn't realize what's going on."

She'd showered and had changed into the pajamas

that had been brought over for her. They'd been pulled from a stash of extra supplies in case guests forgot something at home.

"Good. You found them." The all-white cotton pajama pants and simple matching V-neck button-down shirt fitted her as if they were hand-tailored, highlighting her soft curves.

Dallas forced himself to look away after he caught himself watching a bead of water roll down her neck and disappear into her shirt.

Coffee.

He poured a cup, black, and then paused.

"Think you can sleep?" he asked.

"Probably not," she said with a sigh.

"Coffee sound good? Because I can have some tea they serve at the main house delivered if you'd prefer," he said.

"Coffee's fine. Maybe just half a cup."

"Cream's in the fridge." He pulled out a jar of sugar and set it on the counter.

She thanked him.

"Can I ask you a question?" Kate perched on the countertop and took a sip of her coffee.

He nodded.

"What's your actual connection to Safe Haven?" Her eyes studied him.

"I already told you that I was investigating them." Not a total lie, but not the truth, either. Dallas drummed his fingers on the counter. "I was in a relationship with someone."

"Susan." Kate's gaze didn't falter. "And you had a baby?"

"There's where everything gets dicey." He paused

long enough to see the confusion on her face. "She had a baby. Said it was mine. I'm not so sure."

"You didn't get along with her?" Kate asked, with more of that shock in her voice.

"It's more complicated than that, but the answer would be no."

"What happened?" Those blue eyes stared at him and he wanted to be honest with her.

"I thought she was seeing someone else, and it would have been next to impossible for me to have fathered a child with her," he said. This was awkward, but not as strange as talking to Tommy or the thought of opening up about this to one of his brothers. Why was that? Dallas had known Tommy since they were three years old. And he and his brothers couldn't be closer.

Being the oldest, Dallas had always felt a certain responsibility for taking care of the others. Was he afraid he'd somehow be letting them down by admitting his mistakes?

"Why did she go to Safe Haven?" Kate asked.

"That's a good question. I don't have the answer to it. I had others, so I hired a PI to investigate," Dallas said.

"Wayne Morton," she said.

"That's right. He started digging around. Told me that she'd had a baby and there's a tie to Safe Haven, but I have no idea if the baby was put up for adoption or not."

"I can't even imagine," Kate said, and there was agony in her voice. "That must be the worst feeling in the world."

"Hell can't possibly be worse," he admitted. "Even

though I know there's barely a chance I could have a son out there, I can't sleep at night."

"It was a boy?" Kate said, glancing at Jackson's blanket on the couch. "Do you have any idea how old the baby would be now?"

"Maybe three months old," Dallas said, eyeing her reaction.

She glanced at the blanket again and then her gaze fixed on him with a look of sheer panic.

Yeah, he'd noticed the slight resemblance between him and Jackson, but that didn't mean... Did it?

That look of determination came back as Kate squared her shoulders and took a sip of coffee.

"He's not mine," Dallas said, trying to convince both of them. "All we have to do is swab us both if you want proof."

"I don't need it. Jackson is my son until someone proves otherwise," she said defensively. She hopped off the counter and then walked to the sliding glass door.

It was dark outside, so she wouldn't be able to see a thing. "Don't do that, Kate," he said.

"What?"

"Close up like that." He should know that was what she was doing. He was the king of shutting people out.

She whirled around and there was fire in her glare. "Is that why you've been so nice to us? Because you think Jackson is your son?"

"Hell, no," Dallas said, closing the distance between them in a couple of strides. "And for the record, I *don't* think he's mine. I have more questions than answers, and to say my relationship with Susan was brief puts it lightly."

Kate was too stubborn or too daring to look away, even with him standing toe to toe with her.

And Dallas noticed the second her anger turned to awareness. He could see her pulse beating at the base of her throat, her uneven breathing.

If she planned to walk away, then she needed to do it soon, because he'd made an enormous mistake in getting so close. Close enough that her scent filled his senses and he couldn't think straight anymore.

Before he could overanalyze it, he dipped his head and kissed her.

Her flat palms moved down his chest until her hands stopped at his waist. She gripped the hem of his T-shirt and he helped her pull it up, over his head and onto the floor.

Dallas spread his feet in an athletic stance, preparing himself to call on all his strength and tell her that this would be a very bad idea. One look in those hungry blue eyes and he faltered.

That was all it took? *Seriously, O'Brien? Way to be strong.*

He brought his lips down on hers with bruising need and delved his tongue inside.

She tasted like a mix of the peppermint toothpaste he kept in the guest room and coffee.

Dallas stopped long enough to close the blinds behind them.

Kate wound her arms around his neck and he caught her legs as she wrapped them around his midsection, their bodies perfectly flush, and then he carried her to the kitchen island.

There wasn't a whole lot of cloth between them as

he positioned her on the granite, and he could feel her heartbeat against his bare chest.

Need overtook logic when her fingers dug into his shoulders, pressing him against her full breasts.

Dallas took one in his palm and his erection strained when she arched her back.

He groaned, which came out more like a growl, and felt himself surrender to the moment. He'd never felt so out of control and yet so in the right place in his life. Sex with Kate was going to blow his mind.

An annoying little voice asked if this was a good idea under the circumstances. And he'd be damned if that unwelcome little voice didn't make a second round, louder this time.

Nothing inside him wanted to stop this runaway train, so he needed Kate to.

He pulled back enough to press his forehead to hers and force his hands on the countertop beside her thighs.

"Tell me this is a good idea," he said, and his breathing was ragged.

Her fingers trailed down his back, stopping at the waistband of his jeans.

"I want it, too," she said, breathless. "But it's a terrible idea."

He sucked in a breath and made a halfhearted attempt to step back.

Sure, he could back off if he wanted to, but the problem was he didn't. He wanted to nestle himself between those silky thighs of hers, free his straining erection and bury himself inside her.

Dallas trailed his finger along the collar of her cotton shirt and down the V. So far, he was the only one with any clothes off. That was about to change. He undid the first pair of buttons on her nightshirt.

Her chest moved up and down rapidly, matching the pace of his own breathing, as he reached up and freed her right shoulder.

Dallas bent low enough to brush a kiss there and then one on her collarbone.

Kate was perfection.

"You're beautiful," he whispered, drawing his lips across the base of her neck, pausing long enough to kiss her there, too.

She made a move to touch him, but he caught her hands in his. He kissed the fingertips of both before placing them on either side of her.

"No. I get to touch you first."

Her breath caught.

He slicked his tongue in a line down to her breast and gently captured her nipple between his teeth.

"Dallas," she started, her body rigid with tension.

He stopped long enough to catch her eye. "You can tell me to stop at any time and I will. It won't be easy but I won't force this."

"Oh, no. I want you to move faster."

"I can't do that, either," he said. "I move too fast and this will be over before it gets good. And I'm a hell of a lot better than that in bed."

He ran his tongue across her nipple one more time before taking her fully into his mouth, his own body humming with need.

Kate didn't give up control to anyone. Ever. Except for reasons she couldn't explain, she felt completely safe with Dallas O'Brien.

His hot breath on her skin sent shivers up and down her body and caused desire to engulf her. Maybe that was what she needed to clear her head…a night of hot sex with a handsome cowboy.

In some strange way, it felt like she'd known Dallas for more than just a day. But she didn't. He was practically a stranger.

That thought put the brakes on.

She froze and he reacted immediately by pulling back.

"I want to do this, believe me, but I can't." She buttoned the top buttons of her shirt, still trying to convince herself that stopping was a good idea. She had never felt such a strong pull toward someone she didn't know or allowed a situation to get out of control so fast. "I'm sorry."

Chapter 9

"Tommy just called," Dallas said to Kate as he walked into the living room, thoughts of last night and their almost tryst still a little too fresh in his mind. He figured their emotions were heightened from one seriously crazy day and that was half the reason their hormones got the best of them.

"What did he say?" She was on the couch feeding her son a bottle.

Dallas knew she didn't get a whole lot of sleep last night because Jackson had cried at 10:00 p.m. and then again this morning at three. It was just before eight and he was eating again. Three feedings in ten hours?

For someone who didn't sleep a lot, Kate looked damn good.

"He was able to reach your lawyer," Dallas said.

"What did Seaver say?"

"He made an appointment to drop by Tommy's office today at noon." Dallas crossed the room into the open-concept kitchen.

"I'd like to be there to hear what he has to say."

Dallas nodded. "You want a cup of coffee?"

"That sounds like heaven right now," she said, trying to suppress a yawn. "I usually don't sleep this late."

"This is late for you?" Dallas asked from the kitchen, where he'd started making a fresh pot. Eight in the morning was late for him, too. Work on the ranch began at five in the morning. He hadn't wanted to make noise, so he'd spent the morning recapping the prior day's events.

"I've always been a morning person," she said. "And since Jackson has me up anyway, I'm usually the first one at the soup kitchen. That reminds me. I need to check in at work. I'm sure yesterday has everyone on edge and I still feel horrible about what happened to Allen."

Dallas poured two mugs and brought one to Kate. "You need to keep an eye on his relationship with you."

She thanked him and immediately took a sip. Based on her expression, she wasn't ready to have that conversation.

"Do you really want to work with someone who is fixated on you?" Dallas continued. Knowing he should leave the topic alone didn't stop him from pressing the issue. He was man enough to admit to himself that he was jealous.

"Honestly, work is the last thing on my mind right now," she said, and she sounded defeated.

"You want me to finish that?" he asked, gesturing to Jackson and his bottle.

A moment of hesitation was followed by "No, thanks."

Did she still think he believed Jackson might be his son?

"Last night, about him…" Dallas said. "Well, I just want to reiterate that the probability he's mine is low. I'm offering to help right now so you can have a cup of coffee, not so I can see if there's some parental-child bond between us. Truth is, I'm more than a little uneasy at the thought of holding something that tiny."

The tension in her shoulders relaxed a little as she smiled. "I thought about it all night and maybe we should have a DNA test done today. If your—" she glanced at him "—Susan's child was adopted out through Safe Haven, then we can't ignore the possibility that Jackson *could* be yours."

"It's not impossible but that would be a huge coincidence." Dallas took a sip, enjoying the burn on his throat and the strong taste on his tongue. He thought about the way Kate's kisses had tasted last night. She was temptation he didn't need to focus on.

"Questions are bound to come up and we'll have the answer ready this way."

True. She put up a good argument.

"Chances are strong that I don't have a child at all," he said. "I'm almost certain that Susan was close to someone else at the time we were going out. He may have been the real reason she'd relocated to New Mexico and not to be close to me."

"You didn't confront her about it?" Kate asked.

"Honestly, no. I probably should have but I figured she could see whoever she wanted, given that we weren't exclusive."

"Your girlfriend seeing another man while the two of you were dating was okay with you?" Kate balked.

Dallas couldn't help but chuckle at her reaction. "We weren't serious at the time," he said. "She wanted more and I couldn't give it, at least not then. I thought we could take it slow. Apparently, she had other ideas."

"You didn't break it off?"

"I did," he said. "And then she called a few months later saying she was pregnant and that we should get married."

"Wow. That seems awfully presumptuous. If she was seeing another man, there was no way you could've known for sure the baby was yours." Kate set the empty bottle down and then placed the baby over her shoulder in a fluid motion. She might not have been a mother for long, but she seemed to have the hang of it.

"I'm not making excuses, but when I asked to slow things down until we could get a paternity test, she disappeared," he said.

"Sounds suspicious if you ask me," Kate muttered, bouncing Jackson gently.

"Either way, I need to know." Even if Susan had lied, she sure didn't deserve to be killed, and he hoped that wasn't the case.

"Did you know the guy?" Kate asked.

"No. Didn't want to."

"I can understand that. What about her friends? Think they might know?"

"We don't run in the same circles." She was onto something. If Susan's friends knew who else she'd been dating then they might be able to give them a name, except that his PI had been killed digging around. Maybe he shouldn't involve anyone else.

The baby hiccuped and then burped.

"He's a hearty eater." Dallas changed the subject, eyeing the little boy.

"That's what his doctor says." Kate beamed. Motherhood looked good on her.

"I called the hospital this morning to check on Stacy, by the way," Dallas said. "She had to have surgery on her shoulder yesterday to remove the bullet. All went well and the doctor is expecting a full recovery."

"That's great news," Kate exclaimed. "And such a relief."

"I had flowers sent over and I thought we could stop by and check on her later."

"I'd like that very much." Kate held Jackson in her arms, looking like she never wanted to let go of him.

Dallas filed that away. There was no way they could bring the baby with them today. It was too dangerous. When he really thought about it, it was too dangerous for Kate, too. She'd been adamant about going yesterday, but after that close call she might change her mind. If Dallas had anything to say about it then she'd stay right where she was. But knowing her, she wouldn't dream of being left out.

"Maybe we could make a detour on the way to the sheriff's office," he said.

"Great."

"Hungry?" Dallas asked.

"Breakfast would be nice."

"I'm not much of a cook, so I had one of my brothers bring over some of Janis's homemade muffins this morning," he said, setting his mug on the side table and moving toward the kitchen.

"Is that what smells so amazing?" she asked, propping Jackson up on a pillow next to her.

Dallas brought in the basket filled with blueberry and banana nut muffins.

"Janis makes them fresh every morning."

"She could run her own bakery, based on the smell alone," Kate said between bites.

"Don't tell her that or we might lose her," Dallas teased.

"Must be hard to find good help," Kate said with a smile.

"My brothers and I kicked in and gave her a share of the ranch. She's worked just as hard as the rest of us in making the place a success." They had figured that she deserved a cut far more than their aunt and uncle, who hadn't put in an honest day's work in their lives.

"That was really nice of you guys." Kate looked impressed.

"It was the right thing to do."

Unfamiliar ringtones sounded, breaking the morning quiet. Dallas quickly realized they were coming from her diaper bag.

She looked around, panicked, and Dallas realized she was trying to figure out how to get to her phone across the room without leaving Jackson alone on a pillow.

"You want me to get that for you?" Dallas asked.

"Would you mind?"

He retrieved her cell and handed it to her. The ringtones were pulsing loudly, but he felt more than their vibration shoot through him when their fingers grazed.

"It's my brother." She looked up at Dallas. "What should I do?"

"Answer it."

* * *

Kate took a deep breath and answered.

"What's going on with you?" Carter was frantic. "I've been trying to call and you haven't been answering. A deputy showed up at my house and at Mom's, asking questions."

"We had an incident yesterday morning, but the baby and I are fine."

"Why didn't you call me immediately?" he asked, and she hated the worry in his voice. She still felt like she'd let him down by leaving the business they'd created, and this didn't help.

"I'm sorry, Carter. Yesterday was a whirlwind and I was exhausted." It was partially true. That wasn't the reason she hadn't called, but she didn't want to say that the sheriff had asked her not to.

"Mom is a wreck," Carter said.

"You talked to her?"

"What choice did I have when a deputy knocked on both of our doors? You could've given me a heads-up, Kate." Carter still sounded concerned, but there was something else in his voice she couldn't quite put her finger on. Anger? Frustration? Hurt?

"What did they say?"

"No one told us a thing. They just started asking all these questions about you and Jackson," he said.

What could she tell him? The last thing she wanted to do was lie to her brother.

"Is Mom okay?" she asked.

"After popping a pill and having a glass of chardonnay, yeah. This came as a shock. I mean, you'd think if something happened to you that you'd be the one to let us know," Carter said, and there was a snide quality to his tone.

Was he upset? Concerned?

Maybe that was what was bugging Kate. He seemed more distraught that he and their mother had been surprised than worried about her or Jackson being hurt.

"We were shaken up yesterday, but we're fine now. Thanks for asking," she retorted.

"I figured you were okay, since you answered the phone," Carter snapped.

"What has you so upset? If you're worried about Jackson, he's fine, too," she stated. She didn't like where this was headed one bit.

Had she overestimated her brother's love for her? At the moment, he seemed more concerned with being surprised by a deputy. Then there were his overprotective feelings for their mother.

That stung.

It had always been she and Carter against the world during their childhood and they'd been thick as thieves.

Then again, maybe he resented her more than she realized for leaving the business. She'd sold her shares to him and he'd seemed to be on board with her plan once he got used to the idea.

The times they'd talked, he seemed to be handling work stress fine. He had a lot on his plate, though, and she figured some of that was her fault.

"Everything okay, Carter?" she asked when he didn't respond, that same old guilt creeping in. Normally, it was reserved for conversations with her mother.

"Sorry, Kate. Mother is just freaking out and I haven't slept in days. We have a new program going live next month at work and I found a hiccup in the code," he said. Now he was beginning to sound like the old Carter. "I've been working twenty-four/seven for a solid week."

Once again she felt bad for leaving him holding the bag even though she'd prepped him far in advance. Still, she knew the stresses of running a business better than most, and of the two of them, she was better at dealing with it.

While she didn't miss the day-to-day operations or the stress, she did miss seeing her brother. Now that they didn't work together and she'd been busy with Jackson, she and Carter had practically become strangers.

"How is the little rug rat who stole you from me?" he finally asked.

"Growing bigger every day."

"Is he allowing you to get any sleep yet?"

"It's better. They don't stay little forever," she said, ignoring Dallas's raised eyebrow.

Their relationship probably did seem odd to an outsider.

"Tell him to hurry up and get big enough to work at the business so his uncle can finally get some sleep," Carter said.

"Sorry. He already said he's going to be a fireman and has no plans to spend his life at a keyboard." Kate could only imagine how this conversation sounded to Dallas, coming from such a close-knit family. *Odd* would most likely be an understatement.

"Mom will be fine," Carter said. "You know her. Breaking a nail is cause for a red alert."

Sadly, that wasn't too much of an exaggeration.

"Have you been spending more time with her

lately?" Kate asked, hoping to ease some of her own guilt.

"Not really. Work has been holding me hostage. She'd like to see you, though." Was he trying to make her feel worse about her non-relationship with their mom? Since when was he taking up Mother's cause? "In fact, I better head to the office."

"Oh, where are you now?" Kate asked.

"Nothing. Nowhere. Just out and about," Carter said, and she picked up on the same tone he'd used when he was trying to hide the last candy bar from her when they were kids.

Maybe Mother and Carter were becoming closer now that she was at odds with Kate.

Kate decided not to press the issue, but it ate at her anyway. She should be glad her mom had someone to talk to, since she and Kate's dad hardly ever spoke about anything important. So why did it gnaw at Kate that her mother and brother were on good terms?

Other than the fact that protecting Carter had been half the reason she and her mother had been at odds most of Kate's life?

This suddenly close relationship felt a little like betrayal. Because when Carter had wanted to quit the soccer team at twelve, it had been Kate who'd fought that battle for him, taking on both their parents.

It had been unthinkable for them that Carter wouldn't want to play sports at all. In fact, he'd pretty much hated anything that required him to compete physically. He'd never been the tall, masculine child with a solid throwing arm his father had hoped for and had tried to make him be. Carter had topped out at five foot nine, which pretty much ruled out basketball, a sport their dad had played.

Carter had been great at math, so their parents decided he should be a doctor. That idea fell apart when he couldn't stop vomiting in his high school anatomy class.

It had been Kate who'd stood up to them time and time again on his behalf. She'd let him talk her into the start-up, had worked crazy hours and had sacrificed any kind of social life. Not that she regretted it one bit. She and her brother had been able to do something together that hopefully would last for many years.

"I better go," she said to him now.

"Be careful," he said.

She ended the call, deciding she hadn't had nearly enough rest lately, because she was reading too much into the phone conversation with her brother.

"I've been thinking that maybe you should stay here with Jackson today," Dallas said.

He'd been watching her reactions on the phone and she figured he'd have questions about her family.

"Believe me when I say that I seriously considered it. In fact, that's just about all I've been thinking about for the past few hours," she said.

"It's risky for you to leave the ranch. And there's no way we can take Jackson with us," he added.

"Both good points," she agreed. Those had been her top two after tossing and turning for a few hours last night.

Jackson started fussing. She picked up her son and cradled him in her arms.

"It would be nice if I had more of his toys here," she said, wishing this whole nightmare was over. "You can't imagine how helpful it is to be able to set him down once in a while."

"I'd be happy to hold him," Dallas offered, and there was just a hint of insecurity in his voice. "On the off chance that I am a father, I probably need to start getting my arms around taking care of a baby, because I have no clue what to do with them."

Actually, he was making a lot of sense.

"It's best if you try this for the first time while sitting down." She stood and walked over to him.

He held out his arms and she placed Jackson in them.

Wow, did that kick-start her pulse.

There was something about seeing such a strong man be gentle with such a tiny baby that hit her square in the chest like a burst of stray voltage. She hadn't thought much about Jackson missing out on having a father before. It struck her now.

Maybe it was the lack of sleep or the thought that it might actually be nice to have a partner around to help raise her son.

Ever since that little angel had come into her life, she questioned pretty much all her decisions. It would be nice to be able to talk her ideas through or just bounce them off someone else for a change.

Why did all that suddenly flood her thoughts now? She and Jackson had been doing just fine before. Hadn't they?

Wishing for something that wasn't going to happen was about as productive as sucking on a rose petal when she was thirsty.

It didn't change a thing and she'd end up with thorns on her face.

"I hear what you were saying about me sticking around the ranch for safety's sake today. I'd like to be there when the sheriff questions Seaver and I want to visit Stacy in the hospital. It might be nice for her to have another woman around. I didn't get the impression she had anyone to talk to," Kate said.

"Same here," Dallas said.

"Plus, I feel guilty that those men showed up at her office to begin with. I'm worried that my car drew them to her," she said.

"When they didn't find Jackson with us, they disappeared." Dallas looked down at the baby. He was beginning to look more at ease.

Her son being in the cowboy's arms filled her with warmth.

"I'll need to figure out something to do with him while we're gone," she said, chalking her emotions up to missing her brother.

"Janis offered her assistance when I asked for baby supplies," Dallas said. "She doesn't know who's here, but I'm sure she suspects it's you, since she met you yesterday."

"She's one of the few people I would actually trust with my son," Kate said, and she meant it. Plus, there was the fact that she was already at the ranch and the security here was top-notch. Dallas had given Kate the rundown. There were armed guards at all three entrances and cameras covering most other areas, especially near the houses.

Although the entire acreage couldn't realistically be completely monitored, and there were plenty of blind spots, no one would get anywhere near the houses without being detected.

That thought would've let her sleep peacefully if the handsome cowboy hadn't been in the bed right down the hall.

Chapter 10

"I meant what I said earlier." Dallas shifted the baby fidgeting in his arms. Was the child just as uncomfortable as him? Was that why the little guy was squirming?

Sure, holding Jackson felt good in a lot of ways. But he was so little that Dallas was afraid he'd break him without realizing it. Could he break a baby?

This felt like middle school all over again, when he'd had to carry that egg around for a week. Dallas had broken his on the first day. And he'd already seen how many broken bones his brothers had endured while playing with him.

Jackson started winding up to cry and Dallas's shoulders tightened to steel. "I'm afraid I'm not very good at this." He motioned toward the baby with his head. He was afraid to move anything from the neck down.

And it didn't help that Kate was cracking a smile as she walked toward them.

"You think this is funny?"

"It's just a relief to know I'm not the only one who was nervous when I held him those first few times. I thought it would feel so natural to hold a baby, but it didn't." She reached his side, but instead of offering to take her son, she perched on the arm of the leather chair.

"I'm glad my pain bolsters your self-image," Dallas quipped, feeling even more tense as the first whimpers came.

"Sorry. It just reminds me how hard it actually was for me in those early days and how far I've come since then." She placed her hand on his shoulder. "I'm convinced babies can read our emotions. The more we relax, the more they do."

Relaxed wasn't the first word that would come to mind if Dallas was trying to describe himself.

Jackson wound up and then released a wail. Dallas felt a little better knowing that Kate's presence had done little to calm the child.

"And then sometimes he just needs a good cry," she said, finally taking him from Dallas.

As she did, he got a whiff of something awful smelling. She must have, as well, because her nose wrinkled in the cutest way.

"I think someone needs a diaper change," she said as she moved Jackson to the couch and placed him on his back.

"You need help with that?" Dallas asked.

She waved him off and went to work.

"Have you ever done this before?" she asked.

"Nope." He was mildly curious and figured he'd need to know all about it at some point when he became a father.

"Me, either. Well, not until Jackson." She finished taping the sides of the fresh diaper and then tucked his little legs inside his footed pajamas. "I put the first one on backward and didn't realize it until he had a leak. I'd also bought a size too big."

"Sounds complicated."

"You get the hang of it," she reassured Dallas, neatly folding the used diaper. "We may not want to keep this inside the house."

He held out his hand.

"You sure about that?" she asked.

"I'll have to get used to it at some point in my life, right?"

She nodded.

When he returned from taking it to the garbage out back, she was pacing. "When should we go?"

"Anytime you're ready, if you're certain you want to leave the property."

"Part of me wants to stay right here and never leave," she said, pensive. "I feel safe here and I don't want to let go of that feeling. But whoever is trying to take Jackson away from me is still out there and I need to do everything I can to find him or my son will never be safe."

Dallas understood that logic. He could see all her emotions in her determined blue eyes.

And he tried not to focus on the other things he saw there...

* * *

Dallas's boots clicked against the tiled floors of the hospital wing. The nurse had said Stacy was doing fine when he'd called to check on her last night. He needed to see for himself.

There was a secondary reason for his visit. Maybe there was additional information he could get out of her. Yesterday had felt like a waste of time and he wanted to do everything he could to help locate Morton's killer. Adding to Dallas's guilt was the feeling that he'd put Stacy in harm's way by showing up at her office with Kate.

Stacy was sitting up when he and Kate reached the opened door.

"Come in," she said. Her eyes were puffy from crying and she had a wad of tissues balled in her right fist. Her hair was piled high on her head and she wore a blue hospital gown.

The room was standard, two beds with a cloth curtain in between. It was opened, since the second bed was empty. Stacy's was closest to the window.

"How are you feeling today?" Kate asked, making it to her side in a beat. She had a way with people that made even the worst situation feel like everything would work out all right.

He chalked it up to motherhood. Kate had the mothering gene. Not everyone did. He couldn't imagine that Susan would have that same effect on people. She had good qualities, but was more the invite-to-happy-hour personality than the soothing type.

Of course, being close to Kate brought up all kinds of other feelings Dallas didn't want to think about. And the sexual chemistry between them was off the charts.

He mentally shook off the thought, focusing on Stacy instead.

"Thank you so much for the beautiful flowers." She motioned toward the bouquet on the side table.

Dallas nodded and smiled.

"Did they catch those guys?" she asked.

"Afraid not," he said. Tommy had promised to call or text the moment they were in custody, and so far, Dallas hadn't heard anything. Whoever was behind this had sophisticated ways to disappear when they needed to and that set off all kinds of warning bells for Dallas.

It had also occurred to him that Susan could've gotten herself into some kind of serious trouble. Now that his investigator was dead, there was no one chasing her trail aside from Tommy. And the problem with that was the fact that his friend wouldn't be able to share a whole lot of information about a murder investigation in progress.

So Dallas needed to come up with a plan of his own without stepping on the sheriff's toes.

"Did you get a look at the men?" Dallas asked. He'd been able to give a basic description to law enforcement of dark hair and medium build, before Stacy had blocked his view, which didn't rule out a lot of people in Bluff.

"No, it was a blur," she said. "Everything happened so fast. All I remember seeing was the end of a gun and then a blast of fire, followed by a burning sensation in my shoulder. Once I put two and two together, I honestly thought I was going to die."

Dallas could see why she'd focus on the barrel, given that the gun was fired at her a moment later. "I want to catch these bastards but I need your help," he told her.

"What can I do?" Her gaze bounced from him to Kate and back.

"I'd asked about secret files before. I know you'd never want to betray Wayne's trust, but I need to see mine and any others he has."

"If he had files like that, I didn't know about them." She glanced down, which usually meant a person was lying or covering.

"What about his laptop?" Dallas asked.

"It was in his car," Stacy said, which meant Tommy or one of his deputies was already tearing it apart.

Dallas paced, trying to think of another way to come at this, because he was fairly certain Stacy was holding back. Since his straightforward approach was bringing up an empty net, he needed to take another tack.

"It's okay if you don't know," Kate assured her. "He just wants to find the guy who did this to Wayne."

Stacy glanced at Kate and the softer approach seemed to be baiting her. "Isn't the sheriff already working on it?" she asked.

"Yes, he is. And we would never do anything to get in the way of that. But these guys are dangerous and they might come back for you if they think you know something," Kate said calmly. "And I think we can help with the investigation."

Stacy stared at the door.

Dallas turned to look out the window, because whatever Kate was doing seemed to be working.

"They have his laptop from the office," Stacy finally started, "but that's not where he would keep a secret file, because it would be the first place people would look if he was subpoenaed."

"He's smarter than that, isn't he," Dallas said, turning toward her.

Stacy half smiled and a deep sadness settled in her hazel eyes. "Yes. He was."

Dallas gave her a minute to recover. "I lost someone very important to me a few months ago," he finally said. "Actually, two people."

"I remember reading about your parents in the newspaper and thinking it was a tragic accident," Stacy said wistfully. "I'm real sorry about that, because I'd always heard they were fine folks. Real down-to-earth types. It must've been hard to lose both of your parents like that and especially…"

She glanced up at him with an apologetic look on her face but couldn't seem to finish her sentence without breaking down.

"Thank you," he said. "I know what it's like to have people taken away before their time. And, yes, the upcoming holidays make it worse. Believe me, very soon, once the initial shock wears off, you're going to be angry."

Stacy nodded, blowing her nose into a wadded-up tissue.

"You already want answers and so do we," Dallas said. She was getting close to trusting him; he could tell by the change in her demeanor. "You already know that I could have a child, a son. And I need to know if Wayne found something that got him in trouble while working on my case."

Shock registered on her face, but to her credit she recovered quickly.

"Family has always been important to an O'Brien, and I'm no different. Losing my parents makes me value it even more," he said. "I have selfish reasons for wanting to get that file. Wayne was most likely killed because of my case…because of something he found. If I know what that is, I have a chance at finding out if I have a son and nailing Wayne's killer. Plus, the whereabouts of my son's mother are unknown. She might be in trouble. You and I both know the sheriff may never figure it out since he has to work within the law. And even if he does, it might be too late."

Dallas believed Tommy could dissect pretty much anything given enough time. But that was one luxury they didn't have. As sheriff, he would have to go through proper channels and file paperwork that could take days, weeks or months to process.

"I hired Wayne," Dallas said. "His death is on me. And I need to find out what he knew."

A tear rolled down Kate's cheek. She quickly wiped it away.

Stacy was already blowing her nose again. "He spoke very highly of you," she said. "I didn't know at the time that it was *you*. He referred to your case as Baby Brian. Now I realize it was because of O'Brien."

"Help me find the jerks who did this to him, who shot him in cold blood," Dallas said. "You have my word you'll be the first to know when I do."

Stacy sat there for a long moment, her gaze fixed out the window.

"Will you hand me my purse? It's in the bottom drawer over there," she finally said, motioning toward the nightstand near the bed. "The deputy brought it to me last night when he stopped by."

Kate retrieved the Coach handbag and Dallas noted the designer brand.

Stacy glanced up at Kate and then Dallas as she reached for it. "This was a gift from Wayne." She finally dropped the pretense that the two of them had had a strictly professional relationship.

Kate reached over and hugged her, and the woman sagged onto her shoulder.

"He was all I had," Stacy said. "I never really had a family. He took a chance when he hired me five years ago, because I was nothing. I didn't know a laptop from a desktop. He said he could send me to training for that. Loyalty was the most important thing to him. I could do that. Our relationship was a professional one for the first three years and then, boom, something happened."

"You fell in love," Kate whispered.

"It was like a lightning bolt struck one day and there was no going back," she agreed. "We kept things a secret because Wayne was afraid of someone using me against him."

Kate touched her hand and Stacy looked up with glassy, tearful eyes.

"I'm sure he wanted to do whatever was necessary in order to protect you. He must've loved you very much," Kate said with calm reassurance.

More tears flowed, and even though Dallas was in a hurry to get information, he didn't want to rush out of the room. He was glad that he and Kate could be there for Stacy, and especially since she'd lost her entire support system in one blow.

"I don't know what I'm going to do now," she said. "I don't have a job or a purpose. Wayne showed me his will last year. He left everything to me, but what do I do when I leave here without him?"

There was a lost quality to her voice that seared right through Dallas.

"If you ever want to work again, there'll be a job waiting for you at the ranch," he said. "Once you get your bearings."

"You would hire me without knowing anything about me?" Stacy looked almost dumbfounded.

"Wayne was a good man. I trust his judgment," Dallas said. "Call my cell whenever you're ready and let me know what you decide."

He pulled out a business card and dropped it on the nightstand.

"And the soup kitchen always needs good people," Kate offered.

"That means a lot," she said. "I'm not sure what I'll do at this point, but this gives me options."

Loyalty was important to Dallas, too. And Wayne was right. An employee could be trained for pretty much everything else.

Stacy rummaged around in her purse until a set of keys jingled. She pulled them out and held them on her left palm. With her right hand, she picked through them until she stopped on one.

"This is the key to our house," she said, locking eyes with Dallas. "I'll write down the address for you."

He nodded before she returned her attention to the keys and thumbed through a few more.

"I kept all the keys on one ring, but I also made a duplicate just in case." She pulled out a piece of paper and pen, and then she scribbled the address.

"This little baby right here opens his office door at home," she stated. "There's a house alarm. I'll give you the code. And another one for his office."

Dallas would expect nothing less from an investigator of Morton's caliber.

Next, she dumped the contents of her purse onto the bed. She had a matching wallet, a pair of Ray-Ban sunglasses, a pack of gum and sundry items like safety pins and paper clips.

As she turned the bag inside out, Dallas saw a glint of something shiny inside. Metal? A zipper?

"This purse was made special," she said, unzipping it.

She shook the bag and a key fell out.

Chapter 11

"This one unlocks a compartment in a book called *Save for Retirement*. It's on the bookshelf behind his desk in his office, on the second shelf. It should be the second volume from the right. It works like a diary," Stacy said, motioning toward the key. "There'll be a flash drive inside. I never looked at it, wasn't supposed to, so I didn't. I can't tell you what's on that drive for certain. But whatever he found out about your case, I'd bet my life it would be there."

She held out the keys toward Dallas.

"Thank you," he said as he took them.

Kate hugged Stacy again and he could plainly see that she didn't want to leave the woman alone.

"Mind if I send someone over to keep an eye on you while you rest?" Dallas asked. "I don't like you being here without protection."

"Guess I didn't think about it, but you're right. I'd appreciate that very much," Stacy said.

Dallas made a quick call to Gideon Fisher to put the wheels in motion and then settled in to wait for backup to arrive. Fisher said he'd send Reece Wilcox.

Stacy was on medication, and even though she seemed wide-awake and alert, he didn't want to risk her falling asleep and being vulnerable until Reece arrived.

Kate retrieved the remote and put on one of those home decorating shows to provide a distraction for Stacy. Mindless TV was the best medicine sometimes.

"Can I get you anything from downstairs?" Kate asked. "Or order out?"

"No, thanks. I'm fine. The food here isn't horrible." Stacy paused long enough to wipe at a tear. "You can't know how much I appreciate you both."

For the next twenty minutes, they all sat and watched a kitchen makeover in comfortable silence.

By the time Reece showed up, Dallas and Kate were due at the sheriff's office.

They said their goodbyes to Stacy and promised to visit again as soon as they could.

In the parking lot, Kate put her hand on Dallas's arm.

He stopped and turned to face her, but before he could speak, she pushed up on her tiptoes, wrapped her arms around his neck and kissed him. Hard.

Kate had meant to brush a quick "thank you" kiss on Dallas's lips, but her body took over instead and she planted one on him.

His arms looped around her and dropped to her waist, pressing her to his muscled chest.

Dallas O'Brien was the very definition of *hot*. But he was also intelligent, kind and compassionate. Traits she didn't normally associate with a rich cowboy. He also had a down-to-earth quality that was refreshing. Her body seemed to take notice of all Dallas's good qualities because heat flooded through her even though it couldn't be much more than thirty degrees outside.

When he deepened the kiss, she surrendered.

Instead of fighting her feelings, she tightened her arms around his neck and braided her fingers together. The motion pressed her breasts against his chest even more and her nipples beaded inside her lacy bra.

Neither made a move to break apart when he pulled back a little and locked his gaze with hers.

They stood there, only vaguely aware that it was frigid outside, because inside their little circle was enough warmth to heat a room, and Kate's heart filled with it.

She'd never known this kind of appreciation and acceptance from anyone.

Certainly not from her mother or father. During her childhood, when the two spent time with her, it had felt sometimes as if they were ticking off boxes on a duty list rather than spending real time with her. And then there was her failed marriage to Robert. He'd been handsome and they'd been attracted to one another, but she'd never felt…this, whatever *this* was. More than anything, he just seemed ready to take the next step when the time came. Had their relationship, too, been a box he'd needed to tick off at that point in his life?

Gazing into Dallas's dark, glowing eyes, she saw something she'd never seen when looking into another man's. Rather than analyze it, she kissed him again, because Dallas O'Brien stirred up emotions she didn't even know how to begin to deal with.

And she lost herself in that kiss.

Dallas pulled back enough to whisper in her ear, "You're beautiful, Kate."

She loved the sound of her name on his lips. "So are you."

He laughed at being called beautiful. But he was, inside and out.

His phone dinged, and he checked the screen and then showed it to her.

William Seaver had just checked in at the sheriff's office.

"This is to be continued later," Dallas said, taking her hand in his, lacing their fingers together. He led her to his truck, which had been retrieved by a member of security last night, his gaze sweeping the area as they walked.

Ten minutes later, he parked in the lot at the sheriff's office.

"I hope we didn't miss anything," she said.

"If I know Tommy, he'll hold off the interview until we get inside." Dallas surveyed the lot before ushering her into the office, a reminder of how dangerous their situation still was.

Tommy greeted them in the hall before leading them to his office. "I spoke to Mrs. Hanover last night."

"What did Susan's mother say?" Dallas asked.

"That the last time she heard from her daughter was three months ago," Tommy said.

"What did she remember about their conversation?" Dallas perked up. He seemed very interested in what Tommy had to say and who could blame him?

"She told her mother that she was going out of the country for a while and not to worry about her," he said. "Told her she'd get back in touch when she could."

"That makes me think she planned to disappear," Dallas said. "She knew that she was in trouble."

"That's my guess," Tommy stated.

"This is the first positive sign we have so far that Susan could still be alive," Dallas said.

"Would she just give up her baby and take off?" Kate asked. Those actions were inconceivable to someone like her, but Dallas didn't seem surprised.

"If her child really had been mine, it seems out of character that she'd give up so easily on proving it to me," Dallas said after a thoughtful pause.

"She would've had the paternity test done, the results made into a necklace, and then worn them on a chain around her neck," Tommy stated.

Dallas nodded. "Gives me a lot to think about."

"Sure does," Tommy said. "Let's see what Kate's lawyer has to say."

Tommy urged them into his office. Then he brought in the attorney.

"You already know Kate Williams," Tommy began, "and this is Dallas O'Brien."

Seaver barely acknowledged Kate. What was up with that?

He looked guilty about something, but Kate couldn't pinpoint the exact reason.

Her lawyer's eyes widened when he heard the O'Brien name, a common reaction she'd noticed and figured was due to the status of Dallas's family. Even she'd heard the name before she moved to Bluff, albeit briefly, and that was saying something.

"You represented Miss Williams in her adoption from the Safe Haven Adoption Agency, correct?" Tommy asked.

"Yes, I did." Seaver's eyebrows arched. "Why am I being asked about that? Miss Williams is right there and she can tell you everything."

"We appreciate your patience with the question," Tommy said, redirecting the conversation. Seaver was midfifties and wore a suit. His round stomach and ruddy cheeks didn't exactly create the picture of health.

"Did you know that Miss Williams's home was broken into yesterday?" Tommy pressed.

Seaver seemed genuinely shocked. "Why would I know that?" he asked, crossing his right leg over his left. "I don't live around here, Sheriff. Have you looked at anyone locally?"

"Whoever did this walked straight to her desk. Isn't that strange?" Tommy continued.

"I guess so. Maybe they were looking to steal her identity," Seaver guessed but he seemed tense.

"People usually search the trash for that information," Tommy said.

"What does any of this have to do with me?" Seaver asked.

"Nothing, I hope," Tommy quipped. "But on that file, the stolen one, was her adoption records. Now, why would anyone want those?"

"Good question. And one that I don't have an answer to," Seaver said, but his eyes told a different story.

It struck Kate as odd because he was practiced at presenting his side of an argument and maintaining a blank face, having done so a million times in court. And yet he seemed unnerved.

"A man tried to abduct Miss Williams's son yesterday, as well. Guess you don't know anything about that, either," Tommy murmured.

Pure shock and concern crossed Seaver's features. His top button was undone and his tie was loose around his neck. He leaned forward. "Look, I never dealt with the guy, but this sounds like the work of Harold Matthews. I've heard rumors about him setting up adoptions and then staging abductions. He works for Safe Haven and that's the reason I specifically requested Don Radcliffe. I don't know if any of the rumors are true, mind you. But that's where I'd look first."

"Could Radcliffe and Matthews be working together?" Tommy asked.

Seaver took a second to mull it over. "It can't be ruled out. I've placed a dozen babies through Radcliffe and this is the first time anything like this has happened."

Tommy asked a few more routine-sounding questions before asking for the list of clients with whom he'd placed babies from Safe Haven.

"I can't do that without a court order," Seaver said, tiny beads of sweat forming at his hairline.

"I'm asking for your cooperation, Mr. Seaver," Tommy countered.

"Look, I don't mean any disrespect, but I'm not about to expose clients who have requested and paid for private adoptions to anyone, not without a signed order from a judge," he said, folding his arms and then leaning back in his chair. "And especially not for a failed abduction attempt and a break-in."

"Then you must not have read today's paper," Tommy said.

Seaver blew out a frustrated breath. "Where is this going, Sheriff?"

"A man was murdered yesterday in connection with investigating Safe Haven Adoption Agency," Tommy said matter-of-factly.

A startled look crossed Seaver's features before he quickly regained his casual demeanor. "I've already told you everything I know. But for my money, I'd locate Harold Matthews." The lawyer pushed himself to his feet. "And if there are no more questions, I have other appointments to attend to today."

"I'll be in touch," Tommy said, also standing.

"I have no doubt you will, but you want to talk to Matthews, not me," he said as he walked out the door.

"I think he's lying," Dallas said when he'd left.

"What makes you say that?" Kate asked.

Before Dallas could answer, Tommy called Abigail into the room. "See if we can get a subpoena for William Seaver's client list as it relates to Safe Haven," he said.

"The judge has been downright cranky lately," she said. "I'll do my best to convince him."

Tommy thanked her. "Another thing before you go. I need everything you can get me on Harold Matthews. Search Don Radcliffe, too. If either one of those men have had so much as a parking ticket in the past year, I want to know about it."

"Will do," she said, before padding out the door and then disappearing down the hall.

"There's another way to go about this," Tommy said, turning to Dallas. "We need to step up our efforts on connecting the existing kidnappings to Seaver. It might take some time. If there's a link, we'll find it. Don't leave until I get back."

"I have a new theory," Dallas said, stopping his friend at the door. "What if Seaver is the kidnapper? He was a little too quick to pass the blame and give names. And he sure as hell seemed nervous to me."

Tommy leaned against the jamb, folding his arms. "I noticed that, as well."

"Has he been to the soup kitchen?" Dallas asked Kate.

"Yes. That's where we met right after the adoption," she said, still stunned at the thought.

"Was Allen around?" Dallas asked and she immediately knew what he was thinking. Seaver might've set up Allen as cover. But why would the lawyer try to take Jackson?

"As a matter of fact, yes," she responded. "But how would he know about Allen's feelings for me?"

"It's obvious to everyone," Dallas said quickly, and there was a hint of something in his voice. Jealousy? "Seaver knew you and could have easily arranged to set up Allen with the pictures," he added.

"I'm still missing motive," Tommy said.

"He might not be the one pulling the strings," Dallas said.

Tommy was already rocking his head. "If whoever was behind the kidnappings thinks Seaver arranged an adoption they didn't want to happen, then they could be pressuring him to find the infant."

"Exactly what I was thinking," Dallas said.

"Which would confirm our earlier thoughts that someone wants their son back and they're willing to do whatever it takes to find him," Kate said. An icy chill ran up her arms.

Deputy Lopez's voice boomed from the hallway.

Tommy ushered him inside his office.

"Three more of the adoptions shared the same lawyer," Lopez said.

"Let me guess... Seaver?" the sheriff asked.

Lopez nodded. "But here's something you don't know. Two of the babies were found today..."

Kate cringed, waiting to hear the next part as she prayed for good news.

"Both alive," Lopez said.

"Where?" Tommy demanded, before anyone else could.

"One was left at a baby furniture store two towns over, in one of the cribs for sale. An employee discovered the sleeping infant an hour after she opened, and called local police, who were able to make the match," the deputy stated.

"And what about the other one?" Tommy asked.

"He was left at a church, discovered before service began. Pastor said he'd been in the chapel half an hour before and there was no baby."

"Neither boy was hurt?" Tommy asked, with what could only be described as a relieved sigh.

"Not a hair on their bald heads," Lopez quipped with a smile.

"How long were they missing?" Tommy asked.

"A few days."

"Enough time for a proper DNA test," he mused.

This was good news for everyone except Kate. Some kidnapper was trying to find his own son and checking DNA of all the possibilities before giving them back. And that was fantastic for all the mothers of those babies, because it meant they were in the clear. Jackson, however, was still in question. There was a scrap of hope to hold on to, since the babies were being found alive. Extreme care was being taken to ensure that the infant boys were being located quickly.

Except what if Jackson was the one they were searching for...?

Kate closed her eyes, refusing to accept the possibility.

Tommy excused himself and the deputy followed.

"Seaver lied about not knowing the other family whose baby was abducted," Kate said.

Dallas nodded. "I picked up on that, too."

"What do we do now?" she asked. Dallas hadn't told his friend about the keys from Stacy and Kate hadn't expected him to, given that they'd received them in confidence.

"We have to wait for dark for our next move," he stated, with a look that said he knew exactly what she was asking.

Which meant they'd spend at least another whole day together.

"It's only a few weeks until Halloween. You have a party to help plan. I don't want to get in the way of your family," she said. All she had in the house was a three-foot fake ghost that said "Happy Halloween" and then giggled every time it detected movement. She'd nick-named him Ghost Buddy and he was all she'd had time to put out. Even though she knew Jackson wouldn't remember his first Halloween, she wanted to find a way to make it special. Ghost Buddy was her first real decoration and she figured that she could build her collection from there.

The thought of going home scared her because the more they dug into this case, the less she liked what they found and the more afraid she felt.

The only bright spot was that a couple more of the babies had turned up and they were fine.

Tommy returned a moment later. "I agree with you, by the way. I think Seaver's lying."

"Which means he's either involved or covering for someone who is," Dallas said.

"He gave us a name," Kate offered.

"That might have been meant to throw us off the real trail, buy some time or take himself off the suspect list," the sheriff said.

"Or dodge suspicion," Dallas added. "He seemed awfully uncomfortable."

"I noticed. I wanted to keep him here but he knew better than anyone that I had nothing to hold him on." Tommy nodded. "At least we have a few leads to chase down now. In the meantime, I think it's safer for the two of you on the ranch."

"You have my word that we won't leave unless we have to," Dallas said. "What did you learn when you interviewed Stacy last night?"

"Not much," Tommy said with a sigh. "She didn't recognize the guys and couldn't give much of a description other than what the gun looked like."

"Sorry that we couldn't help with that, either," Dallas said. "Unfortunately, my back was turned for the few seconds we were in the room, and Stacy blocked my only view of their faces, brief as it was."

"She's going to be okay," Kate interjected. "She's strong."

"I sent over security," Dallas said. "Wasn't sure if the guys would come back and I didn't want to take any chances, just in case someone got worried she could testify against them."

Tommy thanked him. "I'll let you know if we get the subpoena or any hits on linked cases," he added.

"What can you tell me about the murder scene yesterday?" Dallas asked.

"Nothing stood out. It will take time to process the site, but it looks like a standard forced-off-the-road-and-then-shot scenario."

Kate winced. How could any of that be run-of-the-mill?

And then it dawned on her why the voice at Stacy's office sounded familiar. "It was him. The other day at Morton's office. The guy who tried to take Jackson."

Dallas's head was rocking. "I couldn't put my finger on what was bugging me before. That's it."

Tommy added the notation to the file.

Dallas's phone vibrated. He checked the screen and the brief flicker of panic on his face sent her pulse racing.

He muttered a few "uh-huh"'s before saying they were on their way and clicking off.

She was already to her feet before he could make a move. "What's going on?" she asked.

"There was a disturbance on the east side of the property. A motorcycle tried to run through the gate," he said, quickly reassuring her that no one got through and everyone was just fine.

She wished that reassurance calmed her fast-beating heart. It didn't.

"You want me to send a deputy?" Tommy called, as they broke into a run.

"I could use an escort," Dallas shouted back.

Kate's chest squeezed and she couldn't breathe.

No way could she allow those men to get near her son.

Chapter 12

Dallas raced through the city with a law-enforcement escort clearing the path. He'd enter the property on the west side near his place, because there was more security at that checkpoint. The earlier ruckus had been on the opposite side, miles away, and if he was lucky, he and Kate would be able to slip in from the west before anyone else could realize what he'd done.

Things were escalating and the kidnappers seemed to be zeroing in.

The thought did occur to Dallas that the attempted breach could be a distraction meant to get him and Kate out in the open. Or someone inside, if he took another vantage point. The latter wouldn't succeed, because there was plenty of security at all the weak spots on the ranch. If the former was the case, then it was working, and he had to consider the possibility that he was playing right into their opponents' hands.

Still, he had to take the chance. One look at Kate and he knew she needed to hold her baby in her arms after the disturbing news about Seaver.

He had her pull out his cell and call his head of security. "Put the call on speaker," he instructed.

She did and he could hear the line ringing almost immediately.

"We're close, about five minutes out," Dallas said to Gideon Fisher, his security chief, when he answered.

"I'll be at the gate and ready, sir," Fisher responded. "Ryder and Austin are here, with a team of my men."

"Excellent." Dallas knew all the extra security at the gate would alert anyone watching to the possibility they'd be coming in that way, but his brothers knew how to handle a rifle and Dallas wanted the extra firepower in case anything went down. "Where's everyone else?"

"Tyler's up front. Colin's roaming."

It sounded like his brothers were ready to go, in addition to the staff of eight...well, seven, since Reece stood vigil in Stacy's hospital room.

A sport-utility vehicle with blacked-out windows roared up from behind.

Dallas's truck was sandwiched between the deputy in front and the SUV barreling toward their bumper.

"Hold on," Dallas told Kate, just as the SUV rammed into them, causing their heads to jolt forward.

"Sir?" Gideon said.

"We have company and we just took a hit," Dallas replied.

"Roger that, sir."

Dallas could see the entrance to the ranch in the distance. Once inside, they'd be safe, but it was dicey whether or not they could get there.

He flashed the high beams to alert their escort to the trouble brewing behind him. The deputy must've noticed because he turned on his flashing lights. "Black SUV, stop your vehicle," the officer called out over his loudspeaker.

The SUV rammed them once more, again throwing their heads forward.

"Change of plans." Dallas gunned the engine and popped over into the other lane of the narrow country road. He was lucky that there was so little traffic in the area and this stretch of road was straight and flat, so there'd be no surprises.

The deputy slowed to allow Dallas safe passage, but the SUV whipped into the left lane, as well, maintaining close proximity to Dallas's bumper.

Even repeating the message over the bullhorn didn't work. The other driver persisted.

Dallas got a good look at him in the rearview and he wore similar clothes to the kidnapper at the soup kitchen. He'd bet money it was the same person.

Worse yet, when Dallas moved into the right lane again the SUV pulled up beside him, blocking his turn.

Austin stepped onto the road and aimed his rifle directly at the oncoming vehicle. Dallas pointed and the driver must've noticed, because he hit the brakes. Before the deputy could respond, the SUV had made a U-turn and was speeding off in the opposite direction.

The deputy followed in pursuit, lights flashing.

Dallas turned onto his property, and that was

when he finally glanced at Kate, whose face had gone bleached-sheet white.

She didn't speak and he didn't force the issue.

As soon as he parked in front of his house, she practically flew out of the truck. "Is Jackson in there?"

"Yes." Dallas followed her inside as she ran to her infant son.

Janis met her in the living room, a sleeping Jackson in her arms, and immediately handed him over. She seemed to know that Kate wouldn't care if the baby woke. She had to hold him.

The look on Kate's face, the same damn expression from yesterday morning, cut a hole in Dallas's heart.

Jackson wound up to cry, then belted out a good one. The boy had strong lungs.

Kate cradled her son while Janis excused herself.

The crying abated a few minutes later as Kate soothed her baby, and the sight of the two of them together like that stirred something in Dallas's heart.

He didn't want to have feelings for anyone right now.

The timing was completely off, now that he was chasing down what had happened to Susan. Besides, he was busier than ever, between the ranch and the business. He was helping Kate and didn't need to confuse his feelings for more than that.

Dallas excused himself to work in his home office.

He hadn't turned on his computer in a few days and that would mean an out-of-control inbox. He'd seen the emails rolling in on his smartphone, but he'd been too busy to give them much thought.

Then there was the ranch to run, and Halloween Bash just around the corner.

After answering emails until his eyes blurred, he

stretched out his sore limbs while seated in his office chair.

The stress of the past few days was catching up with him and at some point he'd need to sleep. There wasn't much chance of that as long as Kate was in the house. His mind kept wandering to her silky body curled up on the bed in the guest room, her soft skin...

Just thinking about it started stirring places that didn't need to be riled up. Especially since there was no chance for release.

So he focused on his inbox again, wishing he'd receive an email or text from Tommy stating that they got the guys in the SUV.

The next time he glanced at the clock, it was three o'clock in the afternoon. The house was quiet. He'd worked through lunch, which wasn't unusual for him. His stomach decided it was time to eat.

Work might have distracted him for a little while, but more and more he wondered what had happened to Susan. Given Morton's death and both their associations with Safe Haven, Dallas feared the worst.

There were 437 messages in his spam folder and he checked each one to see if Susan had tried to contact him but her note had gotten hung up in his filter.

Nothing.

He pulled the set of keys Stacy had given him from his pocket, set them on his desk and lazily ran his fingers along them.

Granted, he and Susan had no business being a couple, but he still felt angry at the possibility of something bad happening to her.

Was she in trouble when she'd called him and told him about the baby? Had she been hoping for his protection? He'd assumed all along that she was trying to trap him into marriage, and she had been, but now that he'd seen the look on Kate's face when it came to a threat to her son, another reality set in. Susan might have been desperate and looking for protection. Marriage to Dallas might've been a way for her to secure her son's future.

She had to know that Dallas would've figured out the truth at some point if the child hadn't been his. Then again, if her life had been in danger, she might have figured she'd tell him after the deal was sealed.

Saying he was the father could've been the equivalent of a Hail Mary pass in football, a last-ditch effort to save the game.

Frustration nipped at his heels like a determined predator. Dallas searched his memory for anything he could remember about the last conversation they'd had before she'd gone missing, and he came up empty.

His cell phone buzzed. The call was from Tommy, so Dallas immediately answered.

"I have news," his friend said.

"What did you learn?"

"We got a few hits today. Of the six abductions that we know about so far, four of them used Seaver," Tommy related.

"So most likely he was involved in the others," Dallas reasoned.

"True. And there's something else."

"Okay," Dallas said.

"Don Radcliffe was found dead in his apartment in Houston."

"Isn't that who Seaver worked with at Safe Haven?" Dallas asked.

"It was."

"Any word on Harold Matthews?"

"We can't locate him. But he's roughly the size and shape of the man you described as the kidnapper from yesterday morning," Tommy replied, then paused for a beat. "Are you alone?"

"Yeah. Why?"

"I have personal news." The ominous tone in his friend's voice sat heavy in Dallas's thoughts.

"What is it?" he asked.

"At first I thought I should wait until all this is over, but I figured you'd want to know the minute I found out. It's about your parents. I got a report from the coroner a couple of days ago that indicated your mother had a heart attack," Tommy said quietly.

"What are the chances of both my parents having a heart attack on the same day?" Dallas asked.

"It made me suspicious, too, so I requested a lab workup. The toxicology report came back showing cyanide in both of their systems. Enough to cause heart attacks," Tommy said.

"What does that mean, exactly?" Dallas was too stunned to form a coherent thought beyond that question.

"I'm opening a formal investigation into their deaths and I wanted you to be the first to know."

Those words were like a punch to Dallas's gut.

"I know it's a lot to process right now, and I may not find anything, because ingestion could've been accidental," Tommy added. "But I'm not leaving any stone unturned when it comes to your parents."

Dallas sat there. He couldn't even begin to digest the thought that anyone could've harmed his parents.

"Dallas, are you still with me?" his friend asked.

He grunted an affirmation, then drew a deep, rasping breath. "Is it possible that their accident might have been staged?"

"Yes, but I'm not ready to jump to any conclusions just yet."

The line went quiet again. Because the implication sitting between them was murder.

"You know I'm here for you anytime you want to talk," Tommy said at last.

Dallas realized he was gripping his cell phone tight enough to make his fingers hurt. "Any word on the SUV? Because the driver easily could've been the kidnapper from yesterday."

"It disappeared and we lost the trail."

The night was pitch-black and the temperature had dipped below freezing. The wind howled. At least Jackson was with Janis, in a cozy bed sound asleep.

Kate's teeth chattered even though she wore two layers of clothing underneath her coat.

She and Dallas had decided to wait until after dark to go to Wayne's house, reasoning that if they left too late, then dogs in the neighborhood might give them away. He'd parked four blocks over.

Ever since she woke from her nap, she'd noticed something was different about Dallas. His mood had darkened and he'd closed up.

Was he preparing himself for the news as to whether or not he was a father?

He had to have considered the possibility that if he'd had a son, the boy could've been targeted in the kidnappings, as well.

At nine o'clock, lights were still on and households busy with activity. Dallas put his arm around Kate's waist and even through the thick layers she felt a sizzle of heat on her skin.

Wayne Morton's house was on a quiet lane in a family neighborhood. Smoke billowed from chimneys on the tree-lined street of half-acre lots. The crisp air smelled of smoke from logs crackling in fireplaces. Halloween lights and decorations filled front yards.

There were enough neighbors about that she and Dallas could slip in and out of Morton's house without drawing attention.

As Kate walked down the sidewalk, tucked under Dallas's arm, she could see kids in the front rooms watching TV or reading on couches, their mother's arms curled around them.

Someone whistled and then called out, "Here, Dutch. Come on, boy."

A tear escaped before Kate could sniff it away. She turned her face so Dallas wouldn't see her emotions, while wondering what it must be like to have a mother's unconditional love and acceptance. She wished that for her and Carter.

Another person half a block down was rolling a trash can onto the front sidewalk for weekly garbage pickup.

"Morton's place is on the next street," Dallas said in a low voice, interrupting her thoughts.

When she didn't respond, he glanced at her.

A second, longer look caused him to stop walking. He turned until they were face-to-face.

Another errant tear escaped and he thumbed it away.

"Are you okay?" He spoke and she could see his breath in the cold air.

Instead of speaking, she nodded.

Dallas's thumb trailed across her bottom lip and then her jawline. Kate had never known a light touch could be so sweet, so comforting.

A set of porch lights turned off across the street and they both pulled back.

Dallas laced their fingers together as they strolled down the lane.

As Morton's house came into view, Kate couldn't help but notice it was the only one on the street that was completely blacked out. That image was sobering and a sad feeling settled over her, making walking even more difficult.

Thinking of Stacy in the hospital, how sad she'd been, made Kate feel awful. Would she come home to an empty, dark house in a few days when she recovered? How would she get past this? Wayne, her job, seemed to be her life. She'd said they were all she had. Before Jackson had come into Kate's life, she could relate to feeling empty inside. And now with Dallas in the picture, she'd never been more aware of how alone she'd been when she was married to Robert.

Dallas stopped at the bottom of the stairs, clearly as affected by the scene as Kate was. She could see guilt so clearly written in his expression. There was something else in his eyes when she really looked closer. It dawned on her what: he might be about to find out if he was a father.

Worse yet, if his child had been adopted out to a stranger, then Dallas might never find the little boy. Given the nature of closed adoptions and the privacy of all involved, it would take moving heaven and earth to locate the baby, and Dallas O'Brien didn't strike her as the kind of man who could live with himself if he had a child out there somewhere and didn't know him.

"Are you ready for this?" she asked.

A car turned onto the street two blocks down.

Dallas glanced around. "As ready as I'll ever be."

The layout was just as Stacy had described. Dallas ushered Kate inside, closing and locking the front door behind them as she disarmed the alarm. The office was to the left of the foyer and had double French doors with glass panels.

There was enough light coming from the surrounding houses with the Halloween lights on for them to see large objects like furniture.

Dallas slid the office key into the lock and then paused to take a fortifying breath.

Here went nothing…

Chapter 13

Dallas stepped through the door and quickly found the next keypad, to punch in the code for the office.

They kept the lights off so as not to alert anyone who might be driving by or watching the place that they were there.

Inside the office, Dallas located a few books and brought them to the window. Stacy had said the volume they wanted would be on the second shelf, two books from the right. She hadn't told them there would be a wall of bookcases to choose from.

A beam of light flashed from outside. A cop?

That would so not be good. Kate froze and held her breath until the beam moved across another window.

What the heck was that?

She didn't know and didn't want to ask questions.

Fear assaulted her as memories from yesterday invaded her thoughts. The men, the guns…

She took a deep breath to calm her frazzled nerves. Getting worked up wouldn't change a thing. They'd still be in a dead man's house going through his things. And even that didn't matter as much as getting back to Jackson safely. Janis had taken him to the main house to sleep tonight, and Kate's heart ached being away from him. Even though she wouldn't see him until morning, being back on the ranch would calm her racing pulse.

She moved to another bookshelf and pulled out a couple of volumes, making her best guess where the right one would be. Then she stepped next to Dallas at the window, where there was more light. One of the books was definitely less heavy than the others. She'd noticed the instant she'd slid it from the shelf.

Disappointment filled her when she opened the lighter book. Nothing.

She and Dallas moved on to other bookcases and flipped open more volumes, placing them back as closely as possible to their original spots.

"I think I have it," he said at last, making tracks to the window to get a better look. He held his offering up to the light. "Yep. This is it."

A noise from the alley caught their attention. Dallas grabbed her hand and moved toward the door in double time.

"It's probably just a cat, but we don't want to stick around and find out," he said.

"What if someone's watching the house?" she asked, ignoring the sinking feeling in the pit of her stomach. Adrenaline had kicked in and her flight response was triggered. She needed to get the heck out of there more than she needed to breathe.

"Stay calm and pretend like we're supposed to be here." Dallas checked the peephole before opening the door. So far, the way looked clear, but he couldn't be certain no one was out there. He tucked the book under his coat, thinking about the meeting he needed to set up with his brothers in the morning to deliver Tommy's news about their parents.

Right now, he needed to get Kate and himself the hell out of there and back to the ranch.

After locking the door behind them, he led Kate down the few steps to the porch. That was when he heard the telltale click of a shell being engaged in the chamber of a shotgun.

"Where do you think you're going?" a stern male voice said. "Turn around and put your hands where I can see them."

"Don't panic," Dallas whispered. "Do as he says and we'll be fine."

Dallas turned slowly to find himself staring down the barrel of a shotgun. Behind it was a man in his late sixties with white hair and a stout build. Dallas had spent enough time around law-enforcement officers to know that this guy had been on the job. He wore pajama bottoms, slippers and an overcoat.

"What are you doing here?" the man asked.

"We just stopped by to check on the place for a friend," Dallas said, figuring this was more a friendly neighborhood-watch situation than a real threat. He couldn't relax, though. This guy looked like he meant business.

"Does this friend have a name?" the man asked, business end of the shotgun still trained on Dallas.

"Wayne Morton," Dallas replied, hoping that would be enough. "He and Stacy are out of town and asked us to keep an eye on the house."

"That right?" The guy eyed them up and down suspiciously.

Kate stepped closer to Dallas and put her arm around him. "They're friends of ours and I'd appreciate it if you wouldn't point that thing at us."

The man lowered the barrel, much to Dallas's relief. It was too early to exhale, however.

"You should turn on the porch light," the man said. "And it's dark in the alley. There's a light back there, too."

"Will do," Dallas said, although he'd pretty much agree to anything to walk away from this guy without raising suspicion.

"Honey, we have to go. Babysitter's waiting," Kate said, twining her fingers in his.

"Thanks for the tip," Dallas said with a nod. His chin tucked close to his chest, staving off the cold. He decided keeping it there would shield his face. A man who used to be paid to notice things wasn't a good one to have around.

"When's Morton coming back?" the guy asked.

"In a few days," Dallas said, praying he hadn't read today's newspaper.

That seemed to satisfy the neighbor. Dallas could hear his feet shuffling in the opposite direction. He glanced back just in case and was relieved to confirm the man was heading home.

If this guy was watching the PI's house, then others could be, too. And that got Dallas's boots moving a little faster.

Another sobering reality struck him.

The data on the thumb drive tucked away in the book he held on to could change his life forever.

The weight of that thought pressed heavy on his shoulders as he drove back to the ranch.

"I don't think Stacy should go home until we figure all this out," Kate said, breaking the silence between them as he pulled onto the ranch property.

"Agreed," Dallas said, thankful to focus on something else for a minute. Another thought had occurred to him. The information on that drive might tell him what had happened to Susan. And at least one area of his life could have resolution, even as more questions arose in others.

Whatever was there might be valuable to someone. Morton could be dead because of the information gained since he was on an investigation for Dallas when he was killed.

And then there could be nothing relevant on it, too. Dallas was just guessing at this point, his guilt kicking into high gear again. There were so many emotions pinging through him at what he might find on that zip drive.

Dallas gripped the steering wheel tighter as he navigated his truck into his garage.

"I doubt I'll be able to sleep without Jackson here," Kate said, and he could hear the anguish in her voice.

"You want me to have him brought over from the main house?" Dallas asked. "I can make a call and he'll be here in ten minutes."

"No. I don't want to wake Janis after she was nice

enough to help care for him in the first place." Kate sighed wistfully. "He's probably asleep anyway, and waking him up just so I can look at him seems selfish."

"I can send a text to have her bring him over first thing in the morning, as soon as they wake," Dallas offered, turning off the engine. "In fact, she probably left a message already, letting us know how the night went. I silenced my cell phone before we left."

He fished the device from his front pocket and then checked the screen as he walked in the door to the kitchen. "Yep. Here it is," he said, showing it to Kate.

Her eyes lit up and they felt like a beacon to Dallas. Everything inside him was churning in a storm.

There was a picture of her sleeping baby, with one word underneath: *angel*.

"Thank you," Kate said, tears welling.

"I didn't mean to make you cry." Dallas held the phone out to her. "You can hang on to that if you want. I need to check the contents of this drive."

"Mind if I come with you?" she asked. "Or I can stay out here if you'd like some privacy."

Normally, that was exactly what he would want.

"I'd rather you be with me when I take a look," he said, and he surprised himself by meaning it. As crazy as everything had been in the past few days, and as much as his own life had been turned upside down even more in a matter of minutes, being with Kate was the only thing that made sense to him.

She set his cell phone on the counter, took his hand and once again laced their fingers together. Rockets exploded inside his chest with her touch.

"Ready?" she asked.

"As much as I can be," he said, and the look she shot him said she knew exactly what he was talking about.

They walked into his office hand in hand and Dallas couldn't ignore how right this whole scenario felt. It seemed so natural to have her in his home, which was a dangerous thought, most likely due to an overload of emotions.

Dallas sat in his office chair and Kate perched on one of his knees. He had to wrap his arms around her to turn on his computer, and that felt so good. A big part of him wanted to lose himself in her and block out everything else.

Another side of him needed to see what was on that flash drive.

His computer booted up quickly and he mentally prepared himself for what he would find. There could be nothing at all, and that would bring a disappointment all its own.

Dallas needed answers and yet there was a healthy dose of fear exploding inside him at finding the truth.

He plugged in the device and a few seconds later a file popped up in the center of the screen.

Dallas clicked on the icon with a foreboding feeling. He scanned a couple of documents.

"Okay, from what I can tell so far, Wayne tracked a baby to Safe Haven and that's where the trail ends," Kate said. "Which is what we already knew."

That about summed up what Dallas had seen, as well. And, no, it wasn't helpful.

"Here's the odd thing. Once the baby was born, Morton seems to think Susan disappeared," Dallas noted. He also realized that the dates didn't rule out the possibility that Jackson was his son.

"And, like, seriously vanished," Kate mused. "No more records of her exist anywhere. I mean, I guess I can see that she might have had a closed adoption, and the agency would have coded her file so as not to give her identity away. That happened with mine. The birth mother wanted a sealed adoption and I was in no position to argue. Plus, I thought it would be better anyway. But there should be some trail of her somewhere—an address, credit card, cell-phone record."

"Her bank account has been closed. There's no record of her existence."

"It's almost like she died," Kate said.

"But then, wouldn't there be a record of that?" Dallas shoved aside the thought that Kate's baby could actually be Susan's.

This was not the time for that discussion. First things first, and that meant Dallas needed to figure out if he was a father.

He opened the other documents one by one, scanning each for any link to his and Susan's baby. If there was one.

There was nothing.

Morton had been thorough and yet… Dallas opened the last file. It was labeled WS.

"Morton questioned your attorney the day before he was killed," Dallas said.

Kate's eyes were wide. He could see them clearly in the reflection from the computer screen.

She opened her mouth to speak but no words came.

"We need to have that DNA test. It's the only way we'll know for sure that you're not Jackson's father," she said.

"If that's what you want. I can arrange one in the morning," Dallas told her.

She muttered something under her breath. She'd spoken so low, Dallas wasn't sure he heard right.

Should he be offended?

"I hope you know that I'd make one hell of a fine father someday," he said, a little indignant. His emotions were getting the best of him.

Kate turned those blue eyes on him and his chest clutched.

"I didn't mean to insinuate that you wouldn't be a good father. You would." Her eyes were filled with tears now. "It's just Jackson's all I have. My relationship with my parents is practically nonexistent. My brother and I used to be close and now he's siding with my mother, which stinks, considering how little she supported either one of us growing up."

Dallas's arms tightened around Kate's waist, and that was a bad idea given the mix of emotions stirring inside him. A very bad idea.

Tears streamed down her beautiful face. Dallas wanted to say something to make it better, and yet all he could manage was "I'm sorry."

"No. I don't expect you to understand, and I'm embarrassed to say anything. I have Jackson now and he's my world," she said.

"I can see that he is," Dallas assured her.

"And he's enough. All I ever wanted was to have a family. Is that too much to ask?" She buried her face in her hands and released a sob.

"It's not," Dallas said. "And I understand more than you know. Because I have an amazing family, I know exactly how much we build each other up, rely on each other. I can't imagine where I'd be if I didn't have my brothers by my side, and especially since we lost our parents."

He lifted her chin until her gaze met his, ignoring the rush of electricity coursing through his body. It took heroic effort to turn away from the pulse throbbing at the base of her throat.

"You're an amazing mother," he stated, and she immediately made a move to protest. "Don't do that to yourself. You are. Jackson is lucky to have you and you're doing a great job. Don't doubt that for a second."

"I'm scared," she admitted, and it looked like it took a lot to say those words. Someone as strong as she was wouldn't want to concede to a weakness. Dallas knew all about that, too.

"It's okay," he said reassuringly.

"What if I lose him? What if my adoption turns out to be illegal and someone has a claim on my son? I've read stories like that." She stopped to let out another sob.

"It won't happen."

"That's impossible to say right now," she said. "I could lose him and that would destroy me. He's all I have."

"You might not have had friends when you came to town and you might've been too busy to make any since. But you have me now. And any one of my brothers would stand behind you, as well. Plus you've found a friend in Stacy."

"You're kind to say that, but we've only just met," she said, her gaze searching his to find out if there was any truth to what he was saying.

"We may have known each other for just a few days,

but that doesn't mean I don't *know* you," Dallas said calmly. He considered himself a good judge of character and any woman this devoted to her child couldn't be a bad person. She put Jackson first every time. Period.

In some deep and unexplainable part of his heart, he knew Kate.

There was something about Dallas O'Brien's quiet masculinity and deep voice that soothed Kate's frazzled nerves. It shouldn't. She shouldn't allow it. But *shouldn't* walked right out the door with self-control as she leaned forward and kissed him.

The instant her lips touched his, Kate knew she was in serious trouble, and not just because she might be sitting across a courtroom from this man someday fighting for custody of her son. Everything in her body wanted to be with Dallas, and that should stop her.

He deepened the kiss and his hands came up to cup her face.

And there wasn't anything she could do to resist what her body craved. With him so close, his scent filled her senses and heat pooled between her thighs. It had been a very long time since she'd had good sex and her body craved release that only Dallas could give. Normally, it took time to get to know a man before she'd let her guard down and allow him to get this close. But she'd never been *this* attracted to anyone. With Dallas, it felt right, and her brain argued that there was no reason to stop. From a physical sense, her brain was right: she was an adult; he was an adult. They could do whatever they wanted. Her heart was the holdout.

Except that the logical voice that generally stopped

her from making life-changing mistakes was annoyingly quiet.

And she wanted Dallas O'Brien with her entire being.

Her hands tugged at the hem of his gray V-neck shirt. The cotton was smooth in her hands as she pulled it over his head and dropped it onto the floor.

This time, there was no hesitation on either of their parts. No stopping to make sure this was right.

Her shirt joined his a moment later and the growl that ripped from his throat sent heat swirling.

"You're incredible," he said, his hands roaming across her bare stomach.

And then he cupped her breast and it was her turn to moan. His lips closed on hers as though he was swallowing the sound.

His hands on her caused her breasts to swell and her nipples to bead into tiny buds. Her back arched involuntarily and she wanted more…more of his hands on her…more of his touch…more of his clothes off.

Kate stood, unbuttoned her jeans and shimmied out of them, kicking off her shoes in the process. Her bra and panties joined them on the floor.

And then she stood in front of Dallas naked.

His hands came up to rest on her hips and he pressed his forehead against her stomach.

One second was all it took for him to decide. No words were needed.

And then in a flash he was standing and she was helping him out of his jeans and boxers.

He lifted her onto the desk and rolled his thumb skillfully across her slick heat.

"I'm ready." It was all she needed to say before the tip of his erection was there, teasing her.

She clasped her legs around his midsection as he drove himself inside her. She threw her head back and rocked against his erection until he filled her. She stretched around his thick length.

"You're insanely gorgeous," Dallas groaned, pulling halfway out and then driving deep inside her again. She met him stroke for stroke as he stroked her nipple between his thumb and forefinger, rocketing her to the edge.

She grabbed on to his shoulders, her fingers digging into his muscles to gain purchase.

Stride for stride, she matched his pace, until it became dizzying and she was on the brink of ecstasy with no chance of returning.

The explosion shattered her, inside and out, and she could feel his erection pulsing as he gave in to his own release. He stayed inside her as she collapsed on the desk, bringing him with her, over her.

He brushed kisses up her neck, across her jawline, her chin.

And then he pulled back and locked eyes with her.

"You know one time isn't going to be enough, right?" And the sexy little smile curving his lips released a thousand butterflies in her stomach.

Chapter 14

Dallas woke at five o'clock the next morning, an hour before his alarm was set to go off. Kate's warm, naked body against his in his bed made it next to impossible to force to get up.

The moment he eased from beneath the covers, he regretted it. He walked lightly to his office so he wouldn't disturb her sleep. He needed to make a call to Tommy and fill him in on what they'd found out last night. And there was so much information making the rounds in his head after learning the news about his parents. He was doing his level best not to jump the gun straight to murder when it came to them, knowing he might be grasping at straws to shift the blame away from himself.

He threw on a fresh pair of boxers and jeans and then moved into the kitchen to make coffee.

"Seaver's involved up to his eyeballs," Dallas said to Tommy over the phone, taking his first sip of fresh brew. His friend had always been an early riser, awake and on the job by five.

"Do I want to know how you know this?" his friend asked, and there was more than a hint of frustration in his voice.

"Morton visited him the day before his death," Dallas insisted, not really wanting to go there with the lawman.

"That's not exactly an answer."

"Just talk to him again. Believe me when I say it'll pay off," Dallas said.

"I'd love to. The problem is I have to walk a fine line with him," Tommy stated. "And it takes time to pull together evidence."

"He killed Morton to silence him. I'm sure he did." Dallas knew full well his words weren't enough to go on. They required proof.

"That may be true, but I need more than your hunch to get a search warrant for his house or his bank accounts," Tommy said. He blew out a frustrated breath.

Dallas knew his friend was upset at the situation and not at him. He shared the sentiment 100 percent.

"I hear what you're saying and I know you have to do this the right way to make it stick, but trust me when I say he knows more than he's telling." Could he share what he'd found on the data drive? He hadn't obtained it illegally, and yet he felt Stacy should be the one to make the call.

"I can put a tail on him. That's about the best I can do under the circumstances." Tommy blew out another frustrated breath.

Speaking of Stacy, did Seaver know about her and Wayne? Dallas wondered.

"I'm probably going to regret this, but what makes you think he shot Wayne Morton?" Tommy asked.

"Believe me when I say it's more than a hunch. Can you check his tire treads to see if they match the ones at the scene?" Dallas asked.

"Already getting someone on it," Tommy said, sounding like his coffee hadn't quite kicked in yet. "Did you get any word on Susan?"

"As a matter of fact, I did." He could share that, since, technically, he'd paid for that information and part of the data belonged to him. "Here's the thing with her. When she disappeared from New Mexico, it's like she vanished. No more paper. One day she was there and then it was like she never existed."

"She get involved with a criminal who made her go away?" Tommy asked, his interest piqued.

"Wouldn't there be a paper trail? Apartment lease? Something?" Dallas asked. "I mean even in the worst-case scenario there'd be a death certificate."

"True." Tommy got quiet. "Not to mention the fact that she was living in New Mexico. Why use a Texas adoption agency?"

"I'm figuring that she was hoping her child would grow up close to home," Dallas said. "I'd have to think there'd be a missing person's report on her somewhere, right? But you checked and there isn't."

"Where'd you get your information?" His friend clicked keys on his computer. "Never mind. Don't tell me. I don't want to know."

"Is there anything you can use to link Seaver to

Morton's murder?" Dallas asked. "Any evidence that might've been overlooked?"

"Tire tracks are iffy, at best. I doubt I could convince a judge to give me what I want based on just that little bit of evidence, so even if they match he'll say so do the tracks of a hundred other vehicles," Tommy muttered. "I'll check to see if Seaver owns a gun. Might get lucky there and get a caliber match from ballistics."

"I've been thinking a lot about Allen Lentz," Dallas said. "About him being set up. Seaver met him, and my instincts say he decided to take advantage of that crush Lentz has on Kate."

"Given his computer skills, Lentz should've been able to cover his tracks better," Tommy agreed. "Maybe I can find a link there."

"We know the kidnapper didn't act alone. If this was a crime of passion, then Allen would've acted on his own, wouldn't he?" Dallas asked, ignoring the knot in his gut as he thought of another man making a pass at Kate.

"That's a safe bet. Allen seemed to think there was still a chance with Kate. If all hope had been lost then he might be motivated to do something more extreme. She seemed to be dodging his advances without outright rejecting him," Tommy said.

"The guy attempting the kidnapping was fairly young. I'm just trying to cover all the bases, but is there any chance Allen could've hired someone?" Dallas asked.

"Nothing from his bank account gives me that impression. No large withdrawals in the past few months."

"What about neighbors?"

"Everyone alibied," Tommy stated.

"Seems like Lentz can be safely ruled out as a suspect," Dallas said.

"That's where I'm at with him," Tommy confirmed. "Good to look at this from all angles, though."

That gave Dallas another thought. "Could someone else be pulling the strings with Seaver?"

"That's a good question," his friend said. "One I hope to answer very soon. So, yes, it's a definite possibility."

Dallas hoped to have an answer, too. Because Kate's future was hanging in the balance.

"I'll do my best to track down Susan using my means," the lawman told him.

"I'd like that very much," Dallas said. "And thank you for looking into my parents' situation. I'll tell the family this morning."

"I'm not making any promises, but if there's something foul, I'll figure it out," Tommy said.

Dallas thanked his friend again, ended the call and then checked the clock. It was almost five thirty. He'd received a text from Janis. She and Jackson were up and she was about to give him his bottle. She said they'd be there around six.

He could wake Kate up for another round of the best sex of his life before the baby showed up. Or he could fix another cup of coffee.

He stood up and turned toward his bedroom.

Kate on his bed, in his bed, had Dallas wanting more than just a night or two with her. But what else? When this was all over, he needed to sort out his emotions and figure out exactly where he saw this relationship fitting into his already overcrowded life.

Relationship? Was that what was happening between them? Something was different, because for the first time in his life, Dallas had no clue what his next move was going to be.

She stirred and they made love slowly this time.

"I'll grab you a cup of coffee," he said, kissing her one last time before leaving the bed.

"Really?" She stretched and the move caused her breasts to thrust forward. The sheet fell to her waist as she sat up, and all he could see was her silky skin. "'Cause I could get used to this."

"Good," he said, thinking the same thing as he forced his gaze away from that hot body and walked toward the hallway.

By the time he fixed her coffee, Kate was dressed and Jackson was coming through the front door in Janis's arms. Dallas couldn't help but notice that the older woman was beaming.

"Thank you for taking care of him," Kate said, reaching for the baby.

He smiled and that was all it took for her to beam, too.

"It was truly my pleasure. I married young, but we never were able to have children," the older woman said wistfully. "Lost my Alvin to the war and never found anyone I could love as much."

She waved her hand in the air and sniffed back a tear. "No need to get sentimental before coffee. I enjoyed every minute spent with this little man and I hope you'll let me watch him again real soon."

Janis cooed at Jackson, who smiled as Dallas grasped two mugs of coffee.

"You staying?" he asked Janis, gesturing with a cup.

She was already waving him off. "No. I better get back to the main house. There's been a lot of excitement lately and it's best if everyone feels like it's still business as usual."

"You sure? I make the best coffee on the ranch," he said persuasively.

She held out a hand and pretended to let it shake. "Already had half a pot. If I drink any more we'll have an earthquake going."

"Keep me posted if anything happens at the main house," Dallas said.

"I have a few appointments scheduled, planning for the Halloween Bash. Should I have them rescheduled, or plan to meet those individuals for lunch in town?" she asked.

"Off property might be best for now," he agreed. "Until we can sort out everything that's happening and be sure everyone's safe."

"I thought you'd say that," she added, as she excused herself and moved to the front door and then looked at Kate again. "He's an awfully gorgeous baby. Don't you think so, Dallas?"

"As far as babies go, this one's all right," he said with a wink to Kate. He set her coffee mug next to her and looked at mother and child.

Could the three of them, and possibly four, if he was a father, ever be a family?

He'd known Kate Williams for just a few days and was already thinking about a future with her?

That made about as much sense as salting a glass of tea.

Dallas mentally shook off the thought. He'd gone without sleep for two nights and it had him off balance.

Plus there were the holidays and the recent news about his parents. He was grateful his ringtone sounded, providing a much-needed distraction.

It was Tommy.

Dallas answered. "I'm putting the call on speaker so Kate can hear."

She looked up from where she sat on the floor playing with Jackson.

"I have news about Susan," his friend said.

"What did you find out?" Dallas moved closer to Kate.

"Your guy was right. She disappeared. As in cleaned out from the system," Tommy revealed.

"What does that mean? A person can't just vanish, can they?" Kate asked, astonished.

"There's only one way I can think of," Dallas said. "Could she have been placed in a witness protection program?"

"It's the only thing that makes sense," Tommy agreed. "I should be able to pull up some record on her, but they just stopped right around the time her baby would have been born. And there's no report of her hospitalization."

"So she knew she'd be going into the program during the pregnancy," Dallas said, realizing that was most likely why she'd wanted to get married. She wanted the baby to have a normal life, and Dallas was the only person capable of protecting her son. Which brought him back to his initial question... Was he the father?

"Seaver's missing. We'll bring him in for more questions as soon as we locate him," Tommy added.

"Wait a minute. I thought you put a tail on him." Dallas took a sip of coffee, needing the jolt of caffeine.

If he understood things correctly, finding Susan was a complete dead end. People in the witness protection program didn't randomly show up again. The only way to figure out if he was the father of her child would be a DNA test of the baby, but he had no idea where the little tyke was or whom he was with.

Speaking of Susan, she'd said a few things to him that made Dallas think she must've wanted a normal life for her child, and that was why she'd given him up for adoption. Dallas would bet money that she'd used Harold Matthews at Safe Haven to handle the paperwork for her or handle the adoption without paperwork. Even if Tommy could get a subpoena for Safe Haven's records, which was highly doubtful, that paperwork most likely wouldn't exist. The agency administrators would be smart enough not to keep records for an under-the-table adoption, especially if the Feds were somehow involved.

Seaver must know something about Susan, and that was why he was involved.

Pieces started clicking together in Dallas's mind.

"I have a theory about what might've happened," he said. "Susan was in over her head with someone. This person was involved in illegal activities and she decided to turn state's evidence against him, putting her and her baby's lives in danger. She didn't want that for her son, so she arranged an adoption through Safe Haven."

"Why Safe Haven?" Kate asked. "Why not somewhere far away?"

"She loved this area, grew up here. When she asked me to marry her, she wanted to move back home with the baby. I'm guessing she wanted her son close to her hometown so she could keep an eye on him when she returned at some point later down the road," Dallas theorized.

"Makes sense," Tommy agreed. "She might've given the stipulation to her handler that her son would be allowed to grow up in or near Bluff, Texas. If the guy she was involved with found out about the adoption, he could be targeting babies here."

"To get back at her or draw her out of hiding," Dallas finished. The one bright spot in this crazy scenario would be that Susan was alive and doing well in the program.

"There's another possibility worth considering. The bad guy might be the father, and he found out about the baby," Tommy said. "The recent spate of kidnappings could be him or his henchmen looking for his son. There was a child discovered in his carrier in the baby-food aisle of a Piggly Wiggly last night. A DNA test this morning confirmed he was one of the boys abducted from an adopted family."

"Which means that all the boys who were kidnapped have been returned home safely?" Dallas said, glancing at Kate.

He wasn't quite ready to let himself off the hook with Susan just yet. Sure, she might've been grasping at straws in telling him he was the father, but there was still a slight chance that it was true. He hoped that she was alive, thriving somewhere else, and that her baby was safe. "Until we know for sure, I'm going to stay with the assumption that the boy could be mine."

"I understand your position," Tommy said. "And that's fine to think that way. I'm looking at the facts and I have to disagree."

"What's the next step?" Dallas asked. He appreciated his friend's perspective, hoped he was right.

"Locate Seaver. Get him in for questioning and try to trip him up," Tommy replied. "I already sent someone to pick up Harold Matthews. You mentioned before that you knew Susan was seeing someone else when you two dated. Think you can work with a sketch artist to give me a visual of the guy?"

"Yeah, sure."

"I don't like you leaving the ranch, so I'd rather send someone to you with a deputy escort."

"What time do you think you can have someone sent over?" Dallas asked. He had a few things he needed to take care of in the meantime. Top of the list was calling his brothers together for a family meeting.

"I can probably have someone over by lunch," Tommy said.

"Let me know if you get Seaver in for questioning between now and then. I'd like to be on the other side of the glass when he's in the interview room," Dallas said.

Tommy agreed and they ended the call.

"I'd like to go see myself what Seaver has to say," Kate said, holding Jackson. "I just wish there was something to identify him at the scene of Wayne's murder or connect him in some way."

"So do I. Speaking of which, I want to check on Stacy this morning." Something was gnawing at the back of Dallas's mind.

Kate nodded. "I need to check in at work afterward. Make sure everything's going smoothly at the kitchen. I can't relax, because I have the feeling that I'm dropping the ball somewhere."

"The curse of leading a busy life. It's hard to slow

down long enough to notice the roses, let alone stop long enough to smell them," Dallas agreed.

"Do you work all the time when you're not helping strangers?" she asked with a half smile.

Kate was beautiful and her looks had certainly made an impression on Dallas. There was so much more to her. She was kind, genuine and honest to a fault. Intelligent.

There wasn't much she couldn't accomplish if she set her mind to something.

"Do you have any idea how amazing you are?" He kissed her forehead, wishing he could whisk her into the bedroom again. Not an option with the little guy around. Besides, Dallas needed to get his brothers together and then work until the sketch artist arrived.

She rolled her eyes and smiled up at him. "I doubt it."

She'd built a successful company from the ground up. She ran a successful nonprofit while taking care of one of the cutest darn kids Dallas had ever set eyes on.

He had a hard time believing that she could feel inadequate in any way.

If he had to describe her in one word it would be… *remarkable*.

"You're kidding me, right?" he asked.

"Growing up in my childhood home didn't inspire a lot of confidence." She rolled her shoulders in a shrug.

"Then I wish you could see the person I see when I look at you." And Dallas needed to figure out how she fit into his life when this was all over.

Chapter 15

Kate made a few calls to check on work and then spent the balance of the morning playing with her son. She had always believed that she needed work to keep her busy, to feel fulfilled, and was surprised to realize that being with Jackson was enough.

Maybe once she got her donor base full, she'd consider cutting back to working half-time. She couldn't imagine stopping altogether. Being a mother was incredibly rewarding, but feeding people filled another part of her heart.

The one thing she'd realized when she'd cashed out of her start-up was that wearing the best clothes or paying two hundred dollars to have her hair colored and cut did nothing to refill the well. Did she enjoy looking good? Of course. She still thought it was important to feel great in what she wore and how she took care of herself. But she'd figured out that she could still look pretty amazing with just the right color sweater. And a ponytail and pair of sweats were all she needed to impress the little man she was holding. Jackson didn't even care if her socks matched, which some days they probably didn't since he'd come into her life.

Her work at the kitchen was important. It felt good to make sure people were fed, to know she was making a difference for others on a most basic level.

Then there were other feelings she was having a harder time getting under control, feelings for Dallas O'Brien.

The rich cowboy was smart, handsome and successful. And he did things to her body that no man before him had come close to achieving.

It was more than great sex with Dallas. There was a closeness she felt with him that she'd never experienced with anyone else.

And yet a nagging question persisted. What did she really know about him?

Like what was his favorite color? Was he a lazy Sunday morning person or did he get up early and go out for a jog? When did he have time to work out between running the ranch and taking care of his business in New Mexico? A body like his said he must put in serious time at the gym. Heck, she didn't even know his favorite meal, dessert or alcoholic beverage.

All the little details about each other that added up to true intimacy were missing.

The one thing she knew for certain was that if she was in trouble, then he was the guy she wanted standing beside her. Dallas O'Brien had her back. And he was capable of handling himself in every situation.

Kate placed Jackson on his belly on the blanket Dallas had spread out on the wood floor. The few toys Janis had brought were keeping her son entertained.

And she wondered how long she could keep him safe like this.

The reality of their situation hit fast and hard, like lightning on a sunny day. They were in hiding in a near stranger's house. Her mind argued that she and Dallas couldn't possibly be strangers anymore, but she pushed logic aside.

She focused on her boy, shuddering at the thought someone could want to take him from her. Rather than give in to that fear, she sipped her coffee.

There were so many facts and theories rolling around in her head. If what they'd talked about earlier was true, then she had to consider the possibility that Jackson's father was a criminal. She wouldn't love her son any less either way, but that would complicate their lives, given that this criminal seemed intent on finding his son.

If he found Jackson, and Jackson turned out to be his, she wouldn't have to worry about courts and judges, because this guy could take Jackson and make a run out of the country. He'd eluded law enforcement so far.

Kate's chest squeezed as she thought about the possibilities.

There was another option. Dallas could be Jackson's biological father. That thought didn't startle her as much as it probably should.

"Don't do that to yourself." Dallas's voice startled her out of the dark place she'd gone.

"You scared me," she said, avoiding the topic.

"Sorry. The deputy and sketch artist are on their way here." He sauntered across the room toward the kitchen with his coffee mug in hand and Kate couldn't help but admire his athletic grace. She also thought about what he looked like naked and that sent a different kind of shiver down her back.

"Don't get tied up with what-ifs," Dallas said, pouring a fresh cup of coffee. He held up the pot. "Want more?"

She shook her head.

"It's hard." She looked at Jackson. He was such a happy baby and her heart hurt at the thought of him being taken away, let alone never seeing him again.

"My mother used to tell me that it was her job to worry," Dallas said.

"Then I'm overqualified," Kate quipped.

He smiled and it was like a hundred candles lit up inside her.

"It would be impossible not to worry under the circumstances," he conceded. "And I think it comes with the territory of parenting."

She locked on to his gaze. "I can't lose him."

"If I have anything to say about it, you won't." The sincerity in his voice soothed her more than she should allow, because nothing about their current situation said that Dallas could protect them forever.

There was a comfort in being with him that she'd never known with anyone else. "How's work? I can't help but feel we're keeping you from your own life," she said, trying to redirect her thoughts.

Dallas eyed her for a minute before he spoke. "It's no trouble. I have everything covered here and in New Mexico."

"I appreciate all you're doing for us," she said, stiffening her back. "In case I haven't told you that lately."

"Don't do that. Don't bring up a wall between us." Hurt registered in his dark eyes.

"I'm sorry. I just don't know how to deal with this," she said, her gaze focused on the patch of floor in front of her. Feeling a sudden chill, she rubbed her arms.

"How about we take it one day at a time," he suggested. He covered well, but she detected a note of disappointment in his voice.

The last thing Kate wanted to do was hurt the one man helping her. The emotions she felt for Dallas confused her, and even though it made no sense, they felt far more dangerous than anything else they faced.

"I don't know if I can do that," she admitted.

"Will you at least tell me why not?"

"I'm scared."

"Then let's not overthink whatever's happening between us," Dallas said, moving to her and then kissing her forehead.

She smiled up at him, which wasn't the same as agreement, and his heart stuttered.

His cell phone buzzed. He fished it out of his pocket and answered, deciding the two of them needed to have a sit-down when this mess was all over to talk about a future. Dallas had no idea what that meant exactly, but he wanted Kate and Jackson in his life.

After saying a few "uh-huh"s into the phone, he ended the call.

"Doc's here," he said, moving to the front door.

He opened it before she could knock. Dallas was ready to get an answer to at least one of his questions.

After introductions were made, he asked, "What do you need from me to get the ball rolling?"

Dr. McConnell smiled, winked and set down her bag. "A swab on the inside of your cheek should do the trick."

Kate brought Jackson over, sat on the couch and then put him on her lap for easier access. She dropped his toy at least three times before the doctor managed to obtain his swab.

"How long before you'll get the results?" Dallas asked, mostly wanting to ease Kate's concern.

"I'll walk this into the lab myself as soon as I leave here," Dr. McConnell said as she secured the samples. "So I should have news tomorrow around this time."

Kate's eyes grew wide and then she refocused on her son. Dallas could almost feel the panic welling inside her.

"Thank you for taking care of this personally," he said, standing to offer a handshake.

"You're not getting away that easily," Dr. McConnell said, pulling him in for a hug. She and his mother had been close friends. "I said it before, but I'm sorry about your folks. I miss my friends every day."

"Same here," Dallas said, appreciating the sentiment. "There's something I need to tell you before you go."

She looked up at him.

"It'll be in the news soon enough, even though Tommy is doing his level best to suppress the story, and I told my brothers this morning," Dallas said. "I thought you should know before everyone else."

"What is it, Dallas?"

"The toxicology results came back with a suspicious substance, cyanide. Mother and Pop were poisoned," he said.

It looked as though the doctor needed a minute to let that information sink in.

"That would explain your father's heart attack. He was in excellent physical condition and I couldn't shake the feeling that something was off about him having a heart attack while driving." Dr. McConnell touched his arm and drew in a deep breath. "I'm so sorry."

"Me, too."

"Why? How?" Her voice was soft. Tears streamed down her face. "They were such good people. I can't imagine anyone wanting to hurt your parents. Is there any chance the substance was accidentally ingested?"

"That's the question of the day." Dallas brought her in for another hug. "No matter what, I pledge to get to the bottom of this. If someone killed my parents, then I won't rest until they pay for what they did."

"I'd like to have the poison expert at my hospital take a look at the report. Give another opinion." Dr. McConnell wiped away her tears and straightened her rounded shoulders.

"Any additional eyes we can get on the case, the better," Dallas said. "Any help you can give is much appreciated."

"This happened the day after the art auction," she said. "So they were around a lot of people that night and the next day."

"If they were murdered, we'll find the SOB," he said, his mind already clicking through possibilities. He'd have Tommy request all the pictures taken that night so he could figure out exactly who had attended the party. The guest list would be easy enough to locate and there'd be dozens of others—waiters, bartenders and cooks.

There was a professional photographer hired for the party, as well as Harper Smith from the society page of the local newspaper.

"I can't think of one person who would want to hurt your parents," Dr. McConnell said, still in disbelief.

"Me, either," Dallas stated.

She took a breath, pursed her lips and nodded. "If I can be of any help, you know my number."

"I won't hesitate," Dallas said.

She hugged him again before taking up her bag and saying goodbye to Kate. Stopped at the door, she shifted her gaze from Kate to Dallas. "I hope everything works out the way it's supposed to."

Dallas saw the doctor out, then turned to Kate. "Are you doing okay?"

Her shoulders sagged and sadness was written in the lines of her face. "I didn't know about your parents."

"I just found out yesterday. I'm still trying to process the news."

"From Tommy?" Kate seemed hurt that he hadn't shared the information with her sooner.

Dallas moved to her side and sat down next to her, ignoring the heat where his thigh pressed against hers. "The only reason I didn't bring it up last night was because there was so much else going on."

"It's okay, Dallas. You don't have to tell me anything," she said, trying to mask her pain and put on a brave face.

"I'd planned to tell you, but with everything else happening I was trying to process the news myself and then tell my brothers. I overloaded last night, and being with you was the only thing keeping me sane."

He leaned forward and pressed his forehead to hers. "I just hope you can understand."

She didn't say anything right away. She just breathed.

"I do," she murmured at last, and Dallas finally exhaled.

The deputy and sketch artist stopped by next. It took Dallas only fifteen minutes with the artist for him to capture the image in Dallas's mind. He thanked them before walking them both out.

For the next hour, Dallas played with Jackson on the floor alongside Kate. He sensed that her nerves were on edge.

"I wasn't expecting to feel this stressed about the test," she finally admitted.

"One phone call is all it takes to make it go away, if you don't want this to go any further," Dallas said.

"Between you and some random criminal being Jackson's father, I'm hoping it's you," she said.

"That's quite an endorsement," he responded, and he couldn't help but laugh despite all the heaviness inside him.

Kate joined him, a much-needed release of nervous tension for both of them, despite the tragic circumstances.

"Well, if I have to have a child out there, this little guy isn't a bad one to have," Dallas said. "You hungry?"

"Starving," she said. "I need to feed Jackson and put him down for a nap first."

"What sounds good?" Dallas asked, ignoring her

comment. He might not be able to take care of Jackson on his own, but he could order lunch.

"A hamburger and fries," she said, making a little mewling sound.

Dallas remembered hearing a similar one earlier that morning while they'd made love. He cracked a smile, thinking how much he'd like to hear it again.

Early the next morning, the door to the guest room opened a crack. Kate pushed up to a sitting position, careful not to wake Jackson.

"Thought you'd want to know that Stacy's going home this morning," he said in a whisper.

"That's great news," Kate said. "Or maybe not. I'm worried about her being home alone."

"I'm sending Reece to stay with her just until this case is resolved," he said, and then his expression sobered. "I got a text from Tommy that Seaver has been picked up and is being brought into the station. From what I've been told, he's not real happy about it. Janis is on her way over to stay with the baby. I'll put on a pot of coffee."

Kate kissed her son, got dressed and met Dallas in the kitchen.

He walked up to her, gaze locked on hers, cradled her neck with his right hand and pressed a kiss to her lips.

"There," he said, after pulling back. "That's a better way to start the day."

"I couldn't agree more," she said, smiling. "I missed you last night."

He kissed the corners of her mouth as a soft knock sounded at the door.

"I'll get the coffee." Kate had already noticed the travel mugs on the counter.

Dallas opened the door for Janis.

"Is my baby sleeping?" she asked.

"Yes. But probably not for much longer." Kate filled mugs and brought them with her into the living room.

"Then I'll read quietly. Is he in the guest room?"

Dallas nodded as he took his mug from Kate. "Ready?"

"Let's do this," she said.

"We'll take my brother's Jeep. Colin drove it over this morning for us," Dallas said.

He had a big family. She'd met Tyler so far. She wanted to get to know the others, too.

As she said goodbye to her son and hauled herself into the Jeep, Kate wondered what it must've been like growing up in such a large family. It had been only she and Carter as children. Maybe that was why his recent closeness with their mother seemed like such a betrayal.

Dust kicked up on the road, which was barely visible in the predawn light.

"We're going to exit on the east side of the ranch, near Colin's place. He's similar in height and build, so I'm hoping no one will recognize me. You might want to get in the backseat and lie on your side until we clear the area safely."

Kate unbuckled her seat belt and climbed into the rear. "Tell me when to duck."

Chapter 16

The ride to the sheriff's office went off without a hitch. Dallas's plan to throw off whoever might be watching by switching vehicles seemed to be working, and Kate finally breathed a sigh of relief when they pulled into the parking lot.

Facing Seaver had her nerves on edge, knowing he was somehow involved if not completely behind the abduction attempt.

Tommy met them as soon as they walked through the door. "He's confessed to everything," he said.

"What?" Kate could hardly believe what she was hearing.

"We're making arrangements for Seaver to turn state's evidence against Raphael Manuel," the lawman added, ushering them into his office. "Manuel was Susan's boyfriend. We connected him using the sketch you gave us yesterday.

"The man you identified is a known criminal who's wanted for murder in New Mexico and Texas. And Seaver confessed that he happens to be the father of Susan's child."

Kate's head spun as she tried to wrap her mind around the information coming at her at what felt like a hundred miles an hour. It occurred to her that while Dallas was in the clear, her son's situation still hung in the balance. Susan and this man could be Jackson's parents.

"You know this for certain?" Dallas asked.

"One hundred percent," his friend declared. "There's no way you fathered Susan's child."

The paternity-test results would prove that, but Dallas was relieved not to have to wait. "What about Susan?"

"Found out from the marshal who will handle Seaver that she is safe and tucked far away until the trial," Tommy said. "She broke off her relationship with Manuel after she caught him engaging in criminal activity, and made a desperate call to you. The Feds have been building a case ever since. With her and Seaver's testimony, Manuel will go away for a long time."

"How is Seaver involved?" Dallas asked.

"Manuel had his henchmen kidnap babies, but he learned from Harold Matthews that some of the adoptions were kept off the books at Safe Haven. Manuel tracked several to Seaver and threatened to kill the lawyer's family if he didn't help locate his son."

"And he had worked with me and Jackson," Kate said quietly.

Both men nodded.

"Which accounts for the change in MO," Dallas said.

"Seaver is deathly afraid of guns and he didn't want to take the chance that someone would get killed. The assignment was to take the babies and test them, not hurt them or their mothers," Tommy explained.

"So, Seaver arranged Jackson's abduction," Dallas said.

"And admitted to setting up Allen to throw us off the trail," Tommy stated.

"Which almost worked," Kate mused.

"Where's Manuel?" Dallas asked.

"We don't know. The marshal is processing a warrant right now so they can pick him up."

"They have to locate him first," Dallas said.

Tommy's cell buzzed. "Hold on. I need to take this."

Dallas's arms were around Kate, and for the first time in a long time, she felt a glimmer of hope.

And then Tommy looked at her with an apologetic expression. Her stomach dropped.

"Manuel must've followed Seaver's trail to your brother. Carter has been abducted."

"What?" Kate's heart sank. This could not be happening. She'd spoken to him just yesterday. Carter had to be fine.

The only thing keeping her upright was Dallas's arms around her. Her head spun and she could barely hear the quiet reassurances he whispered in her ear.

"We have to find him," she said, her knees almost giving out.

"They want Jackson," Dallas said, holding her tight. "They won't hurt Carter." His words wrapped around her, kept her from succumbing to the absolute panic threatening to take her under.

She gasped. "My phone. What if Carter tried to call? I have to get to my phone."

"Where is it?" Dallas asked.

"In the diaper bag at the ranch." Hold on. She could check her messages from anywhere.

Dallas must've realized what she was thinking, because he made a move for his own cell. "Try this."

She put the call on speaker.

Carter's voice boomed into the room. "Kate, don't do anything rash. He wants Jackson."

A male voice she didn't recognize urged Carter to tell the truth.

Her brother hesitated. "He says he'll kill me if you don't deliver Jackson to one of his men."

The line went dead.

The automatic message system indicated that the call had come in at four o'clock that morning.

"Can you trace it?" Kate asked Tommy.

"We'll do our best. Manuel most likely has a program to scramble his signal, though," the lawman conceded.

"They're somewhere local," Dallas said. "Manuel would have brought Carter here."

"What makes you so sure?" Tommy asked.

"This guy is desperate to find his son and he's narrowed his search down to this area. I'm sure Morton told him about the other local adoptions," Dallas said. "A man who goes to these lengths to find his boy would want to be right here."

Tommy nodded. "Good point. I'll check in with local motels."

Dallas held his hand up. "I might already know where he'll be."

"Morton's house." Kate gasped. "Stacy."

"Reece is with her. He's very good at his job. She'll be fine," Dallas said, his thumbs moving on the keyboard of his phone. "I just asked him to call me."

Kate immediately realized that Dallas wouldn't want Reece's cell tones to give him away, or he would have phoned the security agent himself.

Her heart pounded against her ribs.

Dallas pointed toward the landline. "Call your mother. Tell her to get out of the house and not come back until we say it's safe."

Kate did, unsure what kind of reception she'd get.

Her mother picked up on the first ring.

"Mom, it's Kate. I need you to listen carefully. Go next door and stay there until I call."

Her mother must have grasped the panic in Kate's tone because she stuttered an agreement. "What is it, Kate? What's going on?" she finally asked.

"I need you to go now. I'll explain later."

"All right," she said tentatively. "I'll wait next door until I hear from you."

"Tell Dad to be careful, too. He should stay at the office until I give the all clear."

"I'm worried. Are you and the baby okay?" It was the first time her mother had asked about Jackson.

"We're good, Mom. I'll explain everything when I can. Just go, and be careful, okay?" Tears streamed down Kate's face. She and her mother had had their difficulties, but she couldn't stand to think of anything awful happening to her.

"I will. I love you, Kate. And I'm sorry. If anything happens to me I need you to know that."

"Me, too, Mom. And I love you." Kate held in a sob, promising herself that she'd stay strong. "Call my cell when you get to the neighbor's and leave a message. Let me know you got there safely."

Kate's cell was at the ranch, but she could check the message when she retrieved it or call voice mail again using Dallas's cell.

"Okay. Take care of yourself." Her mother paused. "And give Jackson a kiss from Grandma."

Kate had wanted to hear those words from her mother for months. She promised she would do as asked, then ended the call.

Thankfully, her parents were safe. At least for now.

Dallas was urging her toward the exit as soon as she hung up.

"Any chance I can talk you out of walking through that door?" Tommy asked.

Dallas stopped at the jamb and turned.

"I didn't think so," his friend said. "Okay, fine. But we're going in with my tactical unit."

"I'm dropping Kate off at the ranch first," Dallas stated.

"They might hurt her brother if they don't see her." Tommy looked from Dallas to Kate.

"You can't take me back there. Not when my brother needs me," she declared.

Dallas's jaw clenched and every muscle in his body was obviously strung tight. "They're going to want to see a baby."

Tommy called down the hall and a deputy showed up a few seconds later cradling something in his arms.

The plastic baby looked real from a distance. Kate took it from the deputy. "He sees me with this and he'll assume it's Jackson."

"I won't use you as bait," Dallas muttered.

"Neither will I, but I want her in the car nearby," Tommy said, before she could argue.

"We brought Colin's Jeep. I'll let my brothers know what's going on," Dallas said.

"This one needs to stay quiet," Tommy said. "There's no one I trust more than your family, but we're taking enough of a risk as it is."

Tommy called in his unit. "Kate will be in the Jeep with Dallas, here." He pointed to a spot on the Google map he'd pulled up on his computer screen. "We'll come in from around the sides while she makes contact. Our perp will be watching the front and back doors, so we're looking at side windows."

Kate glanced at Dallas, not bothering to hide her panic. "We have to get there before Stacy and Reece do."

"I know." But the expression in Dallas's eyes said it was probably already too late.

Very little was said between Dallas and Kate on the ride over. He had agreed to give Tommy's men a ten-minute head start, which wasn't much time.

Kate regretted having this go down on such a quiet suburban street. It was afternoon, but thankfully a weekend, and she hoped the cold and nearness to the holiday would keep everyone inside.

The sun peeked out from battleship-gray clouds as they approached.

"That's Reece's car," Dallas said. "But this is good. If they surprised him then we'll have someone on the inside. If I know Reece, he's already planning an escape route, and he'll keep Stacy safe."

"She's been through so much already," Kate said under her breath, hating that so much bad could strike such a good person all at once. Stacy must be terrified.

Kate cradled the pretend baby in her arms, making sure anyone watching could see. The look of panic on her face was real.

Dallas eased down the quiet road and then parked across the street from Morton's house, just as they'd planned.

The porch light flickered on and off a couple of times.

"They're signaling," Dallas said.

"What do we do now?" Kate asked.

"We wait."

But they didn't have to sit for long. There was a loud boom inside the house and smoke billowed out one of the windows.

"Stacy's in there," Kate said, her hand already on the door release.

Dallas stopped her. "We have to let Tommy do his job."

"We can't just sit here," she argued.

Dallas's door opened just then and the barrel of a gun was pressed to the back of his head.

The noise inside the house, the smoke, must have been meant to be a distraction while Manuel grabbed his son.

"I'll take that baby," a male voice said, and it had to be Manuel, based on the sketch Dallas had provided.

Kate pulled the plastic baby to her chest to shield its

face from the man. If he got a good look, he'd shoot. "I'll come with you."

She made a move toward the door handle, and at the same time, Dallas jerked the guy's arm in front of him, pinning it against the steering wheel. A shot sounded and Kate's heart lurched.

"Run, Kate," Dallas cried, wrestling the gun out of Manuel's hand.

Dallas must've been putting a ton of pressure on the guy's arm, based on the look on his face.

Kate bolted. She ran straight to the house, flung open the door and shouted, "He's out front!"

Another crack of gunfire sent her stomach swirling. *Dallas.*

Tommy ran out the door toward her.

By the time the two of them reached Dallas, he had Manuel facedown and was sitting on his back while twisting his right arm behind him.

The criminal was spewing curse words.

Tommy dropped his knee into Manuel's back as he wrangled with flex-cuffs. Kate frantically searched for the gun and noticed, as Dallas turned, that he had blood on his stomach.

"Dallas," she cried with a shocked sob.

His gaze followed hers and he pressed his hand against his abdomen.

Tommy was already calling for an ambulance as Dallas lost consciousness. He slumped over onto his side as Kate dropped to her knees, unaware that she was still clutching the plastic doll.

It took ten minutes for the EMTs to arrive. Kate was vaguely aware of Stacy and Reece comforting her.

Reece drove her to the hospital behind the ambulance in his SUV. Being told that the kidnappers had been arrested did nothing to settle Kate's nerves, not while Dallas was in trouble.

She could see the gurney Dallas was on as it rolled into the emergency entrance. She asked Reece to stop, bolted out of the SUV and rushed forward.

One of the EMTs turned around. "Are you Kate Williams?"

Her heart clutched. "Yes."

"Good. Will you come see this guy? He hasn't stopped talking about you since he opened his eyes in the ambulance."

Kate nodded, tears streaming down her cheeks as she ran toward Dallas.

She had never been so happy as when he looked at her and said, "We did it. Jackson's safe."

"I love you!" It was all she could manage to say before he squeezed her hand and was wheeled away.

"Test results are in," Dallas said as he entered the room, his hand fisted around something that Kate couldn't readily make out.

"You shouldn't be out of bed," she fussed. "The doctor won't be happy when she hears about this."

He'd been a trying patient at best since Dr. McConnell agreed to let him recuperate at home.

"Well, if you aren't the least bit curious, then I'll head back to our room," he said, turning.

"Dallas O'Brien, you better stop where you are," Kate muttered.

He did. "Good to know you have that 'mom voice' perfected," he teased. "We already knew I wasn't Jackson's biological father," he continued. "Manuel is."

"Which means he's Susan's child," Kate said. "What if she wants him back now that this is all over?"

"She doesn't," Dallas said. "Said he would remind her too much of her mistakes. All she ever wanted was for him to be brought up in Bluff by a loving family. He's your son and Susan has no intention of trying to change that."

Relief flooded Kate hearing those words. The child of her heart was hers to keep.

"I heard you on the phone earlier with your mother," Dallas said.

"She's making a real effort," Kate said, beaming up at him. "Once you're well, I'd like to invite her and Dad over for dinner."

"I think that's a great idea," he said. "And what about Carter?"

"It'll be tough to drag him away from his company, but I'm determined to spend more time with family."

"About that." Dallas kissed Kate as he struggled to bend forward. He set a small package next to her. "Christmas is a couple of months away."

"The doctor said to take it easy," she warned.

"And what's my punishment if I don't?" He winked.

"An even longer wait before we resume any more adult-only playtime," she teased.

Dallas laughed it off and grunted as he managed to sit down next to her. He made a face at Jackson, who cooed in response, causing her heart to swell.

Kate stared at the roughly two-by-two-inch Tiffany-blue box beside her.

She opened her mouth to speak, but was hushed by Dallas.

"I know what you're thinking. You don't want to

rush, because you think we need to get to know each other better," he said. "I disagree, because I know everything I need to know about you. I intend to spend the rest of our lives together bringing up this boy, our boy. I don't need a test to prove he's my son. He's yours and that's good enough for me."

Tears welled in Kate's eyes. More than anything, she wanted to say yes. Everything in her heart said this was right. "So before you say anything, here's the deal. I love you, Kate. I want to spend the rest of my life with you and Jackson. And that's all I need you to know for now. Sometime before the end of next year, I plan to ask a very important question, but the only thing I'm asking today is…will a year be enough time for you to feel like you really know me?"

"Yes." Happy tears streamed down her cheeks.

"Then hold on to that box as a promise from me," Dallas said. "When you finally do feel like you know me well enough, I want the three of us to be a family. I love you, Kate. And I want you to be my wife."

All Kate could do in answer was kiss the man she loved.

* * * * *

Chapter One

Maintaining a white-knuckle grip on the steering wheel while
negotiating the treacherous curves up Prescott Mountain on his
daily commute was typical for Ryland Beck. *Smiling* while he
resolutely refused to look toward the steep drop on the other
side of the road *wasn't* typical. Nothing, not even his phobia
of heights, could dampen his enthusiasm this chilly October
morning. Today he'd begin his investigation into a serial killer
case that had gone cold over four years ago.

Bringing down the Smoky Mountain Slayer was the challenge
of a lifetime. No suspects. No DNA. No viable behavioral
profile. In spite of the lack of evidence, Ryland was determined
to put the killer behind bars. He wanted to give the families of
the five victims the answers and justice they deserved.

Unfortunately, what he couldn't give them was closure.
Closure, as he well knew, was a fictional construct. The death of

a loved one would always leave a gaping hole in the hearts and lives of those left behind. But knowing the victim's murderer had been caught and punished would go a long way toward making the excruciating grief more bearable.

He continued winding his way up the mountain toward UB headquarters as he considered the limited information he'd found on the internet about the killings. The Slayer's modus operandi was consistent: all of his victims were strangled, their bodies dumped in the woods in Monroe County. But aside from them being young women, the victimology was all over the place. Their educational and economic backgrounds varied, as did their ethnicity. Some were married, some weren't. Some had children, some didn't. All of that made it nearly impossible to build a useful profile to help figure out who'd murdered them.

The detectives from the Monroe County Sheriff's Office had deemed the case unsolvable. But here in Gatlinburg, Ryland had a unique advantage: an über-wealthy boss who knew firsthand the suffering a victim's family endured when a murder case went cold.

Seven years after his wife was killed and his infant daughter went missing, Grayson Prescott had given up on the stagnant police investigation. He decided to create a cold case company called Unfinished Business. Just a few months later, UB had solved the case. Now, the thirty-three counties of the East Tennessee region had formed a partnership with UB and were clamoring for them to work their cold cases.

Don't miss
Serial Slayer Cold Case *by Lena Diaz,*
available March 2022 wherever
Harlequin books and ebooks are sold.

Harlequin.com

Love Harlequin romance?

DISCOVER.

Be the first to find out about promotions, news and exclusive content!

f Facebook.com/HarlequinBooks

𝕏 Twitter.com/HarlequinBooks

◉ Instagram.com/HarlequinBooks

𝓟 Pinterest.com/HarlequinBooks

You Tube YouTube.com/HarlequinBooks

ReaderService.com

EXPLORE.

Sign up for the Harlequin e-newsletter and download a free book from any series at **TryHarlequin.com**

CONNECT.

Join our Harlequin community to share your thoughts and connect with other romance readers! **Facebook.com/groups/HarlequinConnection**

HARLEQUIN

Heartfelt or thrilling, passionate or uplifting—Harlequin is more than just happily-ever-after.

With twelve different series to choose from and new books available every month, you are sure to find stories that will move you, uplift you, inspire and delight you.

SIGN UP FOR THE HARLEQUIN NEWSLETTER

Be the first to hear about great new reads and exciting offers!

Harlequin.com/newsletters

HNEWS2021